P9-BYV-771

The Spanish Promise

Karen Swan is a *Sunday Times* Top Five bestselling writer. She is the author of fifteen other novels, although she's been a writer all her life. She previously worked as an editor in the fashion industry but soon realized she was better suited as a novelist with a serious shopping habit. She is married with three children and lives in West Sussex.

Come to find her at www.karenswan.com, or Instagram @swannywrites, Twitter @KarenSwan1 and Facebook @KarenSwanAuthor.

Also by Karen Swan

Players
Prima Donna
Christmas at Tiffany's
The Perfect Present
Christmas at Claridge's
The Summer Without You
Christmas in the Snow
Summer at Tiffany's
Christmas on Primrose Hill
The Paris Secret
Christmas Under the Stars
The Rome Affair
The Christmas Secret
The Greek Escape
The Christmas Lights

The Spanish Promise

KAREN SWAN

MACMILLAN

First published 2019 by Macmillan
an imprint of Pan Macmillan
20 New Wharf Road, London N1 9RR
Associated companies throughout the world
www.panmacmillan.com

ISBN 978-1-5290-0617-9

Copyright © Karen Swan 2019

The right of Karen Swan to be identified as the
author of this work has been asserted by her in accordance
with the Copyright, Designs and Patents Act 1988.

All rights reserved. No part of this publication may be reproduced,
stored in a retrieval system, or transmitted, in any form, or by any means
(electronic, mechanical, photocopying, recording or otherwise)
without the prior written permission of the publisher.

Pan Macmillan does not have any control over, or any responsibility for,
any author or third-party websites referred to in or on this book.

1 3 5 7 9 8 6 4 2

A CIP catalogue record for this book is available from the British Library.

Typeset by Palimpsest Book Production Ltd, Falkirk, Stirlingshire
Printed and bound by CPI Group (UK) Ltd, Croydon, CR0 4YY

This book is sold subject to the condition that it shall not, by way of
trade or otherwise, be lent, hired out, or otherwise circulated without
the publisher's prior consent in any form of binding or cover other than
that in which it is published and without a similar condition including
this condition being imposed on the subsequent purchaser.

Visit **www.panmacmillan.com** to read more about all our books
and to buy them. You will also find features, author interviews and
news of any author events, and you can sign up for e-newsletters
so that you're always first to hear about our new releases.

For Trish
With love and thanks for giving this writer such a beautiful view whilst writing this book

'The true soldier fights not because he hates what is in front of him, but because he loves what is behind him'

G. K. Chesterton

Prologue

Madrid, March 1937

He stared back at her with eyes that burned like black stars, his hands hot around hers as they stood there, joined together. Just a solitary candle flickered, their faces draped with a pale golden light; no more than that could be risked for fear of being glimpsed from the street.

'. . . by the powers vested in me, I now pronounce you man and wife.'

A smile of delight escaped her. It was done? He was hers and she was his? He stepped forward, cupping her face in his hands and staring down at her as though she was heaven-sent. 'I will love and protect you always,' he said with quiet fierceness.

'And I you.'

He kissed her, the tender press of his lips pushing a button inside her and waking her up. She didn't need to be afraid any more. They had been together for only three days and four nights but already she knew she could face anything with him by her side. Their love was fiercer than any war, and now when she looked into the sky, it wasn't to check for bombs but to follow the birds, to catch rainbows, to wish upon the stars.

A nearby sound of metal on metal, like a door latch falling, made them all startle.

'What was that?' the priest whispered, looking around abruptly.

No one replied, listening instead to the sudden and distinctive sound of feet, running; so nearly silent, but not quite. The two men instinctively closed in around her, scanning the windows for signs of lights, ropes, missiles, both reaching for the guns in their belts and pointing them around the chapel, weapons primed. Everyone was a soldier these days – the grocer, the carpenter, the locksmith, the priest.

They waited but the silence held. Had the danger passed? Was it so improbable to believe it could have been a child playing?

Yes.

'Quick, this way,' her newly minted husband whispered, grabbing her wrist and pulling her towards the back of the nave so fast her feet could barely touch the floor. 'Get behind the choir,' he said, pushing her roughly down behind the giant carved mahogany structure, the tenderness of the previous minute already lost to the art of war. She cowered behind the solid screen as he crept back towards the altar, his gun held in steady hands. She didn't want him to leave her but she reminded herself he was skilled in stealth, able to creep like a cat, light-footed and sure. Her breath was coming hard as the adrenaline pumped and she fought to control it, eyes closed as she tried not to imagine the danger that was creeping around the chapel and encircling them.

There! Her eyes flew open as she heard it, the tiny, single click of a gun's hammer being pulled back. She looked around her wildly, paling as she saw the east door. It was supposed to be bolted – indeed an attempt had been made on their way in, but in their rush to be married, the tip of the bolt was barely nudging up to the barrel.

She broke cover, running fast towards it with no time even to crouch, her terror growing with her speed as she saw the thin crack between the doors begin to widen. Open . . .

'No!' Her scream propelled her, she almost had a hand to it but as she threw herself forwards, it was suddenly flung back. She felt herself fly, the sound of a gunshot whistling through the air with her. But she had seen his face, and a single thought formed in her mind before the world went black.

'You.'

Chapter One

Canary Wharf, London, 9 July 2018

'Gentlemen. Ms Fairfax. We have a problem.'

Charlotte watched as the president of the bank bestrode the room, his footsteps silent on the plush rug. He took his seat at the head of the table and looked down the long expanse of burred walnut at his senior team. She imagined it must look like a fairground hall of mirrors to him: matching navy suits and 'short back and sides' rippling all the way down, thighs splayed and broad hands on the table. She alone broke the rhythm – long dark hair held back in a Chanel-beribboned low ponytail, discreetly polished fingernails, narrow shoulders, putty-coloured dress.

'Carlos Mendoza.'

Even she knew the name. She didn't need to be on the permanent payroll here to know he was one of the firm's biggest clients, which was saying something for a private bank dealing only with ultra high-net-worth individuals. The family was Spanish aristocracy, with a dukedom or two and owning vast tracts of the Andalusian countryside. They had made their fortune many generations back breeding fighting bulls, diversifying over the years into large-scale fruit farming, property investment and, latterly, medical technology. Off the top of her head, having read a profile on them in the financial press a few months back, she recalled their worth as being somewhere around the £750 million mark.

'I've just taken a call from his son, Mateo. I'm sorry to say the old boy's on his way out. Stage-four pancreatic cancer.' He tutted with what was supposed to indicate pity but she heard the subtext too: his dying was in some way inconvenient to them.

Hugh Farrer sank into his seat at the head of the table and stared back at them. At only fifty-four, he was the bank's youngest ever president and its most ruthless. Profits were up by a third in the twenty-eight months since he had taken the helm but it had come at a cost: the labour force beneath him had been trimmed by 21 per cent and he had closed down four satellite offices throughout Europe, centralizing operations at their headquarters here in London.

'The medics are saying he's got a month, six weeks at most, which doesn't give us much time.'

Us? Charlotte saw how the backs along the line stiffened slightly at the words as though they were reined together. She tilted her head to the side, watching, waiting.

Farrer took an exasperated breath. 'On Friday evening, Carlos suffered a mini-stroke. He is currently being treated in hospital and is, I understand, still unconscious. They are cautiously optimistic that he will recover – or at least make some form of recovery – from this. However, during this crisis, when Mateo assumed power of attorney for his father, as has always been customary, he learnt his father had been midway through drawing up paperwork donating the entirety of his estate to one Marina Quincy.'

Farrer let the name soak into the walls, raking his scrutiny over each of them in turn, like a pianist dragging his hand over the ivories. Marina Quincy. Marina Quincy. But it wasn't a name with any obvious material connections – not a Rockefeller or Rothschild, Spencer or Goldsmith. She wasn't Someone, a name they should automatically know. No green lights were flashing to make immediate sense of the directive.

'Mateo had never heard of her. We're awaiting a full report but all we know right now is that she's forty-five and working in a cafe in Madrid,' Farrer added.

Forty-five? Charlotte frowned. Carlos Mendoza was very elderly, late nineties if she remembered correctly.

'Could she be an illegitimate daughter?' someone behind her piped up.

Farrer gave a barely perceptible shake of his head. 'According to Mateo, his father had a vasectomy in his late thirties which he understands to have been successful.'

'So then she's his mistress,' Dan Milton stated beside her with characteristic frankness. It was the obvious assumption and Milton was nothing if not obvious. Thirty-one and already head of private banking for continental Europe , he wouldn't know a euphemism from an embolism. Chicago-born, with a Harvard business degree and an MBA from INSEAD, he had joined the London team eight months earlier and the aftershocks of his blunt managerial style were still rippling through the office.

Farrer settled his gaze upon his protégé, which was always a disconcerting experience. Almost albino-blonde, his eyelashes and brows were so pale as to appear bleached, creating a piscatorial impression. Milton had told her once, during a shared lift ride, that it was like being eyeballed by a trout. 'Mateo Mendoza is adamant he'd met all his father's mistresses. He's put a researcher on to it and they're working up a profile as we speak, but there's got to be something more to her than just that. Dying old men don't just give away their fortunes to hot women, no matter how much they fancy them.'

'Well if she is the lover, then the family has a very strong case for contesting it,' Milton said, confidently clasping his hands together and beginning to assert his authority. He had had a brief stint running the team in Madrid before this. 'Spanish inheritance law strongly protects the immediate family. His wife would automatically get fifty per cent, with the rest parcelled up in forced shares or *legitimas*' – he pronounced the word with a strong Spanish accent – 'for both antecedents and descendants. There's simply no way he can just dump the lot on his girlfriend and rob his legal family of their birthright.'

Farrer arched an almost-invisible eyebrow. 'You're quite right, Dan, he couldn't do this – if it was a bequest.'

Milton's mouth opened a little, as he realized too late he'd tripped up over semantics, his ego running away with him.

'But as I said, it's a donation. Or *donación de bienes*,' Farrer said, matching Milton's pretentious accent with one of his own.

He pulled his gaze off him in a dismissive manner and invited other suggestions but the room stayed quiet: no one else wanted to walk into one of his booby traps; mines were laid everywhere, beneath every word.

Farrer's stare hardened. 'It goes without saying what this potentially means for us. Mendoza is one of our biggest investors and with the shareholder meeting coming up in September and sterling weak against the euro right now, the timing could not be worse. Unfortunately, it is fully within Mendoza's gift to part with whatever he likes, *during* his lifetime and if his money leaves the family—' He stopped, giving everyone a sombre stare. 'Then it may well leave this bank too.'

The tension in the room ratcheted up a notch.

'Having said that, Carlos's lack of time might swing to our advantage – merely delaying the transfer may be all that's needed to make this problem go away.'

Charlotte felt a flicker of dislike twitch her eye. That he was actually suggesting Carlos Mendoza might *oblige* them all by conveniently dying whilst they placed just enough obstacles in his path to prevent him from fulfilling his dying wish . . . ? It was just another Monday morning at the bank but she shifted in her seat, glad her meetings here were infrequent. She always came away feeling grubby.

Farrer looked at the guy sitting to Charlotte's right, the head of legal. 'Paul, get your team on to the small print now, they need to find something, anything, we can use to stall: agreements, tie-ins . . . We need to find a way to spin this out: if he dies before the donation can be signed off, then the wills will stand.'

'Sure,' Paul said brusquely but looking charged by the directive.

Farrer looked back at Milton again. 'Milton, I want a full work-up on the Mendoza trusts and assets. In the event we can't block, what can we lock down and safeguard? We need to see what we can move, diversify, bury – now.'

'On it,' Dan nodded.

'Ms Fairfax.'

She looked up to find Farrer's gaze on her.

'Thank you for coming in at such short notice.'

'My pleasure,' she murmured.

'Mateo Mendoza is going to feed back to us on this woman's identity by the end of the day – which means I need you in Madrid.'

Shit. 'Okay.' She kept her face impassive; this wasn't going to go down well with her mother.

'I need you to make contact with her, sound her out, bring her onside. It's not yet clear what exactly she knows – no one knew what the old guy was up to. Although it seems unlikely, it may be she doesn't know about the gift either, in which case make no mention of it while we spin things out this end and find out more. On the other hand, she probably knows exactly what she's in line for and she's sitting there with her hand out. Either way, we need you to be our eyes and ears on this.'

Charlotte nodded. This wasn't her usual brief. The windfall usually came first, then the counselling, not the other way round.

'If the worst case does come to pass and Carlos gifts the bulk of the estate out of the Mendoza family, we need to be in position to make sure that, regardless, the money stays banked with us. Get close to this woman – she needs to trust you, listen to you, be guided by you. She likely won't know the first thing about finance at this level and I don't want our counterparts getting wind there's a new heiress on the block.' He looked straight at her with his pale gaze. 'I want you doing that thing you do.'

'Connecting?' she asked, the wry note showing in her eyes only.

'Exactly that,' he nodded. 'Bring her in to the mothership, Charlotte. Losing three-quarters of a billion pounds doesn't look good on anyone's CV.'

'Was that a threat?' Milton asked her as they walked down the corridor together.

'Naturally.'

Milton missed a beat and she knew he was smiling. She also knew he found her intriguing, his braggadocio style in complete contrast to her quiet confidence and serene reserve.

'You seem pretty calm, given that he's putting it all on you to make sure she keeps the investment with us.'

'You think it's all on me?' Her arms swung lightly as she walked, her back straight, chin up. Various people nodded at him – them – as they passed. 'Funny. My take was he's got to go through you first. You and Paul are my . . .' She looked at him quizzically. 'What's the terminology in American football, when you put the battering rams in front to protect the guy running with the ball?'

'Blockers.'

'Right. It's *only* going to come down to me if legal can't find a way to block the donation, which I'm sure they can. And of course we all know you know exactly how to make his liquid assets infinitely more 'fixed', so that even if the donation actually did come to pass, I doubt there'd be much left for me to have to save.'

'You're flattering me again, Charlotte,' he chuckled as they reached his office, the view of the oxbow meander of the Thames looking sluggish below the hazy sky. A tall, rangy man was already sitting on his velvet sofa and idly flicking through a copy of *The Economist*. 'Oh, Lord Finch, apologies! My meeting overran.' He strode across the room in four strides, looking important and dynamic, holding out a fleshy hand. 'Good to see you. Good to see you.' His eyes shone with the excitement that came from personally knowing a peer of the realm. 'Hey, allow me to introduce you to Charlotte Fairfax. I've been wanting to put the two of you together, she's our wealth counsellor. I think she could have some very timely advice for you in light of your recent . . . alimony woes.'

The tall man met her gaze and smiled, bending down to lightly kiss her on the cheeks. 'Lotts, how are you, you exquisite creature? It's been too long. You said you'd visit in Klosters.'

'I know, but I didn't get there at all in the end. An emergency at work.'

'Sorry – you know each other?' Milton asked, sounding incredulous.

'Oh, we're forever bumping into each other at this and that, aren't we, Lotts?' Lord Finch asked, just as her phone rang.

She glanced at the screen. 'I'm afraid I need to take this. A call I've been expecting,' she smiled apologetically, reaching up on tiptoe to kiss him goodbye again. 'Let's have lunch in August. Will you be in Positano?'

'Darling, does the pope shit in the woods?'

Charlotte laughed. 'You're outrageous! I'll call you.' And she turned and left, catching sight of Milton's dumbstruck expression on her way out.

'I'll keep you posted!' Milton called after her as she headed down the corridor.

She raised an arm in acknowledgement as she connected the call. 'Rosie?'

'Hi, Charlotte,' her PA's voice replied. 'Good time to speak?'

'Absolutely.' She walked down to the lifts and pressed the button, staring out of the plate-glass windows that gave over London. 'I'm just leaving Steed now. They need me to go to Madrid tomorrow. Can you reschedule my appointments and get me on the first flight out in the morning?'

'Sure. Hey, Madrid, lucky you – you can top up your tan before the wedding.'

'Oh yes, lucky me,' Charlotte replied drolly.

'You don't sound too enthused.'

'You aren't the one who's got to tell my mother I can't make the final dress fitting tomorrow night.'

'Ah.' Rosie was very well acquainted with her mother. 'Well, does that matter? They've got your measurements.'

Charlotte missed a beat. 'Yeah. It's just a couture dress, you're right. They can wing it.'

Rosie chuckled, also very well acquainted with Charlotte's dry sense of humour. 'Well at least you can take your foot off the gas for a bit while you're out there. A bit of distance from all the wedding prep might help you to relax.'

'Are you saying I'm uptight, Rosie?'

'I'm saying you're getting married next week and you've not had a hen party, a lunch, not even a hair appointment. You're only taking a few days for the honeymoon—'

'Because we're both frantic at the moment. We can take one later when things have calmed down a bit. Has he called, by the way?'

'Not yet. Do you want me to try him?'

'No. No, it's fine. I'll catch him later.' She and Stephen never spoke much in the day – one of them was invariably in a meeting – but she was looking forward to a quiet night in with him tonight. Even if she hadn't had to go to Madrid tomorrow, they'd been on a carousel of parties lately, everyone urgently getting together for last hurrahs in the capital before they split for the coasts of Provence, Formentera and Esmeraldas, where they would reconvene to do it all again. She could think of nothing nicer than a rhubarb gin and tonic, a foot rub and an evening on the sofa wearing his pyjamas. 'I'm on my way back now but can you ping me Lucy Santos's file? You remember, Roberto Santos's wife.'

'The Chelsea footballer.'

The lift arrived and she stepped in. 'Ex-Chelsea. Real Madrid now, remember?'

As if she could forget. Rosie was well-acquainted with her

boss's ambitions. Chelsea Football Club was already one of her top clients and it was how Charlotte had met Lucy initially, helping the Santos family to settle as they moved down to London from Manchester. Naturally, Real Madrid had their own variation on the services she offered, an in-house wealth management team, but Lucy liked the personal relationship she had built up with Charlotte and had been adamant that continued access to her was stipulated as one of the conditions of her husband's transfer deal. Eager to secure their new star player, Madrid had happily agreed to his family's demands and Charlotte had worked hard to help them settle quickly in the hope it might lead to the Spanish club becoming another of her clients too.

'This'll be a good chance to touch base with her seeing as I'll be in the neighbourhood. Last time we spoke, she was still struggling: language barrier, the press, school issues . . . The FaceTime sessions aren't enough; I think she needs more proactive support and this will be a good opportunity to try and get some time with her, before everything kicks off in earnest with this Mendoza problem.'

'Mendoza?' It was a name everyone knew. '*Is* there a problem?'

'Could be,' Charlotte nodded. It wasn't every day a bank's liquidity was thrown into question. 'Listen, I've got to go, I'm in a lift. I'll be back in ten.'

'Oh – but what do you want to do about the dinner on Saturday? Will you be back for that?'

The doors closed.

'Oh God, yes, good point. Saturday,' she said, pulling a grimace. How could she have forgotten about that? Charlotte bit her lip. Stephen's parents were throwing a pre-wedding dinner at the Savoy for the core guests. 'No it's fine, leave everything as it is. I'm sure I'll be back by then, but if not, I can fly back for the night if necessary.'

'Or they could come to you,' Rosie quipped, her voice beginning to break up. 'No biggie.'

Charlotte smiled at the prospect of one hundred of her closest friends all decamping to Madrid for the party. 'Quite. We'll charter a jumbo.'

The connection was lost as she heard Rosie laughing. As if she'd been joking.

'I'm home!' she called out, throwing her keys into the trinket dish on the console table and pausing, listening for signs of life as she quickly threw a glance up the stairs and into the drawing room. Nothing. But Stephen's briefcase was on the chair where he always left it when he came in. 'Stephen? I'm back. And I'm wearing nothing under my coat!' She walked down the hall and into the kitchen. 'Oh, hello, Mother.'

'Darling,' her mother smiled, lifting her chin so that Charlotte could reach her cheek more easily.

'Where's Stephen?'

'Just in the cellar, getting some more Pinot.'

'Oh.' Charlotte frowned as she took in the sight of the half-chopped vegetables and a dish of rock oysters on the worktop. '. . . Did we make an arrangement I've forgotten about?'

'Not at all. I just thought I'd look in on my way back from the facialist and Stephen asked me to stay for supper.'

'Ah.' She gave a tight smile. So much for an evening in her pyjamas with her feet up. 'That's sweet of him.'

'As I reminded him, we still need to pin down the more errant of your friends who think RSVP is a cognac.'

Oh good. Charlotte poured herself a glass of water as they waited for the wine. 'How was your facial? You look glowing.'

Her mother took her personal grooming very seriously and was always the first to sign up to any new cosmetic procedure that offered to whip away the years. Her once-blonde hair was now a silvery ash but she still wore it in the curled-under bob she had favoured since her forties, and her blue eyes, though undeniably droopier at the brow, had a youthful twinkle that ensured she was still sought after at dinner parties in London's smartest postcodes.

'Just wonderful. Marie's hands are always so cold, I swear her touch alone makes my skin firm up,' her mother said, dabbing at her cheekbones lightly.

'Mmm.'

Stephen walked in, carrying a bottle of Domaine Leroy Musigny Grand Cru. 'Ah, you're back. You're late,' he said all in one breath as he came over. She reached up for a kiss but he pecked her on the cheek instead; he didn't believe in PDAs, as he called them, and particularly not in front of her mother.

'Yes. I had some paperwork to catch up on before I left.' She watched as he uncorked the bottle between his knees. He had changed into his chinos and a fresh shirt, no tie. It was about as informal as he got.

'How was the meeting at Steed? Farrer fire everyone?' As a broker himself, he was well aware of the rumours about the currently testy atmosphere within the bank.

'No. It was interesting.' She watched as he began to fill her a glass. God, she was thirsty; it had been a long day. 'They need me to go to Madrid for a couple of days.'

'What?' Stephen asked, faltering as he handed over her drink.

'When?' her mother demanded, looking aghast.

'Tomorrow.'

'But the dress fitting—' her mother exclaimed.

'The dinner . . .' Stephen added.

Charlotte stared back at their horrified faces and counted to five. Sometimes she thought *they* were the couple and she the naughty child. 'It's fine. I'll push back the fitting to the weekend when I'll be back in good time for the dinner. Don't worry. I'm hardly going to miss my own wedding party, am I?'

But they both stared at her with expressions that suggested they weren't quite sure. 'It'll be *fine*,' she reiterated, having a sip of wine for strength.

'I don't know why you put yourself through this,' her mother sighed, sitting back in her chair with a disappointed expression.

'Through what?'

'All this stress.'

'I'm not stressed.'

'Of course you are – all these *meetings*, all the *travel*, all this *rushing about*.' Her mother's hand twirled through the air in despairing flourishes. 'No wonder you always look so strained.'

'I don't look strained,' she protested, but her hand had risen protectively to her cheek as though looking for physical proof. She looked over to Stephen for support.

'To be honest, you haven't been taking care of yourself recently,' he shrugged. 'You've lost weight—'

'Every bride loses weight.'

'Plus you're distracted and always late for everything.'

'Yes. Because I'm busy.'

'Busy doing things you don't *need* to be doing,' her mother interjected with a tone of finality, as though that settled it. 'I realize you like the idea of having a job but surely the novelty's worn off now? Frankly, darling, you're spreading yourself too thin. Stephen was just telling me before you walked in, about how he could do with you supporting him by being more at home.'

Charlotte shot him a furious look. Had he? He had the good sense to look away and get busy with prepping dinner again. 'I simply said life would be easier if you weren't working too,' he said quickly.

'What would you prefer I do? Shop? Lunch? Play tennis?'

'And what is wrong with that?' her mother asked sniffily. 'Must you always display such disdain for the way you've been raised? Honestly, Charlotte, sometimes I think you're a closet socialist.'

Charlotte stared at her mother before looking back at her fiancé again; it was hard to keep up with which one of them she was actually arguing with. Seemingly both. 'That's offensive.'

'Absolutely it is!' her mother agreed, completely missing the point.

Charlotte sighed, topping up her glass and too weary to argue. 'Look, I'm not even sure what we're debating here – or why. My career is important to me, that is all; I've worked hard to get the consultancy to this point. It's not simply some sort of daily distraction.'

'I just think you should be thinking about what's best for Stephen's career, before your own. How can you support him when you're running yourself ragged?'

'Hardly ragged.'

'You're off to Madrid tomorrow.'

She sighed; her mother's couture week schedule would put her own to shame. 'Stephen's fine. If he wanted a little wife sitting waiting around at home for him, he'd have proposed to someone else and not me. Isn't that right, darling?'

She looked hopefully towards her fiancé, who appeared to

be concentrating hard on slicing a lemon. He looked up blankly. 'Hmm? . . . Oh, yes, quite.'

It was one of his characteristic non-answers, his chosen method for agreeing and disagreeing with them both unspecifically at once. As a former brigadier in the army, he had survived sniper fire from the Taliban and mortar shelling in Damascus but he still went to great lengths to avoid openly disagreeing with her mother.

'I'm going to have a shower and change into something more comfortable,' she said, setting down her glass irritably. 'My feet are killing me.'

'Well don't be long, please. We need to finalize the buttonholes. Did you see Pip's email? There's been a disaster with the twister roses. Plague of whiteflies apparently, such bad luck. We need to go back to the drawing board . . . She suggested ranunculus,' her mother called to her retreating back.

Charlotte raised a feeble hand in acknowledgement and climbed up the stairs, her mother's crystal tones still wafting enquiringly behind her. Happy Ever After came at a high price.

Madrid

'I feel like I'm going mad.' Lucy Santos's pretty plumped mouth settled into a bitter line. 'No one in this house speaks English. Not her.' She nodded towards the housekeeper polishing a juicer. 'Nor her.' She nodded towards the nanny, playing with her four-year-old in the garden. 'Rob said it didn't matter, that it was a good thing because it forces Leo to speak Spanish, but if there's anything important *I* need to communicate, I have to get Rob to say it when he gets in.'

Charlotte frowned, she had distinctly overheard the housekeeper speaking in English on the phone when she had popped to the loo earlier. 'First off, fire the housekeeper and get one who *does* speak English. Secondly, have you started the Spanish lessons we discussed?'

Lucy snorted. 'For all the good it's doing me. *Hola. Que tal.* That's about it.'

'Keep at it. You'll be surprised what a difference it makes, being able to understand and be understood.'

Lucy's gaze flickered to her resentfully. 'I bet you're fluent.'

There was judgement in the pronouncement; defensiveness; insecurity. 'I came here a lot as a child, which helped, and I did do a Spanish module at university,' Charlotte conceded.

'Let me guess – Oxford.'

'Cambridge,' Charlotte shrugged. 'But don't assume that means anything. I got a third.'

Lucy's eyes twinkled with delight. 'Seriously?'

'Having too much of a good time, I'm afraid.' Charlotte gave a secretive smile.

The admission made Lucy relax somewhat. 'Well it obviously didn't hold you back. Look at you now: wealth counsellor for a fancy private bank. Who even knew that was a thing?'

'Trust me, for as long as there's money in this world, there'll be people who need me. Money is like beauty: a blessing *and* a curse; people think it's the answer to everything but it destroys as many lives as it saves. Any rich person will tell you that money is a prison.'

'Ain't it just,' Lucy muttered under her breath. She was curled up and almost lost from view on one of the vast cream leather sofas. Absolutely tiny, her five-foot-one frame was gym-whittled and elevated by cork wedges, her long balayaged caramel hair giving another inch of height. An enormous aquamarine ring kept glinting on her finger, and the rips on her sprayed-on jeans were so numerous as to suggest she'd been attacked by wolves.

But in spite of the fact it was almost thirty-five degrees outside, her hands were wrapped around a cup of hot, almost-orange tea and she kept dipping her head every few moments to take a sip, losing her train of thought each time. She was distant and distracted, a pale imitation of the bubbly, excited young woman Charlotte had known in London a few months before. Back then, she'd been bursting with impatience to get over here and 'be in the sun at last'.

This was the dream and certainly on paper the move had been seamless. The club had sold £67 million of Santos-branded merchandise, already recouping almost half their outlay on him, and he had settled in well, scoring seven goals in the last nine matches. And behind the scenes, the living was easy: the house was fresh from the pages of *Architectural Digest* – all modernist polished concrete floors, wrap-around windows and cedar cladding, a pale pristine pool with swallows swooping over the surface. In the middle of the kitchen, a copper island the size of an emperor bed was being buffed by another maid in a pale-grey dress. But the mistress of it all was floundering. Unhappy, isolated and resentful.

From her spot on the opposite sofa, Charlotte watched Lucy gazing out at her four-year-old son Leo, playing in the bespoke tree house, the nanny looking up at him from the ground and imploring him to come down.

'D'you think she's pretty?' Lucy asked her, jerking her head towards the young woman outside. Charlotte glanced over. The nanny was wearing jean cutoffs and a white t-shirt with *Déjà vu* written on the front, her long dark hair pulled into a high ponytail. She was in trainers and wasn't wearing any make-up that Charlotte could discern.

'Sure,' Charlotte shrugged. 'Do you?'

'I guess so . . . I mean, she's not *ugly*.'

Charlotte watched Lucy watching her. 'Do you think Roberto thinks she's pretty?'

Lucy's head whipped round, her attention back in the room. 'Why would you ask that?'

'Because it felt like there was subtext to your question.' Charlotte tilted her head slightly and waited. 'Was there?'

Lucy was quiet. 'I dunno,' she muttered finally. '. . . Maybe.'

Another silence settled, filling the room like an invisible expanding foam, filling in all the crevices. They both knew the injuncted stories that swirled around the players – they were always either cheating or secretly gay; no one could ever just be happily married. 'How's he settled here, do you think?'

'Rob?'

Charlotte nodded.

'Rob's Rob. At home wherever he puts his boots.'

'Still, it must be easier for him being here than you – the language barrier doesn't exist, for one thing.'

'Colombian Spanish is different from Spanish Spanish.'

'Yes, but there are more overlaps and parallels than not, surely?'

'I guess.'

'Whereas for you, even just buying a pint of milk is tricky.'

'I have people to buy milk for me,' Lucy shrugged.

'And perhaps that's part of the problem,' Charlotte suggested.

'What? How's that a problem?'

'Once you stop doing little things for yourself, things change. It's a luxury and a privilege having staff, naturally, but becoming disconnected from the basic rhythms of everyday life is also risky – it can be isolating. Alienating. These small routines ground us, we need to stay connected to the mechanisms of our own survival, even if it's just something as insignificant as buying the milk.'

'No chance.' Lucy shook her head. 'You don't know what it's like here. It was hard enough going anywhere back home, but here, it's tenfold. *Galáctico* is another word for god here. People are always staring, watching, judging, filming us even. We took Leo out for lunch last weekend, just a burger, but so many fans came up wanting their photo with Rob, his autograph . . . We ended up having to leave. Leo was in tears, bless him.'

'I can imagine how hard that must be for you. Loss of anonymity can be particularly difficult to adjust to.'

'I'll never get used to it. Me and Leo, we never asked for any of this.'

'Of course not.' Charlotte took another sip of her tea and watched the little boy play too. So much of her job consisted of just listening to her clients, really hearing what they were telling her. 'And of course it works on multiple levels, doesn't it? The general public, invading your privacy with endless gawping, albeit harmless; but it happens on the inter-personal level too, when new people come into your orbit. They know you're Rob Santos's wife—'

'And that he signed for ninety-five mill. I can see it glowing in their eyes when they talk to me.'

'Big boob syndrome,' Charlotte nodded. 'It's all they can see.'

Lucy let out a peal of sudden laughter. 'Yeah. Big boob syndrome, that's it! That's it exactly.'

Charlotte smiled, knowing there was no joy in her laughter. 'It can be hard knowing who to trust: do people like you for you, or because of Rob, or because of your lifestyle? That's incredibly emotionally isolating. Plus you live in a gated community with guards and patrol dogs, and for good reason – your wealth makes you targets – but the upshot is you're as much kept in by these high walls as the public is kept out. And that's physically isolating.'

'Yeah.' Lucy's face fell again as she looked around at the perfect house. 'But then I feel guilty, don't I? We've got so much, more than I could ever have dreamed. What right do I have to moan?'

'Having money at this level can be a profoundly lonely experience, Lucy, and on top of that, you're a young mother, living in a foreign country, far from home, away from your own family and friends, isolated by the language, not to mention being trailed by the paparazzi . . . Who wouldn't feel overwhelmed by that?'

Lucy nodded, looking close to tears.

'The challenge for you is to weed out the people only looking at your boobs and find those people who're interested in you for other things.'

'But how?'

'By doing things that interest you. Go for the experience first and the friendships will follow.' Lucy looked back at her blankly and she shuffled forwards slightly in her chair. 'Okay, back home, what was your favourite thing to do – away from Rob, I mean? What made you happy?'

Away from Rob? The concept seemed to confuse her. 'I dunno.' She gave a hopeless shrug. 'Shopping. Doing up the house. Drinks with the girls. Normal stuff.'

'Any hobbies?'

'*Hobbies?*' Her snub nose wrinkled again. 'You mean like knitting?'

'Or photography. Or pottery. Were you a member of any

book groups? A running club? Floristry workshops?' Lucy looked back at her like she was mad.

'I've got my fitness sessions,' Lucy offered. 'Pilates, HIIT, boxing. I bloody love boxing.'

'Okay, so great – are you doing that out here?'

'Course.'

'And where do you do that?'

'Here.'

Charlotte hitched up a finely shaped eyebrow. 'You've got a gym in the house?'

'Mm hmm.'

'With a trainer?'

'Of course.'

'So it's just the two of you? You're not going out to a class. Meeting other people? Having a coffee afterwards.'

'Oh.' The tiny body deflated again. 'No.'

'What about the other players' wives? Have you met any of them? They're in the same boat as you.'

'They're not like me though. Most of them married their fellas once they were famous. Me and Rob have been together since he was brought over to the youth academy at Man U. I'm not about the money. We properly love each other.'

'I know. I can see it between you. You're a real couple. A real family.' Charlotte thought for a moment. 'Okay, answer me this. What do you think you'd be doing if Rob wasn't a professional footballer?'

Lucy thought about it for a moment. 'Hairdresser.'

'Okay. And what would you do if you *had* to work, but you could do whatever you wanted?'

This time, Lucy didn't hesitate. 'Artist.'

'Really?' Charlotte was surprised, and she saw the

embarrassment climb over her client and sit on her like a child. 'What sort?'

'Portraits. I like looking at faces.' She regarded Charlotte with an intense stare suddenly. 'I'd love to do you.'

Charlotte laughed, taken aback to find the attention suddenly on her. 'Oh I'm sure you can find better subjects than me!'

'No, there's . . .' Lucy stared at her closely, her eyes travelling over her face like she was a dot-to-dot graph. 'There's something about your face . . .'

Charlotte had never thought there was anything particularly beguiling about her face, not really: light-brown eyes, good brows, neat nose, unspectacular mouth, sprinkling of freckles. She was, to her mind, simply pretty, nothing more. Stephen had once told her she was 'tidy-looking'.

'Haggardness?' she asked, recalling her mother's words last night.

'Hardly,' Lucy guffawed. 'Nah, it's . . .' She trailed off, scrutinizing her.

'What?' Charlotte asked, intrigued but also trepidatious.

Lucy's gaze narrowed thoughtfully. 'I don't know – you've got sort of . . . sad eyes.'

The smile froze on Charlotte's face. 'Oh—'

'No, no, I don't mean it as a diss or nothing,' Lucy said quickly. 'Oh, I can't find the right words for it. It's just a bit of a sense I get with you, you know? Some people you meet and they're like old souls, aren't they? You feel like they've been here before.' She widened her eyes spookily. 'But with you, it's like, no matter how smiley you are, there's still something . . . sad in you.' She wrinkled her nose. 'Sorry, no offence. I don't mean to keep calling you sad. I can't think of the right word.'

'None taken,' Charlotte said, keeping her smile fixed. 'But please don't worry about me. I really am perfectly happy. Very happy in fact. Not sad at all.'

Lucy's face brightened further, as she remembered something. 'Oh my God, that's right. Last time I saw you in London, you'd just got engaged.' She leant forward, reaching for Charlotte's hand. 'Ooh that lovely ring he gave you. Let me see it ag—'

Her voice faltered as she saw the bare ring finger. She looked up at Charlotte in alarm.

'It's fine!' Charlotte smiled, seeing the panic on her face. 'I'm just having it resized. It kept spinning round on my finger.'

'Oh my God, thank *fuck*,' Lucy laughed, slapping her hand to her chest. 'I really thought I'd put my foot in it there.'

'No, don't worry, we're absolutely fine.'

Lucy gave a small snort. 'That's what I say to my mum when she rings. "I'm fine."' She looked up suddenly. 'It's the most common lie in the world, did you know that?'

Charlotte shook her head, feeling her heart flutter slightly, like a child startled in its sleep.

'Yeah, I read that somewhere.'

Charlotte kept her face neutral, but her gaze down. She didn't want Lucy seeing her eyes now. Because if 'being fine' was a lie, only one of them here was going to admit to it.

Chapter Two

The apartment was west-facing, the Spanish sun pooling on the parquet floor; the bank reserved it exclusively for senior executive use – and favoured consultants. Charlotte sat with her legs outstretched, bare feet on the ironwork railings, skirt hitched up to tan her thighs – watching as the city six storeys down ran through its rush-hour cycle: red tail lights stretching along the boulevards, cyclists weaving down through one-way streets and narrow alleys, the distant rumble of trains underscoring the bad-tempered traffic. The wine glass was weighty in her hand; beads of condensation matched the sweat on her upper lip. The temperature here always took some adjusting to, especially coming straight from London.

'Hey! Finally. I thought I'd never get hold of you,' she said into the phone, the ringtone against her ear immediately switching to another background soundtrack of traffic.

'Oh, Charlotte, I'm just rushing off.' Stephen sounded harried.

'Where are you?' She sipped the wine, watching as an elderly lady walked her dog.

'Piccadilly.' She could tell from his breathing that he was walking briskly. He still walked like a soldier: shoulders back, chest out, chin up, straight arms. You could take the man out of the military . . . 'Just en route to drinks at the Reform. Heatherwick's back in town.'

'Ah, Charlie, how is he? Still living with tribes in the Andes?' She had only met the man himself once before on a one-night layover between St Petersburg and Panama, but Stephen had regaled her many times with tales of their time in the field together, playing poker inside tanks and singing along rugby songs to his pocket harmonica. When Charlie had decided not to renew his commission after a particularly gruelling assignment in Helmand Province, Stephen had been devastated. Was it coincidence he himself had left after the next tour of duty? He had said it was because he had met her by then and wanted to settle down to a normal life, but sometimes she wondered if the catalyst hadn't been the prospect of a new life with her so much as losing his old one with Charlie.

'Apparently so. I've bought him a tie in case he's forgotten how to dress properly.'

'He's ex-Sandhurst,' she said drily. 'That's impossible. I bet he polishes his fishing spear to a shine.' She lapsed into silence, listening to the rapid beat of his shoes on the pavement. It was his upright bearing that had first caught her eye, when they met. It seemed so . . . reassuring to meet a man who held his head that high, as though nothing the world could ever throw at him would make him duck or waver.

Behind her, in the background, music played softly through the speaker system.

'Where are you? What are you up to?' She could hear the frown in his voice.

'Chilling in the apartment. I'm only just back.'

'Decent place?'

'Decent,' she agreed, blind to the mushroom silk curtains and minimal Armani furniture.

'Good. And how was today?' She knew what he really meant was, have you concluded your business there?

'Fine. I just caught up with another client this morning and popped into the bank's offices for a quick meeting this afternoon. The real work starts tomorrow.'

She heard him tut. 'Just so long as you remember you need to be back by Friday, Charlotte.'

The dinner wasn't till Saturday but she knew better than to point out that detail. Friday was her deadline. He wanted her back in London by then, regardless of anything else. 'I will be.'

'It's a bloody nonsense them sending you away on a project at a time like this.'

'I'll be back, don't worry.' She heard him 'harumph'. He was never any good on his own. 'What are you doing for dinner? There's some lamb in the fridge.'

'I'll play it by ear with Charlie boy. See if he fancies going on somewhere. I should imagine he's in dire need of a bloody steak after all those agave leaves.'

Charlotte smiled. Her fiancé was the sort of man who believed that survival depended upon red meat at every meal and he looked upon vegetarians – much less vegans – as utter lunatics.

'I'm going to have to ring off. I'm just coming up to the steps and you know what they're like with technology in there. My phone will be on silent so unless it's an emergency . . .'

'It's fine. Go see Charlie – feed him up – and I'll call you tomorrow.'

'Okay. Have fun over there. Cheerio.'

Cheerio. It was another of his quirks that had made her smile when they first met, an attempt at levity instilled into him by his own mother. 'Love you, darling.'

'Yes, yes, love you too.'

The line went dead, London transposed for Madrid again, and she sat a few minutes longer, her toes waggling in time to the beat, her gaze flighty and restless as she looked from one rooftop to the next, from the street to the sky, tracking birds, pedestrians, cars, nothing at all. This was relaxing, right?

She watched the sun set for a few minutes more – as if proving a point – before turning back into the apartment. It was immaculate save for the orange net bag puddled on the table; she had bought just enough provisions to get her through tonight and tomorrow morning: coffee pods, milk, a bottle of rosé and a box of cereal that looked to be three parts sugar to one part grain.

Frankly, she was tempted to have the cereal for supper. In spite of playing it down to Stephen – last night's conversation with him and her mother still rankling – hers had been a long day. After the face-to-face with Lucy Santos, she had headed straight over to the regional office for a four-hour meeting with the head of HR. Food and drink had been brought in at regular intervals but to all intents and purposes, they hadn't lifted their heads as they went through the Mendoza file with a nit comb. It was vital she understood the background of the family and how they had built up their fortune to become the dynasty they were today.

Marina Quincy, though. A nobody. A line in a phone book. Charlotte had done her own brief internet search, finding nothing on Google, Facebook or Instagram; it only piqued her interest further; the name had been lodged in her mind since the initial meeting. It was distinctive. Curious, even.

She turned her head to the right and caught sight of the file sticking out of her tote. Rosie had sent it over as she was leaving the office this evening – the preliminary investigative report Mateo Mendoza had commissioned on his father's mistress, as she was now commonly assumed to be. Charlotte, despite her better judgement, had printed it out to take home with her. She knew she ought to leave it till the morning. This was now *her* time. She was supposed to be relaxing, getting ready for the wedding: she still had to make final decisions on the napkin colour and her mother would not rest until they had a verdict on the buttonholes. The wedding was coming round at a gallop and Rosie was right – she did need to switch off from work and give it some attention.

And yet, she found her hand reaching for the file anyway as she passed by to curl up on the white leather sofa. Just a quick look-see . . .

She flicked through the pictures first. Marina Quincy was a strikingly beautiful woman, the sort to make men stare open-mouthed and turn their heads in front of their wives as she passed. From what Charlotte could make out from the somewhat grainy photos taken of her waitressing at a cafe, she was tall and rangy but there was a mannishness to her looks too: she was no run-of-the-mill *femme fatale* with her big hands and feet, thick eyebrows and tawny skin pulled tight over angled planes. Her dark hair was almost black and worn up in a messy bun with wispy tendrils fluttering at her neck. She wore several silver rings on both hands and had a tiny tattoo of a swallow on her left inner wrist, her white shirt straining slightly at the bust and across the shoulders. An old plaster was wrapped around her left pinky finger and the multiple studs, cuffs and small hoops at her ears looked tarnished.

There was nothing polished or refined about her. She looked tired, weary, worn-down. And yet, in the images, though her eyes were cast down as she collected plates from a table, Charlotte could see several onlookers watching her going about her business. Was she aware of the power she had over other people, Charlotte wondered, or oblivious to it?

Charlotte thought not. To transfix a man like Carlos Mendoza, ancient though he was – and he was ancient; two years off a century according to their files – would have been no mean undertaking; she surely had to understand the weapons in her arsenal.

She wondered how long the relationship had been going on for – a glance at the profile told her Marina was forty-five. It surely couldn't be a new thing? Not with his age. If they had met when she was in her early thirties and he in his mid-eighties though . . . ? It was still a hell of a stretch but he might well have been a vigorous older man, carrying his years well? A silver fox? Charlotte had seen the Rolling Stones playing at Twickenham the year before and watching Mick Jagger race up and down the stage for two hours had redefined what 'seventy-something' looked like to her. It was certainly possible, she supposed, and a fortune the size of his was a proven aphrodisiac to many young women before her.

But it wasn't just the age group that struck her as odd. The fact that she was still waitressing . . . It might have been how Carlos had first met her, but Charlotte would have assumed a man like him would want to keep his lover in fancier style than this. Unless Marina insisted upon it – keeping her job, her old life? Was it a principled stand or a tactical play? And if the latter, it begged the question, did she know what her lover was intending for her: wealth she could never hope to count, land she could never hope to cover?

She read through the profile more closely: Born and bred Madrilena. Divorced, ex-husband Miguel Hermoso, a carpenter, no kids. Two brothers, one now dead – testicular cancer. Aunt to three nephews and two nieces. Mother dead, father a mechanic, remarried and living in Bilbao. She had had multiple jobs – working at the laundromat, a hotel maid at a three-star hotel, dog walker, checkout clerk at supermarket. But . . . this was interesting; Charlotte peered closer: she had graduated with a hospitality qualification four years ago.

Charlotte mused on it. She would have been forty-one back then – that was pretty late in the day to decide to go for a professional qualification. Why the new direction? Was Mendoza trying to 'better' her, playing Professor Higgins to her Eliza Dolittle? And if he was the one encouraging her, paying for the course, then why was she still, four years later, waitressing in a tourists' cafe?

She went back to the report, trying to rein in her questions: Marina owned an apartment in a down-at-heel pocket of town – it wasn't rough as such, just not polished. She had credit card debt of 23,600 euros and had defaulted several times on her monthly credit card payments in the last year.

Charlotte let the papers fall in her lap as she tilted her head back and digested what she had read: so, her client was a beautiful divorcee with practically no assets, financially insolvent and insecurely employed; she had an extended family that may or may not need supporting; she was unmanicured and exhausted-looking – all of which suggested Mendoza wasn't bankrolling her; her bank records also showed there was no drip-feed of payments, no top-ups or handouts.

But that made no sense. Why else would she be with him? This wasn't a love story, clearly, how could it be? The man was ninety-eight! He might be infatuated with her but no one would believe that her interest in him could be anything more than financially motivated; a mutually beneficial arrangement. And yet she clearly wasn't taking his money.

A theory occurred to her: if Marina was refusing to accept his help, living by her 'principles', making him watch on as she slaved long hours at the cafe and slept in an un-air-conditioned room at night . . . Charlotte nodded her head, seeing the game: she could well imagine that would be torture to an infatuated Mendoza – he was used to his money solving problems, sanitizing his landscape, buying things and people. But if she wouldn't let him merely 'help out' then she was forcing him into something bigger, something bolder; he would have to give her everything to save her completely, rescue her from this plight.

It was one theory, anyway.

Her eyes flickered up to the windows: Madrid was glowing, the old stone buildings looking aflame in the sunset. Lights stippled the baroque facades, silhouettes beginning to pass in front of windows, the rush-hour roar settling into a background thrum. She felt the city fade away as she cradled the wine glass in her palm and thought back to how she too had tried to rescue someone once. And how someone had in turn tried to rescue her. How they had all failed. And how Life had beat on anyway, regardless . . .

She woke up frowning, the blue light flashing like a beacon in the still-dark room. Her hand reaching blindly for the phone, she then recoiled as the white screen glared back at her angrily: one missed call from Lucy Santos. One from her mother, from Stephen, from Milton, her sister. Why on earth were they all calling her so early? What could possibly have happened? What time was it?

Eleven twenty—

Eleven twenty-five? How was that possible? She couldn't sleep past the dawn chorus in London! She glanced across at the interlined Armani Casa curtains, only a thin blade of light peeping through at the furthest edge. It was their fault.

She swung her legs out of bed, knocking over the wine bottle she'd left on the floor. It was empty, thankfully – or perhaps not, her hand flying to her head as the dull thud began to impress itself upon her. Okay, so maybe it was the rosé's fault too.

She staggered into the shower, feeling light-headed with panic. It was too late to reset her morning to its usual determinedly mindful state via the yoga flows and green juice Stephen always found so baffling, and she grabbed an espresso on her way out instead, leaving the building an impressively quick fifteen minutes later with her ponytail ribbon tied in damp hair, the blue light still flashing on her phone.

She crossed the street, her new Celine shades on and her earbuds in as she joined the busy-busy crowds already halfway through their mornings, intermingling and becoming one of them and trying to get back on track again. She walked quickly, pressed voicemail and listened to her messages, desperate to catch up with her morning. She felt rattled and edgy. How could she have let this happen? Why had she allowed herself to wallow in the past like that last night? She was usually so disciplined.

'Charlotte? It's Lucy. Listen, I've been thinking about what we talked about yesterday, and I reckon you're right, maybe I should do more of what I love. So I've done a bit of a search and uh, there's an exhibition on at the Prado at the minute that I'd love to see. But . . .' She cleared her voice, sounding embarrassed. *'Well, thing is, I've not got anyone to go with. I don't suppose you'd be up for it? Just an hour or so? Call me.'*

She pressed to listen to the next.

'Darling, it's Mama. Have you left already or are you back? I can't keep up. Anyway, we really must thrash out the menus as they need to go to print this afternoon. It was just the font we were

sticking on – I know you felt the Kunstler was tricky to read but really we're all grown-ups, aren't we, and I do think the Bookman is just too . . . dull.' She drew a breath. *'Anyway, ring me back, darling. But not before two. I'm in with Dr Faroodh for some more plumping—'*

The timer ran out, cutting off her mother mid-flow, which always happened when she left a message. Charlotte was convinced her mother clean forgot she was talking to a machine and not a live person on the other end of the line. She pressed delete and waited for the next message.

'It's me, are you in meetings already? Call me back.'

Delete.

She crossed at an intersection, looking for a cab. Madrid was already sizzling in the midday sun, dust kicking up on the streets and a heat haze coming off the bonnets of the cars waiting at the lights.

'Charlotte, it's Milton. Look, call me when you get this. I know it's not strictly your remit but we need to talk before you go in to see Mendoza. Latest is we've managed to shore up a hundred mill but I don't think there's hope for much more. I'll send through the charts so you can show him the detail; he'll be pissed but just remind him that's a significant chunk now tied up for ten years – more than enough time for the lawyers to get things dragging on in the courts. This is a good news story, get that across to him but, sorry – I can only block so much, the rest will be down to you after all.'

A cab came into view, its light on, and she shot her arm up, watching with her hand to her ear as it rolled to a stop at her feet. 'Club de Campo,' she said to the driver, not needing to give him the address; everyone knew it, it was the most exclusive country club in Madrid.

'Lotts, it's Mouse.' Her little sister's trademark husky voice made her smile. Her sister Antonia had been called Mouse

since they were toddlers, although no one was quite sure why any more; the original reason had long since been consigned to history and the name seemed to have become a fond misnomer, for her sister had the loudest mouth and dirtiest laugh of anyone she knew. '. . . *I've just seen the underwear Ma's had sent through for the bridesmaid dresses. She's fucking joking, right? Granny Banana wouldn't have worn knickers as big as those! You could parachute with them, I'm not even joking! Call me straight back, I mean it.*'

Charlotte sat back in the seat, the sound of her sister's panic allowing her own to subside. No major emergencies then? The world was continuing to turn? Her errant 'morning after the night before' was already slipping out of sight below the radar, no harm done.

In fact, a small smile began to spread on her lips as she ruminated on these cameos from the people she loved, all of them in her life – and it was a good life, wasn't it? It was busy and focused and diverting.

Yes, this was enough. She was happy enough.

She watched the city roll past the windows, feeling the caffeine kick in, her headache gradually recede, her hair beginning to dry. Minute by minute, life was becoming ordered again; the mask was back on and the night's grasping shadows were already receding in the bright July light.

'Señor Mendoza? Charlotte Fairfax,' she said, holding out her hand.

'Mateo, please.' The man's grip was strong, his black-eyed gaze direct. 'Shall we sit?' he asked in faultless English. He pointed to the club chairs – bleached wicker with ivory cushions, a giant coral on the table between them. They settled themselves comfortably in the shade and looked out across the undulating greens. Beyond the veranda could be heard the distant sounds of tennis balls being volleyed, electric golf carts zipping between trees that were casting stubby shadows on the perfect ground. 'Thank you for agreeing to meet with me here.'

Charlotte indicated the pastoral scene. 'The pleasure is all mine.' She looked back, taking in his attire: white breeches, tan boots, a pale-blue shirt with a white saltire cross. 'You keep horses at the club?'

'My polo ponies, yes. We have a full season coming up.' He had thrown one stocky leg over the opposite knee, fingers loosely interlaced as he took her in, and she knew he was assessing her as the person upon whom his fate seemed to rest. 'Do you like horses?'

'I do,' she replied, examining him back. His hair was salt and peppered, with thick sideburns and equally impressive eyebrows, his face dominated by a bulbous nose. He was not a handsome man but there was something compelling about him: an intensity, an innate sense of confidence. Charlotte knew he was approaching his sixty-sixth birthday and was seven years into a second marriage with a former Miss Spain that had produced a longed-for son; his first wife had given him 'only' three daughters.

'Do you ride?' he enquired.

'I did as a child. Not so much these days. I travel a lot and my work keeps me too busy for hobbies.'

'Nonsense. What is life without hobbies? Just drudge surely?'

Drudge. Yes, that was the word. She smiled. 'I get by okay. A yoga mat is a lot more transportable than a horse.'

He chuckled. 'Come as my guest this weekend, I insist. We have a match against our fiercest rivals, Real Sociedad. That will revive your love of these magnificent beasts, I guarantee it.'

'Thank you but much will depend on whether I'm still here and what happens in the next few days.' There didn't seem to be any point in mentioning the small issue of dinner for a hundred at the Savoy with her as the guest of honour.

The waiter came over and Mateo gestured for her to order.

'Sparkling water, please,' she murmured.

'And for me, Miguel, but add my usual.' He patted his midriff lightly, looking back at her. 'Chilli flakes, good for the metabolism.'

They waited for the waiter to leave before picking up the thread of the conversation they were both here for. 'Yes, as you were saying . . . shall you still be here by the weekend? Will the nightmare be ongoing? It is the question we all want the answer to, is it not?' He looked over at her with a hooked eyebrow. 'You have seen the report I commissioned?'

'Yes. I went through it last night.' That and the rosé.

He leaned forward in the chair. 'And from what you read, do you think she will take an offer and go quietly into the night?'

Charlotte didn't hesitate. 'No.'

'No?' It was not the answer he had wanted to hear. He slumped back again, agitated and displeased.

'Assuming she is your father's mistress, or that he's in love with her at least, then there's a lot that's not adding up here. Looking at her current financial situation, place of employment, where she lives . . . all of this would suggest she should be an easy target; she's in a vulnerable position. And yet the fact that your father has made seemingly no impact on her circumstances suggests to me she is playing a long game and holding out for more.' She looked directly at him. 'I assume your father would usually provide an apartment for his lady friends, somewhere discreet they could meet?'

'Of course.' Mateo looked pained, as though this was a point of honour when cheating on one's wife.

'Well, the fact that Ms Quincy *hasn't* accepted that offer would suggest she won't settle for the usual titbits.'

'So then you think she does know of my father's intentions to hand it all over to her?'

'Quite possibly, yes. She might even have been carefully navigating him to that position herself.'

Mateo pushed himself back into the cushions, muttering something under his breath in Spanish which suggested he assumed she couldn't understand. Charlotte decided not to dissuade him from that idea. He looked back at her again. 'You will have to excuse my anger but this is hard to take. Who does she think she is to come in and rob us, his family, of everything that is ours, everything we have all worked for and striven to protect?'

'I agree. It's a terrible predicament to be in, but also –' She wondered how to phrase it delicately – 'highly unusual in this instance, on account of your father's age I mean. Do you recall when his health started to decline?'

'I'm sorry?' Mateo looked flummoxed by the question.

'There weren't any specific medical incidents or concerns before the cancer diagnosis? Was he in generally good health before that?'

'Why yes, the best! He was as strong as a bull. Nothing could topple him, no one could ever believe he was in his nineties. He swam every morning until he was ninety-two!'

'Wow.'

'Yes. He always said we Mendozas are as strong as our bulls.'

Charlotte nodded. 'And understand you've never met Ms Quincy?'

His lip curled. 'I'd never even heard of her until last week!'

'And you never had suspicions he was keeping a mistress?'

'No. Well, not after Carmen—'

Carmen? Charlotte hooked an eyebrow, waiting for more.

'They were together privately for many years, he was very fond of her; my mother was too.' Charlotte kept her face neutral. 'But after she died – several years ago now – even for a man like my papa, I did not think he was still . . . that it would be . . . possible to be . . . active.' His voice faded out as he struggled and failed to find the right euphemisms.

She nodded. 'I thought the same thing: this can't possibly be a sexual relationship,' she said, getting straight to the point. 'Which is why I'm wondering if Ms Quincy has been around for quite a while – *before* your father's health declined, even before Carmen died. She could well have been; she's forty-five now but this relationship makes a lot more sense – in fact, it *only* makes sense if it started ten, fifteen, even twenty years ago. If he was still swimming every morning at ninety-two, I imagine he would have been a "robust" man at seventy-eight.'

'Of course. But Carmen only died seven years ago.'

Charlotte watched him. 'So you don't think he would cheat on his mistress?' Was that really the pertinent point?

Mateo looked dumbfounded by the thought. 'I . . . I didn't think so.'

'Well I think we must consider all possibilities,' she said as Miguel came back with their drinks, iced towels rolled on individual trays. 'Thank you.'

She watched as Mateo pressed the towel to the back of his neck before shaking it open and pressing it over his face for a moment. The heat was blistering today, even in the shade, and suddenly London's gentle grey rendition of summer didn't seem so bad. 'What is the latest from your lawyers? Are there any loopholes to work with?'

'None so far. The law is agonizingly clear – he can give what he likes to whoever he wishes during his life. Of course, I have a trust, my own investments, shares in the company and so forth. I shan't be left destitute. But in terms of the bulk of the estate, I am still merely the heir; everything else is in my father's name.'

'I'm sorry.'

He glanced over at her, distracted, despondent. 'It is ironic – all my life, money has been something I have never had to even think about. And now, as I approach old age, I must start counting pennies?' He looked genuinely pained. 'Papa and I are close, there has never been a feud or a problem between us. Why is he doing this?'

Charlotte shook her head sadly. 'Love and money have always been uneasy bedfellows.'

'But this is not love! He does not love her.'

'No. An infatuation is more likely, but to him perhaps, I don't know . . .' She shrugged, trying to imagine what on earth his father might be feeling. 'Maybe it makes him feel alive. Young again.'

'He is making a fool of himself. Out of all of us. Once this gets out, the family will be disgraced. A laughing stock. For generations, the Mendoza name has meant something. Now we will be known for the tawdry headlines—'

'That's not going to happen. Firstly, this is all strictly confidential. The only people who know about this issue are your lawyers and banking team, all of whom are bound by secrecy agreements.'

He nodded, looking like a boy wanting comfort from his mother.

'Secondly, some of the money has already been put out of

reach. Not all, not by a long stretch, but I've just been told by Dan Milton, who's the head of private banking for continental Europe, that they've managed to lock down almost a hundred million euros; it's been moved into long-term investments that if Marina Quincy did try to get her hands on, she'd be forced through the courts – which I don't think is something she'd want.'

Mateo looked at her with a concerned expression. 'Legally, how defensible is that? Can the bank hide my father's money, knowing he was intending to give it away?'

'Well, obviously this is outside my remit, I'm not a banker per se. But my understanding is it would be a matter of what could be proved, if necessary. Steed's line is that, *officially*, they know nothing about the intended gift. This information has come to the bank's attention only through private conversations with you, not your father himself. Now, as their client of many years standing and chairman of the Mendoza Corporation, you are authorized to make trades on your father's behalf and they haven't received any official or formal directive from your father rescinding that authority or asking them to change or cease their trading patterns for him. Clearly, he must have been intending to inform and involve the bank in the disbursement of the gift – there's no way he couldn't – but the stroke has obviously prevented that from happening, for the time being anyway. So as things stand, it's business as usual and the bank's position – if challenged – would be that they've simply looked to protect his investments from a particularly volatile market: Brexit, trade wars with the US and China . . . They'd say they've been conservative, nothing more.' She gave a hapless shrug.

He looked at her intently, beginning to seem reassured. 'Okay, so they've protected one hundred million. But what about the rest of it – if and when my father wakes up and finishes what he's started . . . What then? There's half a billion euros still at stake.'

'Well that's why they've brought me in. If the lawyers and the bankers can't stop your father from giving the money, I can work to stop her wanting it.'

He looked confused. 'I don't understand. How can you do that?'

'There's a thing called sudden wealth syndrome. You tend to see it in people who experience sudden windfalls – lottery winners for example. Almost without exception, a few years down the line, they'll be divorced where they were previously happily married, lonely when they were previously sociable, suspicious where they were previously open. Because what people don't realize is wealth doesn't change attitudes to money, it exaggerates them. You've heard of the saying "caught, not taught"?'

He gave a shrug. 'Sure.'

'Well for someone like Marina, who has always had to dig in for what she's got, had to get her hands dirty and fight . . . becoming rich overnight is not going to be the answer to all her problems, it'll be the start of them. For someone who's grown up having to take to survive, how will she cope with friends asking her to help them out, family members wanting her to pay off their mortgages, buy them a car? She doesn't know how to be a donor, a benefactor. It doesn't matter how good her intentions start out, in no time she's going to become resentful that they're asking, embittered that she feels guilty for saying no, suspicious they all want more from her, paranoid they're only with her for the money, isolated because who can she trust . . . It happens all the time. Living happily with wealth is something that has to be caught, but from what

I can glean from the report, she has no one to guide her, no examples to follow.' She gave a pitying shrug. 'She has no idea how difficult her life would become.'

'I'm beginning to wonder how I've struggled through,' Mateo said wryly.

'Ah, but you're third-generation rich, that's different; you're native to it and that makes all the difference in the world. Did you know that ninety per cent of families fail to pass down their money beyond three generations?'

He looked less glib about that fact. 'Well, we may yet conform to that stereotype then.'

'No, this is by no means a done deal.' She shook her head firmly. 'I'm going to start by introducing myself. Get to know her. See what makes her tick.'

'But why should she believe what you say? For someone in her position, these are pennies from heaven. She will take her chances, no matter what you say. You can't *talk her out* of becoming a multimillionaire.'

'Quite right. But I'm hopeful that once she's been shown the full reality of what that amount of money can do, we can perhaps negotiate her down to a token amount that will prove to be in everyone's best interests – manageable for her, palatable for you.'

'You really think you can do that?'

She nodded. 'I know better than anyone how money screws people up, Mr Mendoza, and it's my job to highlight these pitfalls to her.'

He sighed, looking only vaguely mollified. He sipped his drink, looking out over the lawns, and she let the silence settle; there was a lot for him to digest. '. . . If I could just speak to him. If he could just tell me *why* he was doing this,' he murmured. 'It's the not knowing anything that makes it so hard. Why would he give everything to this woman no one's ever met or heard of? Carmen, I could understand, but why her? Who is she? When did she come into his life? And why is she more important to him than everyone else? We are his family.'

Charlotte was quiet for a moment longer. 'Well, perhaps this isn't about Marina, per se; maybe it's about him. The urge for philanthropy can become increasingly strong as people approach the end of their lives, particularly when they've enjoyed such . . . ease. I've seen it happen before, almost as a barter, a way to minimize the guilt that's almost inevitable when one has so much and others so little. Equally, other people can feel a sense of guilt for the way the fortune was created – historic Nazi collaboration, arms dealing, the tobacco industries . . . Feelings of guilt are particularly prevalent in inheritors, rather than the first-generation wealth creators.'

'But my father has worked hard all his life,' Mateo said defensively. 'He wasn't just some spoilt little rich boy. It was he who diversified the business after the war; he who foresaw the end of bullfighting and predicted the rise of large-scale fruit farming.'

'I'm not disputing it. I'm just saying he was born into money too. His starting point was different from most people's and the guilt of having been "born lucky" into the right family *may* be an impetus in all this.' She gave a sigh. 'But as you rightly say, he was also a wealth creator and perhaps his drive to give back is originating from there . . .' She trailed off. How could they possibly know which way to turn with this? The man's reasons were his own secrets, zipped shut in a frail and unconscious body. An idea came to her. 'You know, perhaps that's where we should be concentrating our efforts.'

Rather than just looking at a cure for this problem that

Marina Quincy presents, we should be looking for the source of it – investigating the root cause of your father's urgent need to divest himself of his fortune.'

'But how? He is unconscious in hospital. None of us can ask him anything right now.'

'I know, but we could engage the services of a research specialist.'

'That's already been done. We employed our own researchers.'

'Yes, your investigators built up a profile on Marina Quincy, but let's forget her for a moment. I'm talking about calling in a historian – someone at PhD level who can sift through the layers of your family's history and go right back to how the fortune was amassed in the beginning.'

'We know how. Bulls. Our family grew rich from breeding bulls.'

'Things are never that linear though, are they, Mr Mendoza? There are always digressions, transgressions . . . Something might have happened in the past that could account for your father's sense of guilt – *if* that's what it is.'

He looked offended by the insinuation. 'So you want to look for dirt on my family? Bring out the skeletons in their closet? Absolutely not.'

'I'm not saying there are necessarily any skeletons, and anyway, it may not even be required. Who knows? Marina might turn out to be conducive to an offer and this can all go away.' Mateo looked sceptical. 'But if it does drag on and she holds out for the full gift, we'll need to consider alternative strategies that probe your father's motivations. I've worked with a history professor at Carlos III University a couple of times. He's very professional, very discreet. I could set up an initial meeting so you can meet and get a sense of him first if you like. When I've commissioned these searches in the past, it's been to help families appreciate and understand what it took to create their fortunes – the personal journeys their forebears took, their struggle, setbacks, risks and breakthroughs, the human story behind the bank balance if you like. But in this instance, where the head of the family is seeking to *rid* himself of that very privilege . . . I do think we need to examine the reasons why that may be.' She shook her head. 'Because something's not adding up. No matter which way we turn it, this just doesn't feel like a straightforward sugar-daddy story to me.'

'No?' He frowned. 'What does it feel like?'

It took her a moment to find the right word. 'A purge.'

'A *purge*? But why?'

'At this point, there's really only one reason I can think of.' She sat back in the chair and inhaled slowly. 'Shame.'

Chapter Three

Ronda, Andalusia, August 1932

She sat in the cradle of her favourite tree, back braced against the mighty trunk and one leg stretched out on the branch, the other dangling, kicking back and forth, back and forth. She was watching the farmers peel the oaks, their axes swinging into the bark with just the right amount of force so as not to damage the inner living tissue, the outer layers coming away in great curved sheets to reveal tender, terracotta-tinted cores.

'Give me some more,' Santi shouted up.

She ignored him. She was watching his father, Juan Esperanza, climbing higher into the tree, the fabric of his trousers flapping around his thin legs, his rope-soled shoes finding grip on the bark. It was always a spectacle to her, seeing how the men moved so confidently without ropes, balancing on branches and swinging their axes through the air. Three years ago there had been a nasty accident when old Pablo Morales had slipped, his axe falling after him into a soft landing. The ensuing tales of gore had been enough to get her brothers here to watch with her for the next two seasons, just in case, but to their disgust, the men were more careful than ever and there had been not so much as a broken fingernail since.

It wasn't why she came though. She loved the sound of the

harvests: the axes thunking in rhythm, the farmers' chatter and songs, the creak of the bark as it split and gave, the melancholic haw of the donkeys as their backs were laden with the fresh cargo; but more than anything, she loved watching the spectacle of the old cork oak forest changing colour, the newly reddened trunks like sunburnt arms, matching the brick earth. In the distance, where the land rose up from these gentle slopes, she could see the *pueblo blanco* in the valley, its tiny, primitive houses little more than white dots from here. Her own house was out of sight from here, hidden in the shade of—

'Nene!'

She looked down. Santi was on the bough below, his hand outstretched for another segment. He had already eaten all three of the oranges she had dared to pilfer from the grove for him on the way through, and now he wanted the last of hers. But his limbs were so skinny, his brown eyes so big in his face, how could she refuse? She tossed the rest of the orange down to him, seeing how his face split into that signature grin which always spelled trouble, his oversized teeth bright against his tawny skin.

'I'm bored. Let's go,' he said, juice dribbling down his chin and onto his shirt as he crammed the orange into his mouth, a half at a time.

'And do what?'

'Go swimming,' he managed, the words muffled.

'Swimming?' she scoffed, even though her skin felt tight and dusty. 'You're a fool, Santi Esperanza, the lake is dry. And you know we can't go near the house. Papa is home.'

'So then let's see Leviatan again. I bet I can make him chase me this time.'

'Ha! You're so small, you're not worth the effort. He may as well toss a grasshopper as you.' But she climbed down from the tree anyway, her skirts tucked into her knickers to free her legs. She detested wearing dresses – they were hot and got in the way; the only thing they were good for was hiding the scabs on her knees from when she fell during their races.

'Santi, where are you going?' his father called after him as they jumped to the ground.

'We are just taking a walk.'

His father hesitated, looking first at his son and then at her. An uncertain look flickered in his kind eyes. 'You must stay near, you hear me? I will need you shortly.'

'I will, Papa. We won't be long.'

His father looked unconvinced, concern still stretched across his lined face, but he gave a polite nod as his eyes met hers.

'I'll make sure he comes straight back, Señor Esperanza,' Nene smiled at him, and it must have been infectious for his face split into a friendly grin too, as though suddenly reassured.

'Thank you, Nene, you are a good girl,' he nodded, pretending, like the other farmers, not to notice her unladylike, leggy display.

That was another reason she loved hiding out up here, she didn't have to be something she wasn't. She could be free, be herself for once.

'Why does he always look so worried?' she asked as they walked off. 'Does he think I will hurt you?'

'He knows you could never hurt me! You're a girl!' Santi scoffed.

'I'm bigger than you!' she said scornfully. Her shadow was taller than his now, even though he was already thirteen by four months and it would be another season before it was her turn. But her shape was changing faster than his, becoming more rounded, undulating whilst he remained stick-thin and twiggy. Santi had pointed and mocked her when he had glimpsed the hair under her arms the last time they had swum together – it was after the last rain in May, when the lake was still full and the almond trees shook with pink blossom – and she hadn't spoken to him for a full eight days afterwards. But she never could stay mad at him for long and she knew his contrition was sincere when he left, in their secret hiding hole in the jacaranda tree, his most treasured possession – a shark's tooth given to him by a passing-through fisherman. She wasn't sure she particularly wanted it, for it had given him the ambition to see the sea one day and that always made her stomach feel funny. What if he sailed away and never came back? They were of the earth, both of them, scrambling up trees, racing in the dust—

'Anyway, it's not you. He's always worried,' he said, looking wistfully out to the horizon, arms swinging high as they strode through the long grass. He paused, hesitated, as though he had something to say but didn't know how. '. . . He says I must go to live with my cousins in Oviedo.'

'Oviedo?' she cried, her feet coming to a stop. 'But that is almost another country! Why must you go there?'

He gave a hapless shrug. 'Because they have rain. And crops. And land we can work. He says I must learn.'

She stared at his face – that impish, thin, naughty face that belonged to the joint-first most important person in the world to her. 'You must say no!'

He arched an eyebrow. 'Like you do to your father?' They both knew first-hand how savage his temper could be when he was defied. The last time he'd caught them playing together, he had boxed Santi so hard around the ears he had been deaf for three days afterwards, and she had been birched and quarantined in her room for all meals for a week.

She picked up an acorn and threw it at him. As ever, she scored a bullseye, hitting him straight between the eyes.

'Ow!' He rubbed his head, glancing over at her, but he didn't throw anything back, seeming to know that behind her anger there was pain. Real pain in her heart.

He turned and began walking again, taking extra slow steps as she stared after him, her shoulders heaving up and down with silent despair, before she began following after him.

They fell into step again, Santi grabbing at a tall blade of grass and pulling it through his palm. 'He says it is only for a few years. Just until I become a man and then I can come back here and look after my mother.' He glanced back at her, his eyes adding something silently that didn't need to be said.

Nene didn't reply. It would be an epoch before he became a man but they were both powerless to stop it. '. . . When will you go?' Her voice sounded funny.

'Before the leaves turn. He says they will need me for the harvest.'

She turned her head away, not wanting to discuss it further. She couldn't imagine her life here at La Ventilla without him. He was the only person who could make her laugh, the only one who could run faster than her. Other girls her age simply wanted to play with hair ribbons or dolls, and her brothers were brutes who were good only for shooting rabbits. Who would she talk to? Who would she test her jokes on? Who would leave surprises in the jacaranda tree whenever they had a fight?

They wandered through the cork oak fields in distracted silence, deliberately meandering beneath the heavy-headed canopies for moments of shaded relief, their hands still absently grabbing at long blades of grass as they walked down the hill.

They covered the rough ground at an idle pace. There was never any point in arriving anywhere early here, it would only hasten the next question: 'What now?' But as they walked, gradually the landscape changed beneath their feet, levelling out and becoming greener – the tangled cork oak forest where the older Mala Fes bulls rooted for acorns replaced by neat rows of orchards, olive, orange, peach and lemon trees planted in strict lines, leading up to the low stone walls that heralded the grazing fields where the famed, gleaming herds roamed. The bulls' hides glistened like velvet in the sun, rich shades of chestnut, dove grey and a blacker-than-black black. They moved their great bulks slowly, nosing the ground unperturbed, their distinctive horns pointing ever upwards in silent warning.

The saying went that second-generation matadors were always terrified of the bulls, but in their family – who simply bred them – there was no such weakness, her three brothers, Montez, Vale and even Arlo, charging around them on horseback with a fearlessness that left their poor mother shaking.

For Nene, though, it was the horses she loved most: their soft whinnies in the stables, combing out their manes, the way they picked their hooves high in the training ring. But more than anything, she loved the feeling of freedom she felt whenever she slid her foot into the stirrup – not riding side-saddle like the grand Amazonas Españolas her father wanted her to ape, but (out of sight) astride, like a real warrior: muscles braced, the hot air streaming over her as she galloped through the woods and outfields. Her best moments were always the hidden ones.

They skirted the far wall, still far enough away from the hacienda to be confident of moving unseen. They could already see the prize bull in the furthest field; he had to be kept alone – at two tonnes he was by far the biggest bull they had ever bred and would be easily capable of killing more of his brothers than any matador. It was her father who had called him Leviatan. He was high in the shoulder, barrel-chested, with horns wider than her arms' span, and he could turn as fast as a polo pony.

'Shh!' Santi said suddenly, pulling her sharply behind a tree.

'What is it?' she hissed, watching as he peered around the trunk. It was only a juniper – crooked and slim-legged: whatever they were hiding from, they wouldn't be well hidden here.

'The conocedor,' Santi hissed back.

Her eyes widened. As her father's foreman, Pedro Martin was also spy and informant. If she was seen consorting with Santi, after her father's express orders never to speak to him, she would be for the lash.

She pinned herself behind him, smelling his particular odour of sweat and pines. His shaggy dark hair was sifted a pale coffee colour from the dust and she saw his mother had repaired his shirt again, for surely the fifteenth time. But it was his only one. It would have to keep making do.

'Did he see us?' she asked, her hands resting on his shoulders, her voice by his ear.

'I don't think so,' he whispered, his eyes pinned to their enemy.

'What's he doing?'

'See for yourself.'

Carefully, she tipped her head round the tree and saw the foreman cantering up to a bull on the ground. The smear of red on its flank was visible from this distance.

'Is it dead?' she asked, watching as he jumped down from his horse and walked carefully around it: these animals, dangerous at the best of times, were never more deadly than when they were injured.

'Looks like it.'

Nene knew as many bulls were killed fighting each other in the fields as died in the rings; the young calves were particularly bad, always wanting to prove themselves and move up the pecking order. It was the conocedor's job – or one of them – to protect them from themselves.

They watched as he crouched down, examining the wound, swatting away the flies that buzzed at its eyes and mouth. He looked up and around him as if looking for help but no one else was around that he could see and, clearly, moving the beast on his own wasn't an option. He straightened again, his hands on his hips, the brim of his hat obscuring his face, but Nene didn't need to see it to know what his expression would be; he only ever smiled when her father was around, the rest of the time his thin face was folded with scowl lines, his hand ever-ready at his hip to grab the riding whip coiled at his belt. This was bad news. Each bull was worth 1,200 pesetas – more money than he earned in a month, more money than most of the peasants earned in three years. Five.

'Oh no,' she whispered, watching as Pedro walked back to his horse, throwing the reins back over its head. 'He's going to tell Papa.'

'Of course. He has to, doesn't he?'

'Yes, but . . . couldn't he wait until after dinner?' Every accidental or unearned death was costly, sending her father into a spiral of rage; she already knew he would be angry at the table tonight, his forceful glares suppressing everyone, even her brothers, into silence.

They heard the sound of hooves begin to drum the hard earth. Santi stepped out from behind the tree, his curiosity getting the better of him – as it always did – eager to get a better look at the mortal wound.

'Santi, wait! Has he really gone?' she whispered.

But he had already frozen on the spot and she felt herself grow cold at the sight of him, stock still, inanimate.

'Run,' he whispered, trying not to move his lips.

'No!'

He looked back. 'He's seen me. Just go. Now.' And when she didn't move, he kicked his leg out sideways, catching her hard on the shin. Tears immediately rushed to her eyes. 'And stay down . . . *Hurry.*'

She ran in a half-crouch behind the stone wall, wanting to turn back to see if Santi was following, but knowing he was rooted to the spot. They both knew it was more than his life was worth to take flight now. Feeling her lungs gasp in the hot air, thighs burning from the hunched posture, she ran the several hundred metres as stealthily as she could, hands clawing at the ground as she stumbled, finally getting to the old *alberca*, the vast metal water store in the far corner of the field. She hid behind it with a frightened sob, her slender frame easily hidden now whilst Santi stood as rooted and exposed as the trees.

She didn't dare peer round to watch. She could hear the timbre of their voices – the conocedor's angry shouts, Santi's meek, deferential responses that were so unlike him – but not what they were saying. Spare words drifted over on the breeze – 'thief', 'criminal' – but how could that be? He had done nothing wrong. He was just standing by a wall. Harmless. What could he possibly be accused of stealing?

Daring to take a peek, she saw the old foreman on horseback and bearing down over Santi, the stone wall between them looking pitifully inadequate. He was pointing his crop at Santi's chest – and more specifically, to her horror, at the orange juice that had spilled on it.

No! Immediately she knew which so-called 'crime' he was

being accused of and she went to spring forward, to cry out, to explain – but an arm jerked her back in the same moment, a hand clasping over her mouth.

'Don't.' The voice was low, hushed and deadly serious. Eyes wide, she looked back at her brother, Arlo, his arms tight around her just as she heard the crack of the whip – how it whistled through the air, the stinging slap against skin, and then the cry, Santi's cry.

She couldn't bear it, wanting to cry out herself, and she struggled to get free again but Arlo's grip only increased, her tears instantly running down her cheeks and over his hand as the whip spiralled through the air, once, twice, three times. She wanted to turn and see Santi, to make it stop, to run over and comfort him, but she could do none of those things as instead she was held in a vice, both of them huddled down beside the water tank until the whipcracks stopped and moments later they heard the sound of hooves drumming the hard ground once more.

After a minute of silence Arlo dared to raise his head above the wall. 'They've gone,' he said quietly, releasing her.

Nene sprang free like a wildcat, desperate to see Santi – but he was already running in the opposite direction, towards the *pueblo blanco* in the distance. He was stumbling and limping badly, his hands outstretched as though ready to break a fall, but he was still fast – faster than her – and she could see his shirt had split across the back, revealing the red seams on his skin beneath.

'Santi!' she screamed.

But nothing could be heard above the galloping horse, nor seen through the plumes of red dust its feet kicked up.

'It was me!' she cried, whirling round to her brother instead, enraged, desperate. 'Me! I took those oranges from the grove!'

'It would have made no difference. If not the oranges, something else.'

'*Why?* He did nothing wrong.' It was the brutal simplicity of his words that hurt her the most, the brazen acceptance of the status quo.

'He was there,' he shrugged, as though that was reason enough. 'You know how Papa will react when Pedro tells him about the bull.'

'So he hurt Santi because Papa will hurt him?' she cried, incredulous.

'He could have just as easily hurt him if he had seen Santi walking with you – and he would have been justified that time. Look at you!' He gestured down to her bare legs, her skirt still tucked into her undergarments and hanging in loose billows like old-fashioned bloomers.

Furiously, she pulled the skirts free. 'We were just climbing trees and watching the harvest!'

'You know what Papa has said about you talking to the *campesinos*. They are dangerous.'

'No, they are hungry! They have not been paid for months now.'

'That is not your concern, Nene. Papa has said these are things we cannot yet understand.'

'Papa says, Papa says . . .' she catcalled. 'I tell you what I understand. I understand it is not right to make people work extra hours for no extra money! To make sure they have no land to grow their own food! How can they survive? They are starving, Arlo!'

He gripped her by the shoulders again, seeing how her voice rose through the octaves. 'Nene, control yourself. These are not matters to concern you.'

'Why? Because I'm a *girl*?' she spat.

'No. Because you are a Mendoza.' The words hung like a death sentence – stifling, oppressive, immutable. 'There are standards to uphold. Other people look to you for an example. They must see through you – through *us* – that there is an order to things. And where there is order, there is safety. For everyone. It has always been this way. Why should it change now?'

'You sound just like Papa,' she sobbed.

He loosened his grip on her shoulders again; it was the worst insult she could have hurled at him. 'I am trying to protect you, Nene. I don't like to see Santi whipped any more than you do. He is your friend, I know that.'

'So then why did you *let* it happen? You could have stopped Pedro! If not me, he would have listened to you!'

Arlo tipped his head to the side sadly. 'I worry about you. Your impetuousness. Your passion – it will lead you into danger. You have to learn to pick your battles, Nene. You cannot fight them all.'

'You don't fight any!' she spat.

'That is not true. I will always fight for you.'

'I don't need fighting for. I can look after myself.' She wiped her tears away furiously, inadvertently smearing the dust into muddy streaks over her cheeks.

'No. You are ruled by your heart, Nene, and that frightens me. Consequences mean nothing to you.'

'So you think *you* are the one to protect me?' she cried mockingly. 'You? You are weak, Arlo! It is you who needs me.'

'Nene, wait, come back!' he cried as she began walking away. But she didn't turn around, and though the sobs wracked her frame, her arms sliced the air like blades and her legs struck the ground like swiping swords.

Chapter Four

They stopped at the crowd of people huddled around the Velásquez painting *Las Meninas*, both of them staring up at it in silence for several moments. 'So this is pretty much the most famous painting here,' Charlotte said in a low voice. 'The Prado's equivalent to *Mona Lisa*.'

'Yeah . . .' Lucy murmured in agreement, before her neat little nose wrinkled. 'I'm not loving it though.'

Charlotte looked across at her. 'No? Some believe it's the best painting in the world.'

'Huh. I mean, I get that it's a big deal but . . .' Her eyes roamed the giant canvas. 'Is that a *dwarf*?'

'Yes, she was a maidservant.'

Lucy stared at it, looking more and more baffled. 'There's way too many people in it.' She counted. 'Jesus – eleven. Eleven figures. I mean, why? It's hardly the Last Supper.'

'No, but which figure is your eye drawn to?'

'The little girl in the middle.'

'Exactly. The Princess Margaret Theresa, she was the king's only surviving child. The other girls are just her maidservants. See the king and queen in the mirror there?' Charlotte pointed to the figures in the background. 'Velásquez was the court painter, an incredibly ambitious man both professionally and socially. He had to reflect the importance of the Infanta, as well as pay deference to his sovereign. The little princess was actually betrothed to her uncle so these paintings were sent to him, as updates if you like, to show how she was growing up.'

Lucy pulled a face. 'Eww, that's so creepy!'

Charlotte laughed. 'Yes, in this day and age it really doesn't translate well, does it? But it was their equivalent of a photograph.'

They continued walking again, eyes alighting on the baroque frames of the vast murals, the rich colour palettes, stiff costumes and stylized scenes.

'Nah, not sure this is my vibe either,' Lucy sighed as they stopped below Bosch's challenging triptych, *Garden of Earthly Delights*. 'I like it all a bit . . . looser. Airier. More relaxed. Less hell and damnation and burning brimstones.'

'Well, let's keep walking. They have some stunning Fortunys through here. We could go see them if you like?'

'Fortuny? Sure, why not,' Lucy shrugged, her Valentino sneakers squeaking on the tiled floor. 'How come you know so much about art anyway? Cambridge again?'

'No, I read history there. I guess it was my parents I have to thank for this. They were always keen, forever dragging me and my sister round galleries as children.'

'Including here? You seem to know this place well.'

'Yes, here too. We visited every time we came to Madrid. My father always loved *The Fable of Arachne*. Do you know it?'

Lucy shook her head.

'It's not the most accomplished painting by any means but there are a few riddles in it that kept drawing him back.'

'Huh. My mum only took us to the National Gallery once and that was because it was free and raining outside.'

Charlotte smiled. She was a big fan of these 'walk and talk' therapies; people opened up so much more when they weren't subjected to direct eye contact, if the body could be distracted whilst the mind roamed . . . Sometimes, she thought the best thing she could do for her clients was take them on a road trip: London–Glasgow for the lesser afflicted; New York to San Francisco for the tougher cases. 'You seem a lot brighter today. I was concerned about you when I left yesterday. Is this new optimism just down to remembering your love of art or has something else happened?'

'Bit of both maybe: Rob got back early from training last night. He said he was playing like a numpty.' She shrugged. 'I don't care, it was just nice to have him around for a bit. We had a barbie and then the three of us watched that new Marvel *Avengers* movie.'

'Sounds great.' Certainly better than her evening had turned out, anyway, dwelling on the past over a bottle of rosé. 'And did you talk to him about how you've been feeling?'

Lucy looked across at her like she was mad. 'No! Why'd I do that? We were having a nice time. Why spoil it with a downer?'

'You don't think it's important he knows you're feeling lonely?'

'Not really,' Lucy mumbled, looking sharply to the left and studying the *Adoration of the Magi*, her face turned away from Charlotte.

'Lucy, do you think your feelings don't matter?'

'Well he's the important one, let's face it.'

'He's the breadwinner, that's a different thing. And it certainly doesn't make him any more important than you. Your role in the household is crucial too. Vital, in fact.'

'Listen, you just caught me at a low ebb, that's all. I'm fine.' As if as proof, she held up her arms, the designer shopping bags swinging from her hands à la Julia Roberts, evidence of her productive morning before their meeting here.

Charlotte wasn't at all convinced, but they left the room and walked down a long, vaulted, light-filled gallery. Black velvet ropes were looped along the run, keeping the hordes from getting too close, weary visitors slumping on benches, backpacks at their feet as they gazed up in cowed admiration at the epic depictions overhead. A troupe of schoolchildren were moving en masse to an audio tour, headphones on as they sloped from one painting to the next, talking too loudly whenever they wanted to ask a question or make a comment.

Charlotte tried a different tack. 'So, back to painting – how are you going to set about getting into it again? Do a course?'

'Oh nothing like that. I was just thinking I'd get some brushes and canvases and give it a go at home.'

'I would strongly recommend doing a course.'

'Why?'

'It's sociable, for one thing. You'd get to meet other, like-minded people.'

'But then they'll find out who I am—'

'And who's that? Lucy, a twenty-three-year-old English woman, married and mother to a little boy, relocated to Spain for her husband's work. That's all they need to know. This is an arena where you can be you in there and *not* Roberto Santos's wife.'

Lucy wrinkled her nose. 'It never works out that way though. People always find out.'

'Not everyone is impressed by money or fame.'

'Everyone *we* meet is.'

'So then change your social landscape. You might be surprised to find that anyone you met on a drawing course would be far more interested in you as an artist than in your husband. To them, your marriage should be just a detail, incidental. You have to stop defining yourself through the prism of Rob's career. At the moment, that is *all* you see yourself as: his wife. But it's suffocating you and you need to see that is only one side to who you are. Who are you in your totality? Mother, wife – yes. But what else? You have so much more to offer.' She saw the doubt in Lucy's still-unlined face. 'Do an art course, join a class. I really don't think you'd regret it.'

'But what if I *can't* do it? It's been years since I've even picked up a brush—'

'Art is instinct. You either can or you can't and if you could once, then you can again.'

'But where would I begin? I don't know where to buy cotton earbuds in this city, much less find an art class.'

Charlotte smiled. 'Leave it with me. I know a few people in this field. I could make some calls for you.'

'Yeah?' Lucy looked at her, the expression on her face bemused. 'Honestly, how do you *know* all these things, all these people?'

'Life,' Charlotte said lightly.

'Helluva life,' Lucy said drily.

A crowd of Japanese tourists, all wearing matching navy caps, were standing with a guide before what at first glance was the *Mona Lisa*.

'Eh? I thought she was in the Louvre?' Lucy mused, wandering over distractedly. Charlotte already knew it was the anonymous copy by one of Da Vinci's own pupils which had been painted at the same time as the master version, but she stood by patiently as Lucy stopped walking to listen in on the talk. She checked her messages on her phone: another two missed calls from Stephen and one from Rosie asking her to call back when she could. Seeing Lucy was engrossed, she rang the office.

'Hello, Charlotte Fairfax's office.'

'Rosie, it's me,' she said in a low voice, turning and beginning to pace lightly in small figures of eight.

'Oh, Charlotte, hi.' Her PA's voice inflected with relief. 'There's been a couple of calls. Dr Ferrante rang back from Carlos III University; he's available and very interested.'

'That's great. Send him the preliminary Mendoza family profiles so that he can get started and arrange lunch for as soon as possible – tomorrow ideally. I want him to meet Mateo and hopefully settle his nerves. Warn him we've got a very jumpy client right now.'

'Okay, I'll pass that on. And Hugh Farrer's office called, requesting an update. Specifically . . .'

But Charlotte didn't hear what she said next. Her eyes had fastened onto a small still life further along the gallery. There was no crowd loitering in front of this one, everyone instead making their way to the headline pieces, but her feet took her there soundlessly and she stood before it, her hand falling slightly, taking the phone away from her ear.

She didn't need to read the placard beside it to know it was by Chardin and titled *Basket with Strawberries*. Her eyes took in the familiar image: a low round basket piled high with a pyramid of strawberries, two white flowers laid before it, a glass of water to one side and to the other, some cherries and a peach. She absorbed the moody background light, the richly textured wooden tabletop, the succulent gloss and rich, ripe colours of the fruit. She knew it so well it was like looking at an old family photograph, memories of a long-ago time stirring within her. She felt deeply buried emotions begin to vibrate and hum in the pit of her stomach, a sudden longing of piercing intensity smashing through the smooth crystalline shroud that had become her protection.

Her mind was whirring. Why was it here? How could it be here? This couldn't be right—

'Charlotte?'

The voice sounded far away and it was a moment before she remembered Rosie on the other end of the line. 'I'll have to call you back,' she mumbled, hanging up before she'd even finished the sentence.

'Charlotte?' She looked up at the echo of her name again, bewildered and disoriented as Lucy came over, her curious expression changing to one of concern. 'Hey, are you okay? What's wrong?'

Charlotte pulled herself back from the past, forcing a smile that felt more like a rictus. 'Nothing. Just . . . work stuff.'

Lucy looked across at the painting that had elicited such a strong reaction from her. 'Wow, that's gorgeous. Do you like it?'

Charlotte nodded dumbly, daring herself to look back at it again – but the memories snapped at her from it like crocodile jaws. *Beauty in the small things.*

She stepped back abruptly, drawing herself taller and forcing a smile. 'Lucy, I'm so sorry but I'm afraid I have to go. Something's come up and I need to get back to the office.'

Lucy's face fell. 'But the Fortuny exhibits . . .'

'I know. I feel terrible. Can we regroup?' she asked, hearing the urgency in her own voice. She just had to get out of here.

Lucy shrugged helplessly, disappointment beginning to swim in her eyes. 'There's nothing in my diary,' she said flatly. 'Whenever you want.'

'Great. So then I'll call you when I'm back at my desk and we'll get another time in.' She was walking quickly backwards now, Lucy growing ever smaller in her frame of vision.

'Okay.'

'I'm really sorry,' she called, beginning to turn away and hide her face; the mask was falling off again and she was nearly exposed. She couldn't afford for anyone to see what was really there: absolutely nothing at all.

She walked without thinking, travelled without seeing, her feet pounding the street and the hot air drying her eyes. She felt scorched inside, desiccated, as the facts and the questions rebounded within her, chasing one after the other. Seeing the painting again, seeing it *there*. How could it be hanging on those walls? And how long had it been there: one week? Eight months? Four years? And what did that mean?

But in her gut, she already knew.

Her hands pulled into fists, her breath coming fast as she wove down the street. Her phone rang and she reached for it almost in relief. To have something to distract her . . .

'Hey,' she said, forcing brightness into her voice as she saw Stephen's name.

'Where have you been? I've been trying you all day.' He sounded irked.

'Sorry, frantic day.'

She could hear his frown. He hated not being able to reach her. 'Where are you?'

'Between meetings,' she panted lightly. 'I was just with a client at the Prado and now I'm . . .' Where was she? She looked around, getting her bearings and remembering herself. She was across from the Puerta del Sol, not far from the cafe where Marina Quincy worked. She had planned on coming over here after leaving Lucy. 'I'm just en route to see another.'

'Well I've had your mother on the phone. She can't get hold of you either and she's going ape wanting a decision on the bloody napkins: scalloped or . . . Christ, I've forgotten what the other thing was.'

She rolled her eyes. She'd wanted distraction, hadn't she? 'Can't you deal with it? I'm busy.'

'Right. Because I've got an opinion on napkins.'

'And you think I have?' she snapped, feeling fraught. 'Look, I don't care either. They're napkins. Tell her to choose whichever she thinks looks best.'

'You tell her. She's your mother.'

'Ugh, Stephen, I'm up against it right now. I'm not over here for fun. I'm trying to get things sorted quickly so I can get back in time. This is your wedding too. Just deal with it, can't you?' Her voice had risen an octave and she realized she had stopped walking, that her hands were pulled into little fists. She was ostensibly a toddler having a tantrum in the middle of the street. She covered her eyes with her hand. What was wrong with her at the moment?

There was a frustrated silence. '. . . Fine.' They were both tetchy and irritable. Did he have a hangover too? Had he just been punched in the stomach by his own past? 'So any idea yet when you are coming back?' he asked.

'I don't know, I've only been here a day and a half. I'll be back by the weekend latest, don't worry.'

'I'm *not* worried. I just don't want your mother on my case.'

'You're the one who invited her to stay for dinner on Monday night.'

'I was being polite.'

She suppressed a sigh; they could do this all day. 'Look, I've got to go. I'm at my next appointment. I'll call you tonight.'

'Fine.'

'. . . Love you.'

'Yes, yes. Speak later.'

He hung up without ceremony, and she stared into space momentarily, feeling her past, present and future all colliding around her. She felt strangely unrooted from the ground, off-balance and unsteady as though the world kept spinning first one way, then the other. She was getting married next week but suddenly fragments of her past were bubbling up like secrets sunken in a lake.

She tossed her head determinedly, banishing them from her mind again; she had a 'strong mental game' as Stephen had once said – one of his more romantic compliments – and she resumed walking, rounding the corner into a golden-glowing narrow street and catching sight of the distinctive green and gold doors of San Ginés, the red *chocolatería* sign already lit on the corner wall; there was a queue of people waiting to order through the hole-in-the-wall. It was just gone four but still too hot for her to sit outside, even in the shade, and she slipped into the cool interior, the scent of caramelized sugar acting as immediate anaesthetic on her raw emotions.

After scanning the space for a moment, she chose a small table in the corner, just near the kitchen door. She picked up the menu but the repertoire was both well known and justifiably restricted: churros and chocolate with a side order of espresso was the combination that had made this place famous, and frankly it was exactly what she needed. In the rush of oversleeping this morning and running straight to her meeting with Mateo Mendoza and then on to Lucy, she had straight-up forgotten to eat.

Letting the menu drop again, she took in the surroundings. The cafe had been going for a hundred years, and the art deco interior felt both dated and yet still elegant – diners perched on dainty green-seated chairs at white marble-topped tables, their reflections repeated infinitely in the mirrored panelling on the walls. Cups and saucers were stacked in neat towers on the counters and the white-tuniced, black-trousered staff moved about with efficient briskness.

Charlotte looked around for the striking woman from the photographs in the file, but she couldn't see her. There was a younger girl clearing the outdoor tables and two guys behind the tills unloading a dishwasher, another coming through from the kitchen with a tray. Charlotte leaned forward, hoping to sneak a glimpse, but the door swung too quickly on its hinges, betraying nothing more than a brushed-steel preparation table and black aprons hanging from a hook. Perhaps she wasn't working a shift today?

One of the guys from behind the counter spotted her and came over, and she placed an order for the porras (a chunkier version of the churros – she needed the carbs), chocolate and an espresso. She carried on watching and waiting for Marina; her heart wasn't in it but Hugh Farrer's PA had called. He wanted an update and she needed to give him something, she had to make contact at least.

'Hi, is Marina Quincy working today?' she forced herself to ask as the waiter came back with her order a few minutes later. Perhaps she'd been on an earlier shift, she thought. Working as Charlotte overslept . . .

'Marina? Sure, she is upstairs.' He jerked his chin towards a staircase.

There was an upstairs? 'Oh. Well is it okay if I take this up there then?'

The waiter looked irritated but merely shrugged. 'As you like. You can pay your bill there.'

'Thanks.'

Trying not to spill the chocolate cup, she climbed the stairs and found another spot to sit at. It was emptier up here – only one other table was taken – and she could instantly tell why, for it was stuffier too. Taking the nearest seat, she scanned the room and immediately found her target. It wasn't hard, she was standing by the clearing station in the far corner, her back to the room as she wiped down some menus. Charlotte ate, watching as she shuffled the menus into a straight pile, boredom in the movement even from behind.

Finally Marina turned back to the room, tucking a tendril of hair behind her ear and tugging on her too-tight shirt. Watching from beneath lowered lashes, Charlotte could see she was every bit as striking in the flesh as her photographs had suggested, although it was easier to gauge her age in the sunlight; those strong looks that looked so dynamic on film were rather more hard-bitten in the flesh.

Catching sight of Charlotte, she came over wearily before she saw, too late, that Charlotte already had a full order before her. 'Oh—' she started, looking a little baffled, for no one else was serving up here.

'Sorry, I ordered downstairs and then decided to come up here,' Charlotte said in faultless Spanish, trying not to scrutinize her too obviously. She noticed she had three piercings in her left ear and that her ring finger on her left hand was still narrow at the base from her old wedding ring. There was a pale tracheotomy scar at her throat too and it struck her that Marina's body had collected battle scars on her journey through life; Charlotte had the distinct impression it hadn't been a smooth one thus far – all of which made for a powerful motive to come by easy money.

'Okay.' Marina gave a careless shrug and turned to leave again.

'But I wondered—' Charlotte said hurriedly.

'Yes?' She turned back, bored.

'Are you Marina Quincy?'

Marina's eyes narrowed, serving to make her look even more impressive somehow. 'Who is asking?'

'My name's Charlotte Fairfax. I'm a freelance consultant for Steed Bank in London.'

Marina turned to face her fully but the name clearly meant nothing to her. It meant nothing to most people. Theirs wasn't a high street offering. Ten million was the minimum investment with them. 'Okay,' she shrugged.

Charlotte decided to go in hard and see what she came back with. Her immediate response would be the most revealing. 'I've come to offer my services to you. I'm a wealth counsellor.'

'A what?' Marina squinted, folding her arms over her chest now.

'I help people adjust when they come into vast sums of money.'

Marina laughed out loud at that, dropping her arms down. 'That must be a nice problem to have but I'm afraid you've got the wrong person. Vast sums of money are not a problem for me.'

'Not yet maybe. But soon perhaps – in the next few weeks?' She watched Marina's features closely, looking for a narrowing at the eyes, a tightening sinew in the neck, a flattening of the mouth as she realized the game was up, her masterplan exposed . . . 'Ms Quincy, do you know Carlos Mendoza?'

Marina was still for a moment, bafflement followed by recognition. '. . . You mean *the* Carlos Mendoza?'

'I do.'

Marina shrugged, giving a dry little laugh. 'No.'

'Are you quite sure?' Charlotte watched her closely, scanning her body language for clues she was lying. 'I appreciate your connection with Mr Mendoza might be considered "sensitive", but I assure you I'm here to act in your best interest.'

'Connection . . . ?' There was a long pause as Marina weighted her words. Finally, she shifted her stance. 'I think I would know if I had bumped into a billionaire recently.'

'He's not quite that, actually. Not far off but not quite,' Charlotte said levelly, still gauging her responses in microscopic detail.

The two women fell quiet, both weighing each other up, assessing, scrutinizing.

'So you're quite certain you don't know him?' Charlotte asked after another pause, making to sound weary herself as she pulled a fifty-euro note from her purse and laid it on the table, beneath the espresso cup. Regretfully, having had only one bite of her snack and a mere sip of her coffee, she stood up.

'Yes. Like I said.' Marina's eyes looked down quizzically at the note before looking back at Charlotte again. The bill was for twelve euros.

Charlotte nodded. 'Okay. Well that's a shame, sorry to have bothered you. I must have the wrong person,' she said, deliberately keeping things oblique. 'Thank you for your time.'

She took her bag from the back of the chair and walked past the woman, sensing the weight of her stare on her back, almost able to read her questions hanging unspoken in the air.

'Wait – your change!' Marina called after her.

Charlotte looked back casually, almost lazily and smiled. 'It's fine,' she said with a shrug. 'You keep it.'

Chapter Five

Ronda, June 1936, four years later

Indigo carried his head well during the pirouette, his neck arched and staying on the bit, and he maintained his cadence through the move, but Nene felt her legs and back aching from the unnatural position, the pommel between her thighs beginning to bruise the tired muscles.

'Sit up, up. Straighter,' the instructor barked, the long training whip trailing in the sand as he walked in tight circles in the centre of the ring, his eyes narrowed into thin slits as he scrutinized her and the horse's forms – their silhouettes, comportments; they had to flow as one to succeed together. She was nothing without the horse and he nothing without her; they were truly the sum of their parts and sometimes she felt she was only important, visible even, when she was on his back, as though he was a base lifting her up into her father's line of sight.

For Nene, it had been love at first look, *un coup de foudre* as the French said, and she had all but begged for her father to buy him when chance brought them into each other's orbits. The magnificent blue-black stallion had originally been a birthday present for the daughter of one of the most powerful men in the land – Don Bartolome de Palencia, who was a personal friend of exiled King Alfonso; Don Bartolome had dreamed his daughter Pepita would make him proud and become an Amazona on Indigo, but the weakly girl was terrified of the beast and had humiliated herself and her father when, at the fiesta at the de Palencia *latifundio*, she had screamed in fright trying to feed him a carrot. A carrot!

Nene had no such fear, forever clasping her hands around his muscular neck and whispering into his ear as she fed him barley sweets and sugar cubes, laughing as the prickly hairs on his soft muzzle tickled her palm; sometimes, she could even forget Santi had left and that her best friend was on the other side of the country from here. Most mornings, if her father was out with Señor Martin, she was able to bribe the grooms into letting her comb his mane and pick out his hooves herself. At 15.2 hands, he was as big a horse as she could physically manage; her mother had been opposed to the purchase, worrying he would run off with her or throw her from his back like a rag doll but Nene knew he would never do such a thing – she had looked into his deep chocolatey eyes that day at the fiesta as she ran to 'rescue' Pepita and she had felt their souls connect. Don Bartolome's fearful daughter would never have been able to handle him; he was a king of a horse – majestic and noble – and he needed a mistress who understood his might and magnificence. He could not be wasted on a girl who whimpered every time he whinnied or pawed a hoof on the ground; he deserved a rider who understood him. Even this – dressage – although a noble art, was a parody of his immense dignity, and the happiest moments of both their lives were when they went galloping bareback over the far fields, out of sight of the hacienda, her hair streaming behind her as his heart hammered against his ribs, the side-saddle on which she rode out of the stables unstrapped and left hidden in the long grass.

'Now, collection into volte,' the instructor commanded, his body tense and wired, primed to pick up the smallest deviation from form, the tiniest error, for a lot was hanging on their official performance. It was early June and her father was throwing a birthday party for her mother at the end of the month; he had invited all the grand Andalusian families, partly so that they might admire his wife's beauty, and partly to show off Nene too, his eligible daughter who was rapidly coming of age. More than once, the 'b' word had passed his lips at the dinner table, causing her brothers to snigger and make quips about the 'poor boy' to be 'burdened' with her.

She felt Indigo's carriage brace, his strides shorten and lighten as he headed towards the perimeter and began to walk the circle.

'Now up to medium pace, taking the centre line,' the instructor called. 'Keep him soft and relaxed through the jaw. Don't let him get excited.'

She gave a tiny twitch of the reins but Indigo needed barely any instruction, carrying her faultlessly through the handsome shapes, making her look good and knowing a surreptitious sugar cube would be his reward later. They both knew the flying changes were coming up, where he switched lead leg mid-canter; it was an exciting and advanced move they had been working on for seven weeks now and it was intended to be the centre-point of the routine, a display of the perfect symbiosis between girl and horse.

She clicked with her tongue, Indigo's signal to ride more forward in the change, and she felt the slight pull in the lead rein as he went to switch legs. But a sudden shout – shouts – threw him off his stride. He tossed his head, pulling back into his hind quarters and rearing slightly. Nene instinctively threw her weight forward, shushing him with her voice and calming him down from the unexpected fright as the clamour quickly grew. Her heart went into a gallop of its own; the sound of angry men was becoming increasingly familiar. Most times it was their shouts and taunts and threats that made her recoil, but when her family drove into town for Mass these days, it was the silence of the *campesinos* that frightened her most, the resentment glinting in their eyes as the car swept past, throwing up dust clouds in its wake. Even those families she knew, and who knew her, now turned away whenever she approached, their old friendliness gone.

She squinted, trying to see through the narrow gap between the roof and the sand school walls to the fields beyond, but thanks to the angle of the setting sun, she could see nothing more than bleached-out rectangular strips.

Another flurry of shouts, growing in heat, made Indigo step back again, tossing his head agitatedly and getting ready to rear. Sliding off the saddle, she hurriedly led him to the far corner, away from the direction of the fracas, and tied him to the post, fishing in her skirt for his sugar cube. She fed him, shushing in his ear, but the clamour was only growing in intensity.

'Take him back to the stable, please,' she said to the instructor, beginning to stride out towards the fields.

'But, señorita—'

'Please. Get him to the stable before this gets any worse,' she said sharply, breaking into a run.

As she approached, the glare dimmed, the sun sliding behind the tree-line and setting the melee into silhouette. There must have been twenty, maybe thirty, men there, all of them holding farming equipment – scythes, threshers, pitchforks – but which, in their hands here now, looked like weapons.

Señor Martin, her father's foreman, was standing on the steps outside his office, his legs planted wide, his hands on his hips as he stared them down, seemingly unafraid of the mob. The more they bayed, the more still he seemed to become, and he made no attempts to placate or calm them, merely watching instead as though this were somehow 'interesting' – his eyes skating over them and taking in who were the leaders, who the muscle, who the stragglers.

'. . . is our right!' Juan Jose Perez was yelling, the sinews in his neck taut, his eyes bulging from a gaunt, leathery face. 'The law is on *our* side and we have come to claim what is ours. You cannot keep this land as grazing for your bulls, when people are starving at your feet!' His face was twisted with contempt, spittle flying as he spoke and landing on the parched ground.

From behind the pillar where she hid, Nene's eyes rose up to the vista behind them. The lush and vividly green pastures were being watered, as they were every evening thanks to the new state-of-the-art irrigation system her father had invested in, the droplets catching the light in the sunset and throwing out prismatic rainbows. In the next field over, the hides of the velvet-flanked herd gleamed as the animals shuffled slowly in the dying heat, heads down, horns up. It might have been a bucolic scene but for this confrontation, shattering the crowning peace and throwing it down on the ground in great, jagged shards.

Still unseen from her hiding place behind the post, she watched as the men jostled on the spot, their arms jerking their weapons spasmodically but their feet rooted – for now – as they jeered and heckled, spitting towards Señor Martin's feet, repeating their calls for the fields to be turned over. Anger twisted their faces, violence glittering in their eyes, but they were still yoked, still reined in – just. This was still a protest, not yet a mutiny.

Nene knew exactly what they wanted. Even as protected

as she was, she had overheard the countless pleas for land on which to cultivate crops that would feed their families. People were starving through lack of land and lack of work too, for far from their rights being protected, anyone at La Ventilla found in possession of union papers was summarily dismissed from the Mendoza payroll.

Every time her father called a meeting with her brothers, she stood on the other side of the closed doors and listened to them talk business. She had heard them admit that by law the labourers should not work sixteen hours but eight, that they should get extra pay for extra hours, that union papers gave them protected rights. All of this was official decree, and yet the law appeared not to apply to them. The Civil Guard never enforced the new Republican government's mandates and the estate guards were never punished for the extreme violence they meted out to anyone caught gathering acorns, windfall olives or collecting up firewood . . . Somehow, they were free to do as they pleased. The law didn't apply to them.

Montez and Vale, her eldest brothers, now twenty and twenty-two, were only too eager to reinforce the status quo. Occasionally she heard Arlo try to speak up, to offer a compromise viewpoint to their totalitarian position, but he never got more than a few sentences out before he was silenced, his opinion as the third son almost as unimportant as hers.

Almost, but not quite. As a girl, she had the least power of all – whenever she had tried intervening, beseeching her father to give up one field, just one to keep the peace, he swatted her away like a bothersome fly, even slapping her one time when she had been too forceful, telling her that this was men's business, she couldn't understand . . .

The building drum of hooves made her look up, and with a sinking heart she saw the plumes of dust herald the arrival of two riders, her brothers coming in from their final recce of the fields for the night. Everyone turned and watched as they pulled back from a canter into a trot, the wide brims of their Cordobes hats throwing their faces into shade but their nobility and prowess revealed by their upright seats and thrust chins.

The peasants lapsed into a sudden hush as the riders drew up, surveying the unusual scene with growing suspicion and displeasure.

'What is going on here?' Vale demanded, effortlessly dismounting the horse and throwing over the reins to a groom who had hitherto been hiding in the stable block. As the eldest and the heir apparent, he carried the full weight of his father's authority and the pack of labourers took a step back as he walked provocatively between them and Señor Martin.

He looked back at his father's conocedor for an explanation.

'These men are demanding that you give them your fields.' The wry tone in his voice intimated how ludicrous this proposal really was.

'Are they indeed?' Vale asked, his head tipping to the side. 'And when you say demanding, you mean to tell me, they are not even asking politely for such a gift? They simply *expect* it?'

'I'm afraid so, Don Vale. As you can see, they have brought weapons with them in an attempt to threaten and intimidate us.'

Vale looked back to them again, his eyes narrowed. 'Yes, I can see that is very intimidating,' he agreed. 'There are just the three of us here and we are vastly outnumbered by – how many men would you say? Fifty? Sixty?'

'Sixty at least, Don Vale,' Señor Martin agreed.

'It looks like sixty to me,' Montez said from his elevated perch. He was still on his horse, his arms crossed languidly at the wrists, the reins slack in his hands.

The peasants took another step back and Nene felt a deep stirring of unease in the pit of her stomach. She too retreated further into the shadows. Threat carried on the air like salt in the sea wind and she willed the men to give up their fight, to turn around and go back to their families.

Instead, one of them stepped forward: old Juan Esperanza, Santi's father.

She stiffened, gripping the post harder. What was he doing?

'What we are humbly requesting is not unreasonable, Señor Mendoza. We are hard workers. Many of us come from families that have worked your land for generations. But we are dying here, the drought is killing us, we cannot afford to eat, much less pay these new rents. Already, many of our menfolk have left for the north, where there is rain and where they can work around the year.'

'Is that so?' Vale asked. 'So then why do you not go with them?'

'I'm an old man, señor, too old to travel so far. And anyway, my heart is here. This is my home.'

'Here?' Vale pointed to the ground beneath his feet. 'This, right here, is your home?'

Juan looked uncertain. 'I meant—'

'Are you trying to tell me that you are *claiming* this land as your own?'

'No, señor—'

Nene swallowed.

'When will it end?' Vale cried suddenly, throwing his arms up as he wheeled around to his brother and the conocedor. 'The impertinence of these people to think they have some right to something that is not theirs! Up and down the country, landowners like us – fair people, decent people – are being coerced into relinquishing land that was rightfully gained by our ancestors through hard work, grit, determination. And yet now we must suffer the insolence of parasites like these who simply want it to be given over, just because they want it?'

'Our children and wives are dying, señor.'

'And that is my fault?' Vale cried. 'You place this at my door that you cannot keep and protect your own family?'

'We ask only that we might work some land off which to live. The bulls do not need all the pastures. The long field has been unused now for nearly five years.'

There was a tense silence and Nene felt the anger in her brother begin to roll, like a distant thunder. 'Because we are resting the land,' he said in a quiet voice. 'What you see as unused we know to be part of a longer-term strategy. Do you think our bulls attract a premium for no better reason than that they are pretty?'

'Of course not, señor.' Nene saw how the other men behind him were standing slumped now, their weapons slack in their hands. One of them dropped his hoe, a literal throwing down of arms, and turned to leave. Juan turned fractionally, watching him go; they had come here on a wave of righteous anger but with all talk and no action their threat was nullified. Impotent.

'Of course not,' Vale repeated sarcastically, bringing Juan's attention back to him again. 'And yet you dare to demand something that is not yours on the mistaken belief that you know about matters far above your station. Or intellect.'

Nene saw how the old man's mouth flattened into a grim line at the insult and he shifted slightly, as though prodded by something from within. Unlike her brothers, she knew that somehow, through sheer force of will and pride, Juan Esperanza had taught himself to read and then taught his children too.

He straightened up, lifting his chin and expanding his chest.

'Above my station, yes perhaps,' he nodded, gripping tighter the cap in his hand as his voice hardened. 'But above my intellect? No.' He raised his head up, the word as sharp as a blade. 'I may be a poor man, señor, but I am no fool. The long pasture *is* unused and I am here to fight for my family. These men with me here are mad with hunger, we cannot go on without change; our requests *must* be met. Nothing works with you – not legal decrees, nor negotia—'

The gunshot rang out, cracking open the sky and sending them all reeling backwards. Nene found herself on her bottom on the ground, her hands in the sawdust as she braced from falling further, her eyes somehow pinned on Juan. He had spun backwards in the instant the bullet hit, turning a full revolution like a drunken dancer until he came back to where he had begun. He swayed for a moment, his head beginning to loll, the men around him all cowering on the ground, their hands over their heads.

Nene looked in horror back at her brothers – Vale and Señor Martin on the steps; Montez still on his horse with the rifle aimed level at Juan's head. For a moment she was too terrified even to gasp, knowing there was another cartridge in the barrel, seeing how her brother's finger twitched at the trigger.

She heard screams – shrill white sounds that shredded the air – and it was several full moments before she realized they were coming from her; that her feet were moving and she was scrambling up again, hurtling forwards and launching herself towards the slowly toppling figure of her best friend's father.

'Nene!' Vale barked, looking shocked and then furious. 'Get away from here!'

'What have you done?' she screamed, ragging her vocal cords as Juan Esperanza's knees buckled and his full weight – though meagre for a man, still far more than hers – toppled forwards. She fell awkwardly, one leg pinned beneath her as she tried to grapple with him, to stop the hot blood flow that was now pumping onto her, the ground, everywhere.

Vale was there in a flash, throwing the dying man off her and roughly dragging her out as though the spectacle was unseemly. She thrashed and fought him, but even through her flailing arms and whip-crack hair, she saw Juan Esperanza on his back, one leg bent at a hideous angle, his breath coming in shallow rasps, his eyes fixed on an unseen point in the beautiful bruised sky.

Santi. What would she tell Santi? *Who* would tell him? He was in Oviedo still, working with his uncle, sending home the money his father had not been able to earn here. She had not seen him in four years and communication had been almost impossible, but they had exchanged a few letters, thanks to the help of a few men from his district when they travelled north for the harvest. In the last one, he had promised to place his beloved shark tooth in their secret hiding place as the signal he was back, and every day she checked it, and every day her loneliness grew. And now . . . Now the tears raged down her cheeks as she thought of his mother alone in their tiny shack in the *pueblo blanco*, waiting for her husband to return. She kicked and bit harder against her brother's vice-like grip, knowing she had to go to her and tell her herself; his mother had to hear it from her – that she was sorry she hadn't stopped it, sorry she hadn't saved him, sorry she was a Mendoza.

She bit down hard on his arm, trying to get free, but Vale slapped her hard, once, across the cheek. 'We had no choice, Nene. You heard him – he was a mad dog, he said it himself. He came here to fight.'

'No!' she shouted, shaking her head furiously. 'That wasn't what he meant.'

'Those were his own words.'

'You're twisting them!' Her body was shaking violently, the sobs and the fury and fear mixing within her; she felt herself growing hotter inside, the adrenaline becoming combustible, and she thought she might explode with rage. And shame.

'Control yourself, Nene.' Vale's grip was tight on her upper arms as he roughly shook her, bruising the biceps. 'These men are animals. They cannot be trusted to be civilized, to do what is right. Do you think they are your friends?' He spat the last word as if it was itself toxic. 'Ha! They would slaughter you for your dinner without a second thought.'

'They *are* my friends,' she screamed, the tears coming as sobs as she saw Señor Esperanza's body lying inert on the ground, his chest still now and the blood flow slowly subsiding. Vale slapped her again, stunning her once again into momentary submission.

Why was no one else fighting? Why were they leaving him lying there?

And then she saw that Montez still had his gun raised and pointed towards the rest of the men – that none of them dared move, neither to save her nor join her. In a flash she understood why. There might be only one cartridge left in the rifle, but he and Vale and Señor Martin all had pistols in their belts too. The *campesinos* knew it as well. The reckoning wasn't necessarily finished. Juan Esperanza might not be the only one.

'Let them go,' she said, sobering suddenly and understanding what Arlo had once said to her – that passion was the real enemy here. Volatility made trigger fingers twitchy and a pitchfork was no match for a bullet. She stood limp, falling still, dropping her head. Submitting. 'You're right, brother, they were animals. But you've made your point.'

She saw the *campesinos*' heads turn in her direction, the

inflection registering their shock as she switched side. But she saw now that if she wanted a voice, if she wanted to be heard, then she had to behave as one of them, a Mendoza. She tipped her head up slightly, nobly, knowing her riding habit gave her a gravitas she could never achieve in her normal clothes.

Slowly, Vale looked back from her to Montez. He indicated for his brother to lower the gun. 'We will show mercy – for you, sister.' He looked back at the men who were warily beginning to pull themselves up, their bodies still hunched, weapons on the ground as they held their hands up. 'Let this be a warning to you,' Vale called out. 'Those who threaten this family – this estate – will be dealt with swiftly and without mercy. We will not tolerate revolutionaries here.' He cast his gaze down and around, eyeballing each and every man, as though committing their faces to memory. 'Now go. And take him with you.'

There was a pulse of inactivity – a moment which hovered between defiance and acceptance. Were they going to take it? Several of the men looked across at her with a black hatred, as though her betrayal had been the greatest of all, before four of them gathered round the body and taking a limb each, lifted Juan Esperanza from the ground like a hunted hind, his head hanging down. Silently, they beat a retreat, their feet shuffling on the ground, heads dipped low as they headed back on the three-mile journey home.

Tears streamed down Nene's face as she watched them go, her body still trembling from the violence she had just witnessed and which supposedly had been done in her name. She had betrayed them to save them but she knew the tale of her treachery would hit even harder perhaps than her brother's brutality, for better had been expected of her.

Santi would never forgive her, she knew that absolutely. She had seen the hatred settle on the men's faces as she switched sides and she was their enemy now – condemned by birth, constrained by a name that spoke for her even when it went against her.

'Get these horses untacked and washed down. Then get that mess cleaned up,' Vale commanded the terrified-looking groom who was still holding his horse. 'It's making this place look untidy.'

The poor groom nodded mutely, as Montez dismounted too and handed over his steed wordlessly. There was still a cartridge in the barrel and he lifted the muzzle into the air, waving it in figures of eight, scanning for a passing bird. He caught sight of a pigeon heading home to roost and took aim and fired, quite unable to help himself, the gunshot ringing out mockingly and no doubt making the *campesinos* run. Nene watched as the bird spun and tumbled to the ground, landing heavily a few yards away.

'Nene?' Vale enquired, but it was really a command. She was to return to the house with them.

Dumbfounded and in shock, she stared down at the twitching bird, its wings flapping desperately in its death throes; she looked at the dropped, abandoned implements – spades and hoes and spindly-fingered rakes that would have been all but useless in a battle – at the pool of arterial blood already blackening on the ground, seeping like tar into the hard-baked earth. The scene was like an old master's still life, telling a story: a bird that had been shot for no other reason than to use up a wasted cartridge; a man killed because he dared to speak up.

And she understood then that the sanctity of life meant nothing to her family, only money and power and influence. And God help anyone who tried to stand in their way.

Chapter Six

Charlotte stared into the fridge. Carton of almond milk. Jar of pimiento olives. Slab of gouda. Pack of serrano. Two avocados. Bottle of Mirabeau rosé. She grabbed the wine and closed the door again. On the counter was a bag of sourdough and a bunch of asparagus.

Deciding to have a drink first, eat later – and she *would* eat tonight, she promised herself – she poured herself a glass and slumped against the kitchen cabinets. The apartment door was locked and she was done with today. It had started badly and limped along from there. She raked her mind over her meetings with Mateo, Lucy, Marina, her scratchy call with Stephen . . . All frustrating and draining in various ways. Had there been any positives? She forced herself to think. Dr Ferrante was available; that, at least, was helpful. Anything else?

But it was hopeless trying to pretend. Hangover or not, her day had never had a chance of recovering from the sight of the Chardin in the Prado. She had felt winded by it, blown off her path by the abrupt reappearance of this memento from another life, as though her past was knocking at the door and demanding to be let in.

Throwing her head back, she drained the glass and poured another, walking through the kitchen, past her woven leather Loewe bag strewn over the dining table with the purse about to slip out, her shoes kicked off and lying on their sides in the middle of the floor. Already she was making the place look untidy, her messy life beginning to disrupt.

Standing at the balcony, she looked down over the city as she had the night before. Ostensibly, nothing had changed: the sun still shone at the same oblique angle, dazzling her as it sliced around the grand neo-classical buildings on the opposite side of the street; the traffic still flowed below her feet up the wide boulevards and out of sight. But she had – only by a few degrees, but her past had come back into her life today as surely as light through an open door. The painting hanging there was an ending thrown at her like a stick, and it hurt. Still. After all this time.

Her phone rang and she answered listlessly. 'Hello?'

'Lotts, it's me,' her sister drawled. 'What the actual fuck? Ma says you're in Madrid.'

'That's right. Something came up at work.'

'So what about our dinner then? That's just off is it?'

'Huh?' Charlotte frowned, before suddenly remembering. 'Oh God! I'm so sorry!'

'For standing me up in the bloody Ritz? Yes, I should hope you are. I'm sitting here right now, on my own, looking like a complete fucking numpty.'

Charlotte sincerely doubted that. Her sister had an innate ability to look completely at home wherever she went, and right now the concierge would be wondering if he'd made a wrong turn to work this morning and was in fact standing in the middle of *her* house.

'I just *completely* forgot. I rearranged the dress fitting for Friday night and . . . ugh, it totally slipped my mind about dinner.'

'Charming. I've been looking forward to seeing you all week.'

'Me too!'

'Liar.'

'Look, it's all just gone a bit crazy, that's all. This project came up last minute for a client and there's been back-to-back meetings since getting here, blah-blah-blah. I just haven't been able to give anything else the mental space. I'm so sorry.'

'Mental space? This is your wedding we're talking about Lotts. You can't leave your final fitting to the weekend. You're getting married in eight days, fuck's sake. What if something happens? You've already got the shrinks.'

'Oh, come on, they've measured me twenty times already. We all know they can just send the dress as it is. These fittings are just fluff to justify their prices. It'll be fine.'

'And fine's good enough for your wedding day, is it?'

'Yes, it really is. It's one dress for one day! I really don't . . .' She sighed, almost collapsing in on herself.

'Care?' There was a long pause as Charlotte realized she didn't have the strength to argue back. Was that really what she'd been about to say? She didn't even know herself.'Look, sis, I'm worried about you.'

'I'm telling you I'm fine! I wish everyone would stop trying to pick me apart.'

'But you haven't been yourself lately. You're . . . distant, all limp.'

Charlotte closed her eyes, feeling her heart begin to thump. 'I told you, work's crazy, that's all.'

'Yeah you said, I just don't believe you. I spoke to Rosie earlier and asked if you'd booked any time off next week and she said you've got a meeting booked in the *morning of.*'

'I agree, it's not ideal, but they just quickly need me—'

'Oh, drop the bollocks, Lotts!' Mouse said, losing patience

now. 'If you're having second thoughts about the wedding, just tell me. There's still time to call it off.'

Charlotte gave a shocked bark of scorn. 'Why would I be having second thoughts? I love Stephen. He's great. We're a great team.' There was another long silence down the line. '. . . Mouse? You still there?'

'. . . Yeah. Yeah, I'm here.' She gave a heavy sigh, a distinctly un-Mouselike sound. 'I just don't want you to make a mistake, that's all. You do know that if you need to talk face to face, I can catch the next flight?'

'You're sweet.'

This time it was Mouse's turn to bark with scorn. 'No I'm not. I'm the bad sister who kisses too many boys and stays out too late. *You're* the sweet one – and that's why I'm worried. We all know I wouldn't marry a man I didn't really love.'

Charlotte felt like she'd been shot, the words physically pushing her back from the balcony and into the apartment. '. . . You can't say that,' she said in a quiet voice, squeezing her eyes shut.

'I know,' Mouse replied, just as quietly, just as sadly. 'So how come I just did?'

'You're back!' Marina greeted Charlotte in surprise as she stepped through the cafe door the next morning.

'You do good coffee,' Charlotte said simply, lapsing easily into her accented Spanish.

'You'd like a coffee?'

God yes, she needed coffee. 'Along with a plate of churros and chocolate, yes please.'

Marina nodded in affirmation but she was regarding Charlotte quizzically, no doubt still mulling over their oblique conversation yesterday and the overly large tip. 'Sure.'

Charlotte watched her go, feeling pleased as she caught Marina glance back at her before she pushed into the kitchen. The casting hooks had attached.

'There you are.' Marina returned a few minutes later with the order, an extra churro spiralled on the plate. Charlotte smiled, even more pleased to see that her generosity yesterday had pierced the skin of this new acquaintance.

'Thanks. I could get used to Spanish breakfasts.'

'. . . Are you in Madrid for long?' Marina asked, loitering awkwardly, her fingertips pressing against the tabletop.

'I was supposed to be but . . .' She shrugged. 'Things haven't panned out the way we expected so I've just got a couple of meetings later and then it's back home again.' She took a sip of coffee and closed her eyes momentarily. 'Which is a shame because I'd been looking forward to a bit more of the Spanish summer. It's raining in London of course.'

But Marina didn't seem to have heard – or at least to care about the English rain. She bit her lip. 'I . . . I've been thinking about what you said yesterday.'

Of course she had. How could she not have done? 'Oh yes?' Charlotte kept her tone light as she dipped the churro into the chocolate pot and began to eat; she could well imagine Marina had done nothing but think about what she had said yesterday.

'Just say I *was* the Marina Quincy you are looking for, why would I need your services? Why have they sent you?'

Charlotte drew in a deep breath as though the question was surprising to her, when in fact she'd been anticipating it. 'Well, because the level of money involved in this instance is very significant. Daunting, even.'

'Daunting?'

'Scary. Wealth at this level isn't a walk in the park. Frankly, it really should come with a health warnings. I've got many – *way* too many – clients who have buckled under the pressure of it.'

Without waiting to be invited to join her, Marina pulled out the opposite chair and sank down into it, her concentration wholly focused on Charlotte alone. 'Buckled how? What happens to them?'

Charlotte kept her tone conversational, chatty, generalized. 'Well, people always make a fundamental mistake with money. They think it makes things easier – easier to pay the bills, buy the car, go on holidays – and when you've got just enough, it does. The trouble starts when the zeros begin to stack up and the money itself becomes another responsibility. You need a financial adviser or even a team to make the money work for you – and that can be complicated and stressful; it's important to get in place people you can trust.'

Marina was staring at her intently, her hand cupped in her chin. It was the closest proximity they had been in to one another and Charlotte saw the focus in her eyes. She was concentrating, learning. *Caught, not taught.*

'That in itself can be easier said than done. You have to find the right synergy between you and your advisers, match up your risk profiles: some people want to grow their capital aggressively and take risks; others want to play it safe and go for the long-term bets.'

'So that's what you do? Matching clients to investors?'

'No, that's the bank's job. What I do is help with the emotional side of wealth.'

Marina looked bemused. '*Emotional* side? Does it have one?'

'Actually, that's the biggest side to it. I help my clients discover the non-financial assets of wealth.'

'I still don't get how being rich can be stressful?' Marina

asked sceptically. Close-up, Charlotte could see those angled cheekbones that photographed so well were amplified by the hollowness of her cheeks. She had known hunger, a battle to get enough food on the table – real problems, not the first-world stresses of an elite.

'Okay, well you basically end up with money one of three ways, right?' She counted off her fingers. 'You earn it, inherit or gain it. And however you come by it, each way comes with its own particular sets of issues. Now unfortunately, because of how the rest of the world regards money – i.e. as something good and desirable – it's a loaded subject. People who can't afford to buy their kids new shoes have no sympathy for a rich person with depression for instance, and that perpetuates a sense of shame amongst these wealthy individuals for being privileged and yet still not happy. People who inherit fortunes, for example, can really struggle to accept that a lottery of birth has left them with so much and everyone else so little.'

'But they could do something about that,' Marina said dismissively. 'Just give it away.'

'Yes possibly. Philanthropy can be a saving grace when done wisely, but it still has its own complications – to whom do you give it and how much? And can you be sure the money's going to be used properly, to get through to the people or causes you're trying to help? There are people in need everywhere you turn and it can be a huge burden if my clients start to feel they are personally responsible for getting rid of these issues, solving all the problems. Money doesn't resolve as much as people would like to think; very often, education is the better tool.'

'They're still in a position to choose, though.'

'Absolutely. And it works both ways – giving feels good, plus philanthropy can really help give them a purpose, which is vital. Can you imagine waking up every day and not having a reason to get out of bed?'

Marina cracked a wry grin. 'Ha. I'd like to try.'

'I know it sounds tempting when you're working shifts and struggling to pay the rent, but believe me, hard though it is, it actually gives you an advantage over the rich man: work forces you into a routine and that routine gives your days, weeks, months and years a shape. It gives you colleagues, another world outside your home. But when your life is stretching ahead of you with absolutely nothing on the horizon, when you don't even need to leave the house because you have staff to buy the food, walk the dog, take the kids to school . . . it's actually terrifying. What's the point in that existence? Everyone needs to have a purpose, a passion; without it, people become depressed, reclusive; they start drinking or taking drugs – anything to shake up the days, change the landscape.'

'So that's why they're all druggies,' Marina said pithily.

Charlotte nodded. 'And *that* is precisely what I mean. Socially, there is very little sympathy for rich people's problems because we tend to think of a successful life in material terms, not emotional ones, so their very human feelings of guilt, purposelessness, depression, shame just spiral . . .' She shrugged. 'They don't feel they can admit to these issues, so it just gets worse. There was a survey done in the States recently and it showed that depression and anxiety rates in rich teenagers are double the national average. I know it's easy to scoff from the outside looking in, but life on the other side of the glass can be suffocating.'

'I think I'd still rather be on that side, thanks.'

Charlotte shrugged, easing off the pedal a little. She didn't need to do a hard sell, she had to draw Marina in to her. She dipped another churro into the chocolate. The sugar rush was exactly what she needed, reviving her beleaguered body; she resolved to get to a soul cycle class that evening and to have only a juice before bed. No more wine. No more mulling on the past.

Marina watched her. 'But you're saying these are the people who are born into money?'

'Inheritors? Sure. That's largely their big issue – guilt, shame, lack of purpose, low self-esteem – how can they compete with their super-successful father or grandfather etc? But they only make up a small percentage of my clients – maybe thirty per cent. Most of my clients have earned their money, and that brings different sets of issues.'

'Like what?'

'Well, perhaps in their heads they'd been striving for so long for life to be a certain way once they'd "made it", and that doesn't necessarily happen – materially, yes, but they can feel disillusioned if some sort of emotional reward or expectation isn't met once they achieve their goals. Equally, the drive and focus that got them to the top of their games can also be detrimental to their personal lives. I see a fair few families in crisis because the breadwinner, be it the mother or father, applies the same aggression and rigour to their domestic lives as their business one – and families don't work like that. A person considered a leader in business can be a tyrant in the home, so they need to learn to relinquish control.' She gave Marina a wry look. 'Much easier said than done. It all comes down to appreciating meaningful relationships and articulating and finding a way of living a purposeful life – independent of money. That's what I mean by the non-financial assets of wealth.'

Marina stared at her, the slight mocking look in her eyes

gone now. She was quiet for a long moment, just watching as Charlotte calmly sipped her coffee. 'You said there were three ways of getting rich.'

They'd been circling the drain but now they were getting to it. 'That's right. Inherit, earn, or gain it.'

'And what's the problem for those that gain it?'

Charlotte sighed. 'Well that usually leads to what's known as SWS – sudden wealth syndrome.'

'It has a *name*?'

'I'm afraid so. A bit like PTSD, the shock can be overwhelming. It's a pretty toxic blend of all the worst elements of the other ways of becoming rich: inheritors' guilt, plus earners' emotional expectation gap. People might crave money, they might dream of never having to worry about a bill again, but when it happens, particularly if it's sudden and they haven't had time to work towards their goals – say they have a lottery win – they're just not prepared; not for the admin and business side of it, nor the emotional vacuum, nor the sudden lack of shape to their days or any kind of impetus to do things. Believe it or not, and I do know how patronizing this sounds, but struggle builds character – it fosters determination, grit, perseverance, and money takes that all away. Seriously, it's tough.' She looked back at Marina levelly.

'And that's why people need you.'

Charlotte nodded. 'People hear the title wealth counsellor and think it's some fluffy job. But that couldn't be further from the truth. Where there's money, there's often crisis.' She held the older woman's gaze, yesterday's conversation vibrating like an invisible thread between them.

'Excuse me, waitress?'

Marina looked up. A couple had sat down at a nearby table

and one was tapping her wrist impatiently. 'I've got to go,' she murmured, looking frustrated.

'Sure. But I have to ask you one last time, before you go. Before *I* go –' Charlotte looked at her meaningfully – 'you're quite sure you don't know Carlos Mendoza?'

Marina tucked a tendril of hair behind her ear. She swallowed nervously. '. . . Yes, I'm sure.'

Her hesitation had been louder than the reply. 'But you are Marina Quincy?'

'. . . Yes.'

'And you live at Apartment 8, 94 Calle del General Garcia de la Herran, Carabanchel?'

Marina gasped. 'How do you know that?'

'The same way I knew you worked here.' She didn't need to articulate that money could buy things other than cars and clothes. Charlotte sat back with a shrug and a sigh, a pitying look in her eyes. 'But if you're really telling me you don't know him, then I'll have to take you at your word.'

They stared at one another and Charlotte could see she wasn't the only one holding back, that Marina was telling her only half-truths. There was more. She knew more. '. . . What if I did know him? What would it mean?'

Charlotte shrugged. 'That's confidential, I'm afraid. Unless you can confirm you are the person I'm looking for, then I'm not at liberty to discuss the details of the situation.'

'Waitress!'

'Fuck,' Marina hissed in Spanish, staring down at the tabletop. 'I have to go.'

'What time do you finish?' Charlotte asked, trying not to sound desperate.

'Not till later. I'm doing a double shift.'

Charlotte tilted her head to the side sympathetically. 'Double shifts are tough,' she said quietly. 'Hard on the feet. Back.'

Marina shifted her weight, bone-aching weariness in the gesture. 'Yeah.' She was exhausted, not just from a day of it, but a lifetime.

Charlotte leaned in suddenly, cornering her quarry. 'Let me come to your apartment this evening. We can talk more then.'

'But—'

'We're running out of time, Marina. Carlos is not a well man. It's important we speak.'

Marina hesitated, then nodded, conflict puzzled across her face. 'Okay.'

'But this time, there will need to be full disclosure – from us both.'

Chapter Seven

'She's lying.'

Mateo recrossed his legs again. They had swapped the country club for his town club, the Casino, but fundamentally they were in the same space: seats on the terrace, the scent of money in the air, drinks between them and a hot anger burning in her client's eyes. 'How do you know?'

'Little things – she repeated my questions, exhibited grooming behaviours.'

Mateo's eyes narrowed with bemusement. 'That is very . . . specific. How do you know about such things, Miss Fairfax?

Milton, whose plane had landed exactly ninety minutes earlier, leaned forward, physically inserting himself into the conversation. 'I've long held a suspicion that Ms Fairfax is in fact a spy,' he quipped.

Mateo chuckled. 'I could well believe it.'

Charlotte smiled as she looked between them both. 'Part of my job is being able to read people. My clients are sophisticated people, easily able to present a veneer to the world. I have to be able to see beyond what they are telling me and read what they are showing me.'

He tapped his finger several times against his lips, watching her closely. 'And you think she knows my father.'

'So far she's only admitted she knows *of* him, although that's hardly exceptional given your family's profile – but yes, towards the end of our conversation, she indicated she might; she was fishing for more information.'

'And what did you tell her?'

'Nothing specific. I mainly explained my role in great detail, showing her the scale of the problems that come with great wealth—'

'Thereby implying great wealth is coming her way.'

Charlotte smiled. 'Exactly. She was definitely tapping me up. But I also made it clear unlimited wealth is a poisoned chalice. When I made initial contact yesterday afternoon, she just denied everything outright: she was the proverbial rabbit in headlights. Deny, deny. This morning, though, she brought extra food with my order, she loitered at my table . . . she'd clearly been thinking about our conversation. She wanted to know more.'

'So what next?'

'I'm going over this evening to give her a final chance to admit to the connection with your father. Now that she's begun to allude to it, it should get easier to draw her out and find out exactly what's going on between them.'

'She's probably realizing that if she has no contact with anyone else in your family, and with your father being so unwell, Charlotte here is potentially her only lifeline to the money,' Milton added.

Mateo frowned at the bluntness of his words. 'Do you think she trusts you?' he asked her.

'I don't think she's a woman who trusts many people, but we're establishing something of a rapport. But Dan's right – if she thinks I'm her only link to the money, that's a powerful incentive to her to come clean with me.'

Milton looked at Mateo, the somewhat obsequious expression he'd worn for greeting Lord Finch on his face again now. 'How is your father? Any further progress to report?'

'I'm pleased to say he is responding well to treatment and gaining strength; he's even trying to talk. The doctors have told us they hope to have him sitting up in bed within the week.'

Milton's expression changed. 'Well I'm glad to hear it, of course. But if your father can sit and talk, then he can also sit and dictate. In theory, he could have that donation drawn up by the end of the weekend.'

'I see, yes,' Mateo said hesitantly.

'Marina doesn't know he's recovering, does she?' Milton looked over at Charlotte who could only shrug.

'She's not admitting to knowing anything right now. I mentioned he was in poor health.'

He was quiet for a moment. 'In which case, let her continue to think he is ailing. She might be more inclined to accept an offer, on the grounds that something is better than nothing.' Milton held his hands out as if it was all so simple. 'I reckon we've been going about this the wrong way, tiring ourselves out trying to move money, find loopholes and second-guess what she knows or is expecting. There's a much simpler, more direct way. Rather than you trying to block your father's actions, Mateo, you need to take decisive action yourself – approach her directly with your own offer but one with conditions attached: if she accepts it, she waives the right to receive *any* further gifts, donations or bequests from the Mendoza estate. You could get the lawyers to draw up the exact wording so that even if your father recovers and proceeds with his gift, even if you can't stop that, she won't be *allowed* to accept it.'

'You mean, we ambush from the other direction?' Mateo asked, looking both impressed and appalled at once.

'Exactly. There's so many other unknowns – with her playing hard to get and your father not yet able to communicate, we have no way of knowing whether he told her of his intentions before his stroke; and if he did, what he told her to expect. All we do know is that right now, she can't contact him and vice versa and that's our strength. Let's run interference between them.'

'But my priority with making contact was to try to understand who this woman is – what she means to my father and why he feels the need to do this for her. I'm not sure I want to . . . cheat her.'

'It's not cheating her,' Milton shrugged mildly, clasping his hands together. 'She's free to sign or not sign. No one's holding a gun to her head.'

Charlotte looked between the two men. 'I think what Dan's saying is that this is a compelling bird in the hand scenario for Marina.'

'Precisely. I think that would be pretty attractive to someone in her straitened circumstances, and it wouldn't take much in real terms to satisfy her needs – even offering an amount far below your father's proposed gift would still prove life-changing. Plus the prospect of court action against someone like you, Mateo, would be highly daunting to her. I'm assuming you would contest the gift if it actually went through?'

'Well I suppose we'd have to but—'

'So then this could save you all that hassle, pain, drama, headlines. Who knows? She could decide to hold out for the whole shebang but you've got nothing to lose at this stage. Why not give it a go and try to head her off at the pass? Get your lawyers to make the offer and see what she says.'

Charlotte watched Mateo closely. He was looking conflicted. His eyes met hers.

'Actually, I think I'd like Charlotte to take the deal to her.'

'Me?' she asked in surprise. 'But I'm not a lawyer or banker.'

'No, but you are the one building a relationship with her, she's more likely to listen to you. Dan's right, this is worth a shot. I'll consult with my advisers and decide on an authorized amount you can go to her with. I'll also get my legal team to draw up any ancillary paperwork so that if she goes for it, she signs a binding agreement there and then – as Dan says – agreeing to waive any future gift or donation from the Mendoza estate.'

Charlotte nodded. '. . . Okay. Well, I'll progress things with her tonight and take it to her, see if she'll bite; but she's a shrewd woman and she may well have a game plan; she might even have anticipated all of this.' Charlotte tipped her head to the side questioningly. 'What if she won't sign?'

'Then it will come down to the matter of time – does my father recover sufficiently to make the donation, in which case we are facing a lengthy court battle? Or does he die before it can be enacted?' He shrugged sadly. 'Neither one is pleasing to me.'

'I'm so sorry this is happening to your family, Mateo. It's already a stressful enough time,' Charlotte said.

'I feel I have begun mourning him already. Whatever happens, it will be hard to get past the sense of betrayal that is attached to the donation – how he could put her before us, his family.'

'Well, I hope at least that is something our professor will be able to help with. It may give you closure on that score.'

'Professor?' Milton asked, sounding bemused and crossing his ankle over his knee, looking across at Charlotte questioningly. He wasn't the sort of man to bend the knee to academia.

'Dr Ferrante, a history professor at Carlos III University. He has agreed to research the family's history for us. He should be here any moment, in fact; I asked my PA to book enough time for us all to talk first, but if we do end up needing his services, it could be very healing.'

'Healing? Really?' Mateo shifted position in his seat, looking uncomfortable again. 'At our last meeting, you said you thought my father was acting from shame, as though there's something we should be ashamed of.'

'That was just a hypothesis, I could be completely wrong. But even if I'm not, Dr Ferrante is an academic, not a gossip and not a journalist. The point of the exercise would be simply to try to identify the reasons why your father is doing this. Is it just about her – an infatuation – or is something else compelling him?'

They lapsed into silence as the waiter set down their drinks – Pisco Sour cocktails – Charlotte taking a moment to soak up the view. They were on the rooftop terrace, a gentle breeze and cream umbrellas softening the glare of the heat, neatly clipped box trees dotting the perimeter as white-jacketed waiters glided between the baroque white-iron tables and chairs. Every table was booked, Madrid's chic set enjoying their aperitifs before they headed down to the mirrored two-Michelin-star restaurant downstairs.

'Well it all sounds intriguing,' Milton drawled, with a tone that suggested it was an amusing diversion. The 'soft' politics of wealth were always lost on him. He was driven by bottom lines, risk and growth. 'He's a history professor, you said?'

Charlotte gave a polite smile. 'That's right; he's attached to the Humanities division at Carlos III University. He's done similar work for me on other clients several times now. It's amazingly interesting. Illuminating even. Mateo, do you have that TV programme here, *Who Do You Think You Are?*

He shrugged. 'I don't watch television.'

'Ah. Well, it's similar to that. Every family has stories that have been forgotten or lost. It's something of a privilege really to be acquainted with your own personalized history.'

'I will have to reserve judgement on that.'

'Of course. But please remember, you're not being judged in any way. Dr Ferrante is a very skilled and discreet man, methodical in his work.'

'But this is an odd request for him, is it not, to do a research project like this? I would have thought he would look down on something like this. Academics are purists, they hate selling out.'

'He told me once he views these projects as history in the singular – the macro-events of the political and social climate of the time, playing out in the confines of the family unit.' She smiled confidingly. 'And let us not forget, every academic has an overdraft. And at this time of year, when the university term is over and they've got a little time to dedicate to a few weeks or so of private work . . .' She shrugged. 'He's got to eat.'

Mateo sighed heavily. 'Well, let us hope your professor is—' He shifted position slightly, just as his gaze caught on something – or someone – behind her, an interested look coming into his eyes. 'Ah, Dr Ferrante I presume? We were just talking about you.' He rose, holding out a hand.

Charlotte leaned forward to set her drink down on the table, moving to turn round.

'Dr Ferrante couldn't make it, I'm afraid. A sudden family matter has come up. He's had to fly to Barcelona for a few weeks and has asked me to stand in for him,' the voice behind her said—

'You're Charlotte, right? Doc Hall's tutee?'

Through the blur of her hangover, she saw a melange of green eyes, a clear gaze, bright blonde unbiddable hair, a gappy smile. He smelled of lanolin soap and coal smoke, his handknit jumper anachronistic against the public school cricket sweaters the rest of college was wearing.

'. . . I'm Dr Marling. Nathan.'

Was he underwater? His voice sounded echoey, distant, as though coming to her in a dream. So many dreams. She turned, her body on autopilot, hand out even though she had no conscious thought of putting it there. Her eyes were swept up by his, like fishing nets scooping her out of the sea, green stars that shone in her sky, day and night, regardless of the rising sun or the waxing moon.

'Doc left a note in my pigeon hole. He can't make it. Emergency root canal. He's asked me to take the tutorial.'

'Has he?' she asked in surprise.

'Yes.'

'But you're far too young.'

A tiny frown puckered his brow. 'I'm doing a master's.'

'Okay. You're too handsome then,' she teased, amused by his earnestness.

The frown deepened. He shifted his weight. '. . . He wants us to discuss free will.'

Where was he from? She couldn't place his accent. She'd never met anyone from outside the M25, not properly. 'Or we could exercise some free will of our own and go to the bar,' she said, guessing the idea of a midday drink would scandalize him. He looked so . . . innocent, somehow. She hugged her books to her chest and leant her head against the wall, giving him one of her sleepy, sexy smiles and letting her hair fall over one eye. It was one of her favourite games, seeing how quickly she could reel them in. 'You do drink, don't you?'

Could he tell she was mocking him? His face betrayed nothing, his gaze open and clear as he took in the sight of her, up close. People always seemed surprised she had freckles, as though they were somehow too bourgeois for a girl like her. 'Of course.'

'Yes? What's your nipple?'

'Excuse me?'

She'd arched an eyebrow. 'What's your tipple?'

'Oh. I . . .' Confusion clouded his features but the word was in his head now, the image . . .

She gave another languid smile, feeling like a cat toying with a mouse. 'What did you think I said?'

He flushed beetroot, his clear-eyed gaze shrouded over now as she swam in circles around him, making him dizzy, tongue-tied. The high colour suited him, though she doubted he had any idea of that, and she watched as a tiny muscle clenched in his jaw. He was getting angry with her and she found she liked it. She liked the idea of pushing someone like him to their limits – someone so opposite to her: always in control, always good, so driven and striving for more. What would it take to break them? To show them how the world looked from her side of the fence?

She stepped into him. 'Come and have a drink with me.'

'I can't.'

'Why not? Don't you want to?'

'It's not that. We're supposed to go ahead with the tutorial without Doc.'

'And do you always do what you're supposed to do, Mr Master's?' she asked, lightly raking a nail down the front of his chest.

His hand caught her by the wrist, stopping her. 'Don't.'

'Don't what?'

'You know what.' His eyes met hers properly then, desire marbled with frustration at her games, and she felt a sudden jolt as she did sometimes when she fell asleep too quickly, her heart shocking herself

awake again. She felt wide awake now – the blurry fuzziness of today's hangover dissipating in a flash as they stood there in the narrow hall, rigid and linked. 'I'm not one of your toys.'

What was happening? It was supposed to have been a joke, another of her signature teases, but somehow she was the one caught in the net. Out of sight around the corner, the sound of a stampede was growing down the hall – bellows and cheers and running feet and doors being thumped – but she was oblivious to it, watching him transfixed as he saw straight past her fakery and bullshit, the party queen crap that kept everyone else fooled and at arm's length. She was completely exposed before him and she didn't know whether it was her fright of being caught in the act or the pity in his eyes that made unbidden tears suddenly bud in her eyes.

'You're worth more, you know,' he said quietly.

'More than what?' she'd wanted to ask, but there had been no time. The rugger buggers were barrelling down the hall now and upon them, Rt Hon. Jules Fairfax scooping her up in a fireman's lift with nary a word and spiriting her away as though she wasn't mid-conversation with someone, as though that someone wasn't even there. And as she was jogged out of sight, down the stairs and towards the bar, her gaze remained on him as she went back to her world, and he stayed in his . . .

A long pause cradled them both, time suspending her endless beat to give them breath. Was this real? Was she awake? Was it really him?

'Hello, Charlotte,' he said finally, his hand clasping hers in a pedestrian motion and undoing her world. 'It's been a long time.'

He had changed. His hair was longer, the muddy blonde side-swept style she remembered replaced by something shaggier and more bookish. He wore glasses too now, heavy-rimmed black ones that served to highlight those eyes that had always transfixed her. Gone too were the studenty sport shorts and t-shirts; today he was in a tobacco linen unlined jacket, pale-pink shirt and ivory chinos.

She watched him talk, filling in Mateo Mendoza with his impressive CV – a PhD at Yale after Oxford, and now a post-doctoral fellowship researching the civil war here. He looked calm and composed, but his eyes kept coming back to her like a bee to the flower. She had said barely a word since he had sat down, trying to soak him up, to absorb his presence, but he saturated her, filling every part of her mind, body and soul, and yet still she couldn't contain him. He overwhelmed her senses and she realized she had been living in a world without colour, sound and taste and she hadn't even known it. There had been no vibrancy, passion nor verve – everything had been automatic and robotic, correct yet not present; something always off like a jigsaw with one missing piece, the world a scrambled image. But seeing him again was like finding a missing part of herself, her shadow having somehow become unstitched from her, and now here it was, unfurled on the chair opposite, darker than ever in the Spanish sunshine.

It was hard to keep up with what he was saying. Her eyes kept scanning him over and over, watching rather than listening.

'Well, you certainly sound supremely well qualified,' Mateo was saying, glancing over at her and giving her a quick nod of approval.

'Over-qualified, even,' Milton said with a dark smile.

'. . . Have you been briefed on our "situation"?' Mateo asked.

'Not fully. Dr Ferrante only passed the case on this morning.'

'Then perhaps I should let Charlotte brief you, seeing as

she is the one who has done this before. It is not a straightforward project.'

It was her cue but for several seconds, she couldn't find her voice; Nathan's eyes had stolen it from her. How could she talk to him as though he was just anyone?

But Milton was watching closely too; he'd never seen her flustered before. She cleared her throat and gave it her best shot. 'Well, it's a delicate issue, I'm afraid. Mr Mendoza's father was very sadly diagnosed with terminal pancreatic cancer a few weeks ago. At best, it is expected he has only a couple of months left.'

Nathan took his gaze off her and it was like the sun going behind a cloud. 'I'm sorry to hear that.'

Mendoza nodded his gratitude.

'Unfortunately, Mr Mendoza's father suffered a mini-stroke last weekend. Mr Mendoza has power of attorney for his father's estate in such times, and it was during the course of those events that it came to light that his father had been drawing up a directive to gift the entirety of his fortune to a woman called Marina Quincy. A woman no one in the family has either met or ever heard of.'

Nathan frowned but said nothing and Charlotte knew he was being tactful, too discreet to state the obvious. Unlike Milton.

'We have made initial contact with Ms Quincy and are currently liaising with her on the matter. It's a delicate balancing act at the moment as we are trying to establish exactly what she knows and expects, but we are hoping in the first instance that we might be able to come to some financial agreement. It's in her interests this doesn't go to court – the family would most certainly contest the gift if it came to pass – and of course, it's in their best interests to keep this out of the press. If a settlement is reached, then we wouldn't need to go any further with you and we would pay you for your time here today.'

'And is a pay-off looking likely?' His gaze was so steady; she felt her heart leap like a salmon jumping upstream.

'Well, at the moment Ms Quincy is denying even knowing Mr Mateo's father. But I am seeing her again tonight and we are hopeful an agreement can be reached.'

Nathan clasped his hands together, sitting back in his chair and pinning her with a look that frankly left her breathless. 'And if it can't, that's where I come in?'

'Yes. We are concerned as to what may be behind Mr Mateo's father's rash behaviour; this is completely out of character for him—'

'Completely,' Mateo reiterated.

'He has always been a loving and devoted husband and father. A family man. This has come like a bolt from the blue.' Mateo nodded at her words. 'One line of thought is that – upon being confronted with his mortality – this has perhaps prompted a need for Mateo's father to make reparations, possibly for something that occurred in the past?'

'You think he feels guilty about something?'

'Perhaps.'

Mateo sat forward in his chair at that, waggling a finger. 'Guilt is not a word I am comfortable with, professor. My father has always been a man of honour. He is a known philanthropist and a great benefactor to the arts. He is held in high regard by all who know him.'

Nathan gave a level smile, correctly reading his fears. 'I assure you, I have no desire to embarrass your family, Mr Mendoza. If something has happened in the past that is responsible for your father's actions, I shall bring it to your attention with the sole intention of helping you, nothing more. Furthermore, whatever I might uncover would remain confidential, between you, Charlotte and the bank.'

Charlotte saw Milton's head turn at the casual, familiar way Nathan had said her name.

Mateo nodded, wringing his hands but looking somewhat appeased. 'So then, what next?'

'Well,' Charlotte said, musing that very same point as Nathan's gaze alighted upon her once more. She had to force herself to wrench her gaze away and back onto her client. 'Professor Marling already has the preliminary profiles that the bank keeps on file of your family, but with your permission we would also send over the information supplied by your researchers on Marina Quincy. Then we would leave him to do what he does best – dig deep.'

On the table, Mateo's phone vibrated and he glanced at the screen before looking away with a weary sigh. 'I'm afraid I must go – another meeting with my lawyers.' He rose to standing. 'And, Dan, you should probably come too. You can talk them through the terms of this offer of yours.'

Milton looked reluctantly between her and the professor. 'Of course.'

'It has been interesting meeting you, professor,' Mateo said, shaking Nathan's hand. 'My mind is put to rest on the matter and I would be happy to engage your services if our Plan A fails.'

'Okay, I'll wait to hear,' Nathan replied, shaking his and then Dan's hand too.

'Good luck this evening. Ring me if there are any developments,' Mateo said to her.

'Of course,' she nodded.

'Likewise,' Milton said before coming back to her, throwing another suspicious look Nathan's way again. 'I'm not flying out till the morning, so let me know if you want to meet up for dinner.'

'Sure,' she smiled.

She and Nathan watched them go, waiting until they were out of sight before turning back to one another. Again she felt it, that zippering of electricity between them as the world contracted to just the two of them—

For three weeks, she lost sight of him. Though she went to all the usual parties, clubs, pubs, hangouts, her eyes searched for him wherever she went – scanning as she walked down corridors and across quads with her glamorous social set for that diffident blonde boy in the hand-knitted sweater.

It was only after she'd been spirited away that she had realized she didn't even know his name, although it had been easy enough to find out.

'Oh you mean Nathan Marling,' one of the girls in her Indian Democracy module had drawled, sweeping mascara onto her lashes. 'He's a supervisor in my Fascism class. Fucking oddball. I am not joking, he actually sits in lectures with a fucking apple on his desk. I mean, who even does that?'

'Right,' Charlotte had murmured, thinking it was charming. That bitch was right – who else did do that?

When she'd found him again, it was in the one place she hadn't thought to look – lying on the banks of the river with Jules and their gang, drinking champagne from teacups and not even pretending to revise, her head had turned, bored, at the collective splash of blades sluicing the river Cam, the slash of wooden seats sliding back on their rails, the heavy breathing of eight men moving in unison, muscles flexed and taut . . .

His hair gave him away instantly and she froze as the boat lunged past in ten-metre increments, the cox huddled in the stern and shouting instructions through a cone. He was the stroke, first in the boat, the one all the others looked to for speed, pace and beat, and as the boat passed by their rowdy group, his unseeing gaze found her. She saw the slap of shock on his face as their eyes locked, but he didn't miss a beat; he kept the rhythm, sliding back and forth, pushing through the pain, pulling himself away from her until within a minute, he was out of her sights again—

'Another drink?' she asked.

'Yes. But not here.' His gaze was level, but entirely different in tone to that of a moment earlier. Nothing more needed to be said. Or explained.

And in that instant, she felt the world settle back into place. 'Let's go then.'

She didn't even know the name of the hotel. He had grabbed her hand and run with her, pulling her through the traffic on Gran Via and across the road to an historic building opposite. There, they had stood at reception and booked a room, trying to look contained as they waited for the paperwork, their eyes on the ceiling as they rode up in the escalator with the poor porter who had nothing to carry but their key. It was the middle of the afternoon, they were dressed for business meetings, they had no bags . . . everyone knew what this was.

He didn't bother showing them how to work the TV or explaining the thermostat in the bathroom, merely handing them the key with an embarrassed nod and beating a hasty retreat. For one moment, alone at last, they had stood in front of one another, neither one of them bothering to take in the view at the window or check the toiletries or the minibar. Their eyes were glued on one another, their breathing shallow, eyes bright like they'd run up the stairs.

But then he had shrugged off his jacket in one seamless movement, letting it lie where it fell, and she was in his arms, back where she was always supposed to have been. Everything was instinctive and urgent between them, words superfluous to touch, to taste, as they reclaimed one another again, trying to close the gap on the intervening years and compress the separation that had left her hollow and him, hungry.

His smell was like a comfort blanket over her, undoing all the pain and loneliness of the past four years, and as they fell into one another, again and again, she wondered how she had ever done what she had done to him, how she had had the strength to break what they had when clearly they were invincible.

She felt herself change as his hands moulded her, shaping her into someone better, brighter, happier, than she otherwise was and her heart thrilled as she heard his groans against her neck. This was a homecoming. This was destiny. This could never have been denied—

Doc Hall poured the brandy, a vinyl of Mahler's Fifth Symphony wobbling around on the turntable, wood smoke puffing back into the small room in occasional downdraughts. The William Morris curtains were drawn but the window was ajar and intermittent shouts and carouses from the quad pierced the homely tranquillity of the tutor's room. She was sitting on a gold velour pouffe, the fringing in one section held up by a safety-pin; Nathan was in the leather club chair on one side of the fire, Doc's Burmese Grey, Mrs Miggins, sitting on the arm and swishing its tail in his face every few minutes. Ordinarily, it would have made her laugh – she loved to laugh; it was the only way not to cry as far as she could see – but she felt stoppered up by his presence, all her feelings tamped down, as if allowing one emotion would allow them all, an unstoppable force waiting to erupt from within her. She hadn't expected him to be here in her tutorial. Had he asked to join it, specifically?

'. . . all begs the overarching question, does History even matter?' Doc Hall mused, handing them a drink each and sitting down heavily in the high-backed gentleman's chair. He was a small, shrewish man, with a taste for three-piece tweed and leather buttons.

Charlotte couldn't stop staring at Nathan, her eyes tracing how the firelight drew him in golden lines. He sat very upright, one hand on his thigh. He was wearing jeans and another jumper tonight, this one an old-school Aran, his face angled in the tutor's direction but his eyes coming back to her every few seconds.

His gaze was inscrutable, the moment of clarity and understanding that had passed between them that day in the hall, a month ago now, increasingly distant. She couldn't feel the connection she had felt back then and it made her feel foolish and embarrassed that a joke gone wrong had let him get so close. Why should she have thought he was different? Special? He was just a geek, a swot scholar who rocked a hand-knit. He would never fit into her world anyway. Her friends were sophisticated, worldly; they spent weekends in London and Christmases in Zermatt. He, on the other hand, travelled everywhere by bike and went home in the holidays to some remote village in the Midlands. For almost a month, she had pinned her hopes on finding and reconnecting with this enigmatic stranger but she had made him into something he wasn't.

Not to mention it had been a one-way fantasy. He hadn't sought her out. They were too different, he instinctively knew that and would never act on it – she could see just from how he was sitting there that he was sensible like that. And besides, everyone knew she and Jules were on-off sleeping together. He wouldn't dare—

But when she'd seen him on the river, in his element, it hadn't looked like it was her boyfriend he was wary of.

'I asked Mr Marling here to join us, Charlotte, because you made some points in your essay, "Does History Tell us the Truth", which I thought might provoke an interesting discussion—'

She forced herself to look back at the professor. 'Huh?'

'—Yes, you said, for example, that History is just a fable agreed upon and that there's nothing to be learnt from the stories of dead men; but I wonder if you've considered the long-term perspective it confers upon the entire human experience? That perhaps it puts the present into context, for example?'

She felt her cheeks burn. She didn't want to debate history with him. 'It would if the history conferred upon us was comprehensive, but the present is being contextualized by only that one narrow version of the past, the one written by the victors, and that is reductive,' she replied sullenly, her voice sounding as perfectly bored as ever. 'The dead can't tell their truth. The full complexity of what really went down is reduced to a headline, an agenda, a policy. Historians can't possibly know every aspect of the truth. No one ever gets to know the whole story. Lives are broken all the time by the things that go unsaid and remain unknown. The full truth lies down in the cracks where we cannot see.'

'So you're saying that History is inherently flawed because what is transferred is just one perspective in what is actually a prismatic experience?'

'Exactly. Same as in life. We're all here, in the same room, at the same college, in the same university – yet our experiences within that framework are completely different.' Her eyes flickered towards Nathan again, she couldn't help it. He was staring at her intently, but his thoughts were impossible to read. 'Whose version is right or the most authoritative? When we leave here and move away, whose should be remembered and passed down as the official Cambridge experience?'

He didn't blink, his eyes never leaving her now, her speech the warrant he needed to watch her.

'So then, taken to its natural conclusion, your view is that History can tell the truth but not the whole truth and certainly not nothing but the truth?'

She blinked and looked back at him. '. . . Yeah.'

Doc Hall allowed a tiny smile to play on his lips. 'Mr Marling, what are your thoughts on the matter?'

'The exact opposite, sir. History is vital because it provides the framework by which the lives of every person on the planet are shaped. Learning from the mistakes of the past is the only way to avoid them in the future.'

'Care to elucidate?'

'To study history is to see Darwinism in action: evolution, survival. The brain is the human species' single greatest weapon; we are unique in the animal kingdom in that we can not just revisit the past, but learn from it and shape our future behaviours too.'

'So you believe it allows the ennoblement of the human race?'

'I do. If we learn from the mistakes of our forebears, we can save ourselves. The mistakes of the father need not be the path for his son. Or daughter.'

Charlotte's eyes flashed up sharply, his words searing her skin; they felt targeted and sharp. Mistakes of the father? That wasn't coincidence. What did he know? Did he know? He was looking straight at her, pity in his eyes.

He knew. He'd heard somehow. The Cambridge grapevine. The press.

She looked away, feeling a white-hot spike of rage. He thought she was some tragic fuck-up because of what her father had done? He thought she could somehow be 'saved'?

Fuck him. She didn't need his pity. She didn't need his patronizing academic theories about how they'd all be okay if they just read some fucking books. She felt her cheeks redden and she knew it was all there on her face for him to read – anger, shame, that for some reason she couldn't hide from him.

She knocked back the brandy in one gulp, wincing as it stung the back of her throat, feeling it burn all the way down to her stomach. That burn, then the numbing . . . it was so familiar, so welcome. She closed her eyes. The room felt hot suddenly. Airless. That roaring fire in this tiny room – it wasn't like there was snow on the damned ground. It was October. She pulled on the neck of her jumper, trying to cool herself, to breathe.

Nathan was watching her but his guard had dropped too and his hand was now gripping his thigh. Looking tense, primed somehow, he absently swatted Miss Miggins onto the ground. She gave a mewl in protest, slinking over to Doc Hall and interweaving herself sulkily between his legs.

'. . . I'll pass that sentiment on to my colleagues, Mr Marling. Many of them are quite certain we are doom—'

A bell started ringing suddenly – loud and insistent – continuously, throughout the college. It made them all jump and Charlotte realized that in fact she had, that she was actually standing. Her body was rigid, as though the alarm had leapt from her own body, out into the world. She had to get out of here.

'Drat that wretched alarm system,' Doc Hall muttered, reluctantly putting down his brandy and pushing himself out of the chair again. 'Okay, we'll have to pick this up next time. File out to the quad. I need to put Miss Miggins back in her carrying crate. The one time I don't bother will be the one time there is actually a fire—'

But Charlotte was already throwing open the door, his words receding at her back as she ran down the corridor. She had a clear path. No one else was yet coming out of their rooms, everyone too lazy or stoned or drunk to want to get off their beds and stand outside in the autumn chill for the sake of a fire drill.

But she needed the cold slap of winter on her skin, she needed the freezing burn of the easterly wind in her lungs. She needed something that would make her feel – not feel better, not feel happier. Just feel.

'Charlotte!'

He was following, right behind her.

She ran faster, throwing open the door and running out into the quad, but he was taller and fitter, easily gaining on her. In panic, she grabbed a bike that had been left propped against the wall and threw her leg over it.

'Charlotte!'

She began furiously pedalling. It had been years since she'd ridden one – not since she was a little girl in fact – and she tore out of the college grounds, through the arch, past the scholars' garden and turning onto the river bank. The Cam lay dark and inert beside her, seemingly scarcely moving, as she flew along the path, travelling beneath the street lamps from one limpid pool of light to the next. Her eyes were streaming but that was from the wind; she wasn't crying. It was the wind. It was.

Breathless, she risked a look behind her but there was nothing to see. He wasn't there, she had left him in her wake. There was nothing to hear either, the desperate clamour of the Clare fire drill now lost on the breeze, but her legs were still pumping. The crisis was over but she wouldn't slow down; she could still hear his condescending theories, feel his patronizing pity. Who was he to judge her? Did he believe life lessons came in a particular order and at a set time too? She had already suffered. She had already lost. Her life – though dazzlingly colourful and bright – was like a kaleidoscope, shattered into tiny pieces that could be arranged into attractive patterns but would never again be whole.

Over the sound of her own breathing, she heard it – the whir of another set of wheels. Glancing over her shoulder, she saw him. He had a bike too. Of course he did, she knew tha—

She didn't see the pothole and she was flying through the air before she even knew it was happening, landing on the grass bank – thankfully soft from recent rain – and rolling dramatically to a stop. From her dazed vantage, she saw that she was by a boathouse, a boat strut still up and a half-drunk bottle of fizzy orange left by the wall.

'Charlotte!' Nathan was there two seconds later, jumping off the bike while the wheels were still spinning and helping her up as she tried to stagger to her feet. 'Are you okay?'

'Let go of me!' she yelled, mortified, humiliated, all her rage overflowing now as she saw the pity in his eyes again.

His hand dropped away instantly. 'I'm sorry.'

'Fuck you! I don't need your sympathy.'

He looked taken aback, startled by her fury. They both knew she wasn't talking about the fall. 'Look, what I said back there, I didn't mean to imply—'

'Yes you did,' she spat. 'You think you know me because of what you've read? You think what they're all saying behind my back is the truth? It's bullshit. That's just their version of the past. I saw it all through the prism. So you can take your fucking theories about ennobling yourself and—'

'I'm sorry about your father—'

'Don't mention my father!' Her hand flew up, slapping him hard.

He stiffened, the instinctive anger flashing through his eyes as the sting spread across his cheek; she saw the muscle ball in the side of his jaw again, the way it had that first time when she had pushed him too far.

'Oh my God . . .' she said, aghast, her hands flying to her mouth. 'I didn't mean—'

He stepped back, out of her orbit, and she could see the effort it was taking to restrain himself, the struggle to override instinct.

'Nathan—'

'Forget it.'

'I'm sorry,' she whispered.

'It's fine.'

But it wasn't. She could see it in his eyes – the disgust at her behaviour, the surprise, the bafflement. Things like this didn't happen in his world. Girls like her didn't exist – wild girls, ferals, falling apart . . .

She felt her shoulders hitch as the oh-so-familiar self-loathing rose up; it was a high tide in her today, the memories coming fast and unbidden. She closed her eyes, trying to black them out, tossed her head, trying to shake them out. But they were stuck to her, part of her; they were her history. Evolution wasn't going to come fast enough to get her out of this mess.

'Charlotte.'

She looked up to find him staring down at her, seeing her suffering, pained by it.

She jerked her gaze away quickly. Christ, she was a mess. She'd lost it. She was making a fool of herself – yelling, hitting him. What was she going to do now? Cry? She didn't even cry in front of her own mother.

With visible effort, she pulled herself up to her full height – not that five foot six was any sort of achievement against six two – and forced a fake smile, pushing her hair back with a trembling hand. 'Well, sorry again,' she said, falling into the slightly bored tone she had long ago perfected, albeit with a wobble in her voice. 'Brandy's never been my drink.'

'Don't.' The word was like a push, forcing her off-balance again, stopping her from saving them both from this. 'You don't have to do that. Not with me.'

She swallowed, looking away, feeling the tears rise up in her, higher and higher. Oh God, yes she did. She had to act it was fine to make it fine, to pretend everything was going to be okay . . . She went to turn away but he blocked her, the bulk of him too much to see round, to get round. He was all she could see. He was her landscape now.

She swallowed, looking up at him again and knowing that with every breath she was coming apart, stitch by stitch. Her gaze fell to the handprint on his cheek and instinctively her own hand followed it there. 'I'm sorry,' she whispered, her voice held aloft as though carried on a sob.

He didn't move for a moment, his eyes never leaving her, as though he didn't trust her not to slap him again or bolt at the slightest stir; but then his hand covered hers on his cheek and he turned his face into it, kissing her palm.

The simplicity of the act, the tenderness in it, the intimacy . . . no one had ever kissed her there before. It was so unexpected, that the tears she had been holding in abeyance suddenly dropped like a curtain on a play, streaming in silent floods down her cheeks.

Without a word, he pulled her in to him and, cupping her face in his hands, staunched her tears with kisses. And kiss by kiss, her sobs steadily became gulps, and then gasps, and then they were lost—

'What are you thinking about?'

His deep voice rumbled against her ear, tickling her. She always had liked lying on top of him, her cheek pressed to his broad chest as she listened to his heartbeat. From where they were, she could see their clothes in a tangle on the floor, Madrid still going about its business outside the windows. It was only their world that had stopped.

She smiled and turned to face him, playfully digging her chin into his chest and wiggling it side to side, before coming to rest on her overlaid hands. 'I was thinking about our first time together.' He was lying on a couple of pillows, his arms splayed out behind his head. Up close, she could see age was suiting him. The delicate, pretty boy features of his adolescence were heavier; he was classically handsome now, and later, in his forties or fifties, when the sharp angularity of his features began to soften and droop a little, she could see he would be rugged. He would always be a beautiful man.

He arched an eyebrow. 'In the boathouse?'

'You remember?'

'Of course.'

She smiled, the memories like an afterglow. 'Do you ever think about it?'

'Not really.'

The abruptness of the admission shocked her. 'Oh.'

'What's the point? It's . . . painful.'

She looked at him, seeing the honesty in his green eyes. Tenderly, she kissed his chest. 'You always were pragmatic. You haven't changed.'

'You have.'

'Have I?' she asked hopefully.

'Absolutely. Where'd all your spark go? You were so . . . polite back there. No use of irony or the F-word at all. I had to keep checking it was really you.'

'Ha-ha. It's called being professional.'

He gave a wry grin. 'I never thought *you* would end up being a professional.'

'Hey!'

'Professional party girl, maybe.'

'I object to that!' She flicked one of his nipples and he laughed again, catching her arms easily as she tried to do the same to the other one, and flipping her off him onto her back. There was playfulness in the movement but something else too, simmering below the surface.

'You're still angry with me,' she said quietly, looking up at him as he looked back down at her in the same way too: his eyes drinking her in, soaking her up like she was water to his roots.

'I'll always be angry with you.' It was a statement of fact, plain and simple.

She felt a stab of disappointment, a red tint of shame begin to bleed into the pristine perfection of their reunion. She didn't want to talk about the past. She didn't even want to think about the future. She wanted to stay in this moment, this one right here, filled up with a golden light. But it couldn't be ignored. The past clung to them like weeds, the bad memories as well as the good. 'You know Jules and I . . . didn't last?' She almost whispered the words, as though by keeping them hollow they would leave no trace on the here and now.

He loosened his grip on her at the mention of his name. 'Well, I won't pretend to be surprised.'

'It was the biggest mistake of my life, you have to believe that. I've never regretted anything more.'

He was very still now and she could see the pain was still alive in the very furthest reaches of his eyes. 'If you say so.'

'I do. I do,' she said urgently, holding his arms harder, pulling him tighter to her. How could she convey to him that for the first time in years she actually felt happy? Fully alive? She had been sleepwalking all this time and she'd never even known it.

Instead they lay there in still and silent communion, gazes locked, suspended in their own private bubble, the pain and exquisite joy of their first love pulsing between them, before he broke the seal and bent down to kiss her lightly, once, twice, three times . . . She closed her eyes in rapture, the kisses feeling like an answer to a question she hadn't even asked.

Her phone rang loudly on the bedside table and, instinctively, they both turned to look at it.

Oh God, no.

His expression changed. His voice too. She actually felt him flinch. '. . . Aren't you going to answer it?'

'No, I . . . no.' She bit her lip and shook her head, but it was too late. They had both seen Stephen's name on the screen.

For several long moments, there was nothing: no movement, no sound, just the uncertain hovering between opposite worlds: past and present, love and hate, trust and despair. He stared at her, his eyes travelling over the contours of her face, before he pushed himself up and off her. Decision made.

He walked across the room – he always had been magnificent, naked; that rower's physique . . . She felt another stab of longing for him. 'Who is he?'

'N-no one.'

He shot her a derisory glance as he stepped into his clothes. 'Don't play me for a fool. Not again, Charlotte. Things are different now.'

'But—'

'We've both got our own lives,' he said, doing up the zip on his trousers. 'It's fine you're with someone else now. I'd expect it. Well, maybe not quite *this*,' he said scornfully as he shrugged on his shirt.

She sat up in bed, clutching the sheet to her. She felt exposed, vulnerable suddenly. 'Nathan, you don't understand—'

'Don't get me wrong, I'm grateful, actually.'

'*Grateful?*' She stared at him.

'At least we got a proper goodbye at last. The one we never got to have first time around.'

'No. This isn't goodbye,' she said in alarm.

But he wasn't listening, moving fast. 'I've always thought it's funny how defining a first experience tends to be, and yet the last one is almost always lost to obscurity.'

She shook her head, unable to keep up. Why was he talking about first experiences? '. . . Huh?'

'Well, you'd expect that it's the last time something happens that has more resonance – it's an ending; that should be more powerful really. Endings are traumatic for humans: we want life to be linear and unbroken.'

Christ, the man always had a theory. Was this really the time to get philosophical? 'Nate, what on earth are you talking about?'

'Take our first time together, like you just said. I never really think about it – but I could if I wanted because by virtue of being the first time it was made memorable. Our last fuck on the other hand . . . ?'

She winced at his language. Swearing had never suited him. And that word wasn't right, anyway. They'd been in love—

'I just can't remember it, can you?' He didn't wait for a reply as he did up the buttons. 'But that's because the last time we slept together, we didn't know it was the last. Or certainly, *I* didn't. And that's because at the time it was actually happening, it wasn't defined as the "last" one because there was everything to suggest we would do it again, that there would be another fuck to come, because I thought we were happy.' He gave a mirthless laugh, as though mocking himself.

'Nate—' she faltered. She felt the ground begin to drop away, the rush of blood beginning to pound in her ears, adrenaline coursing, panic setting in.

'It was only hindsight that imbued it with the significance of being the last time, by which point, the memory was lost. There had been no ceremony for it, nothing to make it stand out at the actual time.' He shrugged as he stuffed his feet into his shoes and stared back at her bewildered on the bed. 'So I guess at least now we have a definitive experience with which to round things off. Something we can both remember and look back on with clarity and fondness.'

Fondness? 'Nate, stop this!' she cried, feeling herself begin to crumple, to fall apart.

But he just picked up his jacket and walked over to the door, looking back at her with an expression she couldn't read. 'You already did, Charlotte.'

Chapter Eight

Ronda, June 1936, four days later

Nene pulled the brim of her hat low. She had stolen it from a peg in the maids' quarters, the thin shawl and dress too. The dress was slightly too tight across the bodice and a fraction too short in the arms and length – she was so much taller than most other women – but comfort mattered for nothing right now. She just needed to move incognito through these streets, to pass through unrecognized and unmolested.

The bells were already ringing, calling out the mourners, and a steady stream of people were wending their way through the hilly cobbled streets to the Church of Santa Maria la Mayor. Dressed all in black, they looked like scurrying ants from this distance.

She hastened her stride, overtaking a family, the parents struggling to move at any speed with their young children, and she took care to keep her head dipped, her eyes averted as she passed. Her heart was pounding with the terror that she would be recognized and outed – for if that happened, she knew her safety could not be guaranteed. There were stories all over the wireless of atrocities being committed with alarming frequency against people being found in the wrong place, at the wrong time. Tensions since the elections in February had reached breaking point, with communities now pitched against one another: Republicans v. Nationalists; Carlists v. anarchists; Falangists v. communists. Skirmishes were becoming fights, protests revolutions. The country was scaling up its anger, the quivering tension becoming tighter every day. The rule of law increasingly counted for nothing and there was talk that even the military was going to revolt.

Nonetheless there had been no question of her not coming here. She needed to pay her respects to the man who had never been anything other than kind to her, who was the father of her best friend in the world; she needed to kneel before God and beg forgiveness that his life had been taken by her own blood without mercy or just cause. She had scarcely slept since it had happened; her appetite completely diminished, she had grown thin even in the space of four days and she knew her older brothers were watching her closely, looking for signs that she might betray them to their father and give the true account of what had happened.

But would he believe her if she did? Would he care? The Civil Guard had not even paid a visit to the estate, not a single question had been raised. Juan Esperanza's death had simply been accepted. He had been inciting violence, fuelling a revolution; it was self-defence, that was the official line, and in the face of the Mendoza brothers' great name and powerful brutality, who would dare refute it?

The peal of the bells lured her onwards, their mournful song beginning to vibrate through her bones as she walked between the giant yew trees that flanked the west door and joined the shuffling mourners filing into the church. It was a deceptively unobtrusive building from outside, the humble plain stone tower offset by balconied colonnades to one side, the narrow arched windows and minaret-turned-tower betraying the building's original Islamic roots.

She kept her head down as she waited her turn in the queue and it was a relief to step into the church's cold embrace, the scorch of the sun on her back immediately quenched as brown marble replaced hot cobbles. As always when she entered this holy space, her eyes were drawn upwards. It was an instinct impossible to resist, for the church's plain facade hid a magnificent interior – the vaulted ceilings frothing with murals and baroque frescoes, an opulent crystal chandelier dangling down as big as a man. The church's very shape was ornate too, the seemingly boxy exterior revealing a polygon clad in reeded marble and dimpled with deep niches and alcoves. But it was the gilded, full-height altarpiece that always rendered everyone mute, reinforcing the supreme majesty of the god they had come to worship.

Nene took a seat in one of the pews at the back, pushing herself into the corner and trying to look unobtrusive. She had never sat here before, her family always front and centre in the best seats, closest to God. From lowered eyes she watched the feet of the mourners shuffling past her on the brown and white marbled floor, the stitches missing in some leather uppers, patches on others, but all of them polished to a shine. The men were in their best suits, the women in their mourning hats, all of them dignified in their unified grief. Nene could hardly lift her head from the shame that they were gathered here because of what her brothers had done – killed a man. Murdered him. Vale had accused Jose of being an animal – but who was the beast really, who was proven the most barbaric and base?

An elderly couple came and sat beside her, easing themselves slowly onto the unforgiving wooden pews, coughing lightly into handkerchiefs, their breath coming in exhausted rasps. The church was almost completely full, the pews filling up rapidly so that soon there would not be enough room to sit. She pulled her elbows in, trying to take up as little space as possible and hoping desperately no one would look at her too closely. She tugged down on the sliver of net that was passing as a veil. Her own mourning mantilla fell to her collar-bone, obscuring her face completely, and would have done a far better job at concealing her identity as well as tears – but it was in itself too decorative, a Chantilly lace from Paris that would have announced her presence as loudly as any speaker.

The congregation sat in almost perfect silence but for the occasional cough or sob, everyone's heads tilted skywards. Nene's eyes scanned the backs of their heads, guessing their identities from their body posture and hairstyles. Manuel Garcia, the barber; Andres Ramirez, the mechanic; Emiliano Dambolena, the pig man. Pablo Lopez, the man who had instigated the quarrel with Señor Martin. He was sitting in the second pew from the front; she could tell him just by the anger in his shoulders which were risen almost up to his ears, his jaw set forwards like a brake. His wife – bony-shouldered and shivering – sat beside him, her head bent low as she worried at some rosary beads, tutting to herself as they waited for the ceremony to begin.

But it was the solitary figure in the front pew – hunched and tiny in black – that stilled the blood in Nene's veins. Santi's mother, Renata. She was as still as the statues all about, as frozen behind her mask of grief as the gilded figures at the altar. Nene had only met her three times – once at the Feria Goyesca bullfighting festival; once in corking season when she had come up to La Ventilla with refreshments; and once when Nene and Santi had walked too far one afternoon and she had set up a small search party. Nene remembered her as a vivacious woman: Santi had inherited his infectious smile from her and the gap between his teeth. Her skin was too tanned (her mother would have said), her face too thin, but she had been a beautiful woman once; Nene had understood that even as a small girl and many times she had wished she could have known her better. But politics, class . . . the *adult world,* had made it impossible. She wasn't supposed to 'consort' with those people, as her mother put it. It was unseemly for her to run about the fields like a campesino, to come in with muddy hands and scraped knees, to laugh with the labourers as though they were her equals, to call them her friends. Her best friend.

Santi.

Shame bled through her, staining her cheeks, and she wrung her hands as she thought yet again about what he must have thought, how he must have felt, when he'd heard his father had been murdered. By her family. It was her torture, to imagine his face . . .

A note sounded, pure and steady, as though an angel was floating through the mihrab, towards the east window and heaven itself. Everyone turned and stood as one, as the singer – a girl not much older than her – came through, her voice expanding into the billowing space as she sang 'Ave Maria'. Behind her, coming at an almost ceremonial half-step, the coffin inched into view and Nene felt a gripping tightness at her chest as she saw the pall-bearers come in, their shoulders sagging beneath the weight.

At the very front was Santi. For a moment, she did not recognize him. He had grown so tall and strong, his skin darker than she had ever seen it; his shaggy hair of their childhood cropped short, revealing those beautiful bones of a face she had loved and missed these four years. But he was different in other ways too – he was a man now. The shadow of stubble prickled his cheeks and jawline, there was a scar on his neck that hadn't been there before, and where once his eyes had danced and laughed, now they blazed, fixed upon the altar as though there were answers there to his questions.

She watched the coffin slide by, her breath held, unable to believe it was her brothers, her blood, who had put a man inside that box. The girl's voice began to soar as the coffin was carried to the front and set down on the trestle, the men grunting slightly as they struggled to make the transition respectfully smooth. They took their seats besides their wives, families. Mother.

Nene watched as Santi leant over and kissed Renata's temple, saw how the older woman nodded and dabbed at her eyes. This was the aftermath – the living with the pain. She had seen the final moments of Juan Esperanza's life: the crack shot that had rung out, sending the birds from the trees and all of them to the ground; the slow-motion stagger as the dying man dropped from his upright position – noble and proud in life – to lie in the dirt until the big bright sky bleached out to nothing. Only a handful of people in this space had shared that experience and now they were here, like her, with him still. The horror of those few minutes had changed something inside her in ways she couldn't yet fully understand and she would have to live with the guilt and the shame for the rest of her life. But it was those two people, sitting alone at the front, who would suffer most of all – more than Juan, or her, or the other men.

The girl finished singing and the priest began, his voice intoning solemnly to the hushed congregation. Nene didn't hear what he said. Her attention was focused entirely on Santi, or rather the back of his head, her eyes scrutinizing every inflection, tilt, freeze. When finally their eyes met again, would she be able to read him still? As children she had been easily able to read his mind. He was as open as a book, she always used to laugh – all his hope, bravado, hunger, mischief, writ large in those limpid eyes his father had given him. But now, the prospect of meeting his gaze and the truth of what her family had done to his lingering between them made her chill. It was crazy even to have come here. One word and he could betray her, and these dignified, unified mourners would become a lynch mob, out for Mendoza blood.

It was a risk she had been prepared to take. She had to believe that he too knew their friendship went deeper than names or associations; he had to know that what her brothers had done, she would never do, nor endorse, and she would risk her own safety to prove that to him for she was in his territory here. Now she was the vulnerable one.

She tried to partake in the service. When they prayed, she prayed harder than she ever had, her eyes squeezed shut, her hands blanched; and when they sang, she looked skywards, in case her Catholic sincerity could atone for her brothers' barbarity. But her chance for redemption had a time limit and too soon the service was over, Santi leading the pall-bearers as they stood to take the weight of his father again.

Nene watched them get into position, steadying themselves and taking a breath before they began the slow walk back up the aisle. Her limbs were leaden, all sound drowned out by the rushing of blood through her head as he drew closer. Closer.

Her head was tilted down but her eyes tipped up, obscured only a little by the net veil, her gaze fastened to him like a pin. He was two arm's lengths away now, his stare locked onto the rectangle of light through the open door. His jaw balled as he walked, one cheek pressed to the pine casket and she saw that not one tear had fallen; his eyes were dry. Determined.

She swallowed, knowing he was about to pass without seeing her. In another second he would be gone and he would never know that she had come here, risked herself, for him. She wanted to reach or call out, cough or swoon – something, anything to catch his attention. But he was blind to all this: these people, the singers, the hymns and prayers; lost in his grief.

So it was all the more shocking then, when suddenly his gaze shifted – instinct kicking in as though he sensed her – and his bladed brown-eyed gaze swivelled sidelong straight towards her. It was only for a second, but that was enough. She saw the startle in his face, and then the deeper shift in his soul, his attention fully fastening onto her and turning his head even as his feet propelled him onwards, out of sight.

Nene felt her breath come in short, ragged pants, her heart clattering erratically as he disappeared from view. She wanted to run after him, to follow him into the plaza and throw herself on his mercy. But that was impossible. She had been able to read him after all and that alone remained the same – but her old friend had become a stranger, changed by fortunes, destroyed by her family.

Tipping her head down again, she pushed against the flow of the crowd, slipping out through the side door. She knew she couldn't stay here or wait to be seen: he would throw her to the dogs. For in that single moment when their eyes connected, she had seen inside his heart and understood there was no longer any room for love or friendship.

He was a man intent on revenge and they were all in uncharted waters now.

Chapter Nine

Charlotte pushed back in her chair and looked out at the Madrid skyline. She had been back at her desk in Steed's Madrid offices for an hour now – having left the hotel as quickly as she'd entered it; she couldn't bear to stay in the room, in that bed, without him – but she had achieved precisely nothing. Her mind kept incessantly, insistently, going over and over the afternoon's events, recalling every last look, comment, gesture. She felt stunned, still. Had it even happened? How could he have just left like that, without giving her a chance to explain? It was almost as though he'd been expecting it, like he'd been looking for an excuse to leave, to get away from her.

As for Stephen . . . She dropped her head again. The thought of him made her feel sick, not from guilt but lack of it – for not at any point in her stolen hours with Nathan had she once thought about him or felt bad about what she was doing. In fact, it had all been so natural, instinctive and primal between them that it was he who had felt like the aberration, the intruder to the natural order of things. The awful truth was that it hadn't been a lie when she'd said he was no one. Compared to Nathan, everyone was no one and he was everything.

And what did that mean? How could she marry a man she—

No. She didn't want to think about it. He was a good man, they made a great team. They'd shared eighteen months together and it all worked – their friends liked each other, their parents got on; he had his own career and seemed to accept (just about) her need for hers . . . It wasn't a dynamite pairing, they weren't the high-octane, party-loving pair she'd been with Jules – and thank God for it. Stephen was the antidote to all that. He kept her steady.

Yes, steady. Plodding. Safe. That was what she had always sought – the life she had never known as a child when strangers wandered through the house at night in their party clothes, when her father's glassy eyes and her mother's shrill nervous laughter were more unsettling than any scream, when Mouse would climb into her bed every night and together they would listen to the crystal smashing.

'Pa?'

The bedroom was quiet, a window open so that she could hear the birds in the oak tree outside, even though it was cold. Freezing in fact.

'Pa, are you here?'

She tiptoed into his sanctuary. She and Mouse weren't allowed in there ordinarily, he needed his privacy, he said, somewhere he could escape the endless demands they all made on him.

'Mouse is hurt, Pa, she trod on some glass . . .'

Her gaze swept around the room in dismay. Disgust. The walls, decorated with silver grey chinoiserie panels depicting exotic birds and blossom trees, were stippled with cigarette burns; a bamboo-style Chippendale chair was tipped on its back; clothes were strewn over every surface as if a gale had broken in and partied in the room. The vast bed she and Mouse had always wanted to make dens on but had never been allowed, was unmade, the sheets grubby and twisted and stained with assorted body fluids she didn't want to think about.

Even she and Mouse kept their rooms better than this. What would Mrs B say if she saw it? But then she wasn't allowed in here either.

'. . . She needs stitches. We don't know where Mama's gone and Mrs B can't drive . . .'

She crept through, into the dressing room, which was more of the same, if not worse: almost every item of clothing was torn off the hangers and piled on the floor in heaps, obscenities scrawled on the mirrors with lipstick and nail varnish.

'. . . Pa? Can you help?'

She was at the bathroom door now and she stared down at the handle. But she couldn't turn it. Her arm wouldn't move.

Because her feet were getting wet.

Yes, there was a lot to be said for safe. Living in the glare of flashlights and headlines, she had had to burrow hard to find refuge in the shadows: she had a different name now, a respectable job and none of her clients had ever guessed just how well qualified she was to preach. She had done what her father could not and found a way to survive.

But Nathan, he threatened that. He always had. He made the world spin faster. He made the colours truer. He was an obsession she would lose herself in and she couldn't afford to live on those boundaries.

She stared down at the desk that was hers for the duration of her trip. It was largely bare, save for the thick and weighty Mendoza files and a few Post-it notes, including a number for Katerina Cedano, her contact at the Prado. She rubbed a finger over the name. She had been at the funeral that awful day five years ago.

'This came for you,' a young executive said, standing by her door and holding a large envelope. A red 'confidential' sticker had been slapped across the seal. How long had he been there for?

'Thank you,' she said briskly, snapping back to attention and holding her hand out for it.

She waited until he was gone before opening it, but she already knew what it was: the offer and contract terms from Mateo Mendoza's office. She read through it all: proof of identity forms, terms and clauses, non-disclosure agreements, all of which, if she accepted, Marina would be obliged to sign on the spot.

She sat back in her chair, staring at the offer and musing upon it. Ten million euros was the kind of sum that would be life-changing for Marina, even though it wasn't remotely within the parameters Mateo's father had outlined for her and which possibly she had originally been aiming for. But ten million euros? Depending on how she chose to live, she could afford never to work again, to buy a place, travel . . . It was enough money to play with but not so much as to be dangerous; she could still keep her identity with a number of this size. It wouldn't swallow her up and define her as it did to so many of her clients, like Lucy Santos for instance. As far as Charlotte was concerned, this offer would be the best thing that could ever happen to Marina Quincy but would she see that, or would her ambition render her blind to Charlotte's persuasions? Would she see that the Mendozas were trying to buy her off cheaply?

Her phone rang and she picked it up on the second ring. 'Charlotte Fairfax.'

'Charlotte? It's Katerina.'

'Kat, hi. I was literally about to call you!'

'Well I saw your office had called and I didn't want to miss you. I know how quickly you come and go from places.'

'Sadly true. How are you?'

'Very well, darling. It is a lovely surprise to hear from you.'

'I know, it's been – what? Two years?'

'More like five.'

'*Five*? Really?' Charlotte tutted. 'God, where did that go?' But they both knew.

Katerina laughed, her voice husky from a lifetime of cigarettes and rioja. Everything about her was flamboyant – her hair, her wardrobe, her zest for living. 'Tell me, how have you been?'

'Oh, you know – busy. Travelling a lot, here, there, everywhere.'

'Yes, I have heard you are much in demand these days. Your name has come up at some dinners recently.'

'Oh? Should my ears be burning?'

'Always!' Katerina laughed. 'It is only good things of course.' The circles Katerina moved in were richly bohemian in mix and her dinner parties were legendary, placing ambassadors next to burlesque dancers, next to teachers . . . Charlotte's father had known her before he met her mother, back when he was a jet-setting bachelor, and Charlotte had often suspected they had been more than friends, at least for a while. She suspected her mother sensed it too, for she had always disapproved of what she called Katerina's 'high spirits' and had firmly vetoed her father's suggestion that she be Charlotte's godmother. 'I'm so sorry I cannot make your wedding next week. But tell me, what happened to the handsome devil that was your first husband?'

'Oh, I'm afraid we divorced a long time ago.'

'But, darling, *why*? He was the most beautiful creature I ever saw.'

'Good looks were about all he had going for him.'

'Tch, looks are underrated, if you ask me. All everyone seems to care about these days is personality and sense of humour. A man that makes you melt, now that's where real happiness lies.' She cackled away; her love of good-looking younger men unabashed and well documented. 'Besides, I was still hoping you might convince him to sit for my students.'

As well as heading up the Neo-Classical Art division at the Prado, Katerina also ran small but very highly regarded life-drawing classes in the loft of her sprawling home; and it was almost impossible to get in – Katerina's policy was one out, one in, prompting people to remark in only half-joking tones that they'd happily kill for a place.

Charlotte cracked a smile at the thought of the wayward Rt Hon. Julian Fairfax sitting for her – not because of the stripping off, he was wildly uninhibited, but of him sitting motionless for three hours. Three minutes would be their lot. 'I'd let that one go,' she grinned. 'Unless perhaps you gave him a sedative first.'

'Don't put it past me, darling.'

Charlotte laughed. 'Actually, it's your classes I wanted to talk to you about. I have a client who's new to Madrid and she's really struggling. I'm keen to get her back into painting again, it was her great passion but she gave up for the sake of her husband's career; I think it would really help give her some focus and get her in with some like-minded souls.'

'Uh-oh,' Katerina murmured, knowing exactly where she was going with it.

'I *know* it's a total long shot, but I don't suppose you've any spaces?'

'Ha! As if! My God. Picasso himself would have to wait.'

'Oh.'

There was a half-pause and then a sigh as though she was acting against her better instincts. 'But for you, darling, anything. You know what your father was to me. I would deny him – and you – nothing. Tell her to come to the studio the day after tomorrow, eight o'clock.'

'Oh, that's great! Thank you, Kat, you are wonderful. Is it still the same address?'

'Of course. And will you come too? Let's have dinner after!'

'I'll be back in London by then. Ma's working herself up into a frenzy for the final wedding prep so I need to be around.'

'I'm sure,' Katerina said lightly. There was no love lost between the two women, though they kept a civil face on it. 'Well listen, if you have time for lunch, drinks, coffee, whatever you can manage, call me. I'm dying to see you and hear your news properly.'

'Well, I'm here on a priority project so I'm rather at the beck and call of the client at the moment but if I possibly can, you know I will.'

'I know you will, darling.'

Charlotte remembered something suddenly, something which had completely slipped her mind earlier. 'Oh and by the way, before I forget – there was something else I wondered if you could help me with.'

'Go on.'

'I saw a painting in the French Art gallery today. A small oil by Chardin. I wondered if you could find out anything about it – like how it came to be with you? Who sold it and when?'

'I can certainly try. What is the name of the painting?'

'*Basket of Wild Strawberries*.'

'Okay. Is it important?'

Charlotte bit her lip, holding her voice firm. 'Only to me.'

Chapter Ten

Marina wasn't at the apartment but Charlotte found her anyway, by chance, forty minutes later as she was walking towards the address supplied by Mateo's report. She would have walked straight past the *lavateria* had it not been for the shouts inside. A man and woman were arguing, the man's arms thrown up in the air as the woman furiously tore clothes from the drum of the machines and dumped them in her basket. It was sheer luck that Charlotte happened to glimpse Marina bent down behind them, behaving as though nothing untoward was happening as she pulled her own clothes free and stuffed them in her own basket. From the look on her face she was unperturbed by the warring couple beside her, merely rolling her eyes in a bored expression as the man's waving arms knocked a shirt from her hands and she had to stoop to pick it up again.

Charlotte watched from the distance, seeing the resignation in Marina's movements; this was the only life she knew: hard, mundane, repetitive, small. It felt almost perverse to Charlotte that she should be standing there, not five metres away, with a letter in her bag offering this woman ten million euros, a one-way ticket out of this.

Marina glanced up, as though sensing Charlotte's stare,

stiffening as she saw that she was indeed being watched. Charlotte instinctively held up her hand in an awkward wave but Marina simply tipped her head quizzically in return and continued pulling her wet clothes from the drum. Had she been expecting Charlotte later?

She decided to wait for Marina outside – what she had to say was better said without an audience, particularly those two.

Marina emerged several minutes later, red-cheeked from the dryers' heat, the laundry basket wedged on her hip, but she didn't approach Charlotte, instead walking in harried steps back down the street, her slippered feet slapping against the pavement.

'Hey.' Charlotte walked over and fell into step with her. She noticed the laundry in the basket was still wet. Couldn't she afford the dryer?

'What are you doing here?' Marina asked sharply. 'You said you would come to my apartment.'

'And I was on my way there when I happened to see you in there. Why? Is there a problem?' Was she embarrassed to have been caught doing her laundry?

'This is harassment, you know that? A violation of my privacy. There are laws against this sort of thing, there must be. You can't just keep turning up at my place of work, at my home, in my street.'

Oh dear. This wasn't the start she'd been hoping for. 'But, Marina, we agreed to meet here tonight, remember? I said I'd be coming over.'

'You shouldn't have my details in the first place! I've already told you – I'm not who you think I am.'

Charlotte was taken aback. What had happened to make Marina so defensive suddenly? Why was she so stressed?

'Look, Marina, we've done this dance twice already. Don't you think it's time we cut to the chase? I'm here to help you, but we're running out of time.'

'But I don't know what you want from me!' Marina replied exasperatedly. She looked panic-stricken. Almost frightened.

'Hey, I *don't* want anything from you. I've got something *for* you . . .'

Marina abruptly stopped walking. 'Why? Why me?'

'Because there's someone you matter to.'

'No.' Marina's mouth curled in a sneer. 'I don't matter to anybody.'

Charlotte's face fell at the bleakness of her words. 'That's not true. Please believe me – I am here because I'm trying to help you. Really, I am. Won't you at least hear me out? I promise that what I have to say to you will be life-changing.'

Marina stared back at her: defensive, aggressive. But the curiosity was beginning to tighten its grip again; Charlotte could see it glimmering weakly in her eyes: Charlotte's sheer persistence, her job title, now this promise of an offer . . . Marina didn't say anything further but she didn't protest further either as she began walking again and after a brief hesitation, Charlotte hurried along beside her.

They didn't speak, lapsing into an accepted silence, Marina's slippers slapping against the pavement as they walked. They went past a bar, the sound of shouts drifting out in punches as a football match blared inside; a ladies' boutique with body-con dresses stretched over white plastic mannequins; a bakery with a beaded curtain at the door and a hole-in-the-wall pizzeria. A giant black and white mural of Cristiano Ronaldo had been spray-painted onto the corner building, the lower sections overlaid with the names of other players, Roberto Santos included in bright blue.

Crossing the road at the T-junction, they took a left off the main drag onto a narrower street. It would be far too tight for cars to pass down – except perhaps an old-school Fiat 500 – but mopeds were parked nose-to-tail in a line along the bollards. The street was entirely in shade at this time in the early evening and flanked by older, umber-coloured buildings with wooden doors and wrought-iron balconies on the upper floors. A few trees softened the unremitting hardness of the urban block, as did the washing tied to some of the balustrades, and, on one balcony, an Atlético Madrid flag. But a collection of overflowing bins halfway down the street had attracted the attention of a stray dog, sniffing for scraps, and one of the ground-floor windows further along had been boarded up, shards of glass still peppering the ground.

Marina stopped outside a tall arched door and fished for a key in her hip pocket.

'Here, let me take that for you,' Charlotte said, offering with her outstretched arms to take the basket. But Marina found the key and let them in, pointedly leading her up three flights of stone stairs with the basket still on her hip, silently reiterating both her independence and pride.

The common quarters were clean albeit tired, with marks on the walls, some of the plaster missing in areas, and cracks like a crazy glaze spidering the paint. A bicycle was propped outside one apartment, several Amazon boxes stacked on the floor outside another; and a broken washing machine had been left on the half-landing two floors above, waiting to be taken away.

'Is that yours?' Charlotte asked, as Marina walked around it and put her key in the door.

Marina looked over at it with disgust. 'It had been threatening to die on me for months.'

'There's never a good time for them to break, is there?' Charlotte mused. Marina looked back at her sharply, as though trying to gauge her tone, before letting them both in.

Marina dropped the basket with a groan onto a small square elm table. 'I expect you would like coffee?'

'No, really. I'm fine,' Charlotte demurred, feeling the oppressive heat in the flat. The last thing she wanted was a hot drink. A glass of rosé on the other hand. Oblivion . . .

Was it really only three hours since she had been in bed with Nathan? Their bodies pressed together, fingers and legs intertwined . . .

'You think I can't look after my guests?' Marina asked defensively, pulling a dirty t-shirt off the corner of a chair.

'Am I a guest?' Charlotte smiled, trying to soften her hostile mood. Inwardly she felt exhausted. Defeated. This meeting was the last thing she needed. 'I did rather invite myself over.'

'You said you have something to offer me,' she shrugged, as though this was the payment in return. 'I will get coffee. Take a seat.'

Marina disappeared from the room, and as she wandered to the sofa, Charlotte took the opportunity to openly look around. It couldn't have been more different from Lucy Santos's home in the La Finca district just a few miles away – that had been all clean angles and space and light; this apartment was its polar opposite: dark, stuffy and cramped with low sloping ceilings. There was no air-con that she could see and one of the eaved windows looked painted shut; Charlotte had to resist the urge to try to open the other.

She sat on the sofa – a sagging, green floral eighties chintz – carefully pushing a pair of kicked-off trainers further under the tiled-top coffee table with her feet. If the flat was basic, attempts had still been made to give it a homely feeling: there were handmade, coloured crocheted-doilies on a sideboard, funky embroidered LOVE cushions on the ecru armchair opposite, the beautiful, original floorboards were covered with a metallic purple shag rug. Several framed black-and-white and bleached-out seventies photos were arranged on top of a bookcase. This place certainly wasn't unloved. Marina may not have much, but she had still made this a home.

Charlotte heard the kettle coming to the boil and she sat forward, straining to see into the next room. Marina was only just visible from behind, efficiently arranging the wet laundry onto a clothes horse. Two minutes later, and she was back in the room, instant coffee poured into two glazed mugs and a plate of churros – taken from San Ginés no doubt – arranged on a small chipped plate.

'Amazing, thank you,' Charlotte smiled as the older woman sat down opposite her, no trace of a smile on her face. She looked worn out and brittle. 'It's lovely here. Have you lived here long?'

Marina shot her a wry look as if to say, must we play this game of small talk? 'My whole life. It was my grandmother's first and my father grew up here too. I lived in my husband's place for six years but when I found him in bed with another woman, I came back here.' Her words were deliberately abrasive, intended to push Charlotte back.

'Wow, so it really is home then,' she said mildly instead. Charlotte picked up the mug but didn't immediately move to sip from it. Her hostess was right; there really was no place for small talk here. 'Marina, what if I told you, you could afford to buy this place outright – and I don't just mean this apartment, I mean the entire building.' Now she sipped the coffee, allowing her words to settle on Marina like a mist, spritzing her, waking her up.

Sure enough, there was a pause. 'I would say you were crazy.'

'Would you? Even though you know what I do? Who my clients are?'

'A private bank, you said.'

'That's right. And one of their clients wants to make a special offer to you. He is prepared to give you ten million euros.'

'Ten—?' There was a stunned silence; Charlotte could almost hear it rebounding off the walls, until Marina threw her head back and laughed. 'Now I know you're fucking crazy! Why? Why would someone do that?'

But Charlotte wasn't smiling now. 'It is being offered on strict conditions which I need you to hear and understand: the offer stands for today only, it is a one-off payment with categorically no scope for further negotiations or subsequent revisions. Furthermore, you can never apply to my client's estate for more; acceptance of this sum would forfeit any future rights to either apply for or receive a gift, donation or bequest from my client's estate. It's very important you understand all that.'

The laughter died on Marina's lips, a look almost of fear creeping into her eyes. '. . . Who is this client?'

'His name is Mateo Mendoza. You know his father, Carlos.'

Marina recoiled, shaking her head. 'No.'

'Yes,' Charlotte insisted, firm now. 'We know everything, Marina. We know about your relationship with him.'

'My r—?'

'Señor Mendoza understands you are . . . special to his father. That is why he is prepared to be so generous. It is why he sent *me* to see you rather than one of his lawyers. He wants to make sure you will be well supported and guided in this

– as I told you before, wealth can be a burden, particularly if it comes suddenly.' She looked down at her coffee and then up again. 'He wants the best for you and asks only one thing in return.'

Marina was staring at her with a confounded expression. '. . . And what is that?'

'That you make no further contact with his father. At all. Carlos Mendoza is a very sick man; these are his final weeks and the family wish to spend together what time he has left. They should not be worrying about legacies and legalities at such a moment. I'm sure you can appreciate that, Marina. I've met you enough times now to see you're a good person.'

Marina didn't reply. She didn't look like she could. The colour had drained from her face and she looked even more tired than she had before.

'Señor Mendoza has taken a great deal of time and effort trying to put together an offer that he believes both fairly rewards the happiness you have brought his father in his final years, and also allows you to live your life without any financial concerns whatsoever. And I have been authorized to work closely with you to help you transition to your next phase, for, believe me, your world is about to change in ways you couldn't possibly imagine. You will never have to bring a basket of wet clothes home from the laundry ever again. You won't have to save up for a new washing machine. You won't even have to see your new washing machine because you can have staff who do the laundry for you.

'And that's not even a fraction of it. Everything is going to change, Marina, for the better. Life is going to become so much easier now. I know how hard you work. I know it's a struggle.' She stared across the coffee table, seeing how Marina's eyes were still, that she was barely blinking. She was in shock. 'Marina?'

Slowly, Marina slid her gaze up to her. 'Carlos Mendoza is an old man.'

'. . . Yes.'

Her voice was quiet. Charlotte wasn't surprised. Being told you were being given ten million euros would do that to most people. 'Why are you so certain . . . ?'

'That you're involved with him?' Charlotte paused, knowing she had to choose her next words carefully, judiciously. 'Because before he fell ill last week, he was instructing his lawyers to make financial provisions for you.' She could not lie, but neither could she admit the whole truth; no one yet knew whether Marina was aware of the full scope of Carlos Mendoza's intentions and Charlotte couldn't afford to let it slip here. 'His wishes were very specific: Marina Quincy, Apartment 8, 94 Calle del General Garcia de la Herran, Carabanchel, Madrid.' She looked up at her. 'That is you, right? You are Marina Quincy? This is your address?'

Marina nodded.

'Then congratulations – you're about to become a very rich woman.' She reached into her bag and pulled out the contract that Mateo's lawyers had drawn up. She set it down carefully on the table, watching how Marina's eyes drifted over it – catching on the words 'ten million euros' which had deliberately been set in bold type.

'I know this is a lot to take in,' she said, wondering privately whether it really was, or whether Marina was still acting the ingenue here; her mask hadn't slipped once, not in any of their meetings. 'But this isn't a joke. This is a legally binding document, bequeathing the sum of ten million euros to you' – she was careful to keep repeating the words, making them real. 'From the Mendoza family trust. Let me be clear: this is not a loan; there are no tricks. Spend it, save it, give it away

– the money is yours to do with as you wish. The only conditions upon you, as I have said, are that if you accept this offer today, you can have no further contact with Mr Mendoza at all; you must cut all contact with him. And you can never make any future claims on the Mendoza estate. This settles your account, if you like, once and for all.'

Marina stared from her to the contract and back again.

'All you have to do is read it and sign, Marina. It's that easy.'

Slowly, Marina reached forward and took the contract from her, looking down again at the white paper, crisp and bright in her hands, and with the power to change her life. Her eyes moved down the sheet, snagging on the baffling legalese she could never have encountered before.

Charlotte sat back in the chair, watching her. 'If there's anything you don't understand, please ask. I can explain it to you. You must be absolutely sure you understand what this means in its entirety.'

Marina read it in silence once, two times, no doubt looking for tricks, something in the wording that was going to take it all away from her again. Finally her gaze came back up to Charlotte's again. 'I'm going to need time to think about it.'

'I'm sorry.' Charlotte shook her head firmly. 'You can take as long as you need to read through whilst I am here but this is a one-shot offer. You either sign today and the money will be in your account within five minutes; or you don't, and the offer is withdrawn. I will leave here and everything will be the same as it ever was.' She gave an easy shrug, hoping Marina wouldn't stop to think and wonder what this offer might actually be obscuring, for it was a glittering unicorn of a deal, there to dazzle and distract her from the real prize, which although bigger was by no means guaranteed.

She watched as the sinews in Marina's neck became more pronounced, the stress building, and as her hesitation stretched, Charlotte saw that Marina *had* known more than she had let on. She knew she was having to decide whether to take this or hold out for more and play for all of it. If she didn't know that was even an option, there wouldn't be a decision to have to make and that contract would have been signed already – for who would turn down ten million euros, unless they knew there was the potential for even more?

'Do you need a pen?' Charlotte asked her, holding out her own, a silver Mont Blanc, engraved with her initials.

Marina took it, her hand trembling slightly.

Charlotte stood up and stepped back, ostensibly giving her a final moment's consideration, not wanting to crowd her. But as she quietly paced away towards the windows – her hand trailing on the bookcase, gaze tripping lightly over the photographs there – she felt her own tension pitch, for a signature on that contract did more than change Marina's life; it would change hers too. With the offer secured and the Mendoza fortune firmly protected within Steed Bank's vaults, she could leave here tonight and return to London, to Stephen and to the life she had carefully, quietly curated until this week.

She would never see Nathan Marling again. He had left without a backward glance and so must she; it had been a last tumble into bed for old times' sake, a chance to say a final goodbye, that was all. Their lives had moved on and she didn't belong here, she didn't belong with him, no matter what her heart said. His life was in Madrid, hers in London. One signature and she could go home . . .

She felt her heart hold its beat as she heard the first scratch of the nib make contact with the paper and she closed her eyes, waiting for the axe to fall.

Marina handed her the helmet but Charlotte just looked at it. 'I'm not getting on that thing until you tell me where we're going. What is this all about?'

'The truth.'

'The truth about what?'

'Just trust me.'

'Marina—'

'I am not signing unless I am clear what is going on and you said I cannot have time tonight to consider it.' She shrugged. 'Therefore you must come with me now.'

Charlotte sighed, exasperated and frustrated. It had been a long and devastating day and she had needed this evening's meeting to be a coup de grâce on this whole Madrid episode, not a drawn-out torture. 'This is crazy.'

Marina put her own helmet on, fastening it under the chin as she pinned her with a wry look. 'You think *this* is the crazy part? It's all nuts to me,' she quipped.

Charlotte pulled the helmet on and straddled the back of the moped.

'Have you ever been on one of these before?' Marina asked over her shoulder.

Charlotte looked down at the dented, scratched black moped with a Greenpeace sticker on it. 'Not sober.'

The older woman chuckled. 'It is easy. Just hold on.'

'How far are we going?' she asked, loosely lacing her arms around Marina's waist as the bike roared into life and Marina kicked out the stand.

'Only a few hours or so.'

'A few hours?' Charlotte spluttered. It was hard to tell

whether it was Marina laughing or the vibrations of the engine that she could feel, but regardless, they glided out of the narrow side street and back onto the main drag. They passed the Ronaldo mural and the football fans' cafe, the laundromat where Charlotte had inadvertently found her, the warring couple now long gone.

The breeze over her skin felt delicious after the cloying humidity of the apartment and she felt herself relax momentarily. So much for making a clean getaway. She still couldn't believe this wasn't a done deal already. Marina had been so close to signing, the first pen stroke already on the paper, the money all but hers. Charlotte had thought she was hearing things when Marina had said those two little words: I can't.

They zipped through the rush-hour traffic, Marina expertly angling the bike and somehow managing to make all the green lights. The city still steamed, its colours rich and deepening in the late afternoon glow, but its citizens moved differently now their working days were done. Coffees in cafes were replaced with beers in bars, women swapping shift dresses for shorts and men pulling the ties from their suits. Everything was loosening. Breathing out.

The city became a blur; she had lost track of where they were, as Marina nipped down side streets and alleys, popping out onto distinctive boulevards before going off-grid again, but it was only ten, fifteen minutes before she felt her begin to slow and look for somewhere to park. She came to a stop beside a bollard and kicked down the stand.

Charlotte jumped off, her muscles surprisingly trembly from the ride; it had always felt the same when she was a little girl, dismounting the horse after her lesson. 'Where are we?' she asked, looking up at the vanilla-coloured apartment blocks. Plate-glass windows reflected the world back on itself, striped canopies over the balconies deflecting the worst of the sun's rays. The buildings, while not run-down like Marina's neighbourhood, had a faintly sour tang, like turned milk; they had been there just a little too long.

'Vallecas.'

Charlotte didn't know it. 'And why are we here?'

'You'll see.' Marina took the helmet from her and locked both in the underseat storage. 'This way.'

Charlotte followed after her, musing on the change between Marina now and half an hour earlier. The woman in that apartment had been resistant, stunned and then overwhelmed; she had been tempted. So what had stopped her? And why, with every step, was she becoming somehow stronger, as though she was growing sure of something?

Charlotte followed her in through a set of double doors. Inside was a lobby with a terracotta tiled floor, some eighties blue sofas and a depressingly poor framed print of Van Gogh's *Sunflowers*. A woman at the reception desk looked up as they walked in and Marina pointed questioningly towards another set of doors, not stopping.

'Oh, hey, Marina. Yes, down there.'

Charlotte caught the woman's inquisitive stare as they passed by and knew she looked incongruous here: too manicured beside Marina (still in her slippers), too flashy in her dressed-for-Casino lunch outfit.

They pushed through the double doors and down a corridor. It was unremarkable – closed doors on both sides, nothing whatsoever to identify it, just a fire evacuation plan and more inferior artwork on the walls.

Marina stopped at a door, so suddenly that Charlotte almost stepped on her heels.

'Oh.'

Marina knocked and waited, after a while pressing her ear closer to the door. She knocked again. After another pause, she turned the handle and looked in.

Charlotte stood on the threshold behind her, waiting to see what was going on.

'You can come in,' Marina said, turning back a few moments later.

Barely able to conceal her curiosity, Charlotte followed, stepping into a dim room – the curtains were pulled to, not quite meeting in the middle, so that a seam of light crossed the floor, over a bed and up the far wall like a transverse axis.

'She's resting,' Marina said in a quiet voice, stating the obvious, as Charlotte's gaze came to rest on an elderly woman asleep in the narrow bed. A quick glance around the room told Charlotte this wasn't a hospital – there were too many personal effects around: photographs on surfaces, more of those coloured crochet doilies, a bag of knitting . . . 'But don't worry. She'll be awake soon. She never sleeps for long. Just catnaps really.'

'Right,' Charlotte nodded blankly. 'And *who* is she?'

'My grandmother.'

Charlotte struggled to keep her patience. Why had they just driven across the city to pay a visit to this sleeping old lady? 'Marina, I've got a plane to catch. Why are we here? Surely your grandmother doesn't have anything to do with whether or not you sign the contract?'

'Actually, she has everything to do with it. That money is meant for her.'

Charlotte sighed. Had this woman missed the entire point of what she'd been telling her? 'Look, if you want to spend the money on your grandmother's care, then you can. There are no restrictions on how or when or where you spend it.'

'No, you don't understand. That money isn't meant for me. It can't be. I've never met old man Mendoza. It must be for her.'

Charlotte closed her eyes, her dream of getting back to London and Stephen tonight, of escaping Nathan's casual abandonment, inching out of sight. They were back to square one. 'I don't know how I can say this any more plainly. It's for you, Marina.'

'It's for Marina Quincy.'

'Exactly,' Charlotte said, exasperated now. Weren't they agreeing exactly the same thing? 'Marina Quincy. Apartment 8, 94 Calle—.'

'And I already told you that was my parents' apartment before it was mine. And my grandmother's before them. It's her apartment.'

Charlotte frowned, trying to keep up. 'You've lost me.'

'I keep telling you – I've *never met* old man Mendoza. Or any of them. So all the facts you've got about me living at that address might be right, but you've made one mistake – the birthdate.' She jerked her head towards the sleeping form in the bed. 'My parents named me after her. She's Marina Quincy too.'

Charlotte's jaw dropped down. '*What?*'

'Yeah. So if that money's meant for either one of us, it's got to be her.' Marina looked down at the sleeping woman, stroking the back of her hand tenderly. 'For some reason, Carlos Mendoza wants to make my grandmother a multimillionaire.'

Chapter Eleven

Ronda, late June 1936

Even by her family's standards, this was something else. Nene stood by her window and looked out at the party, the bodies of the guests swaying lightly to the music, the ladies' dresses billowing in the breeze. She had never seen her home look so beautiful before; always imposing, tonight it was transformed: thousands of white gardenias had been threaded onto cord and strung in an intricate lattice between the orange trees that lined the courtyard; rows of long tables were decked with candles, the crystal and silverware glittering like fireflies as the dusk lengthened. Her eyes flitted to the stone fountain – her father had seriously considered having it replumbed to flow champagne for the night, the statues carefully spotlit in the corners.

Everything was beautiful, elegant, opulent yet refined – like her mother. That had been her father's brief: tonight had to reflect his exquisite wife. He had bought her a white satin Schiaparelli dress from Paris especially for the occasion and it skimmed over her lovely figure, her long dark hair worn swept to the side and secured with a comb of fresh gardenias. Nene too had had a new dress: violet dotted cotton with puff sleeves and an empire waist, a garland of pale yellow rosebuds made especially for her hair.

She had seen the approving way her mother had nodded and looked at her as she had gone into her bedroom for a quick appraisal before the guests arrived, knowing Felix Lacuna was expected tonight. His family owned most of the land between Huelva and Seville, and Nene knew her parents had hoped she would catch his eye. And perhaps she had for he had spoken at length to her about boar-hunting, which he seemed to find fascinating.

But if dull, he was certainly handsome, with a clean-cut appearance that matched hers these days, for she was changed beyond recognition from the girl she had once been, free and running around the estate with Santi. Everything had changed when he had left, the fun falling out of all the activities she used to love to do with him – even Arlo, sweet, gentle Arlo, couldn't engage her, though he had tried; but he was too scared of their father, too quick to appease and play by the rules to be any fun. His spirit was trussed up in chains and though she loved him, she despaired of his weakness. And so, her wild, girlhood curiosity had gradually been replaced by a numbed sedation. There were never scrapes on her knees any more or dirt beneath her fingernails, her hair was always brushed and pinned up, her skirts firmly untucked from her knickers, and her mother believed this meant she had become a lady at last.

But if losing Santi the first time round had stripped her of a comrade, losing him the second time had taken her spirit; she felt as though a light had gone out of her, the shame of what her family had done, what they *were*, dimming her into obsolescence.

He was lost to her, she knew that. She understood it too. Since the funeral eleven days earlier, there had been nothing from him: no messages passed, not a word uttered. Every night she stood by her window, looking for a dark shadow running across the fields or standing by the trees. And every day she looked to see if he had put the shark's tooth in their secret hiding spot, his only way of forgiving her for being a Mendoza. But the deafening silence was intimidating and instead left her listening for footsteps behind her or bracing for confrontations on the steps of Señor Martin's office as his father had done. Her eyes searched for him everywhere. She knew he was still in Ronda – instinct told her – but she did not dare return to the old town. The flash of threat in his eyes that day had been enough to ensure she hadn't left the *latifundio* since.

Not that she felt any safer within the estate. Things had changed since Juan Esperanza's murder. There was an edge now between her and Vale and Montez, a trace of menace lurking beneath their interactions – the next morning after the murder, under Vale's watchful gaze across the table, she found a shard of glass in her breakfast dish – too big to miss but a warning nonetheless; another day they instructed the cook to cancel her dinner altogether, saying she was feeling ill. She felt their gazes on her every time their father walked into the room, not trusting her to remain quiet, but for once, she didn't try to fight them. They had already proved they were capable of anything. What was it Arlo had said? She had to pick her battles? Well now she felt she had no fight left in her. She was defeated.

Moving away from the window, she unbuttoned her dress, letting it fall listlessly to the ground. She stepped into her new riding habit – midnight velvet, again made especially for tonight. It was heavy and would be impossibly hot in this midsummer heat, but the rich brushed pile was so perfect against Indigo's gleaming hide. She fastened the jacket up to her chin, her fingers fumbling with the scarlet frogging. It was close-fitting and stiff and she tugged it down at the waist as she examined her reflection, the full skirt falling around her in deep plush folds.

She was putting on her hat when the bedroom door was suddenly flung open and Arlo fell in. He was the only one of her family who never knocked, feeling he had special dispensation to burst in whenever he liked. That she was a young woman who valued her privacy, and modesty, never seemed to occur to him.

'Woah!' he cried, mid-leap onto her bed as he caught a proper look at her. 'Look at you.'

She looked back at her reflection again. Yes. Look at her indeed. She too was transformed tonight. In the party dress she had looked simply . . . pretty: more than attractive, less than beautiful, she'd have said. But in this habit, even if she did acknowledge it herself, she looked magnificent. She twisted, doing a half-turn one way, then the other, admiring her fashioned silhouette, the dark lines and curves of the midnight velvet.

'Looks like Señor Lacuna won't get the chance to adore you.'

'What do you mean?' she asked, whirling round to him.

'Well, how can he compete when you're far too in love with yourself?'

'Oh, stop it!' she hushed, grabbing a cushion from the chair and throwing it at him.

Arlo laughed and braced as it landed on him. Like he could talk! He was dressed to the hilt too. All the Mendoza men were wearing new black trousers beribboned on the outer leg, elaborate black silk bowknots at their necks and immaculately cut cropped jackets. In fact it was a wonder to Nene her brother was able to move with such abandon, for he looked every bit as corseted as she.

'Are you nervous?' he asked, watching as she began fussing with her hair. The styling was fiddly, looping down to her neck in a net but leaving enough room for the angle of her hat.

'Of course not. Indigo could do this in his sleep.'

'He's unpredictable.'

She tossed her head haughtily, securing the hairstyle with pins. 'For you maybe. He and I understand one another. He won't put a foot wrong tonight. We've been practising for months for this.'

'I overheard Señor Martin telling father they can get a king's ransom for him. They're putting him out to stud, you know.'

Nene shrugged. 'They can do what they like. Even his babies will be pale imitations of their father. There'll never be another horse like him.'

'No? Four legs, tail, black, bad-tempered, highly strung—'

She threw another cushion his way and he laughed again as it hit him square in the face. 'What would you know? All you can think about are bulls. Bulky, stupid, plodding bulls.'

'You wouldn't call them that if they were running behind you.'

She put on the hat, fiddling to get the right angle, casting a nervous glance over her completed look, then turned to him. 'What do you think?' She bit her lip nervously. For all her and Arlo's jokes about her marrying into the Lacunas, she knew that tonight was important to her parents and her show-piece with Indigo was the denouement before dinner and later, dancing: an embodiment of precision, grace, control, power and elegance, it was to represent everything the Mendozas were and wanted to be.

Arlo didn't respond for a moment, pretending to look pained by the sight of her. '. . . Not bad for an ogre,' he shrugged.

'Beast!' she laughed, reaching for another cushion to throw his way but she was all out. 'Lucky for you!'

'Oh, yeah,' he scoffed. 'Or else you'd have me running scared?'

'You know I would,' she said defiantly, a smile on her lips.

'Little Nene, our baby, you are the toughest of us all,' Arlo grinned, jumping up from the bed again. 'Come on, I'll escort you to the stables. I worry for your safety looking like that. Felix Lacuna will want to make passionate love to you as soon as he sets sight on you.'

'Ugh, eeew!' Nene scowled, crumpling her face into a thousand furrows as they swept from her room and along the stone corridor. The skirt was so long, she had to pinch the fabric up as they descended the stairs and, due to the number of admiring glances coming from the staff alone, they slipped out through the kitchens. They would never get through the guests in time otherwise.

As predicted, the habit had her sweltering within minutes – the evening temperature still at thirty-two degrees – as they crossed quickly from the hacienda towards the stable block. Nene patted her pocket, checking for the sugar cube which would be Indigo's reward when this was over, the spirited voices, laughter and music in the courtyard dimming at their backs as they headed for the lush pastures which had been a source of much comment and praise from her father's guests tonight; in this hot summer, green grass was considered a true extravagance.

'Papa has asked me to help him select the bulls tomorrow,' Arlo said as they cut diagonally across the grazing field, the bulls having been moved to the field closest to the hacienda tonight (for their father saw no harm in showcasing his business at his wife's birthday celebrations). The grass had been allowed to grow longer and more tangled here, clusters of wild buttercups and tiny purple flowers – sand viper's-bugloss – dotting the ground into a painter's palette. 'He says it's time I became a *novillero*.'

'Arlo, no,' Nene gasped. For all his bravado and professed obsession with the family's business, she knew it was a ruse designed to attract their father's attention; she knew he didn't share their older brothers' reckless courage.

'No, I'm ready for it. I am,' he said, nodding a little too vigorously, looking more handsome than he would ever know in his new clothes. 'Papa has been waiting for the right moment for me and if he believes this is the time, then I believe it too. He had Vale and Montez out there when they were fourteen and fifteen remember, younger than I am now.'

'Yes, but they are barbarians,' she said forcefully.

Arlo glanced across at her. 'It cannot be put off forever, Nene. I am a Mendoza. Bulls are our blood. I always knew this day was coming.'

She reached over and squeezed his hand. 'Then I will be there with you.'

'No.' His voice was firm as he looked back at her with his clear round eyes – just like hers. 'It would be better if you are not. In case I . . . embarrass myself.'

'You're always embarrassing as far as I'm concerned,' she quipped.

But his smile in reply was only half-hearted and they fell into an uneasy silence, both of them thinking of what lay in the ring for him tomorrow. Montez still had the scar on his left thigh from where he had turned too late his first time.

A sound of a twig cracking made her look across towards the holm oaks, where the bulls liked to stand in their shadows in the midday heat. She had expected it to be a ground squirrel or perhaps a fox, an elephant shrew or even a lynx, for the grooms had told her the continuing drought was forcing the higher-ground animals down to the valleys for water. What she wasn't expecting it to be was a man. Her eyes followed him as he sprinted away, his arms and legs like pistons, something in his hand. Instinctively, her feet stopped moving.

'Santi!' The word erupted from her with such passion, such longing, he came to an immediate stop.

He stared back at her, his new unfamiliar face sending a jolt through her, his dark eyes burning bright. And for just a moment, as his chest heaved and his body recovered from his sprint, she could see a trace of the skinny boy who had once been her dearest friend in the world. He had grown strong and muscular from his years in the fields, his skin tanned a rich chestnut brown, but she knew if he smiled, there would still be that gap between his teeth which she had loved to tease him about as a girl; it would be proof he was still the friend she had once known. If only he would smile . . .

'Please, wait,' she cried, picking up her skirt and making to head towards him. But Arlo grabbed her by the elbow, holding her back.

'Nene, no. You must not. You know you can't.'

Santi's eyes flashed blacker at his words and she saw suddenly that although beautiful, although her old friend, he was also savage. Where she had grown tame and obedient in his absence, there was something feral about him, as though he had cast off more than the powerlessness of childhood. He was an angry young man now.

'Arlo, please.' She tried to tug herself free but he held her firm. She looked over at Santi. 'Santi, please.'

But as he stared back at her she felt the breach between them not narrow but widen, like two tectonic plates being pushed apart, mountains thrusting up as a wall, dividing them forever. She realized how she and Arlo must look to him – dressed to the nines in their formal riding velvets, a party at their backs, whilst he stood barefoot in trousers held up by a leather lasso, his shirt closed with only one button. And in his hand . . .

Her gaze fell for the first time to his hand, just as he turned and sprinted away again, like a deer from the wolf. Her heart began to thud heavily in her chest, her jacket feeling even tighter than before. 'Santi,' she whispered.

'What is it?' Arlo asked, paling at her expression. 'Nene, what is it?'

'Something's wrong.' And before he could ask her what – or how she knew – she began to run too. The velvet skirt was heavy and unwieldy in her hands as she tore across the ground with a pace she hadn't found in years. The stables were only a few hundred yards ahead but it felt like miles, her ribs constricted in the tight jacket, her hat flying off her head and remaining only by the cord at her neck.

Arlo ran after her but even with his greater height and strength he couldn't keep up; desperation was propelling her. 'Nene! Wait! What are you doing?'

She could see the stable-hands now – some of them sweeping the yard, another refilling buckets, several others raking the sand in the training school into neat ridged furrows. The guests were due over here in half an hour and final preparations were well under way.

One of them glanced up, freezing momentarily at the sight of her and her brother racing over the field. He straightened and waited, concern buckling his expression as he too saw hers. 'Señorita Mendoza,' he said politely. 'Is everything okay?'

'Where is Indigo? Where is he?' she cried, running onto the cobbles, her skirt still bustled in her fingers. 'Is he tacked up?'

'Not yet, señorita, I am sorry,' he said humbly. 'It was decided to wait until the last few minutes, because of the temperatures. We did not want him sweating—'

'Is he in his stable?' she demanded, looking wild.

'Yes.'

She looked across the courtyard. Why then wasn't he nodding over the stable door? He always whinnied and barged the door at the first sound of her voice.

'You're sure?'

'Of course, señorita. If you like—'

But she didn't like anything. She didn't want servitude and obsequiousness. As she looked over at the empty stable, she wanted to know where Indigo was. What had Santi done with him? She knew he had done something, that he had found out from someone what that horse meant to her and used him as a way to get back at her. She raced across the yard, feeling panic switch with anger. He had hidden him? He wanted to humiliate her as their guests assembled for the display by hiding her horse? But how could he have pulled that off? No one could have stolen into these stables and simply walked out with the family's prized stallion – not without inside help, or a diversion.

She saw the alarmed looks on the faces of the grooms and stable-hands as she ran past, oblivious to how imposing she looked in her habit. She had no sense of the impression she made to others, only the desolation she felt inside that her horse had been stolen. That it was Santi who had done this.

'Nene, what on earth is the matter with you?' Arlo asked, sounding desperately out of breath behind her.

She reached the stable and as her hand drew back the bolt, she saw over the half-door and felt a punch of sudden joy: Indigo was there, her magnificent beast on the ground and sleeping, his beautiful dark coat rendering him a polished shadow.

'Oh my God! Indy!' she cried, throwing open the door with

a relieved sob as all her panic and dismay dissipated at once. 'I was so terrified—'

Her eyes fell to the thick, hot carmine tide running over the cobbles towards the drain. She stared at it, as though it was an impossible thing to see – a floating lake or pink unicorn, something that defied the natural order. An abomination.

Behind her, Arlo's cry echoed around the yard, bringing the workers running, but Nene was oblivious, her entire being focused on making her brain understand what her eyes were seeing. Her gaze drew inexorably up the wash, towards the source – a thin tributary at his throat – and Nene felt something deep inside her break.

Her magnificent beast was on the ground. But he was not sleeping.

Chapter Twelve

Charlotte was back in the room again, having slept significantly less overnight than the occupant here. The blue curtains had been pulled open, a breeze ruffling the previously fetid air and rippling the pages of a television listings magazine on the sill. The sun was still on the east side of the building, leaving the room in shadow, but it sang out with colour and life in a way that had been obscured last night. Standing here now, Charlotte noticed the round jute rug on the tiled floor, orange gerberas freshly arranged in a vase; the pink floral dress hanging on the door hook, a paste necklace on the bedside table. But more than anything, she saw the woman whose domain this was – *really* saw her, for awake, hers was a magnetic presence. Age had not diminished her. Here sat a matriarch, a woman who had lived and loved. A woman not to be trifled with, nor to suffer fools.

Her eyes, though rheumy, were a startlingly clear grey, her white hair worn short in an almost boyish crop. She was sitting on the bed in a coral linen shift, yellow plastic globes at her ears and a matching bracelet on her wrist. Liver spots speckled her thin arms and legs and she wore heavy black-rimmed spectacles which were reminiscent of the model Iris Apfel. She had that especial avant-garde air which women of advanced age possess when they retain an idiosyncratic sense of style.

Marina was pouring iced water from the jug on the chest of drawers, handing it out to them in plastic tumblers.

'Abuela, Charlotte works for a bank,' Marina said, coming to sit beside her grandmother on the end of the bed. Charlotte herself was perched in the stiff, wingback chair opposite.

'Bank?' Señora Quincy frowned. 'Is there a problem?'

'No. She's come to us with an offer. Well, you. She has an offer for you.'

The old woman's eyes narrowed. 'What kind of offer?'

Charlotte put down her untouched glass of water and leaned forward so that her elbows were on her knees. It made her physically smaller and less threatening; it was also a more relaxed, confiding pose. 'Señora Quincy, there's a lot for us to discuss but perhaps I should first begin by introducing what I do: I don't work for a bank per se; the bank is a client of mine. I'm a wealth counsellor.' She spoke slowly, enunciating carefully, but at the mention of 'wealth' she saw the old woman's eyes narrow further. 'It's a funny title, I know, but actually what I do is very simple and very important: I help high-net-worth individuals – rich people, in other words – manage the emotional aspects of their wealth.'

She paused, letting the old woman absorb her words, for she already knew what her first thoughts would be: why do rich people need help with being rich? It was what everyone puzzled over. But that wasn't what ran through *her* expression and as Señora Quincy looked back at her, Charlotte could see caution in the movement now, a certain shuttering internally. 'I am not rich, nor do I wish to be.'

Charlotte hesitated. She had never met anyone who actively *didn't* want to be well-off. 'Well, I am here because I am obliged to present to you an offer on my client's behalf. You are of course free to refuse it but before I go any further, I must advise you there are several conditions attached.' She waited, anticipating another objection, but when there was only silence, she continued. 'The offer is on the table for this morning only; once I leave here today, it will be withdrawn. Secondly, this is a first and only payment. If you choose to accept, you will have to sign an agreement in which you forfeit any future right to claims on my client's estate. Thirdly, the money is yours to invest or dispose of as you wish. This is not a loan but a gift.' She clasped her hands together and looked into the old woman's clear eyes. 'Do you understand what I'm telling you? Is there anything you'd like me to clarify?'

But the old woman didn't respond in any way – not by the tilt of her head or a frown or a smile.

'Señora Quincy, my client wishes to offer you—'

'I don't want it.'

Charlotte stalled. 'But I haven't told you what it is yet.'

'You don't need to. I don't want it.'

'Señora, I don't think you understand—'

'I understand perfectly. I don't want it.' The old woman stared back at her with eyes as cold as a December dawn.

'Abuela,' Marina said, leaning in to her grandmother. 'Let her finish, please. You must hear what she has to say.'

'I do not need to, child. I already know what this is and I want nothing to do with it.'

'But you don't even know who it's from.'

'Yes I do.' Señora Quincy closed her eyes. 'I do.'

Marina and Charlotte looked at each other. Charlotte bit her lip. She hadn't expected this. It was one thing to refuse the offer, it was quite another to refuse to even hear it.

'Perhaps I should give you and your grandmother some time alone?' Charlotte suggested quietly.

'My looks may have left me, but not my senses,' the old woman said sharply, opening her eyes again. 'I assure you, I can think for myself perfectly well.'

Charlotte looked back at her, the slightly patronizing view she had taken of her upon entering now becoming clearer-eyed, more equal. 'In which case, you will appreciate I am beholden to supply you with the full facts before I can accept your answer. You know the terms but not the offer, nor the identity of my client. Rest assured this is not a whimsical gesture; he has invested significant resources into tracking you down in order to make his proposal, and I must be satisfied you understand what is on the table before it is taken away.'

'Grandmother, please,' Marina implored her. 'Just listen to what she has to say.'

'No good will come of it, Marina.'

'You're wrong!' Marina said forcefully, standing up now. 'It could change everything for us! Look at how we struggle. I had to give up my car because the insurance went up. I can't afford a new washing machine. I work two jobs. I'm exhausted all the time. I can't remember the last time I put on a dress and went out. I'm forty-five but I feel eighty.'

'I wish I did.' It was a quip, a joke, but her granddaughter was near tears, her body tense with panic and resentment.

'You owe it to me to hear her out,' Marina said bitterly. '*I* could have signed it, you know. She came to me first; she didn't know about you. I could have just taken all the money for myself and no one would ever have been able to take it away from me. I could have changed my life, like that.' She clicked her fingers. 'But I didn't, because I love you. Because I had never met the man doing this so I knew it had to be you they were looking for.' She crouched down by her grandmother's knees, looking up at her through teary eyes, and the old woman instinctively reached out to cup her cheek, caressing her beautiful face. 'I knew the money wouldn't interest you. It never has. You're happy here, you have your friends, all you need. But I thought there must be a reason *why* he is doing this. No one gives away ten million euros for no reason. I thought it must be important.'

Charlotte saw how the old woman's eyes narrowed at the figure. She looked . . . angry. 'He thinks I can be bought.'

'Señora Quincy, please listen to your granddaughter. I am not privy to the client's reasons for doing this but you should perhaps know one pertinent detail: my client is dying,' Charlotte said in a low voice. 'Pancreatic cancer. He's been given only a few weeks left to live.'

Her words settled in the room like snow on the ground. Señora Quincy was quiet then for a long time, her crooked fingers absently stroking her granddaughter's curved cheek as her eyes lifted off and stared into the distance, seeing into a forgotten past that had seemingly come roaring back into her life and now pulsed here in this very room. She rolled her lips into a thin line, her clear eyes watering slightly, the free hand in her lap pulling and releasing slowly in small fists.

Finally though, she drew herself back to the present, looking first at Marina, then Charlotte. 'Tell him I don't want the money.' Her granddaughter gasped but she held a hand up to silence her. 'But if Arlo wishes to see me one last time, then I will see him.' Her gaze was level and cool.

Arlo? Charlotte hesitated. Was it a shortening of Carlos? It was just about close enough, and the old woman had come to that name completely unprompted. 'Okay, I will pass that message back to him. But you should know, he suffered a stroke last week,' she said gently. 'He's currently in hospital. He was unconscious but is now recovering fairly well, I understand.'

Señora Quincy flinched at her words, nodding in understanding.

'May I ask what he is to you?' Charlotte asked quietly. 'What is your connection to him?'

At that, Marina Quincy hooked an almost hairless brow. 'You mean to say you don't know?'

Charlotte shrugged. 'We've jumped to one wrong conclusion already.' Her eyes briefly met Marina's. 'I hesitate to guess again: a former friend? Boyfriend?'

'More than that.'

'Husband?' Charlotte asked.

She shook her head.

'. . . Brother?'

'More than that,' the old woman repeated, just as Marina said at the same time, 'My grandmother was an only child. Orphaned in the war.' Marina gasped as she heard her grandmother's contradictory reply.

Charlotte saw the intense look simmering in those grey eyes; something was waking from deep within her. 'I don't understand: how can he be more than a brother?'

'Oh, quite easily,' the old woman said, fire in her eyes and a secret on her lips.

Mateo's white sneakered foot was already twitching anxiously by the time she rushed up the steps. He was dressed in his tennis whites, his signature glass of chilli-infused water beaded with condensation.

'Charlotte, our third meeting in almost as many days. You have good news for me, I hope?'

She shook his hand and tipped her head in a half-shrug. 'I definitely have news.'

'Did you make the offer?' he asked impatiently.

The waiter came over and without pause or ceremony she ordered a Pellegrino. She sat down on the rush seat, the pale-blue cushions a gentle complement to her shell-pink dress.

'A lot has happened in the past twenty-four hours, so I'll get to the point,' she said directly. 'We discovered last night that the Marina Quincy identified in the report was the wrong Marina Quincy.'

'What?' Mateo looked aghast. 'No, absolutely not,' he rebutted sharply. 'Those researchers were working with information directly supplied from my father's lawyers. They haven't got this wrong.'

'To the letter, no. But Miss Quincy is in fact named after her grandmother who, although she's living in a care home, remains the legal owner of the apartment – even though it is her granddaughter who lives there now.'

She paused, seeing how the consternation in his expression changed into confoundment. Two women with the same name, two generations apart, living at the same address? It was an unfortunate coincidence.

She continued. 'I met the older Marina Quincy this morning but I'm afraid she has point-blank refused to accept the offer.'

'So then we're negotiating?' He scowled, a look of disgust deepening across his features.

'No, she says she's not interested in money. The only thing she has said she will do is see your father.'

'*What?*' he thundered, his composure slipping completely and sending a sparrow pecking at his feet, flying back into the bushes. He looked apoplectic. 'That is precisely what we said she could not do. My father is dying. I will not have her coming into the heart of our family and spreading her poison—'

'That's the thing,' Charlotte said gently. 'She *is* family.'

Mateo looked at her as though she'd started talking in tongues. '. . . Don't be ridiculous,' he said quietly, but his face had paled.

'She is your father's twin. Younger by six minutes.'

He shook his head, his mouth hanging open but no words coming out. 'No. This is . . . this is a lie. My father had two brothers, both older, who died in the war. He never had a sister, much less a twin. Don't you think we would know if he had?'

Charlotte chose her words carefully. 'Well, Marina Quincy apparently concealed his presence from her family too. They believed her to be an only child, orphaned in the war.'

'There you go then! She's a fraudster, a chancer!'

'I don't think so. She knew exactly who the client was – who was offering her money – before I had a chance to say your father's name. In fact, I never did name him. She said it to me, unprompted.'

'What?'

'Yes, although she called him Arlo. I assume that's a shortening for Carlos?'

'Yes, but not one that I've ever heard used for my father. In fact he's always been very particular about it.'

'Well, perhaps only she called him by that name? It reminds him of her?' She shrugged, watching as he struggled to make sense of the barrage of information. 'Either way, if they've both lied about their families and kept their pasts hidden, there has to be a very good reason for it. And with your father gravely ill, this begins to make sense of what he's doing: it is increasingly looking like he's reaching out to her, like this is his way of trying to make amends for something.'

Mateo looked furious again. 'Why should we assume he is to blame? If even any of this is true.'

The waiter set down her drink but neither one of them acknowledged him, too deep in the conversation to notice.

'Mateo, I'm not pointing a finger at anyone,' she said calmly. 'These are the only facts I have to hand at the moment and it goes without saying that we will investigate thoroughly and corroborate Señora Quincy's story that she is his twin sister; we can also insist on a DNA test for absolute, genetic proof.'

'Yes. I insist upon it. She could be anyone,' he blustered.

'Possibly. But it is strange that both of them have concealed the other's identities from their own families, don't you think? Clearly, there's something that links them. But your father is the one who has instigated contact, not her, and she appears to have gone to very great lengths to remain hidden from him: if Marina's granddaughter has grown up believing her grandmother was an only child with no other family, then it follows that her father – Señora Quincy's son – thinks the same too; this would suggest that whatever happened between her and your father at the very least occurred when her son was very young, or it even pre-dated his birth.'

Mateo shook his head, denying her words and the implicit blame within them. 'You're telling me that this woman kept her past a secret from *two* generations of her family? As far as I'm concerned, that tells us all we need to know about her: she is a convincing liar.' It was said as a statement of fact. An utter condemnation of her character.

'With all due respect, your father lied in keeping her a secret from you all too. You had no idea he was a twin either.'

Mateo Mendoza's eyes flashed with anger at the assertion but he had no reply to it. He looked at her with hard eyes instead. 'So then, what does she want exactly? Why does she want to see him? What does she expect to get out of it? *More* money?'

'I doubt it; she seemed wholly uninterested in the financial offer. My guess is that she's after closure of some sort. An apology?'

'I've just said, my father—'

'I know,' she interrupted, not wanting to hear another defence of his father. 'But clearly none of us possess the full facts at the moment. We don't know what's gone on between them, only that they've both hidden each other from their own families for a very long time.'

He was quiet for a moment, his eyes on the horizon as he took a long sip of his drink. He was thinking, calculating, considering . . . 'How did she strike you?'

'Well, I spoke with her at length just now and she appears to be in fine health for a woman of her age, although clearly she tires easily and is physically frail.'

'How about mentally?'

'According to her granddaughter, she is not suffering from any mental deterioration, if that's what you mean. She's in the home for physical assistance, nothing more.'

Mateo's face crumpled into a frown, his head dropping forward as though his neck could no longer support the weight of it. 'None of this makes any sense. For the past week I have been going over and over it: who is this woman? Why is he so fixated upon her, above and beyond us? And now we learn she's his twin?' He sighed, looking exhausted and embattled. 'That makes no sense either; even less than before. If she is his blood, why gift her the estate? Legally, she's already entitled to a fixed share when he dies. Technically, she should *already* have a share, after their parents, my grandparents, died.' He looked at her, baffled.

Charlotte shrugged. 'From the financial profile the researchers worked up, the apartment is her only asset – but it's very meagre. If she does already have a fixed share in the estate, it doesn't look like she's ever accessed it. Could there be a hidden fund or a trust? Another bank account perhaps that's been dormant . . . ?'

'There's never been any mention of one, but then why would we look for someone we didn't know existed?' he muttered. 'I'll get Milton and the lawyers to look into it.'

'Or perhaps your father has already done that and that's why he's giving her the gift? Perhaps he knows she won't touch the family estate otherwise? For some reason, she didn't want it then and she doesn't want it now . . . Do you know if he was going to make the donation anonymously?'

He shrugged disconsolately. 'I know nothing about any of it. He never discussed it with me.'

'Well, it would have been tokenism anyway,' Charlotte mused. 'Marina would surely have guessed where the money came from if several hundred million euros suddenly turned up in her account one day.' She bit her lip. 'Maybe he's tried giving her her share before and she's refused . . . ? Perhaps he thinks that by giving her the money on his deathbed, she won't be *able* to return it?'

'Why should he have to try so hard? It makes no sense,' he cried, the exasperation bursting through again as they went round in circles, seemingly never getting closer to the point. 'Are we really supposed to accept that this woman turned her back on her family and left them far behind – not just the estate and her share of it, but the people: her brothers, my father, her parents? What kind of woman could do such a thing? And then, not only did she hide herself from them, but she perpetuated the lie throughout her own family's lifetimes?'

'I agree it's baffling. It suggests that whatever happened between them must have been devastating.'

They were both quiet for a long time, the word sitting between them like a bomb. 'Devastating' covered a lot of ground.

'What do you want me to do?' she asked finally.

He was quiet for a moment, trying to control himself, control the situation. 'Well clearly the financial offer is now redundant. If she's truly a Mendoza, then legally she is already a rich woman, whether she chooses to spend it or not. No, money has no weight here any more.' He narrowed his eyes. 'What is vital now is that we discover what happened between her and my father to make her abandon her family. And why my father is so desperate to bring her back again.'

Charlotte agreed. 'He's certainly gone to a lot of trouble trying to track her down. It strikes me that reconciliation, even forgiveness, is what he needs before he dies.'

'Reconciliation? . . . Hmm.' His eyes slid sidelong to her. 'How is Professor Marling getting on?'

In an instant, her world flipped, landing belly up. The very mention of him was enough to floor her. 'Um . . .'

'Because he had better be as good as his CV suggests. You might have brought him in initially for some background context, but things have changed. Everything now hinges on knowing exactly what happened, when and why. He needs to be thorough and he needs to be fast.'

'He won't let you down. He's meticulous.'

'You said you two knew each other?'

'That's right. We were briefly at Cambridge together.'

'Cambridge?' he frowned. 'I thought he said Oxford.'

Charlotte was impressed he'd picked it up; he clearly had an eye for details. 'Yes, he – uh, transferred, for his final year,' she said stiffly.

'Oh. Well he must have had his reasons. We'll have to put ourselves in the hands of the professor and hope he can find an explanation for why my father's doing what he's doing. God knows, we all need resolution now before he passes.'

'Well, I don't doubt he'll do an excellent job for you. And if I can do anything further down the line, either for you or the two Marinas, don't hesitate to let me know.'

Mateo frowned. 'That sounds like you're leaving.'

She looked back at him in surprise. 'What more is there for me to do? My role was to get close to Marina and find out what she knew and, if necessary, to manage her financial expectations.' She shrugged. 'That she's family means that's all a moot point now. She has certain legal rights; your lawyers will take over from here.'

'On the contrary, you are still very much needed, Charlotte,' Mateo said, shaking his head at her. 'I'm sorry but if she and my father are to be reunited after almost a lifetime apart, then that will take a certain amount of managing and you alone are the bridge between the two sides. You are best placed, I feel, to help our newcomers adapt to the new life in which they are going to find themselves. I need you to be at La Ventilla for the reunion.'

'La Ventilla? That's your estate in Andalusia.' She felt her stomach dip again. Telling Stephen and her mother she was coming out to Madrid had been tricky enough. Now the country pile?

'Precisely. The doctor has said my father can be discharged in the next few days, and he is keen to go home. Clearly he is not well enough to travel any distance so we must bring my aunt to him. If you and she are correct and reunion was what he really wanted all along, then we must honour my father's wishes.'

'But she's very elderly too.'

'Naturally. But you said she is in generally good health? We'll fly them down in the family jet. It will be so comfortable, they will scarcely realize they are travelling.'

Charlotte shifted awkwardly. 'When were you thinking for this?'

'As soon as possible. The day after tomorrow? Time is against us.' He stared into space briefly. 'She must be important to him. Marina's name was the first word he said when he came round.'

'I didn't know that,' she murmured sympathetically. 'The thing is, I'm afraid that's going to be tricky for me. I have plans for this weekend that can't be changed.'

He looked displeased. 'What could possibly be more important than resolving this crisis?'

Charlotte swallowed. 'Well, I'm getting married next week and my fiancé's parents are hosting a formal dinner at the Savoy on Saturday night. I'm afraid that, as the bride, I am very much obliged to be there.'

'Hmm, yes, I can see that you would be,' he said, reluctantly looking at her closely, as though it was fascinating to consider she might have a life outside of managing his. '. . . Congratulations.'

'Thank you.'

He lapsed into thought again. 'When would you need to be there by?'

'In London? Well, the dinner's at eight.'

He thought for a moment. 'Okay. So then you could still

accompany them down there in the morning and get them settled in? I will be in Seville, making arrangements for my father to be discharged and sent home to recuperate, but I'd be happy to put the plane at your disposal to get you back to London for early evening.'

Her heart sank. If she had a private plane at her disposal, how could she refuse? On what grounds? There were none. Her mother would freak, Stephen would sulk, but what else could she do? It would work. Just. 'Okay, thank you.'

'Of course, I'd want you back here the next day. What day is the wedding exactly?'

'Um, it's a civil ceremony on Thursday but I really will need to be in London next week for final—'

'Yes, yes, we'll have you back in good time for all of that, but I'm sure you understand the imperative of making sure the reunion proceeds smoothly. If this is, as you said, my father's dying wish, then we must all do what it takes to make it a success. You, Charlotte, are a vital cog in that wheel.'

She suppressed a sigh, forced a smile. 'I have an appointment on Sunday morning but I can be back by the lunchtime?'

'Good. Our two Marinas trust you, your being there should put them at their ease and help them settle in till my father is well enough to join them,' he said, looking pleased. 'I really feel that between you and Professor Marling we have the best chances of successfully resolving this matter, one way or the other.' He tapped his finger restlessly, staring into the middle distance. 'I will certainly be intrigued to get to the bottom of it all. If they've been estranged for so many years, then there has to be a good reason for it. That is a long time to hold a grudge.' He looked at her, perplexed. 'I mean, what exactly could have happened that was so bad it lasted both their lifetimes?'

*

She stared at the number she had scrawled in red pen on the back of the receipt as Rosie dictated it down the phone. It was just a random jumble of digits and yet it was more than that – it was the hotline to him, the golden thread that could connect her to him wherever he was in the world. It brought him into her life, his voice into her ear. It made him real and flesh and blood again.

Was he expecting her to call? Or after the way he'd left, so abruptly, with such finality, was that supposed to have drawn the line in the sand between them?

With a deep breath and closing her eyes, she pressed dial and brought the phone to her ear. It rang once, twice, three times . . .

'*Diga!*' His voice burst into her consciousness and he was so fully formed to her, it was like he was standing right in front of her. In the background she could hear music, voices, laughter. A woman laughing. Where was he? '. . . Hello?'

'Nathan, it's me.'

The silence that followed was like a gun crack. '. . . Charlotte. I didn't expect to hear from you.'

Expect? Or want? His words hurt and she closed her eyes, pinching her temples as she swallowed hard. 'Really? Why not?'

Another pause, but this time his voice – when he spoke – was harder. 'I would have thought that was perfectly obvious.'

'You didn't let me explain—'

'Because I didn't want you to. It never should have happened.'

'You don't mean that,' she said quietly but her voice was feeble, weak.

'I've never meant anything more.'

Such simplicity. Such brutality. She felt winded by his words and she didn't know how to reach him. He wasn't the boy she'd once known. '*I* don't regret what happened between us—'

'There is no us.'

She faltered again. 'Nathan, please . . .'

'Yesterday was a mistake, Charlotte. This conversation is a mistake. Don't call again—'

'Wait!' He couldn't hang up on her.

'What is it?' She heard the frustration in his voice. The irritation that she was still there.

'It's not that simple . . . We still have to work together.'

He gave an astonished laugh but he didn't sound amused. 'You're joking?'

'No.' She swallowed and tried to rally, to pull her voice into shape again. She might not pull off bored right now, but she could do professional. 'I'm calling to see how your report's coming on.'

'There is no report!'

'Really? Why not?'

There was a stunned silence. 'Charlotte, we cannot work together. It's impossible.'

'Do you want to explain that to the client?' she asked quietly.

He didn't reply and she realized the background din had become muted. Had he moved away, into another room? Outside? She wandered over to the balcony and looked out over the still restless city as though she might just catch a glimpse of him. She wondered where exactly he was. A mile away? One block?

As the silence lengthened, she listened to the sound of his breathing, the pain between them twitching like a raw nerve.

'Look, it doesn't add up anyway. The entire thing is absurd,' he said finally. It was a second before she realized he was talking about the client and not them – able to just click off from her, do what had to be done. 'Even from just an initial read-through, it doesn't ring true that he's donating his estate to his *mistress*. If he was in his sixties or seventies even, it might be plausible, just, but two years off a century? I don't think so.'

'Yes, it jarred with us too but we had to work with what we had,' she said quietly. 'It's since transpired we were working with inaccurate information.'

'Inaccurate how?'

'Birthdate. There are two Marina Quincys: the one we were targeting; and her grandmother, after whom she's named.'

There was a long silence, her embarrassment at the idiotic error only lengthening in the vacuum.

'Right. Well that immediately makes more sense. And how old is Marina Quincy Senior?'

'Ninety-eight.'

'The same as Carlos Mendoza.'

Charlotte rolled her eyes. It would be just like him to have memorized the entire bloody file.

'Is she a former girlfriend then? First wife? There's no mention of another marriage.'

'She's his twin.'

'. . . No mention of that either,' he said tersely, as though they'd been deliberately wasting his time.

'We only discovered it ourselves in the last twenty-four hours, but you can see how that changes things.'

'Hmm,' he reluctantly agreed, but she could hear from his tone that his interest had been piqued again, his academic brain wanting to solve the puzzle. 'Well, this at least makes more sense. But if they're estranged siblings then it dramatically changes the potential timeline. It's one thing researching his life for the last twenty or thirty years but this break between them could have happened anytime from childhood. If they're both ninety-eight, then . . .' his voice trailed off as he did the maths. 'That means going right back to when they were teenagers or even kids from the 1930s onwards . . .' he exhaled, working out dates. 'It'd mean trawling through stuff from the Civil War, the Second World War and any time after in the Franco era, right up to the present day.'

'You're going to be busy then,' she said flatly. 'Mateo is putting a lot of store in your research capabilities. I told him you wouldn't let him down.'

There was another long pause. '. . . Look, Charlotte, this isn't a good idea.'

'No, it isn't,' she said. 'But I didn't go looking for this; I thought I was hiring Jose Ferrante. If the situation could be changed, I think we'd both jump at it, but it's too late now. Mateo wants you.' She cleared her throat lightly, the strain getting to her. 'So tell me where you're up to.'

He was quiet for a long while, clearly looking for a way out – and finding none. 'Jose had done a preliminary trawl through records for Marina Quincy here in Madrid – birth, confirmation, marriage, electoral register . . . Clearly none of that's now relevant given he was working with the wrong date of birth so I'll have to start again on all that. As she's his sister and there's a family history, it'll probably mean going down to Andalusia too; the Mendoza estate, La Ventilla, is just outside Ronda so I'll need to base my searches there as precious little has been digitized. A lot of information was lost during the Civil War; and what does remain, well – when it comes to Franco's version of history, let's just say revisionist doesn't begin to cover it. I'll need to see source material myself which will mean flights, a car, hotel, food etc . . .'

'Whatever you need, just do it. Money isn't a problem.'

'On the contrary – money's always the problem,' he snapped.

His words hung in the air, sparkling between them like chandeliers, beautiful and true.

'You should know things on your side have become a lot more urgent since I . . . saw you,' she faltered. Had it really only been yesterday afternoon that the two of them had raced across that street, hand-in-hand, seemingly running towards their destiny? 'Carlos Mendoza is hopefully being discharged from hospital this weekend and Mateo has offered to fly Marina and her granddaughter down to Ronda in the family plane, ready for a reunion. I'm accompanying them down for the journey tomorrow morning. You are welcome to travel with us if it would help.' Her voice sounded stilted, formal. Like her mother's.

Another silence. 'Fine.' He could hardly argue for a seat on a commercial flight if they were taking a private plane.

'Fine. I'll arrange for the driver to collect you at ten, then.'

Another unhappy silence. '. . . Fine.' And he hung up.

Chapter Thirteen

Charlotte sat in the back of the car, trying to look calmer than she felt. It was a black stretch Range Rover and had looked like a presidential motorcade when it had pulled up outside her apartment. Mateo had arranged for his driver to collect Marina and then her grandmother first – Charlotte couldn't imagine how it had managed to turn down Marina's street – and they were already sitting in overwhelmed silence when she first climbed in.

A little small talk – health, the weather, was the glass really bullet-proof? (yes) – had tided them over for the first few minutes, but they were all nervous and soon lapsed into distracted silences.

'Where are we going now?' Marina asked. 'The airport is that way.' She pointed right as they swung left.

'Yes. But we are also collecting my colleague. Professor Nathan Marling.'

'A professor?' Señora Quincy enquired, like her nephew – an eye for the details. 'What kind of bank is this, that has counsellors and professors?'

'My clients try to be . . . holistic in their approach,' Charlotte said lightly, not wanting to give too much away about Nathan's work. She didn't think Señora Quincy would take kindly to knowing her past was being thoroughly investigated.

'And what is he a professor of?'

Too late. Charlotte swallowed. 'History.'

The old woman's eyes narrowed with immediate displeasure and it was evident she knew exactly what was happening behind her back. They sank into a stiff silence, looking out of the windows instead.

The Las Letras district had none of the flashy townhouses of Salamanca, nor the trendy condos of Goya. Rather it had a bohemian vibe, with boldly painted buildings veering from the usual umber and ochre palette to terracotta reds, hot pinks and oranges. The buildings were functional rather than beautiful – in spite of their exotic colours – and crowded so close together Charlotte thought it must surely be possible for people to stand on their balconies and touch the fingertips of their neighbours across the street.

The car slowed to a crawl as the driver looked for the address, pedestrians having to squeeze past to get by, glancing down at the blacked-out windows with both annoyed and curious looks.

Señora Quincy looked uncomfortable. Perhaps it was the attention, but, more likely, it was the stress of what they were embarking upon – a return to her old home for the first time in . . . well, no one yet knew how many years. In spite of the ivory quilted aniline leather upholstery and the air-conditioned seats, she looked as uncomfortable as if she was wearing a wool dress in a heatwave – her shoulders twitching, hands clasped tightly together, eyes pressed shut as though if she couldn't see it, it wasn't really happening. In fact, she was perfectly attired again – wearing a teal linen shift dress, a pale-pink plastic bangle at her wrist and pink-rimmed spectacles. Forget ninety-eight, Charlotte thought – watching her eyes flicker behind her glasses – she could have passed for a woman twenty years younger, easily; only the utter transparency of her thin, fragile skin betrayed a body that was older than the spirit.

'The address is across the plaza there but I cannot turn into the street,' the driver said, turning slightly so that his face was in profile to her. 'Nor can I park here.'

'It's fine, I'll knock,' she said in a thin voice, undoing her seat belt. 'What is the address?'

He told her, pointing to a corner apartment above a tapas bar on the opposite side of the tiny square.

'Okay, I'll be right back,' she murmured, her eyes already fastened to it as she hopped down. People stared at her as she emerged from the vehicle, clearly wondering if she was famous, or at least powerful, but she didn't register their interest. Only one thing was running through her head: this is where he lives. His life is here now.

His fingers intertwined in hers. Sunlight streaming in. The middle of the afternoon. Twisted sheets—

Her eyes scanned the plaza as she walked quickly, taking in the espresso bar (did he get his morning coffee there?), the old bookshop (he would definitely browse there at the weekends), the artsy jeweller's, selling turquoise and silver earrings (no). There was a gallery too, a long thin bronze sculpture of a man on a pedestal in the window.

'. . . Let's skip the party.' His voice low. Slow.

'And do what?'

A shrug. 'Go to the cottage. Be alone. Just the two of us for once. No one else—'

She was at his door. It was set off to the side, away from the steel tables and plastic-wicker chairs that crowded at the building's base. There was nothing to mark the significance of the place, nothing to indicate that he – once the most important person in her world – lived and ate and slept here.

She pressed the buzzer for Apartment 3, as the driver had told her, and she stepped back, feeling her body brace with the anticipation of seeing him again. The visceral shock of it.

His kisses on her eyelids, the tip of her nose, the dip at the base of her ear…

She waited, then waited some more, trying to allow a respectable amount of time for him to answer, but she felt twitchy and jumpy. Was he doing this deliberately? Had he seen her cross the square, was he deliberately making her wait?

'These parties are all the same. Everyone getting wasted, Fairfax leching over every girl that isn't you . . .'

'You sound jealous,' she grinned.

'Not jealous. Just bored of him trying to turn it into some kind of war between us. Why won't he accept you're with me because you want to be . . . ?'

She buzzed again – just as the green door opened and, suddenly, there he was. It was the same every time she saw him: that sensation of the world tilting abruptly, like a car on a rollercoaster swooping the thrillriders into the next convex whirl.

'Hey,' he mumbled, managing to make it sound unfriendly. He was wearing jeans and a cream linen blazer, holding a black holdall in one hand and, almost immediately, he slid on a pair of sunglasses, creating a barrier as thick as any wall.

She managed only to nod in reply, just as a sudden burst of static made them both startle.

'*Diga.*' The voice flickered, sounding almost mechanical through the ancient intercom, but it was undeniably female.

Charlotte felt her heart constrict. It was the reply to her

extra call up to his apartment. Her gaze immediately flew back to him but he was already leaning forward, urgency in the movement. He quickly, quietly spoke into it, his Spanish faultless and rapid. 'It's fine, I'm down here now. I'll call you when I get there.'

Charlotte stepped back once, twice – her feet wanting to move, to get her away from here, knowing her composure was deserting her. Already. Not even thirty seconds and she was thrown, undone – for the picture was suddenly startlingly clear. *She* was why he had all but sprinted from the bed. *She* was why he hadn't wanted her explanations about Stephen. Was she his girlfriend? Wife?

He looked up. 'Ready when you are,' he said simply, but there were tiny red spots on his cheeks as though he was angry. Angry with her? For finding out? Did he think she would tell her . . . ?

Struck dumb, she turned, leading him quickly across the plaza, only just able to stop herself from breaking into a run. He climbed into the front seat of the car – which was waiting on the opposite corner – twisting round to introduce himself to Marina and her grandmother with an easy smile that he pointedly kept from her. Charlotte saw the flicker of appreciation in Marina's eyes as she shook his hand, the suspicion in the old woman's.

'To the airport?' the driver asked, looking at Marina in the rear-view mirror.

'Yes please.' She looked stiffly out of the window, her arm resting on the windowsill, her hand covering her mouth as they pulled away. How was she supposed to do this? It was like torture, some sort of sick game . . .

But as the car eased away, her stare became fixed on the windows of Apartment 3 above the tapas bar: a woman had come onto the balcony. At this distance the details were hazy, but Charlotte could make out that she was tanned, wearing a black strappy sundress and her long curly dark hair was wild. Even 150 metres away, she looked sexy.

But as the car glided round the corner and out of sight, the last thing she saw was not the woman on the balcony – it was the baby she was bouncing on her hip.

Ronda, 10 July 1936

The snip of the scissors was the only sound to be heard as the dark lengths of hair fell into the white basin, feathering it like a nest. She kept her eyes on her reflection, working fast, not caring if it was level or neat – only that it was gone. What had taken years to grow halfway down her back was being undone in moments, and as the last cut fell she allowed herself the luxury of absorbing her new identity. She ran her hands quickly through the cropped cut, shaking it out and feeling the peculiar new lightness of her own head. It felt boyish and feathery through her fingers, like a baby bird's down, and she was pleased to see there was nothing now to reveal who she was, or rather had been – her luxuriant hair left here not so much unceremoniously as pointedly, all the other trappings of her former life unclipped and pulled off and left in defiant tangled heaps on the mahogany bed.

With one final glance she met her own eyes, seeing the determination within them. She was going to have to find resources she had never needed before; she was going to have to be fast, strong and wily if she wanted to stay safe for there was danger outside these walls, yes – but it was still nothing to the threat that persisted within them.

Grabbing the swollen grain sack she had carefully packed with food – stolen over a week from the kitchens – she hurried to the window and looked out. The dark sky was still peppered with stars, only the faintest blade of light beginning to bleed up behind the distant hills. Throwing one leg over the sill, she took a moment to marvel in the freedom that came with wearing trousers (another steal, this time from Arlo's room). She jumped like a cat onto the veranda of the porch, and carefully scaled down the bougainvillea trellis; she had done it numerous times as a child but as a full-grown woman she couldn't be absolutely sure it would take her weight, and when her foot touched the parched soil she breathed a heavy sigh of relief.

Without looking back, she broke into a sprint, heading for the cover of the cork oaks on the far side of the pasture. Leviatan was in there, somewhere, but she didn't care – tonight she knew she could outrun him; she had something bigger than a two-tonne bull to escape. Her feet kicked up red dust, dirtying her clothes and legs, but she embraced it, for it was yet another small sign of the freedoms now afforded to her. She ran until the house was out of sight and her lungs were burning, keeping crouched down as she vaulted the estate wall. And as the moon slid behind a cloud, she slipped into the open countryside and the big wide world, leaving behind one life and stepping into the next.

Chapter Fourteen

Ronda, July 2018

Charlotte stared down at the landing strip, an anomalous rectangle in the vast plain. It had been a punishing summer and the long grass around it was bleached calico. The pilot had explained that these huge tracts of land had once been the grazing pastures for the bulls that had made the Mendoza family's name and fortune; now, they stood bare – converted into a private airfield – the family's attentions directed these days towards large-scale citrus farming. But then, Charlotte and Nathan already knew all that. They had sheaves of paper on these people: how they'd made their money, how much there was of it, where they invested it. There was only one thing they didn't know about them and it seemed to be the most important thing, the only thing worth knowing: why the prodigal daughter had run.

Señora Quincy was catnapping, one of the chairs converted into a chaise for her, Marina beside her, sitting with her face pressed to the window and fogging the glass. She had been to the toilet four times on the short flight, prompting Charlotte to suspect she was just enjoying looking around and the autonomy of moving about as she pleased. Nathan was sitting towards the front of the plane, keeping to himself and absorbed in reading on his iPad; he had said barely a word in the car and hadn't lifted his head since wheels-up.

She looked down as the plane circled in the hot sky. Even from up here, the hacienda looked impressive: a vast, sprawling white building with peach roof peg-tiles, it was arranged around an inner courtyard with two large and newer-looking wings spanning out at either side. There were numerous outbuildings too: a clay tennis court, two pools, an equestrian arena and what looked from here like a polo pitch. All the toys and trappings in other words, it read almost like an inventory of what the modern magnate's estate should be.

The landing was hard, but then so was the ground, and they were greeted off the steps by a team of young white-jacketed staff who took their bags and fawned over Señora Quincy as though she was a queen returned from exile. Charlotte watched on with interest, wondering what Mateo had told them. Did they know who she really was?

They drove over the arid ground in golf carts; Señora Quincy and Marina were in the one ahead, her and Nathan following behind. Occasionally, his thigh knocked against hers as they bounced over the rough ground but he said not a word and she wouldn't look at him; she didn't trust herself to, the shock of his betrayal seeming all the worse for the fact that he'd tried to cover it up, instead pushing all the blame onto her. She concentrated instead on admiring the 'view', although, as with any airfield, there was nothing to see – just vast expanses of flat, fallow land. She would be gone again in a few hours, she told herself over and over. She could get through this. She would be back with Stephen tonight – her loyal, steadfast fiancé who deserved so much better than this, than her; she would step back into their careful life and it would fold around her and keep her safe. Nathan had a family, yes, but so did she. She could turn her back too.

The grass grew steadily greener as they approached the *cortijo* estate, the human element meaning scrubland became fields, pastures and ultimately lawns. In the near distance she could see an ancient oak forest, old stone walls and the remains of a metal water store; she wondered as to the people who had farmed this land and the stories they could tell. She wondered what had made the old woman in the buggy in front run from here and never come back.

The grass grew shorter, the bosky bushes tamed, clipped and shaped as they drew ever closer until finally they drove beneath a grand arched gateway. The studded wooden gates were almost as high as the main house, with *casitas* incorporated on either side, creating a walled courtyard. In contrast to the arid land outside these walls, within was an oasis – bright blooming bushes of hibiscus and oleander planted in rustic, white-painted stone planters and troughs, a large black dog sleeping in the shade and oblivious to their arrival.

They drew up to the hacienda compound, every one of them looking around greedily at the lush sight. At ground level, the building – though vast and sprawling – was surprisingly low-built, squat even. It seemed somehow friendlier up close, the thick, rough walls punctuated with round-arched windows, like a gingerbread house, and yellow pinned-back shutters. Deep bushes of hot pink bougainvillea were trailed up every wall and around every orifice, the decorative black grilles against the ground-floor windows making pretty lace patterns on the walls, froths of jasmine spilling from giant clay pots at the bottom of the steps.

The cart in front had come to a stop but Señora Quincy was still sitting in hers, taking it all in. Charlotte could imagine it would be emotional even just seeing the house – her childhood home – again, and she could see Marina holding her hand and stroking it.

'Is there a problem?' Nathan asked, tipping his head slightly in the Marinas' direction but keeping his gaze forward.

'I think it's a bit overwhelming for her, that's all,' she murmured. 'She's been away a long time.'

He gave a hard shrug. 'Why? The past is dead. It can't hurt her now.' And he swung himself out, grabbing his travel bag off the rack at the back.

Charlotte watched him go. Her heart felt like a rock in her ribs, heavy and inert. Who was he now? It was clear she had no idea at all.

Forcing herself to put one foot in front of the other, she followed after him to where a woman in her sixties was standing on the steps, her hands folded in front of her stomach. She too was all in white, her dress rather like an old-fashioned nurse's outfit.

'Welcome,' she said, nodding deeply, her hair tucked back in a low bun. 'We are delighted to have you as honoured guests at La Ventilla. I trust your journey was pleasant?'

'Very comfortable, thank you,' Charlotte smiled, aware that Nathan had arched a wry eyebrow, somehow managing to mock her even without words. *A private jet comfortable? It was the height of luxury for most people.*

'Don Mateo passes on his apologies that he could not be here to welcome you himself. He is in Seville this morning.'

'Yes, he said,' Charlotte replied. 'Has Señor Mendoza been discharged, do you know?'

'Soon, I understand.'

'Does he know Señora Quincy is here?'

'I believe not yet.' The housekeeper gave a brief smile. 'Please follow me. I will show you to your rooms.'

'Shouldn't we wait for the others?' Nathan asked.

Charlotte looked over at Señora Quincy, still immobile in the golf buggy. Three members of male staff had rushed out and were assembling a makeshift step to help her navigate her way down from the cart. It would be easier just to lift her down – she must weigh practically nothing – but she could see from the old lady's patience and posture that she wouldn't allow it. Was it a matter of pride? Dignity? As if, having once run from here, she would not allow herself to be carried back in?

'Señor Mendoza has arranged for Señora Quincy and her granddaughter to reside in the west wing. There are some bedrooms on the ground floor there; he felt that would be best for ease of access. The main house has stairs that are difficult to navigate.'

'How thoughtful.'

'He has liaised with Señora Quincy's carers and assigned a medical team to take care of her during her stay here. You and Professor Marling, however, are in the hacienda. Señor Mendoza thought you would like to experience the authentic Andalusian lifestyle?'

'Great.'

'My name is Mayra and if there is anything I can do for you during your stay, please do not hesitate to ask,' she said, as she began leading them up the steps.

'Thanks, Mayra,' they said in unison, the harmony making them both glance at, and recoil from, one another.

'This is the great hall,' Mayra said, fanning her arms lightly as they walked into a dark-panelled, double-height hallway. The floors were laid with terracotta tiles, an intricate staircase winding up and around, the walls studded with the mounted heads of at least a hundred bulls. Charlotte couldn't suppress her gasp in time, nor Nathan his look of disgust. 'The Mendoza bulls are of course very famous. All the heads you see here are of the champion bulls that were granted pardons.'

'Pardons?' Nathan questioned.

'For bravery in the bullring. On occasion, when a bull impressed the matador or the crowd with his big heart, nobility and courageous spirit, he would be pardoned and allowed to live out his days in the pastures. These bulls you see here all died of old age.'

'The lucky ones, huh?' Nathan smiled, but Charlotte recognized the edge in his voice. She remembered how he had clashed with her shooting-hunting-fishing friends at Cambridge; clearly bullfighting wasn't going to become a great love of his anytime soon either.

They walked through the space to a narrower hall, the inner courtyard Charlotte had spied from the air now off to her right. It was laid to lawn, with an ornamental pond and fountain in the centre, elegant orange trees dotting each corner. She spied some benches in the shade and wondered whether anyone ever came out to use them, or whether they were purely ornamental.

'All these rooms are of course available for your use – the card room, billiard room, the library,' Mayra said, gesturing towards the half-closed doors as they clipped past. 'The dining hall and drawing room are on the other sides of the courtyard. Señor Mendoza entreats you to use the house as your home.'

They turned into the corridor at the back of the square, a more modest staircase than the one in the great hall, flanked against the wall. Stone pedestals were topped with church candles in hurricane lamps, a tapestry hanging stiffly from a pole. The low curved ceilings swept down to the solid arches of the windows like sheets caught mid-billow, or the vault of a crypt.

'How old is the house?' Nathan asked as Mayra led them up the stairs.

'The oldest parts are eighteenth-century, with new additions in the last hundred years.'

'It's very imposing,' he said. 'Have you worked here for long?'

'All my life, professor. I came here as a housemaid and never left.'

'Worked your way up, huh?'

'That is correct,' she nodded, stopping outside a carved, carbonized wood door. 'Señora Fairfax, this is your room.'

She opened the door wide and stood back to allow Charlotte to enter. It was large but sparsely and simply decorated with whitewashed walls and a tiled floor, a charming yellow toile fabric dressing the bed and the windows. A walled wardrobe stood proud on the left-hand wall and opposite was the black bedstead, an image of the Madonna hanging above it, and on the far side, a door to the en-suite.

'Uh, it's beautiful, thank you,' Charlotte smiled hesitantly. Was the housekeeper aware she wasn't staying tonight? That she was here simply to drop off the guests of honour? 'But—'

'Professor, you are next door,' Mayra said, leading him onwards. His eyes met hers for a moment as he turned and followed her down the corridor, but Charlotte stood where she was. Curious though she was to see his room too, she couldn't follow; this wasn't some jolly trip with friends – 'Ooh, let me see your room.' She sank onto the bed and remembered to switch back on her phone. She listened to their voices through the open door, Nathan's brief but polite murmurings rolling back to her like a ball.

She felt at a loss. What was she doing here? Every minute in his company felt like torture. She couldn't believe he had lied to her so easily, made her feel so wretched for cheating on Stephen when he – *he* was the one already married, with a child.

She couldn't believe he had a child, that he was a father. Over and over on the plane she had tried to imagine it – him, them – but her mind simply wouldn't allow the image to form and instead she was distracted by the pain in her heart and the sense of panic it brought to her limbs, making her want to flee.

'. . . No, we can't. They'll all be waiting for us downstairs,' she protested reluctantly, pulling away from his embrace and walking over to the window.

'Let them wait. They're dull anyway, and you know it.'

'They're my friends!'

'They're punching above their weight then,' he sighed, collapsing back on the bed. 'All they ever talk about is the going at Goodwood and Mary's latest pair of new shoes. And Julian's latest shag conquest, of course.'

'Oh, Nate, you won't be difficult this weekend, promise me? Let's just have a good time. I know you find them boorish but they mean well. Contrary to popular opinion, Jules gets a really rough time of it at home with his old man.'

'A slap around his head could only be for the good in my opinion. Please don't give me his poor little rich boy story.'

'You've got it all wrong about him, you know.' He had loathed Jules ever since he'd overheard him describing Nathan as 'chippy' in the toilets at the pub on one of their first nights out as a couple. His integration into the group had been awkward, to say the least, and initially it had seemed that Jules had offered the friendliest welcome, making the betrayal all the greater when his true feelings were finally discovered.

'I don't think so – he's spoilt, pampered and entitled. I can't think why you'd want to defend him.'

'Because I know him. The real him. We go back a long way.'

'And are you going to go forwards a long way too?'

She shot him a look. 'Don't be ridiculous. You know it's not like that between us.'

'It was when we met.'

'Precisely. And then we met and I realized how utterly clueless I'd been about love.' She blew him a kiss. 'You're the one for me.'

'Hmm,' he said noncommittally. 'That will remain to be seen.'

'On what?' she asked indignantly.

'On whether I can suffer another of these weekends with your friends.'

'If you love me, you will,' she said coquettishly. She didn't want to fight; they only ever seemed to argue when they were with her friends. Standing at the window, she looked down upon the stepped garden carved into the steep Tuscan hillside, the square white sun umbrellas like unfolded handkerchiefs from this elevated viewpoint. 'Come and see this view.'

'I like it well enough from here.' She turned back to find him lying on the bed, his ankles crossed and hands clasped behind his head, watching her.

'You'd love it.'

'Frustratingly, I love you more.'

'That's because you're a philistine. Anyone with any taste knows Florence is the most beautiful place in the world.'

He arched his eyebrow in that way he always did when she was being provocative. 'You're only saying that because you're too unimaginative to consider anything that wasn't inculcated into you by your snob mother. Real aesthetes know that the most beautiful place in the world is anywhere that has you in it.'

She let the compliment slide, far preferring the combat of the insult. 'Unimaginative, huh?' She walked towards him, letting her dress fall. 'I'll show you how imaginative I can be—'

The sound of footsteps passing made her look up. Mayra popped her head in. 'Please feel free to use the house, walk the grounds and explore the estate: there is the golf course on the western boundary, horses if you like to ride, tennis, and of course the spa: there is a masseuse on call should you wish for a treatment. Señor Mendoza entreats you to feel at home here.'

'Thank you, Mayra,' she nodded. 'That's very kind, but Mateo is sending the plane for me later. I have to return to London by this evening.'

'But you are returning in the morning, I understand?'

'Yes.'

The housekeeper nodded and slipped away, as further down the hall a door clicked shut.

She sat for a moment, wishing she could have a drink, something to take the edge off the morning's revelation, but she got up instead. A shower would refresh her; travelling always left her feeling grubby. She walked into the en-suite, unbuttoning her blouse just as a door opposite opened – it had been all but obscured by a couple of fluffy robes hanging on it.

Nathan stared at her, a towel thrown over his shoulder. 'What the . . . ?'

There was a moment of stunned surprise, followed by appalled understanding, and she watched as the unguarded look in his eyes was quickly veiled with cold hardness again. A Jack and Jill bathroom – how exactly was this supposed to work? Allotted times? A special knock?

Nathan stepped back. 'After you.'

'Thanks.' She didn't bother to politely protest and he didn't bother to wait for it. And as she watched him retreat, she remembered her father correcting her when she was a little girl of a 'common mistake' – that it wasn't hate that was the opposite of love. But apathy.

Chapter Fifteen

Charlotte walked down the hallway, her pale-blue lululemon yoga kit feeling anachronistically urban and millennial in the old dark house. She had no idea where the gym was but, as much as anything, this was a good excuse to explore. There was nothing else to do for the moment: Marina had texted from wherever she was in the estate to say her grandmother was resting and that she was staying in over lunch to keep check on her (Charlotte read that to mean they were both overwhelmed and hiding out in their rooms).

As for Nathan, she had spied him from the bathroom window as she stepped out of the shower, out on a run, her eyes alerted more by the plumes of dust kicked up by his feet on a dirt track than his distant figure pounding through the shades of the far-off oaks.

She had watched him until he had turned out of sight, heading deeper into the trees and towards some hills. He had always been a runner (although not – she thought – ever *that* fast), and at Cambridge he had deplored the lack of gradient and any sort of pitch against which to throw himself. But then he had always been something of an ascetic, clean-living and clear-eyed, associating the worth of reward with the degree of struggle first required. Perhaps that was why he had been so drawn to her in the beginning? She'd been his challenge, his struggle. They certainly had never made sense on paper. Everything about them was opposite – their backgrounds, their views, their taste in music and favourite foods – and yet face to face, it was as though their hearts were tethered as one, tied together like balloons on a string, pulling them along so that they could barely keep their feet on the ground, both of them running on tiptoes – until in the end she had broken free, torn herself from him, because he couldn't help her in the way she needed; he couldn't understand the one thing that determined everything in her world.

Jogging down the stairs, she crossed over to the other side of the quad to which they had walked with Mayra earlier. Apparently the gym was in one of the two wings flanking it, but which? This wasn't a hotel, it wasn't like there were signs.

Her phone rang as she popped her head in one doorway to her right and saw it was a drawing room: red velvet chairs, half-panelled walls, a wide fireplace and a worn tiled floor. No, not there.

'Hello?' she said quietly, switching left instead and finding a door that opened onto a covered veranda, the open garden beyond it, lawns rolling away into the distance and dotted with the shadows of almond trees. Nope.

'What the hell is going on, Charlotte?' Stephen asked, his voice strained; she could tell he was trying not to shout. 'You're not picking up your phone, you're not returning calls.'

She stopped walking in panic. Stephen! In all the upset of dealing with Nathan last night, she had forgotten to call and update him with her new arrangements. It had slipped her mind completely as she'd worked her way through another bottle of rosé, trying to forget the hardness in his voice and how readily he was trying to turn his back on her. 'Oh God, I know, I'm so sorry, it's been so frantic—'

'Enough with the frantic! I don't give a damn how busy your work is. We have got a hundred people arriving in a *few hours* to celebrate with us, and you are nowhere to be found. Do you have any idea how worried we've been? I've been going out of my mind. You were supposed to be back yesterday! No one could get hold of you – not your mother, not even Mouse.'

'I know. I – I meant to call.' She had turned her phone off for the flight.

'So? What happened?'

She closed her eyes. Nathan had happened. Her past had stepped into her present and sucker-punched her off her feet. She had left her phone in her bag and walked straight to the glasses cabinet, piled into a bottle of Mirabeau and tried to block out all the memories of Nathan, her father . . . 'I promise, I'm leaving shortly. I just had to fly down here with the clients to settle them in but I'm—'

'Fly down where? Are you telling me you're not even in Madrid? Where the hell are you?'

'. . . Andalusia.'

'Anda—? Fucking hell, Charlotte!' He never swore.

'But it's okay. I'm leaving again at five. We're landing at quarter to six local time at City and I'll have a car take me straight to the hotel. I'll be there by seven.'

'. . . Seven? This is *bloody* ridiculous.' She could hear that he was speaking through clenched teeth, struggling to regain self-control.

'Stephen, I'll make it up to you, I promise.'

He scoffed. 'Make it up to me? Christ, don't do me any favours! I had assumed you were glad to be marrying me. That you were happy about it.'

'I am! I—'

'Listen, I don't know what's going on with you at the

moment but I can't speak to you right now. We'll talk when you get here.' And he hung up.

Charlotte stared into space, feeling the adrenaline race around her. Was there anyone she wasn't at war with right now? She was at odds with the world, dislocated, alone.

Walking slowly, she quickly rang her sister. 'Mouse, it's me.'

'Fuck, Lotts!—'

'Yes, yes I know, I'm dropping all the balls at the moment,' she said wearily. 'Please don't you have a go at me too.'

There was a pause, her feisty sister wrong-footed by her immediate surrender. 'Christ, now I'm really worried about you.'

'I'm f—'

'And *don't* say you're fine. I know when you're going off the radar.'

Charlotte looked upwards, swallowing back the tears. If she so much as sniffed, her sister would know and the game would be up. Busted. 'Listen, I'm flying back this evening,' she said, concentrating on keeping her voice steady. 'I'll be at the hotel for seven so just keep Ma calm till I get there and then you can all shout at me. But can you do me a favour first – can you grab me a dress and some shoes for tonight?'

'. . . Okay,' her sister replied with a sigh. 'I think I've got a set of keys. What do you want?'

'I don't mean back home. Ask Matty at Selfridges what they've got in that would suit.'

Another pause. 'You mean, you haven't already got something lined up?' She sounded incredulous.

'Well I'd intended to get it sorted this week but there's been no time.'

'Lotts, it's your wedding dinner! How can you not have got this sorted?'

'Because it's just a dinner.' Her voice sounded reedy and thin. 'I only need a dress to wear, that is all.'

'But it's supposed to be special! You should be excited.'

'And I am.'

'No, you're the very definition of *not* excited. I've seen you happier taking out the bins.'

Charlotte didn't respond. They both knew she'd never taken out the bins. 'Okay, I'll be there at seven. Thanks for your help, I'll see you later.' She got off the call quickly just as the first tears fell. She wasn't sure how much she could take. She felt pushed to her limits with wedding demands, work demands: Stephen, Mouse, her mother, his parents, one hundred guests, Mateo, Hugh Farrer, Marina, Marina . . . She was failing them all. And behind all of it, all of them, was the one she had failed most of all. The one who would never forgive her.

She heard footsteps coming down a hallway; they sounded brisk, efficient . . . She didn't want to be found here, crying in the corridor.

Straight ahead was a closed door. She turned the handle and found herself in an extraordinary open space: as in her bedroom, the ceilings were vaulted but down here the distinction between the ceilings and walls seemed to have become even more blurred, with the brick skeilings swooping all the way down to the floor into a series of thick, looped arches.

She walked through, her flip-flops slapping on the stone-flagged floor. An extravagant statement of space for space's sake, everything was textured and layered: the rough-plastered walls, the exposed brickwork, her nose detecting the fragile scent of essential oils before her eyes found the extravagant sprays of white tuberose arranged in splayed planters in alternate arches, strategic lighting illuminating them in moody golden pools. In contrast to the untouched, old-world traditional feel of the main house, with its mounted bulls' heads and dark portraiture, this wing felt impressive by its very unshowiness, an exercise in architectural restraint, an Axel Vervoordt dreamscape.

A uniformed woman carrying a bundle of towels suddenly emerged from one of the doors on the right, stopping as she caught sight of Charlotte and the yoga mat tucked under her arm. 'The gym is the fourth door on the left, Señora Fairfax,' she said, making no sign of noticing her blotchy face.

'Thank you,' Charlotte nodded, walking away quickly. She glanced in as she passed, at the room the woman had just left – Marina was lying on a massage table, her bare shoulders visible above the sheet, her dark hair swept up in a topknot. Her eyes were closed, gentle music playing quietly, and Charlotte wondered how she was coping with all of this. Did she know this was all an illusion? A seduction? For a woman used to working two jobs – a woman who, a little more than twenty-four hours ago, had walked back in slippers from the laundromat with wet clothes she couldn't afford to dry – this was a severe dislocation from normal life: chauffeur-driven cars, a private jet, five-star bedroom and now a private spa treatment. It would read well for now, and for the next few months, as she got used to the idea that this was rightfully hers and that she was family, not merely a visitor. She was one of the famed Mendozas too.

But six months from now, or a year, when the novelty began to pall and the days began to stretch endlessly, when she no longer *had* to do anything . . . that was when the trouble would begin. Charlotte knew it even though she did not, and she felt sorry for her; this wasn't the fairytale ending Marina assumed it to be.

Charlotte stepped into the gym, stopping momentarily to absorb the state-of-the-art equipment. There was a Pilates

Reformer machine, which she knew from experience was also a torture device, aerial yoga slings and even an anti-gravity treadmill. But the visitor's eye was inexorably drawn to the lines of this impressive space, not the equipment within it, those same arches outside in the hall here glazed with giant crittall windows that gave onto the grounds. The glass was tinted a smoky colour, keeping the room cool and subdued, and she rolled out her mat in front of one of them, determined to harness her frantic thoughts and calm her racing mind.

She needed to focus, eliminate the noise. She lay flat, her palms facing the ceiling. She closed her eyes and tried to find her centre, to imagine her breath as a white light rolling through her – starting in her feet and working up, all the way through. But when she got to her torso, her heart, the light stopped as though blocked.

She tried again, keeping her eyes closed. She was agitated, she already knew that. It was why she was doing this. It always worked.

Only this time it didn't.

After the third attempt, fed up with her glowing white knees and resolutely black heart, she opened her eyes again and rolled up, just as agitated as before. Perhaps she should have waited till the end of the session – get her flows in first. Find a rhythm and soothe herself that way.

Jumping up, she stood in the mountain pose, feet in parallel, eyes dead ahead, her hands splayed with the fingers pointing to the floor. As she began to run through the sequence, letting her body move rather than forcing it into stillness, she felt her mind begin to drift. Yes. She closed her eyes, running through the asana twice, three times, just feeling the rhythm and controlling her breath – it was the only thing she could control seemingly . . .

By the time she opened her eyes, her mind was drifting like a boat on water. There was no wedding, no Stephen, no Nathan, no bouncing baby . . . But there was, in a sort of slow-motion comedy sketch, one of the golf carts trundling slowly over the lawn, Señora Quincy sitting in the front, a straw hat on.

Charlotte's gaze snapped back into focus. She was supposed to be resting from the journey. Was she getting some air? Reacquainting herself with the estate? Charlotte wondered how much it had changed in her absence – these wings certainly hadn't been here back then (whenever 'then' was) – but the old woman didn't seem overly curious, her gaze fixed forwards rather than scanning the landscape. Perhaps she didn't want to see the changes, perhaps they challenged her too much, serving as painful indicators of all that she had missed out on?

The buggy came to a stop at one of the decorative flowerbeds that broke up the lawn: a low stone retaining wall encircled a mature jacaranda tree, with profuse oleander bushes clustered at its base. She watched as the driver – one of the male orderlies she had seen helping her with the step earlier – got out, listening to something his passenger was saying. He pointed at the bed and Señora Quincy nodded. The man hesitated, looking uncertain. Then he stepped over the wall and into the bed, up to the jacaranda tree. He looked back at the old woman and yet again she said something that made him point and then move. Charlotte frowned as she watched him carefully encircle the tree, before stopping at a point on the far side from where Charlotte sat, and stooping out of sight. What on earth was he doing?

A moment later, he straightened up and, picking his way carefully back over the bed, handed something to Señora Quincy. Charlotte could see her nod her thanks from the tilt of her hat but she was too far away to see what the item was that she placed in her lap. All she could see, as the driver got back in and turned the buggy towards the hacienda again, was that Señora Quincy had taken the item and was pressing it to her lips as though it was treasure.

'How are you doing?' she asked, as Marina emerged from the spa.

Marina smiled at her languidly, leaning against the door frame for a moment. 'I just had a *three-hour* massage,' she stage-whispered, as though it was a dirty secret.

'Good for you.'

'It was amazing. I don't think . . . I don't think I've ever felt this *limp*.' She seemed almost drunk on the relaxation. 'The girl told me I had the hardest muscles she's ever worked on.' Marina lengthened like a cat proudly.

'Well I'm not surprised. You work so hard.'

'How the other half live, eh?' Marina winked as they began slowly walking together. She glanced at Charlotte, noticing that she was in exercise kit. 'Did you do a workout?'

'Yoga. Just a bit of mat work.' That wasn't entirely true. After seeing Señora Quincy's strange behaviour, she had given up on the yoga and a futile quest for zen, and instead exhausted herself with an aggressive kettlebell workout that would punish her more tomorrow than it had even today.

'I'll go in the gym next,' Marina said, nodding as though she was working through a list. 'Do you know I've never actually been in a proper gym before? I could never afford the fees.'

'Well get someone to show you how to use the machines first then. You don't want to end up with an injury.'

'Perhaps I'll ask Professor Marling. He looks like he works out.' Marina was looking across at her slyly, her tongue poked teasingly between her smiling lips. 'He is pretty sexy, no?'

'Well, I'm afraid he's also married,' Charlotte said, giving as natural a smile as she could muster. She had noticed that Marina's attitude towards her had changed since she had revealed her grandmother's existence, becoming more confiding and intimate – as though Charlotte could be trusted now that she wasn't directly 'after' her. They appeared to be on the same side.

Marina tutted. 'Typical. All the best ones are.'

'Yes,' Charlotte murmured, not liking to point out that he was fifteen years her junior. 'He's got a baby too,' she added for good measure, wondering if the words would be as diabolical, as painful, said out loud as they were swimming in her head. In fact, they were worse.

They had walked out of the beautiful gallery and leisure wing, back into the rear hall of the main house. They passed the stairs that led to Charlotte and Nathan's rooms, and then over to the other wing on the opposite side. It was identically laid out – jaw-dropping curved spaces, rustic textures – but here were the guest suites.

'Check out my room,' Marina said excitedly, leading her into a space which felt almost holy in its virtues: an emperor-sized bed draped with dove-grey linen faced onto the same smoke-tinted crittall windows of the other wing and Charlotte realized that what added to the coolness there, delivered privacy here. Two crushed-linen curved sofas dominated the expanse of space between all four walls, the worn-smooth floor texturized with an antique Talsint rug. 'Isn't it incredible?' Marina sighed, tipping her head back and spinning girlishly, before collapsing onto the bed.

'Stunning. What amazing taste they have.'

'Is your room as beautiful?'

'No,' Charlotte replied truthfully. 'It's very comfortable, but this is . . . special. You are clearly getting the VIP treatment.'

Marina sat up on the bed again, looking flattered, and it was true – her body was different. Relaxation seemed to have changed her molecular make-up: that pushed-forward jaw and tense neck, her jerky energy, now smoothed out into languour. 'What's he like, my cousin?'

'Mateo? Well I'd say he's polite, focused, driven, passionate. Very family-oriented. Loves horses.'

'How old?'

'Sixty-six I believe. Fairly recently remarried though. He has a six-year-old son with his second wife.'

'A six-year-old?' She pulled a face. 'And I thought my mother was old! She was thirty-seven before she had me.' She pulled a face. 'Six miscarriages.'

It was a blunt thing to say to a near-stranger and indicative again of the new dynamic blossoming between them. 'My God, how awful for her.'

'Yeah. It meant she doted on me, though. People say it's not easy being an only child but . . . it never bothered me. She was all I needed. We were best friends.'

Her voice had thinned out and Charlotte walked over to the sofa, hearing the past tense and sensing they were moving into deeper territory. The more she could learn about Marina's family life, the better. 'What happened to her?'

'You mean how did she die?' Marina asked quickly, defensively. Her expression changed. 'Nearly fifteen years ago, sepsis. Died from a cut on her ankle, can you believe it?' It was a rhetorical question, Marina staring unseeing into the garden. 'I still can't, even after all this time . . . It was the most stupid thing ever – a bit of metal from an old door stopper was sticking out and she caught it as she went past. That was it. Then she got sick and never thought to connect it to the cut. By the time they discovered the infection, it was too late. Way too late.'

'I'm so sorry.'

'Yeah.' The hardness had come back into her voice, the familiar rigidity threading her limbs again.

'What about your father?' Charlotte asked.

'What about him?' Marina asked back, defensively. Charlotte couldn't blame her – it was the one question she herself could never bear to be asked.

'Are you close?'

Marina gave a scornful bark. 'Ha! No. He remarried within the year and moved to Bilbao with the new wife – he said there was more work there, but I don't believe that. *She* just wanted to get him away from us. Men, right? They just move on.' Marina's eyes flashed up. 'I've never met her.' Defiance coloured the words, a child's attempts at spite.

'Your stepmother?'

'She's not that; she's not a mother to me in any sense,' Marina said flatly.

'You sound angry with him.'

Marina hesitated. 'Disappointed maybe. He's not a bad man, just weak; he doesn't know how to be alone.' She gave a hopeless shrug. 'I have always said I would prefer to be happy and alone than together and lonely.'

'You're strong. Not everyone can do that.'

'Grandmother says I take after her. When I left my husband, I left behind everything about him – his name, the ring, our apartment. I started again from new.'

'Why did you leave him?'

'He cheated on me, drank too much beer, smoked too much weed. Could never keep a job.' She shrugged again.

'Did he ever hit you?'

'Only once. And I hit him back harder. That was the day I left. And I never looked back.'

'I'm sure he regrets it now.'

'I know he does. He called me up every day for two months trying to get me back. Too bad,' she said with defiance. 'You can never go back, right? Our momentum must always be forwards.'

Charlotte's smile stuck in place and she merely nodded. She looked away, inhaling deeply and trying to steady her own emotions but Nathan's reappearance in her life underpinned everything, destabilizing her world.

'So it's just you and your grandmother? That's why you're so close?'

'Yeah, growing up she always said we were like peas in a pod, the two Marinas. I'm her mini-me.'

'Still, your grandmother must miss your father,' she said simply. 'To have him live so far away when she's so old . . . Even if he's flawed, he's still her son.'

'Maybe.' Marina was silent for a long moment before she gave a quiet exhale, her shoulders dropping and rounding again, the gathering fight dissipating in her. 'Yeah probably. For my sake, she pretends she doesn't but I can tell she does.'

'Did she have any other children, besides your father?'

'No. She said she had always wanted lots of kids but my grandfather was killed in the war and that was that for her – she never remarried.'

'The Second World War?'

'Worse – the Civil War.'

'Right.' So there were no further heirs then, the blood line on Marina's side hadn't split into multiple tributaries. 'Marina, do you have any idea why your grandmother left here all those years ago? Why she never mentioned that her family was alive?'

'No. Like I said, we thought she was an only child.'

'But now that you know the truth, has she still not said anything? To be a Mendoza, I mean, it's not a name you can escape in this country . . .'

'She won't discuss it.'

'And you're okay with that?' Charlotte pushed. 'This is your family too. Your heritage. Don't you think you have a right to know where you come from, to at least understand why the opportunities and advantages that were rightfully yours were taken away from you? Your life could have been very different. Perhaps *should* have been.'

Charlotte watched her, seeing the bitterness in the set of her mouth, and wondered how her grandmother had just looked on – watching her son cross the country in search of work, her granddaughter's marriage collapse into violence, all of it under the strain of poverty, knowing that with one admission, they could step out of these circumstances at any moment and claim their birthright. It was one thing to have fled her family all those years ago – she must have had her reasons, whatever they might have been. But to continue to actively choose this life, in the face of the deprivations and hardships of subsistence living . . . Could what she had left in wealth really be worse than what her own family now endured in poverty?

Marina looked down, plucking at a loose thread on the duvet. 'I should probably go check on her,' she said evasively, protectively. If she felt betrayed by her grandmother's actions, she wasn't prepared to admit to it yet. 'She's been sleeping a long time. I have to watch her or she won't be able to sleep tonight.'

'But—'

Marina jumped off the bed with a focus that said the conversation was over, and still in her dressing gown, a tattoo of a butterfly evident on her bare left ankle, she walked out of the room and into the one next door.

Disappointed to have been rebuffed, Charlotte followed at a distance, hesitantly putting her head round the door once she heard their voices.

'Good afternoon,' she smiled, stepping into a room identical to next door, only here the bed was draped with grass-green linen. Señora Quincy was lying on top of the bed, pillows plumped around her. 'How are you feeling?'

'Just wonderful,' the old woman smiled back. 'I've had the most wonderful sleep.'

'All that time, Abuela?' Marina chided. 'But I've been gone for three hours!'

'The journey wore me out. I needed the rest. I am an old woman, remember.'

Charlotte frowned as Marina fussed over her. 'You'll never sleep tonight,' she tutted, rearranging the pillows for her.

'Then perhaps I'll stay up past my bedtime,' her grandmother chuckled, her eyes flashing up to Charlotte's. She looked bright. Lighter somehow.

Charlotte smiled back but it was forced. Señora Quincy was not the frail, dotty old lady she might like others to believe. She had not slept for three hours straight; Charlotte had seen her with her own eyes heading straight for the jacaranda tree. And perhaps there was a simple reason for it – a long-forgotten childhood relic now reclaimed. But if it was innocent enough, it begged one equally simple question: why lie about it?

Chapter Sixteen

Madrid, 19 July 1936

She was part of the crowd, a single speck in the sea of bodies gathered up and down the length of the boulevard. There were more people than she had ever seen, far more than she could ever count, and she felt wonderfully insignificant and anonymous for the first time in her life. It wasn't just her image that had changed, with her oversized men's clothes and roughly chopped, boy-cut hair; she had given herself a new name too: Marquez, borrowed from her housemaid. Mendoza carried less social heft in Madrid than in Andalusia but she was taking no chances – not only did she need to stay hidden from the people her family would send looking for her, she also wanted to be judged from now on by her values and intellect, not her pedigree.

She let the tide gather her up and spirit her along towards the plaza, the fervour of the crowd's shouts matching the screams that had raged in her heart ever since that day in the stable almost three weeks earlier. Giant speakers had been positioned in front of the Cortes and the crowd swarmed, waiting for the distinctive voice that always put a shape to their thoughts and dreams; her arm joined theirs, collectively punching the sky, as they shuffled ever onwards, some people standing atop cars or climbing on the street lights, making their voices heard and their might felt as they chanted they would rather die on their feet than live on their knees.

Only yesterday, Franco had declared the overthrow of the Second Republic. After months of violent skirmishes and protests, localized revolutions and repressions, suddenly the country was officially at war – with itself. The Republican government's measures to liberalize the political, social and religious landscape were being tolerated no longer by the old Establishment and stories were already coming in that the highly trained and skilled Army of Africa – which for years had been fighting savage battles in Morocco – was preparing to invade the mainland, a prospect that chilled the blood of the most hard-boiled Republican revolutionary. For no matter how angry the starving labourers were, how were they supposed to fight their own army? If there was fervour, there was also fear.

A sudden whine and blast of static made the crowd pause and take a breath as they waited for the low, gathering voice of Dolores Ibárruri. Every single body turned towards the Cortes and the giant speakers relaying the radio broadcast.

'Workers! Farmers! Antifascists! Patriotic Spaniards! . . .'

Marina felt her heart pound as the voice from the loudspeaker vibrated through her bones. This was it! Revolution! And she was here, a part of it. In an instant, she felt the mood of the crowd lift again. Change would come, it had to. The dynastic traditions of centuries past could not continue as they had. The winds of social change had been blowing through the country for six years – the monarchy was now gone, didactic religion abandoned for education, equal rights being advocated for women . . .

'. . . The country realizes the gravity of the current situation through the bulletins being issued by the government and the Popular Front . . .'

Someone trod on her foot, the pain sudden and intense, making her gasp out, and she glanced across to see a woman beside her, hair worn up in looped plaits and wearing dungarees. She was gazing up rapturously at the disembodied voice, a cigarette dangling between her lips.

'Oh! Sorry, was that your foot?' the woman asked, before breaking into a relaxed smile, the cigarette waggling as she spoke. 'Are you okay? I'm so clumsy.'

'Not at all,' Marina demurred. 'It is rather crowded.'

It was a vast understatement, their bodies compressing into an ever-smaller space as the crowds continued to push in at the back. The woman, taking the cigarette from her mouth, threw her head back and laughed. 'Yes, it is rather, isn't it?' she replied in a hoity-toity voice.

Marina admired the woman's bold, frank manner – she seemed somehow fearless – but she realized that she had also inadvertently betrayed herself, her refined speaking style at odds with the coarse and colloquial language of the crowd. She would have to do better at hiding the manners and etiquette that had been steamrollered into her if she wanted to be accepted as a true Republican. This crowd would turn in an instant if they knew who she was: the daughter of an Andalusian landowner.

'. . . *Communists, socialists, anarchists, Republican democrats . . .*'

'She's amazing,' Marina said, jerking her head towards the government building, hoping the woman hadn't noticed.

The woman looked at her. 'Yes. I have seen her before, last month.'

'Really?' Her excitement and admiration was genuine. 'Did you meet her?'

'Not yet. But I intend to.' The woman looked ahead again, her chin raised determinedly. 'I want to learn from her.'

Marina followed suit. Me too, she thought, feeling a sense of belonging begin to claim her in this crowd. Though she had not been born into their world, still she shared their concerns.

'. . . *the soldiers and services loyal to the Republic have inflicted the first defeats on the insurgents, who drag through the quagmire of treason the military honour they have boasted about so much . . .*'

'Want some?'

Marina looked back to see the woman looking at her, holding out her cigarette between her fingers. She hesitated, then reached for it. 'Thanks.' She had never smoked a cigarette before and she felt the cough roil in her throat as she struggled to hold it down. The woman was smiling at her, as though somehow knowing this was her first, that she was an impostor here. Did she sense that Marina was one of the very people this million-strong crowd wanted to see wiped out?

'Where are you from?' Her eyes narrowed interestedly.

'Seville,' Marina managed to reply, keeping it vague as she handed back the cigarette. 'You?'

'Badajoz.'

'What brought you here?'

The woman tilted her head slightly as though what she had to say tipped her off balance and weighted her down. 'My husband was mayor of our town, a place where the landowners refused to give work to anyone unless they ripped up their union cards . . .'

Marina knew from Santi, all those years ago, that the union cards protected the rights of the workers – entitling them to paid overtime, regulated hours and guaranteed jobs to locals. She also remembered Juan Esperanza's pleas for those very things, for fairness and human dignity, on the steps of her father's foreman's office.

'They were literally starving the workers to death, refusing to give them work. So my husband used municipal money to buy them food.' Her expression changed. 'And for that he was found guilty of "misuse of funds", and murdered.'

Marina's jaw dropped down. 'I'm so sorry.'

The woman gave a shrug but the movement was raw and brittle. 'And you?'

'Me?'

'What made you come here?'

She thought of Juan Esperanza, staggering to stay on his feet, eyes wide as the bullet tore through him. She thought of Indigo, slain in his stable – an eye for an eye, the instrument of Santi's revenge – and felt the tears rush up. 'Similar,' she whispered.

The woman lip-read her mouth, seeing the pain still fresh in her face, and she understood. 'Have you been in Madrid long?'

'I arrived this morning.'

The woman arched an eyebrow, raking her gaze over her and taking in her dusty, stained and torn clothes, her ragged hair, the limp sack over her shoulder. 'Did you come on foot?'

'Pretty much, although I managed to hide on the train from Cordoba to Puertollano.' Marina nodded and the woman nodded too, something in her eyes changing, as though evidence of this pluck and grit, of her flash-flood tears, confirmed she really was part of the struggle, in spite of her ladylike manners.

'. . . The whole country roils with fury at those savages who want to plunge democratic and the people's Spain into a hell of terror and death—'

The woman placed a kindly hand on her shoulder. '. . . Got somewhere to stay?'

Marina hesitated. She hadn't thought that far ahead. Just getting off the estate, out of Andalusia and into Madrid had been as far as she'd been able to think. She knew plenty of people in the capital, of course; she had visited many times with her parents over the years and her mother's sisters lived here, as well as some other close friends. But even if she had known where they lived (which she did not, for she had only ever seen the city through the eyes of a child), she could not contact a single one of them; in their eyes, she was a traitor now, that worst of things – a Republican. 'I will. I'm getting myself sorted,' she said determinedly.

'But they shall not pass!'

The crowd erupted into a roar, *'No pasarán!'* being taken up as a chant, making the hairs on the back of Marina's newly exposed neck stand on end. *'No pasarán! No pasarán!'*

The woman looked around at the ignited mob, then back at her. 'What is your name?'

'Marina Marquez.'

'No pasarán! No pasarán! No pasarán!'

'Well, Marina Marquez, I'm Paloma Rivas,' she said, dropping the cigarette to the ground and grinding it out beneath her hobnailed boot. She stuck out her hand welcomingly, as though Marina had passed some kind of test. 'You just stick with me. I've got somewhere you can stay.'

The apartment was in the Salamanca district, at the very top of a grand old peach-tinted building, which gave the impression of blushing in the dusk. Glazed, fully enclosed verandas were stepped all the way up the facade and sycamore trees shaded the streets below, protecting the residents from the harshness of the Spanish sun.

Inside, the genteel nature of the place continued: black and white marble floors, a grand cantilevered staircase, and there was an elaborate cage lift but it appeared to be out of order. The tall lemon tree in the atrium looked dusty and parched.

Marina frowned, feeling a strange twitch in her heart as she followed Paloma up the stairs, catching sight of a broken lace parasol left propped in one corner. No one else appeared to be around, which felt odd coming straight from a crowd of tens of thousands; she knew the city was full to the brim and yet there was an air of abandonment here.

Paloma stopped outside a set of black panelled double doors – they were vast, at least ten feet high – and Marina listened as she gave a series of knocks in sequence, like a code.

A moment later the door opened and a young woman peered out. 'Oh good, you're back. We lost sight of you in the crowd.'

'Hey,' Paloma said, pulling off her cap and tossing it onto a table in the entrance hall, before striding through into another room. Hesitantly, Marina followed after her, seeing how the girl simply stared. Marina nodded cautiously but the girl said nothing, as though it wasn't her place to pass comment.

They walked. Marina heard the door close behind her, the girl's footsteps just behind her own, her gaze raking over Marina's jagged, jaded appearance. It had been nine days since she had last bathed and she hadn't slept or even sat on a soft surface in all that time either, unless the mail sack on the train counted. Her food pack had had to suffice for a pillow for the first few days – lumpy though it had been – but once she had finished her supplies, it had been as comfortable to sleep on as a napkin.

But tired as she was, she felt wired right now, her body on

high alert as she took in every detail of the deceptively lavish apartment – the deeply architraved doorways two men wide, the cornice details on the high ceilings, the Versailles panelled floors. Wasn't this everything she had just run from? Escaped?

She turned into the drawing room, or rather, what had been the drawing room, for only a solitary crystal chandelier still remained. Hanging low from the ceiling – albeit its glittering light long since diminished by thick layers of dust – it stood as a token of the belle époque world that had once gently beat within these walls. Several dead plants stood skeletal in their pots; the walls were rimmed with the outlines of Old Masters now removed to new pastures. Marina had grown up in rooms exactly such as this. She didn't even need to close her eyes to envisage the parties that had been held here – christenings and Christmases and birthdays, women in beautiful dresses that skimmed the parquet floors. She knew these rooms. She knew this one.

Now, though, it wasn't so much a haven as a hive, some sort of headquarters with long industrial tables set up with papers and, on the back wall, a giant map of Spain. Several smaller desks were set by the windows, ugly filing cabinets pressed against the shutters.

A middle-aged woman was sitting at a typewriter, typing fast, the *tat-tat-tat* of the keys punctuating the low murmur of intense conversation: two men poring over something in a folder and arguing amongst themselves as they jabbed at a photograph.

'Hey.' Paloma's voice was assertive, and Marina understood she was a leader here – although of what, she didn't yet know.

Everyone turned. The woman stopped typing, the men arguing, as they caught sight of this new stranger.

'Guys, this is Marina Marquez. We just met in the rally.

She's arrived from Andalusia this morning and has nowhere else to stay. So I've told her she's with us now.' It was said as a statement of fact, not a question. She turned back and squeezed Marina's shoulder like a big sister. 'These fellows are okay, you can trust them, all right?

One of the men straightened up, his eyes narrowing suspiciously. He was a slight man with an underbite and wire-rimmed glasses, but there was a toughness in his expression that made him somehow assume more space.

'This is Sindo Coronella. He is our leader. Sindo has valuable contacts both in the government and in the police. If he says we act, then we act, you got it?' Marina instinctively nodded. 'No second-guessing. Sindo coordinates all our activities.'

Paloma pointed to the man next to him: bearded and all-round bigger but somehow less menacing. 'Ivan Gutierrez. Before this, a mechanic, and before that, a soldier in the army. He knows how to handle weapons – how to strip a rifle, clean it, reassemble it again. It is a rare skill for our fighters and one of our biggest disadvantages against the Africanistas. But do not worry, he will show you too.'

She was to handle a rifle? She remembered the gunshot that had killed Juan Esperanza, and how the sound of it had rung in her head, over and over in the weeks afterwards. Stopping her from sleeping, eating . . . But that was then, a lifetime ago. She was a different person now and this was war. Marina Mendoza may have run from this but Marina Marquez would do what had to be done.

Ivan nodded in greeting and she chanced a tiny smile.

'Luciana here helps with the propaganda side. She writes, prints and helps distribute our posters.' The woman at the typewriter nodded.

'And Marta, behind you, is like us: a foot soldier. We go where we're told and do as we're asked. There are others of course – they come at different times and go again; but we live here. We are the beating heart.' Her eyes were dark and intensely fixed upon Marina's. 'Help us, work with us and you will have a home here. Those are the terms of the arrangement. Will you join our cause?'

Marina hesitated. 'I'm not entirely sure what your cause is,' she said uncertainly.

Paloma threw out her hands as though it was obvious. 'Why, the overthrow of the Nationalist dogs. The eradication of the Carlist elite. Rights for workers. A fair democracy.'

Marina looked back at the strangers watching her – Sindo, Ivan, Luciana, Marta, and of course Paloma. Were they her family now? They wanted the same things after all. She thought of Juan and Santi, of Arlo – all the people she had loved and lost in different ways. The family she had once had. What choice did she have? Who else was there for her in this world? 'Then I'm in,' she shrugged.

Her words seemed to pop the bubble that had formed around her in the apartment, releasing the tension, and she gave a nervous laugh as the others cheerily rushed over to welcome her formally, Ivan clapping her on the back, Marta and Luciana throwing their arms around her as though she was a long-lost daughter. Only Sindo was restrained, greeting her with a handshake: his skin was cool to the touch, his grip firm, reinforcing her initial impression that he was a man not to be trifled with.

'Welcome to the club,' he said in a quiet voice, so quiet she almost had to lean closer.

'Thank you.'

'Andalusia, Paloma said?'

She nodded. 'That's right. Near Seville.'

It was a white lie. Technically, Ronda was closer to Malaga but she needed to walk a tightrope – putting distance between her and her abandoned family, whilst remaining close enough to the area to be able to discuss it familiarly.

'My people are from Cordoba.'

'Oh,' she nodded, feeling her heart beat faster. 'I have never been there. I would like to visit – one day.'

'When the agrarian oligarchy is annihilated.' It was a question. Or perhaps a test.

'Of course.'

He looked at her, his expression partially obscured by the reflection on his glasses, and she wondered – did he know? Could he see past the shorn hair and the dirty face and see she was no poverty-born revolutionary? Did he recognize her? Her family's renown in the region was so great, her father always used to boast the fame of their bulls brought people not to see the matadors but the beasts themselves. Mendoza was a name he would know.

Finally, though, he nodded, looking down the length of her. The food sack, empty now, hung limply across her body. 'That is all you have?'

She nodded, not daring to offer more and reveal she had run away. Most of the Republican fighters travelled with and fought for their families, not against them.

'Then go through to the bedroom and rest. You look weary.'

'I'm ready to work,' she said stoically, even though she couldn't think of anything more enticing than a stuffed mattress and twelve hours of oblivion. It had been so long since she had slept well.

His eyes saw everything, it seemed. 'Rest first. The cause

can wait a few hours. You will be more use to us after a wash and some sleep.'

She nodded, looking down. She turned and walked towards the door.

'The bedroom is the third door—'

On the right, she willed him to say.

'On the left.'

She smiled her thanks and walked out, but her heart was thudding alarmingly now, her eyes tripping over the friezed walls as some of the details came back: had there been a small oil of a mountain scene here? An oval table against that wall there? Perhaps. Or perhaps not, these places must look all the same, surely? But there was one thing she did remember, something even a little girl could not confuse or forget. She walked to the doorway, third on the left, and looked in – and up.

The adrenaline spiked through her, making her hands tingle and her palms sweat, for the celestial skies painted on the ceiling were exactly as she remembered and there was no denying it any more. She could hardly bear the irony of it, the unfairness that she had fled her home and travelled across the country by foot – only to end up here. In her godmother's house.

Chapter Seventeen

NM. SE.

Charlotte stared at the initials carved roughly into the bark of the jacaranda tree; they had been crudely etched and would have been almost completely obscured were it not for the especially smooth wood here of the black fissure, like a necrotic wound, running down the trunk on this side. The carving was conveniently hidden from the house, even though the tree was in plain view of it, sitting front and centre between the two spectacular wings.

Checking no one was watching – it would have been hard to explain why she was standing in the middle of a flowerbed – she crouched down and reached her hand in, feeling blindly for something, anything: nothing. Whatever might once have been there, Señora Quincy clearly had it now. It was remarkable it should still have been there after all this time, even more remarkable that she should have remembered it.

With a sigh, she rose, her fingers tracing over the initials once more as she wondered who had carved them and why. NM – one of the Mendozas? She ran through the names she knew of from the file: Mateo, his wife Cristabel, son Felipe, daughters Isabella and Sofia . . . father Carlos, mother Matilda. No Ns though . . .

She picked her way carefully out of the flowerbed and resumed her stroll around the gardens. It was that point in the late afternoon when the sun hung like a peach, heavy and ripe and blushing in the sky; the worst of the heat of the day had passed and the cicadas were still an hour off starting up their scratching racket. She had left her book and a cool drink under the veranda and she headed back there now, restless, anxious to get on.

It had been a slow day and, frankly, pointless. The Marinas were still hiding out, barely venturing from their rooms, Nathan was missing in action somewhere – she hadn't seen or heard him since his run. As far as she could see, there was no point at all in her being here, whilst perversely, in London, her presence was desperately needed . . .

She had had another shower after her workout, lunch on her own, and now she was just watching the shadows lengthen, killing time and waiting to go. It had been a wasted day. Finally, though, time had obliged her and Mayra had gone to find an estate worker to drive her to the plane; her overnight bag was packed and she could almost taste her escape.

The sound of shoes on the flagstones made her look up expectantly. She reached for her overnight bag and stood in anticipation.

'—Oh, it's you,' she said in surprise as Nathan leaned around the doorway.

'I'm afraid so,' he murmured.

There was a pause and she noticed his gaze managed to land everywhere but her. An awkward silence bloomed. What did he want?

'I understand you're flying out.' She nodded, hoping he wouldn't ask why. 'Mayra's asked me to drop you on my way. They've given me use of the car while I'm here.'

'Oh.' Wasn't there a golf cart she could use? She could drive it there herself. '. . . Right.'

She picked up the bag and followed him down the cool dark hallway, their footsteps out of time with one another. They walked through the main hall, below the pardoned bulls, down the steps into the courtyard and over to a shiny red jeep.

The keys were hanging in the ignition. She got in beside him and busied herself with untwisting her seat belt as he turned the engine on and pulled away, the wheels back-spinning momentarily so that a cloud of dust obscured their departure from the house. The radio station had been left tuned to a channel playing obscure Euro pop hits but he, predictably, managed only a few minutes before switching over to a talk channel.

'So where are you off to?' she asked stiffly, feeling the need to pierce the silence between them.

'Ronda. I'm going to check the local records for someone.'

'Who?'

'A man called Jack Quincy.'

'. . . Marina's husband?'

'I think so, yes.'

'Think so?'

'There could be other candidates but I'm starting with the assumption that Quincy, which clearly isn't a Spanish name, could be American, possibly British. Therefore I've checked the records for the International Brigades and found three Quincys – all American – who signed up to serve.' His voice was flat and toneless. 'One, Edward, died on the ship over. Another, Theodore, fought in Barcelona and returned to the States in early '39. But I've ruled him out – he was gay and lived with his partner in San Francisco until his death in 1972.'

'If he's dead, how do you know he was gay?'

'I spoke to his business partner's son,' he said shortly. 'The last one, Jack, came by ship to Malaga and was killed in Madrid in the spring of 1937. He looks the most likely.'

'What do you know about him?'

He shrugged. 'Former Baptist minister from Oregon. Landed in Malaga as part of the first wave of international volunteers. Seems to have arrived in Ronda sometime in November '36 and helped coordinate a local resistance group before moving on, probably up to the capital.'

'When did he leave here?'

'That's what I'm trying to find out but it must have been early on. This region was one of the first to fall to the fascists. There had been various attempted uprisings against the Establishment in the years before the war and the subsequent reprisals were severe and, let's just say, disproportionate. It was no place for the reds to hang around.'

Charlotte looked across at him, wondering if there was more, but he was staring straight ahead, his jaw set; he certainly didn't look to be offering anything further. She pulled her gaze off him again, looking out of the window as they sped along, seeing how the grass was beginning to lose its manicured edges as they pulled to the further reaches of the estate, the green becoming less vibrant as grass was replaced with hay.

Just a few more minutes and they'd be back at the plane; she'd be heading back to London, away from here and him . . .

She tried to ignore the wafts of his aftershave – Aramis, still – that kept drifting over in the wind; she determined not to notice how he still drove with his hands splayed against the wheel, the upper tips of his fingers free to tap along to the music—

He turned back to her, the excitement clear and bright on his face. Paul McCartney was singing within touching distance of their table and she knew it was taking all his self-control not to reach out and check he was real, that this was actually happening. He hadn't believed her at first when she'd said he'd be performing at her mother's birthday celebrations.

'Are you a fan?' Cecilia Fairfax asked him, sitting on his right.

'Ever since I first heard "Strawberry Fields",' he replied. 'My mother saw the Beatles at the Cavern in '61.'

'Oh? Are your people from Liverpool?'

He frowned. 'No. Sheffield.'

'Ah, I've never been. Always meant to get up there but you know how it is.'

'Any objection if I smoke?' he asked rhetorically, pulling a packet from his shirt pocket anyway.

The question brought her back from the reverie with a start. 'Since when do you smoke?'

'Since forever.'

Define 'forever', she wanted to say. The moment after she'd broken them?

She leaned against the cubicle, light-headed. She had drunk too much again.

Heels clipped in on the Portland stone floor, sequinned evening bags splaying on the marble counter. The sound of rushing water.

'. . . He's an interesting fellow, though. There's something about him, even if he does have that accent.'

'Oh, don't buy into it.' Her mother's voice: bored, manicured. 'This is just her latest rebellion. She's trying to get a reaction from me, falling in love with a boy from the wrong side of the tracks. It'll never last.' Her heart began to race.

'I don't know, Petra, they certainly seem smitten.'

'Precisely. They'll burn brightly and then the novelty will wear off and she'll see what's blindingly obvious to the rest of us – that he doesn't fit. I mean, he's sweet enough, but he's clearly out of his depth. Did you see him at dinner? He had no idea about the fish knife; he was using it upside down, poor chap.'

Cecilia Fairfax tittered. 'Oh, put him out of his misery now.'

They were quiet for a few moments, no doubt rearranging their hair, refreshing their make-up.

'Do you remember when they were little,' Cecilia said in a strange voice and Charlotte knew she was pulling down her lips as she reapplied her mascara. 'We always used to think Lotts would end up with Jules? They just seemed to go so well together.'

'They still do.'

'Mmm. Such a shame they broke up. Jules has really gone off the rails again. I think she was rather a calming influence on him.'

'And vice versa, darling.'

'Jules? Calming?' Cecilia sounded confused.

'Oh, I know he's a little wild but he'll calm down soon enough. It's a phase. And the thing is, he understands her – that's what she needs, although God knows she'd never admit to knowing it.' There was a small pause. 'I'll tell you something I've never said to anyone before,' her mother said, dropping her voice a little. 'But I've always been so worried Charlotte will take after her father. They're so alike it frightens me.'

'You mean—?'

'Their passions, excesses, yes. Life's too easy for them. Everything's a party.'

'So then, couldn't this boy be good for her? He seems very stable.'

'No! On the contrary, he's the very worst thing for her. Don't you see? He's just another of her obsessions, an infatuation, a novelty act. What she needs is someone who comes from her world, who's not impressed by it all. I mean, I really thought at one point that boy was going to invade the stage and piggyback Paul—'

He didn't wait for her answer, lighting it easily, one-handed, as he drove. Practised, deft, angry, she saw he was no longer, in any lingering way, the man-child she'd once known, struggling to find his new place in the world. His beautiful enquiring mind had dislocated him from his roots into her star-dusted orbit, before spinning him out again into another world – this one, in the Spanish heat and dust, with a sexy woman on a balcony and a baby on her hip.

'What's her name?'

She hadn't meant to say it out loud, but it was uncontainable, the question lurching from her like seeds spilling from a pod, as inevitable and natural as a cloud bursting with rain. 'Your wife, I mean.' She looked down at his hand – no ring, but that meant nothing; plenty of men didn't wear wedding rings. Her father hadn't. 'Or girlfriend. The one at the apartment.'

He looked dumbfounded by the question, as though it was somehow scandalous she had dared to ask it. 'That's none of your business.'

'I'm only asking her name, not her life story.'

He glanced across at her angrily. 'You don't need to know anything about her. She's nothing to do with you.'

Charlotte watched his profile as he drove, faster again. 'So – what? I'm not allowed to know anything about your life? Nothing?'

He looked dead ahead. 'That's right. Nothing at all.'

'Why not? What is it you think I'm going to do? Tell her about us?'

'I already told you, there is no "us",' he snapped, his fingertips curling round the top of the steering wheel, tightening. 'I fell in love with you once. It's not a mistake I intend to repeat.'

She stared at him, pummelled by the words. She'd been a *mistake* to him? 'Did you plan it all? All this?'

'Did I *what*?'

'You must have known it was me you were coming to see. Rosie would have given you my details. I was sitting there waiting for Dr Ferrante. But you – you knew it was me you were coming to meet.' She watched him, seeing how his grip tightened on the wheel. 'How long have you been waiting to hurt me back? All that time?'

'I haven't been waiting.' He looked across at her, their eyes connecting even as the car bumped along on the rough track. He shrugged. 'I did it because I could.'

The coldness of his words took her breath away. She had been that easy to play? She had meant nothing at all . . . ? The tears slid treacherously from the corners of her eyes but she couldn't stop them.

He looked away again, his expression setting harder still.

'Has what I did really tormented you that much, that you're prepared to sacrifice your own family, everything that's good in your life, just for the chance to get back at me?' she cried. 'Was it worth potentially losing them . . . ?' The words fell from her, torn from her lips, as she suddenly lurched forwards, her head almost hitting the dash as the car came to a sudden stop. The smell of burning rubber came to her nose and she saw the car had stopped at a skewed angle.

'I'm not losing anything. Not for you. Not again.'

She looked at him in bafflement. The bumper was inches from an old dry stone wall. Had he almost crashed the car to win a fight?

'I didn't ask for any of this, okay?' he snapped. 'I didn't want you back in my life and I didn't go looking for it. I don't want to be here now and I don't want you to be here. I don't even know why you are here! *Why* are you here?' He threw out his hands in utter exasperation. 'You're not a researcher! You can't help! Why the fuck are you here?'

His anger shook her to the core; she had never seen him angry before, not even that day, the last day . . . 'Because the client asked me to be,' she said quietly.

He said nothing for a moment, his eyes roaming her face with a dark expression that left her frozen in its wake; even her tears had stopped mid-track. How had she not seen any of this, lying in his arms? How could she have blinded herself to the truth of what they were now, strangers determined to hurt and wound one another, to inflict death by a thousand cuts.

He turned away, ball pulsing in his jaw as he steadied his breathing and she watched as he stretched his fingers straight, visibly forcing them out of a fist. He took a deep breath and leant down to the ignition, starting up the engine again. 'Just stay away from me, Lotts, and let me do my job.'

Did he know he'd said it? The sound of her pet name in his voice . . . she went cold, goosebumps rippling on her skin, the past keeping pace with them again. She saw the slip register on his features, surprise and then anger flitting over them.

'I'll finish up as soon as I can and then we will never have to see each other again. Until then, we will have to tolerate the situation, which I am doing my level best to do; as far as I'm concerned, you're not even in this car right now.'

It was another moment before she could speak. '. . . Right. Got it,' she said in a half-whisper.

He straightened the car up and drove her the rest of the way in silence, dropping her off at the gleaming plane that was refuelled and waiting for her on the airstrip. She got out without a word and he drove off without looking back. Within five minutes, she was up in the sky, tears she couldn't stop streaming down her cheeks, as she looked out of the window in fragile stillness, her gaze casting down over a field of grazing donkeys, over striped parcels of olive groves, over a red dot that was moving silently and ever further away through the Andalusian landscape.

Chapter Eighteen

London

'Oh my God, I have *literally* been having kittens,' Mouse cried as she ran through the door into the suite three hours later. 'What happened? You said you'd be here at seven?'

'And I was,' Charlotte panted, throwing down her bag and giving her sister a quick hug. She looked sensational in her acid-yellow pleated dress with pale-pink lace inserts, her long brown hair worn back in some sort of intricate but edgy braid. 'There was a security alert at Whitechapel and half of Embankment's got roadworks. I've just spent ninety minutes sitting in a cab, stuck in bloody traffic. Where's Ma?'

'Downstairs with your dearly beloved and the outlaws, trying to pretend everything's tickety-boo.' She poured a glass of Dom Perignon and handed it to her. 'Here, bolt that.'

Charlotte did as she was told, feeling the worst of her agitation begin to dim. Mouse, for all her histrionics and dramas, was the one person who could read her, reach her.

'So how's this?' Mouse held up a dress on a hanger – black silk chiffon with a pink rosebud print, it had a crossover bust, translucent skinny sleeves and long flowing skirt.

Charlotte smiled, feeling her shoulders drop another inch. It was good to be back. 'Nailed it! Sis, you are a star.'

'Yes, well, someone had to take charge. Clearly you'd have just . . . worn that,' she replied, taking in Charlotte's creased khaki linen shorts and white shirt. 'Matty thought it'd suit you. She said she'd been holding it back for you anyway.'

'Yes, I must go in and see her,' Charlotte sighed, sipping from her glass as she began to unbutton her shirt. 'I need some new pieces for next season.' She padded through to the bathroom and showered quickly, emerging minutes later with pink cheeks and brighter eyes – the puffiness had all but gone now, thanks to the protracted taxi ride too. No one would ever guess she'd spent the entire flight in tears.

Mouse had refilled her glass and sat beside her on the chaise, swinging one long tanned leg idly as Charlotte quickly did her make-up.

'Is everyone here?' she asked, carefully applying a nude eyeshadow.

'Everyone who's anyone,' Mouse shrugged. 'All awaiting your grand entrance.'

'Ha, I hope they're not going to be disappointed then,' she muttered.

'As if. You're the peacock in every room, whether you like it or not.' Charlotte glanced over at her. Mouse's own wild partying stage had come late, after their father's death. She had been an awkward teen before that and Charlotte had the sense she had unwittingly cast a long shadow over her little sister, something she'd been trying to make up for ever since. 'Even your ex has made it.'

Charlotte's hand dropped down like a stone. 'What?' Her voice sounded cleaved.

'Jules?' Mouse arched an eyebrow.

' . . . Oh.' She looked down at the dressing table, her eye picking up the microscopic grains of Chanel pressed powder on the glass. She tried to bring her heart rate straight back down again.

'Who'd you think I meant?'

Charlotte shook her head and swallowed. 'No one.'

Mouse frowned, quiet for a moment as she watched her. '. . . I take it you've heard the latest?'

Charlotte didn't stop moving to listen, blending the shadow up onto her brow bone; there was always news of some sort about Jules. 'Nope. What's he done now?' she asked, bored, far more interested in her make-up.

Mouse laughed loudly. 'I can't believe you haven't heard! Honestly, don't you two ever talk?'

'We didn't talk while we were married, why would we talk now?' Charlotte muttered, looking for her brown kohl.

'He's going to be a father.'

She found it, pulling it out and checking the point was sharp enough. 'Really?' she murmured. The news only vaguely surprised, rather than shocked, her. He had been engaged to Jemima Astoria for a few months now, after surprising himself, as well as his intended, by proposing at a party in Ibiza. 'Well, that's great.'

'Yeah. But that's not the thing,' Mouse said, revelling in the gossip, her slim leg swinging faster.

'No? What's the thing?' Charlotte murmured, applying her mascara, eyes pulled wide.

'It's not Jemima that's preggers. It's Violet.'

Charlotte's hand dropped again. 'Her sister?' she gasped, sitting back in the chair in shock.

'I know. Been at it for months apparently, the dirty dog,' Mouse tutted, eyes bright with the scandal of it all.

Charlotte rubbed her hands over her face, feeling somehow

tainted by the news. 'Poor Jem, she must be devastated. She's hardly the most resilient girl.'

'Whole family's gone batshit appaz,' Mouse said, holding her hands up in the air and sloshing champagne onto the carpet.

'I'm not surprised. Is Violet keeping the baby?'

'Must be. Otherwise this could have all blown over quietly, couldn't it? She could easily have got rid of it without anyone ever knowing and things could have carried on between them as they were.'

'Unless she wanted more from him than a fling.'

Mouse wagged her finger. 'Which would be typical of her – she always did want everything Jemima had.'

Charlotte inhaled deeply, feeling the tendrils from her old life reaching out to her and inching ever closer.

'Honestly, what you ever saw in him,' Mouse tutted.

'Yes, well, I think we both know the answer to that one.' She tried to draw a line under the conversation, to move on and away. She got up and slipped off the bathrobe, stepping into the dress. 'Can you do me up?'

Mouse stood, looking six feet tall in her heels, and zipped the dress, stepping back to admire Charlotte's reflection in the mirror. 'Yeah. Nailed it,' she nodded, congratulating herself. 'Stephen Rathbone is going to be the most envied man in London tonight.'

'Hardly.'

'He will,' Mouse said simply, reaching down to pick up her clutch. 'Ready then?'

Charlotte slid her feet into the new strappy black heels left out for her too and straightened up, taking a deep breath as she caught her own gaze in the mirror. She looked transformed:

revitalized; beautiful; free. With almost one and a half thousand miles between her and her past, she felt like she could breathe again, see clearly. Being with Nathan at La Ventilla had been like having her face pressed against a pane of glass – it had been hard to breathe, to focus. But in this beautiful hotel suite, with her sister beside her and the man she was going to marry patiently waiting for her downstairs, she could see the bigger picture again. This was how things were always supposed to have been.

She smiled back at her sister. 'I'm ready.'

It was a fairytale princess moment – not the kind of thing she had ever dreamed about because she had never wanted to be a princess – but special nonetheless, heads turning, everyone smiling and an audible gasp of delight as she entered the room.

'My God, you are worth waiting for,' Stephen said proudly, catching sight of her and coming over. She smiled hard but felt a deep and sudden bolt of shame as he approached. It was the first time she had seen him since being with Nathan and the most striking thing, out there anyway, had been how very *un*guilty she had felt about her betrayal. But standing before him now – could he tell? Sense it?

He came over with his trademark deportment, looking dashing in a navy lounge suit, pale-blue shirt and primrose-yellow Windsor-knotted Hermes tie.

'Traffic, I'm sorry,' she said in a low voice, beneath her smile, as he kissed her on each cheek, as he always did when they were in public.

'We'll discuss it later,' he murmured in her ear and she knew he was still angry with her from their disagreement earlier.

'Darling! You look radiant!' her mother trilled, looking newly trim from her 48-hour flash visit to the Mayr clinic in

Austria, where she had had to chew every mouthful of food one hundred times before swallowing. She always popped over there before any 'big event' and Mouse had made her laugh in the lifts on the way down, impersonating their mother's deeply ingrained need to always keep the small talk going at dinner while everyone was busy counting.

'Hello, Mama, you look beautiful.'

'I'm glowing from the inside, Lotty darling. To see my eldest daughter marrying the man of her dreams has always been my greatest wish.' She reached over and squeezed her future son-in-law's hand. 'You make such a beautiful couple and I just know you're going to be so happy together.' Charlotte stretched her smile wider as everyone nodded. 'Now all I need to worry about is finding someone equally suitable for Mouse.'

'Ha, don't hold your breath,' Mouse muttered with a roll of her eyes and another swig of fizz, before seeing her mother's expression. 'By which I mean, Lotts has snagged the last of the good ones. I swear old Stevie here was the best man left in London.'

'You'll have to travel then,' Charlotte winked, immediately banishing from her mind the pop-up image of Nathan, in Spain, in bed.

She determinedly sipped more of her champagne, allowing her gaze to travel the room. Most of the guests were from the groom's side: friends from school, Sandhurst, the corporate finance world, some High Court contacts of his father . . . She had perhaps thirty people there, most of them friends from school and Cambridge. She hadn't invited anyone from work; unlike her fiancé, she preferred to keep her private and professional lives separate.

It was interesting – amusing, in fact – watching the two sides mix. She could see her friend Bee caught in conversation with Stephen's father, Toby. There was a lot of earnest nodding going on, heads tilted empathetically; Bee looked and sounded the part – her father was a viscount – but Charlotte wondered whether Toby, a High Court judge, would be quite so enamoured by her if he knew that Bee had been their main weed dealer in sixth form.

Stephen's mother on the other hand was excitably holding court with Jules and clearly oblivious to the fact that he was her future daughter-in-law's ex-husband. She watched Harriet's extravagant hand gestures, the feather bouncing wildly in her fascinator – Jules tended to have that effect on women, regardless of age or marital status. He was leaning against a pillar, one hand stuck in his trouser pocket, and letting her talk, regarding her with that insouciant gaze that made most of them capitulate. He was irritatingly beautiful – straight, dark hair, ever-smiling mouth, dancing eyes. It was little wonder he had seduced and impregnated his future sister-in-law too.

As if sensing her gaze, he lifted his eyes without moving his head. She arched an eyebrow that asked what he thought he was doing? His arch in reply said 'why not?' They had always understood each other. It was why it had always been so easy to be with him. Everything about them worked – backgrounds, social circles . . . Their mothers had been right – they just looked well together; like a Ralph Lauren ad, their Cambridge mates had always said. No one seemed to think it was important that he drove her nuts – with his carelessness, his laziness, his spoilt arrogance – and they certainly would never have understood that she didn't fancy him. Yes, he was gorgeous but she had never responded to him on an animalistic, chemical level. The great secret they had successfully kept from everyone – and she knew he had felt it too – was that they were more like brother and sister than lovers.

He winked at her and she gave him the barest smile in return, turning away quickly before her mother-in-law could see who had snaffled his attention.

Stephen was standing in a small group with her mother and her mother's friends. Charlotte wandered over, sliding her arm into the crook of his elbow. 'Mind if I steal him away for a sec?' she smiled, doing just that.

Arms linked, they went and stood by a window overlooking the river. The tide was out, barges resting on mudbanks, giant tyres dangling from chains as make-do fenders on the jetties, the Thames a blonde rope in the evening sunshine, wending its way out to sea.

'I missed you,' she said, looking up at him, one hand resting on his chest, fiddling lightly with his tie.

He didn't reply immediately and she could see the hurt in his eyes, the frustration. 'I missed you too,' he said finally.

'I'm so sorry about this week. I know I've behaved badly, made the wrong decisions. I should have been here, put you first. I promise I'll make it up to you.' This was not the time to tell him she was due back there again tomorrow. Not the time at all.

He watched her fidget like she was a specimen under his microscope. 'I thought perhaps it was . . . symptomatic of something else.'

'Like what?' she frowned.

He regarded her closely. 'Change of heart.'

'What?' She gave a shocked laugh. 'Why would you think that?'

'Come on Charlotte, you've hardly been enthusiastic. I never thought *I'd* be the one choosing napkin colours.'

Another time, it might have been a wry comment, but she saw the questions in his eyes. He had his doubts about her commitment. 'Stephen, I love you, I do. And I can't wait to be your wife. I know we're going to be so happy together.' She pressed her hands to his chest and gazed up at him.

But he was unmoved. 'You sound just like your mother when you say that.'

She bit her lip, feeling the anxiety ratchet up again. 'Okay look, full disclosure: perhaps I *have* been overcompensating for what happened with Jules. First time round, I robbed Mama of the opportunity to plan my wedding, it was something I just hadn't thought about from her point of view and she was so devastated. I thought this time, doing it properly, handing the organization over to her would be a way to make up for that.' She shrugged. 'But perhaps I stepped too far back and that's why I've struggled to feel . . . involved.'

'You're the bride.'

'I know.'

'Everyone told me to expect bridezilla, but instead . . .' His voice trailed off.

'Stephen, I've felt a lot of shame for running off with Jules the way I did. It hurt a lot of people and it . . .' Nathan flickered in her mind again, as bright and alive as if he were in front of her, not Stephen. 'Well, it was devastating in so many ways.'

It was the clatter of baked bean cans tied to the bumper and rattling on the road behind them, that woke everyone up. Lights began switching on, curtains were pulled back. A few voices called across the quad at the sight of the old gull-wing parked at an angle on the grass.

'Fairfax! What the fuck?'

Jules opened the car door and fell out, his palms on the ground to push him back up as he staggered around to open hers. Always the gentleman. It was raining, the water pooling on the cream leather back seats, but they didn't care. They hadn't wanted the top up.

They had liked the feeling of the wind on their faces as they drove back from the airport; she had liked her face being wet as she screamed and laughed and cried all at once, her hair whipping about, her arms above her head, the magnum of Moet wedged between her legs.

She felt distant, disembodied, the growing fuss around them increasingly perplexing as she too tried – several times – to get out of the car. She finally managed it, holding up the bottle like it was some sort of trophy. A cheer went up, some of the bystanders swigging it in their pyjamas, their underwear.

'We got fucking married, man!' Jules was laughing, staggering about and almost falling over as his friends high-fived him. The place erupted. No one was sleeping now. Students were hanging out of the window, listening in, joining in.

Jules came over and slung his arm around her shoulders, almost sending her legs out from beneath her and kissing her messily on the mouth. She'd never been this out of it before. She couldn't even remember exactly what she'd taken, what she'd done. She just knew that she couldn't feel much and that that had been precisely the point.

Some of her friends were squealing, clasping hands as they jumped up and down in the rain, excited by the night's development, and they all began to move as one towards the college. A gang. A pack.

Through the narrow doors, they fell back into smaller groups, couples and single file, banging on doors as they passed, raising the house. Jules was still hanging off her, lurching wildly, sending them both into the walls and then off again. He kept laughing but she . . . she couldn't stop crying. Why was she crying? Her mascara streaking down her cheeks, her hair tangled and wind-whipped.

Up the stairs they went, falling up them, past a door that was already open. Nathan was standing in it wearing just his pyjama bottoms, oblivious to everything but the sight of her. Wrecked.

Their eyes locked and she felt time slow as she passed by, seeing the look in his eyes. Neither one uttered a sound but they both felt it – the shattering of something good, something right, something pristine.

And then he was out of sight, behind her, already part of her past. Another regret.

Her greatest regret.

'I've been just trying to do things differently this time. I don't want to make the same mistakes.'

He looked back at her for a minute as though assessing her for risk. A born soldier. 'Okay, fine,' he said eventually. 'Let's just get through the next week without any further mishaps. Things will settle down again once this wedding business is all done and dusted.'

She gave a thin smile. 'Exactly.'

'Hey! The happy couple.'

They turned to find Jules sauntering over, arms wide, legs bending at the knee playfully.

'Jules,' she sighed, letting him reach over and kiss her cheek.

'Talk of the devil,' Stephen said wryly, pumping his hand with extra grip. 'We were just talking about you.'

Jules held his hands up in surrender. 'Whatever it was, I sincerely apologize, I wasn't in my right mind. I lost that years ago.'

Stephen allowed a bemused tiny smile. He had always somehow understood her ex-husband was no threat, as though he'd got the measure of him. 'Hmm. Well, I'd better mingle. Don't spend too long *reminiscing*.'

He walked off, joining a couple of his father's friends.

'Christ, does he always have to walk like he's chewing a toffee in his arse?' Jules murmured, looking back at her wickedly.

'Oh? Have you got a suite of walks then? One for every occasion?'

He laughed, shooting her a dazzling smile. Her sarcasm had always thrilled him; she was one of the only females on the planet not to fall at his feet and agree with everything he said. 'God, I miss you.'

'No you don't.'

'No, I don't, you're right. You were always far too clever for me. I could never quite get ahead of you. You usually made me feel about this small.' He pinched his index finger and thumb together.

'Careful. People will wonder what we're talking about,' she said waspishly, having another sip of her drink, although frankly she was grateful for the light relief. The conversation with Stephen had left her feeling rattled again, every declaration of love somehow resurrecting memories of Nathan and the terrible thing she'd done.

'You're looking absolutely stunning, by the way. That dress.' He nodded appreciatively, looking her up and down.

She tipped her head to the side and stared at him. 'What is it, Jules? I always know when you're trying to butter me up.'

His eyes glittered as he took a step closer. 'Well, there is this thing I thought you should know.'

'Don't worry, I already know about your "thing",' she murmured, looking around the room again. She knew she was going to have to mingle, she couldn't put it off any longer.

He looked surprised. 'You do?'

'Well, of course. Everyone here does.' She pinned him with another hard stare. 'You know, you really are an utter shit sometimes, Jules.'

He looked blankly at her before realization dawned. 'Oh, you mean Violet?' He pulled an apologetic face. 'Yes, not my finest hour.'

'I should say not.'

'Pretty tricky.' He nodded self-pityingly.

'Sticky wicket if ever I saw one,' she sighed, losing interest. She was glad his problems weren't hers any more.

'Yeah,' he agreed, before suddenly shaking his head again. 'But no – it wasn't that I wanted to talk to you about.'

She looked back at him and was alarmed to see he actually looked nervous. 'What is it? What have you done?'

'Well, funnily enough, for once it's more a case of what I *haven't* done.'

She shook her head briskly, feeling her muscles tense. An apprehensive Jules was a very frightening prospect. 'I don't follow.'

'We have a bit of a problem.'

'Bit?'

'Big. We have a big problem.'

Chapter Nineteen

Madrid, November 1936

They stood in formation, the mops pressed against their shoulders as Ivan patrolled past, checking their placement, bearing and discipline. He kicked at the shin of one woman half a step forward of everyone else but she didn't even flinch, shuffling back in line; discipline was being instilled, slowly but surely.

He was a hard taskmaster, difficult to please, rarely smiling or finding a good word. Sometimes they drilled for three hours straight, their arms trembling from the sustained weight of holding the guns and the motionless poses. But it hadn't been for naught, all the marching, weapons training, target practice . . . She could strip, reassemble and load a rifle in three minutes flat now and she had grown strong and streetwise, her innocence of even three months ago now long since discarded.

Her future survival depended upon the shedding of that youthful skin. The fascists were now at the city gates, their notorious Columns of Death having advanced under Franco from Badajoz in the south, and under Mola from Burgos in the north. Their unstoppable drive on Madrid had only been disrupted by Franco's insistence on relieving Nationalist troops in Toledo as well, giving the Republicans enough time to rally a robust defence of the capital. But if Madrid still stood free, the roads to her were not, the rebels digging in on the city's outskirts and changing tactics from a coup to a siege; they were sitting in for a long, drawn-out war and although their troops had not breached Madrid's front line, they had another advantage in their arsenal – their much-feared Fifth Column, made up of a sizeable population of isolated and undercover Nationalist sympathizers already in the city, were now at work: reporting back on Republican tactics, disrupting supplies, leaking misinformation, and stray snipers were even taking aim from rooftops at churchgoers and cinema visitors. Innocents.

Defeat was not an option. The atrocities committed by the Army of Africa were spreading word-of-mouth up through the country in a metaphorical shudder of revulsion, as refugees fleeing the countryside for the safety of the cities brought their tales of horror with them. It was already clear this was no ordinary war. The usual codes of conduct did not apply: there were no casualties left behind, no prisoners taken. Utter annihilation of the Republic was the aim, sending out one very clear and simple message: this was a purge; every red would die.

As a regular in the People's Army, she had not yet killed, but she knew the moment was coming – it was all that anyone ever talked about in the shops, the cafes and on the wireless: the atrocities, the horror, the capture and fall of villages, towns, whole provinces . . . In the early weeks of arriving in Madrid, her role had been primarily educational, helping Luciana and Marta to distribute the leaflets and recruit numbers to their cause; but as the weeks wore on and the fascists' forces marched onwards and inwards, towards Madrid, the tone had changed, the sense of urgency. Propaganda wasn't enough. Action was needed. Defence.

Paloma, as their figurehead and speaker, drew widespread admiration as well as crowds with her bold rhetoric and charisma – all she needed was someone's attention for two minutes and they were sold. Marina knew now that she too had been one of her converts, their accidental bumping into one another in the crowd, nothing of the sort. But Marina counted herself lucky to have been swept up. Her comrade and leader was gaining a spreading fame through the city, for the Republic's supporters were splintered and fractured, the socialist, anarchist and communist factions all competing against each other for similar goals. Even in their own home, there were divisions. Paloma and Marta identified with the anarchists' cause, Sindo with the communists, and Ivan and Luciana with the socialists. But Paloma was increasingly seen as a consolidating figure, bringing the Left causes together under her umbrella, and there was strength in unity, surely?

Marina wasn't entirely sure which political position she took. The nihilism of the anarchists or the comradeship of the communists? Both or neither? She adopted their ideas, believing in some elements of each, but her real spur was not political faith but vengeance. The fire that burned within her raged at both Left and Right, at her family *and* Santi's, for they had destroyed one another, each side taking from the other something irreplaceable, and she – caught in the middle – had suffered twice over.

She wished she had the certainty of Paloma's convictions. Luciana had told her one afternoon, as they'd been printing the latest batch of propaganda material, that Paloma – smuggled recently over the French border in an apple truck on a covert mission to get weapons – had come back into Spain by jumping out of a plane over Catalonia with the machine guns strapped to her body. For Marina, it had taken everything in her merely to leave, to pick a side, and she knew she could never match the passion of the political zealot. Ideology was pure and uncomplicated. Life was not.

'At ease.'

The squadron deflated at his words, a mass of mops hitting the ground with soft-headed *thunks*. Intimidating they were not. Drills and discipline were one thing, but without weapons they were like children playing at being soldiers . . . Reports of armaments caches being moved to the capital had been circulating for the past few weeks but there had been precious little sign of it so far. An initial delivery of sixteen thousand weapons had proved a white elephant when it transpired only five thousand of them worked, and every attempt since had been foiled by ambushes and slaughter, for the Moors were expert in guerrilla attacks and played dirty with dummy surrenders that led their enemies straight towards them.

It was a grossly uneven and distorted battleground: the Republican loyalists may have had the sanction of the government but they were trying to resist the forces of a sophisticated, militarized enemy, and in its efforts to look peaceable to the foreign allies whose support it needed, definitive action from the Republican government was unforthcoming. With both the Civil Guard and the army supporting the rebel Nationalist cause, the militia had become merely a People's Army: ordinary men and women with no prior combat experience, training to go to war with neither an organized tactical campaign to direct them, nor any weapons with which to fight. Ivan did his best to train their squadron, to explain the basics of warfare and weaponry, to teach mapwork to displaced country labourers who could not read – but even with a squad of sixty, they were no army.

'This was better,' he said solemnly. 'But there can be no room for mistakes. Lack of discipline could cost you your life or, worse, that of your comrade. Keep the line and you will stay strong.' His stare carried over them all and Marina prayed he wasn't going to make them follow up with some target practice. Instead, for once, he nodded. 'Troop dismissed.'

Marina let the air slide out of her as she held on to her mop for support. They had been marching for hours this afternoon and her feet ached, the small hole worn in her sole now considerably larger.

'Come, we must get back,' Marta said, hurrying over and slapping her on the shoulder. 'Sindo has an important speaker coming tonight and we are already late.'

Sindo, a cobbler before the war, had grown in the power vacuum created by the hostilities, masterminding the activities of the communist underground from behind the scenes. His face wasn't known to strangers like Paloma's, his name alien to their ears, but that was how he liked it. A tactician rather than showman, he preferred the shadows, slipping unknown and unseen, often in the dead of night. Marina knew his tread on the floors, for she didn't sleep well. She also knew he didn't quite trust her, that something lingered between them that had never been articulated, a sense, instinct, of suspicion.

Leaving their mops with the fifty-eight others in the shed that had once been the school's coal store, they began to walk back quickly to the apartment, Marta talking nineteen to the dozen: about the blister on her left index finger from holding the mop, a new hairstyle she had thought up herself, her date tomorrow night with the boy from the print shop . . .

Marina smiled as she listened, loving the mundanity of it all. The thing she had learnt about war was that it flipped everything into reverse: making heroes out of ordinary people, making small lives extraordinary, and turning the trivial into the epic. When every day was a fight for survival and just living to see the sun both rise and set again was a victory in itself, these tiny day-to-day details assumed greater importance than they could ever achieve during peacetime.

They were almost home and Marta had moved on to bemoaning the prospect of the meeting in the apartment. It wasn't that her commitment to the cause was waning but all she wanted to do, she said, was to 'fall on the bed and sleep for a week'.

She stopped suddenly, looking shocked. 'Oh! Oh no.'

'What is it?' Marina asked, feeling an immediate ripple of fear. Danger was only ever a heartbeat away these days: the muzzle of a gun pointing from a window; a mortar whistling through the sky.

'I saw old Lopez earlier. He has got some tomatoes.'

'Fresh tomatoes?' Marina repeated, her mouth beginning to water.

Marta nodded. 'He promised to hold some for me.'

'But how did they get past the blockade?' Marina asked, her tummy giving a rumble for good measure.

Marta shrugged.

Food was growing harder and harder to come by. The Nationalists' siege meant supplies from the country increasingly couldn't get past the lines. Many Madrilenos had already packed up their families and relocated to the Valencian coast in anticipation of a further assault on the capital. The city was steadily shutting down and looting was beginning to be commonplace.

Marina looked left and right. The apartment was another quarter-mile to their right. 'But it's in the opposite direction and we're already late for the meeting.'

'I know, but . . .' Marta's eyes brightened. 'Fresh tomatoes, Marina.'

Marina hesitated – to her stomach they were more urgently needed even than guns. 'Okay, fine, let's go. But we must run.'

'No. We can't both be late. Explain for me. I'll hurry.'

'But—'

'It's fine. I won't be long!' She was already tearing away. Marina thought she looked like she had lost weight. Perhaps they all had. Their days were long: working for the cause through the daylight hours and then keeping the team going after dark – cooking, washing and, increasingly, nursing comrades with injuries.

She ran the rest of the way home and let herself into the apartment building, giving the special knock at the door.

Luciana let her in.

'Marta's just getting some tomatoes. She'll be ten minutes.'

'Ssh, they have started,' she said quietly, looking solemn.

Marina hurried in, trying to slip unnoticed at the back, but she saw Sindo's quick gaze catch sight of her, noting her tardiness: her lack of commitment to the cause?

'. . . grave escalation of atrocities. I have personally had sight of a letter in which the devil Queipo de Llano wrote, the executions of our brothers must *proceed with greater energy . . .'*

She looked over at the man talking. It was Sindo's contact, Miguel Modesto. She knew him by sight and reputation, but that was enough; even Paloma called him a thug. A former blacksmith, he was tall and athletic with a high forehead and swept-back light-brown hair, a broken nose and bowed lips. Good-looking, some said, but tales of his savagery preceded him. He had been one of the men to lead the massacre at the Montana barracks in July and his appointment as chief interrogator for the Commissions of Investigation was scant cover for the kangaroo courts in which justice was merely a bit-part. Everyone knew about the sharp increase in 'motorized crimes' under his watch, in which Nationalist suspects were simply driven to the city outskirts and shot. If he had been a dangerous man before, he was even more threatening now that he was sanctioned with official powers. Was it good to have a man like him on their side? Certainly he was a dangerous enemy, but she had heard Paloma tell Sindo several times that he was an equally dangerous friend.

'Greater energy?' he repeated in disbelief. 'What more can they do to us? We know that to prevent any rebellion, they are killing all prisoners, their wives and children too. We know what they do to our women that they allow to survive – violating them repeatedly, shaving off their hair, forcing them to ingest castor oil and then shaming them by making them parade through the towns as they soil themselves.' He pointed a finger. 'No! Do not look away. Hear my words. Feel them.'

Marina felt the tears bud in her eyes. Was this true or propaganda? But she had seen some of the women herself, shorn and trying to disguise themselves under shawls, arriving in the great waves of refugees flooding the city.

Her own ragged cut was already growing out, its shocking roughness softening into a messy style that now swung gently at her ears, though her neck was still bare; Marta had taken to brushing and styling it for her each morning, curling the ends under and pinning it in place by the temples. Unbeknownst to Marina at the time, it was her cut that had first caught Paloma's eye in the crowd, assuming her to be one of the 'unfortunate women' caught and abused by fascist troops, and it had been many weeks before Marina had managed to convince them that she had unwittingly cut it herself by way of disguise.

'Far from the worst being over, this is just the beginning. The columns are advancing and the repression is intensifying. In the north, Navarre and Toledo have fallen. In the east, Huesca has fallen. In the west, Coruña and Lugo, Salamanca and León have fallen. In the south, Cadiz, Huelva, Granada, Cordoba and Sevilla have fallen. Fallen! Our comrades annihilated.'

Marina felt her blood chill, her heartbeat slow. Andalusia was down?

'And now the Falangist dogs are heading here. For me. For you.' His eyes tripped over every one of them, making it personal. 'The fascist scum must be neutralized. There can be no mercy against an enemy that disregards the very humanity of its opponents. Only three days ago, there was a report from Malaga that our brave comrades were rounded up in the bullring – the bullring! – and slaughtered. They shot at them like fish in a barrel.' He took a breath, contempt twisting his face. 'This was not just the landowners' revenge, this was their *sport* . . .'

Marina felt an echo ring against the words – Malaga . . . Bullring . . .

'Where, exactly?' Her voice, refined and feminine, rang like a bell against the cannon-fire of his rhetoric. She felt a spike of fear as every head turned, Modesto's gaze coming to rest upon her, for she hadn't known the words were leaving her until she heard them in the room too.

There was a pause, Modesto regarding her carefully. '. . .

Ronda.' She didn't flinch, though it took everything in her not to react; Ronda was still three miles from La Ventilla; it could have been the Ordonez or Romeros . . .

Modesto's eyes narrowed, his stare weighing heavily upon her. 'By every account I have heard, the *braceros* were starving, previous attempts at uprisings having been immediately and mercilessly staunched. But this summer, they reorganized themselves, invading the estate and reclaiming it for harvest; they slaughtered some of their bulls—'

'Bulls?' she queried again, but her heart was hammering now. She knew what he was going to say.

'Mendoza bulls. Famous for their strength and courage. And, of course – meat.' Modesto looked back around the room again. 'Our brothers wanted merely to feed their families. No different to you or I. But for that *audacity*, they were rounded up and sent in to the bullring, in groups of five, for the landlords to pick them off, one by one. Even the beasts are granted more dignity than that.'

A roar of disgust rumbled through the room, condemning her father, her brothers. She allowed her head to give a tiny nod, but she was shaking, violent tremors barely contained. Because she knew her family had done this in her name, as payback for losing her. Tit for tat. It would never end.

'Why do you ask, señorita?' Modesto's attention was back on her again, his scrutiny upon her disconcerting for he was a man known for his interrogations, a man hired to read when people were lying.

'I am from Seville,' she replied, remembering her initial lie to Sindo. 'I wondered if I might know them. If I could help.'

'And do you?'

She shook her head. '. . . No. I'm sorry.'

He stared at her for longer than was necessary, the tension

in the room growing like an overblown balloon. Did he believe her, or did her voice betray her? 'Well, that is a shame.'

He tore his gaze away and it was like being ripped from the arms of a monster. Luciana came and stood beside her. 'What did you do that for?' she whispered as he started up again, hatred inflecting off every word.

'I wanted to help,' she murmured back.

'How? All you've done is brought yourself to his attention. You know what he's like.'

They looked back at him, holding the crowd with his dogma as he extrapolated on the fascist scum. His colour was high, hair flopping theatrically as he paced, expounding the need for vigilance and action. But every few moments now, his gaze came back to her again, like she was a resting post, somewhere he might tarry a while.

She stared at the floor, knowing her curiosity had left her exposed. She would be remembered. But if she had had the chance to think it through, she would also have done it again, for she knew exactly who had organized their uprising this summer, who had finally dared them to succeed where they – and his father – had failed before. There's no fire that burns so hot as a young man's anger and she saw now that, far from being an end in itself, slaughtering Indigo had merely been the calling card that this was the beginning. In the four months she had been gone, she had missed out on Santi's revolution and his full revenge upon her family. And what a revenge it had been: her mother had lost her only daughter, and then her father and brothers had lost their land. But his victory had been short and reprisal vengeance had been theirs once more, for didn't the Mendozas always win in the end?

And that meant only one thing, something that made her

bones want to snap from sheer despair, even though she hated him now – Santi was dead.

He was dead.

Her old best friend, shot to death by her own family as he ran for his life in a closed-off bullring . . .

Santi . . . She remembered how his eyes had burned the last time they had seen each other. How, for just a moment, she had thought she could reach him still. Until Arlo had spoken, redrawing the battle lines, and he had run, the bloodied knife in his hand—

'Death to the Falangist dogs! Viva La Republica!'

The cheer made her jolt and look up, drawing her out of the thoughts she had sunk into so deeply. How much had she missed?

She saw that the meeting had come to a close, their supporters leaving with fresh fires blazing in their eyes; she remembered she was supposed to be handing out flyers with Luciana as they passed by. Remembering her duty, she went to run to her post by the door—

A hand on her arm stopped her.

'Marina, allow me to introduce you properly.' It was Sindo, and beside him, a full head taller, tonight's speaker. 'Miguel Modesto.'

Up close, he was even more imposing than on the speakers' floor, the intensity he brought to his words carried through with a rough physicality: tobacco, sweat, stubble; cuts and bruises on his hands.

'Hello,' she said simply, still with a hesitation for it had been hard work to break the habit of using the formal introductions she had been raised with.

'Señorita Marquez, I was grateful for your efforts tonight. It is good to see our womenfolk so committed to the cause.'

'I believe many of us are, sir,' she said, sweeping her gaze over Paloma and Luciana, who were still engaging the departing crowds, still exhorting them to rally their peers, their friends, their neighbours . . .

'Sir?' he queried. 'There are no hierarchies in this room. We are all equals, are we not?'

'I apologize. An old habit. My mother raised me to show deference.'

'And what was your mother?'

'A cook,' she said quickly. 'For the local landowners.'

'Not the Mendozas?' His eyebrow was arched but there was a playfulness to it, as though her questions about them somehow bonded them now. A shared joke perhaps.

'No, señor. My people are in Seville.'

He nodded. 'It is tragic what has happened there.'

'It is,' she agreed.

'Are your family safe?'

'I have no family now.' It was a truth, at least. Her heart ached for Arlo and her mother but they had neither one of them been strong enough to act decisively against her father, to make the changes she could not live without, and their apathy had been as effective as the others' brutality in casting her out.

'Well, I am sorry to hear that, though it is a common enough story.' His eyes never moved off her and she could only imagine what it would be like to be questioned by this man with a revolver on the table. 'Which is why it is all the more important to bind closely to our friends and comrades. I trust your supporters here tonight will have taken my words to their hearts and heard the warnings I am giving them. Conditions here are only going to get worse – a lot worse. It is imperative you know who you can trust, who can keep you safe in times like these.'

He seemed to be saying something more than his words, a double-binded message. But was it a promise or a threat? She had heard too much about him to discount the rumours of his violent excesses, and if he was offering her safety, his protection, it was at what cost?

'Marina! We need you here.'

She looked over, to find Paloma and Luciana standing by the doors as the last of the followers filed past. Paloma beckoned her over.

'I'm sorry, I must go. Will you excuse me?'

Modesto smiled again. 'You really do have fine manners for the daughter of a cook, señorita.'

She inclined her head fractionally. 'Then I shall take that as a compliment to my mama.'

Something glittered in his eyes as she turned to leave and she hurried quickly to where the others were standing. 'What is it?' she asked breathlessly, feeling the adrenaline shoot through her limbs now she was free. She felt like a doe that had been released from the jaws of a leopard.

'You looked like you needed rescuing,' Paloma winked, handing her the leaflets to distribute with them.

Modesto made a point of taking one from her on his way out, catching her eye with what seemed to be a meaningful look before he left. When the last guest had gone, they walked down to the bedroom together; Luciana collapsed down on her bed with a sigh – grateful for the brief respite before the work began for dinner. Paloma pulled a cigarette from inside her shirt – she kept them lined up in her bra – and offered one.

Marina took it, feeling shaken. Distraught.

'What was Modesto saying to you?' Luciana asked.

Her voice sounded far away and it was a moment before

the words reached Marina's ear. '. . . Oh. He was offering me protection, I think.'

Paloma's eyebrow arched. 'Don't fall for that. You know what he means, right? You are not such an innocent as to believe he would not want something in return.'

'Of course not.' But she didn't know, nor did she care. It wasn't Modesto who was on her mind. She went and sat on her mattress, feeling drained, the news of Santi's death buzzing in her like a butterfly trapped in a bell jar. She took a deep drag of the cigarette, trying to ignore it. She should be happy he was dead. She *would* be. He had been no friend when he died, but her enemy – he knew the enormity of what he had done when he took Indigo from her. No, it was just the shock, finding out like that, that was all. She would feel happy about it soon enough.

She lay down, her arm outstretched with the cigarette over the floor. The mattress was scarcely fit for purpose, one of the springs pushing up against her ribs, a corner of the fabric torn, horsehair tufts spilling through it and God-only-knew what climbing in, for every morning she awoke scratching, her skin covered with hundreds of tiny red bites.

She stared into the distance, at nothing, seeing not the panelled walls or her sisters in arms, but a boy with black eyes and a gap between his teeth. She hated him. She hated him. She *would* hate him. She would.

Beside her bed was one of the boxes left by the previous owner – her godmother – and which they now used as tables. They had all long since been scavenged, torn through when Paloma and Sindo first requisitioned the space, looking for food, bedding, writing materials, anything that might assist them in their cause; but much of it was useless – extravagant balldresses that could possibly be converted into curtains if only they could sew, hats and ribbons, trinkets and photographs. Some of the candelabras had been deemed useful for the blackouts when the German Luftwaffe took to the skies and they had quickly grown accustomed to eating their peasants' meals off long-pronged silver cutlery.

Unlike the other girls, Marina had nothing on her 'bedside table': not a photograph of her family or beau, nor even a hair-brush. She had taken only food with her and a kitchen knife, just enough to keep her safe and alive on the journey to the capital. But beneath it, innocuous and seemingly irrelevant if anyone should chance upon it, was an irregularly heart-shaped pebble. She had found it in the pocket of the old trousers she had stolen from Arlo the night she escaped and it had become her last remaining tie to him, to the land she had once called home, to La Ventilla, to Santi: they were all interconnected, joined together by a shared childhood. She rubbed the stone, remembering the day she had stolen orchard oranges for Santi, when they had dangled happily in the oaks and watched the cork harvest come in, the same day they had found the dead bull in the field and Señor Martin had whipped him till he bled, the same day Arlo had saved her from their father's wrath but could not save her friend.

She held the stone now, recalling how the joyous and horrific memories of that day intermingled, inseparable from one another and all conjoined by the mere few minutes that separated them. There had been no such thing as a good day or a bad day back then. Life had been marbled, a constant mix of both, and she had longed for the purity of a clear path. But now that she was on it, was it any better? She had picked her side but every day here was unremittingly bad, and if Miguel Modesto was to be believed and his words hadn't just been propaganda – albeit their own – then they were going to grow worse. She was always hungry, barely slept, cooking and cleaning for the team, working for the cause from the moment she woke till she dropped back down here last thing at night.

What did the protection of a man like him actually mean? A full belly and a soft bed? A day to walk in the park and see grass and trees again? Was all that worth it against what Paloma warned, the unmentionable her mother had never discussed with her but which hung like a mist from almost every man she met?

And which man could she trust anyway? Why was he any more of a monster than her father, her eldest brothers, Santi. What made him any worse than them?

Santi.

He was dead. He was dead. When would it sound true? How many times did she have to say it to believe it?

'Marina?'

She looked up with a start, realizing she was rocking, the pebble in her hand squeezed tightly in her palm. Had she betrayed herself? Paloma's voice was questioning, there was scrutiny in the word. With effort, she pushed a stillness through her limbs and slid the pebble under the edge of the box again. She looked up, hoping she looked careless and carefree, that her face wasn't overwritten with the spasms of pain wracking her body like thunderbolts.

'Yes?' she asked. Luciana was filing her nails, a book open on Paloma's lap.

'Where's Marta?'

Marta? Marina looked at them both. In the shock of dealing with Modesto's attentions and Santi's death, she had forgotten all about her. 'She went to get fresh tomatoes,' she said quietly, even as a sudden cold dread replaced the fracture in her heart. 'Why? Hasn't she come back yet?'

Luciana stopped filing. Paloma sat up straighter. 'No. She hasn't come back.'

Chapter Twenty

Ronda, July 2018

'They're just in there, señora,' the driver said, pointing to the vast, over-scaled wooden double doors. 'I will take your bag back to the house for you.'

She stared out blankly. '. . . Thank you.'

She got out of the car and stood on the cobbles for a moment, looking up at the round building. A magnificent bronze sculpture of a bull dominated the courtyard, the curved walls a dazzling white in the ferocious sunlight. She pulled on her wide-brimmed straw sunhat and walked towards it, making for the shadows the first chance she got. It must have been thirty-five degrees today.

'I'm sorry, we are closed for a private tour,' the ticket clerk said as she approached.

'I'm part of the Mendoza party.' Her voice was flat and toneless.

He bowed his head in apology. 'They are in the stadium, señora. Through the doors and up the stairs to the right.'

It was hard to concentrate. She wasn't quite sure why she was here, only . . . there hadn't seemed to be anything else to do. 'Thank you.'

She stepped through the inset door into the outer courtyard

that ringed the arena, her gaze blankly riding up the thick curved walls. A horse was tethered at the opposite end, drinking from a trough. Behind it was a series of low buildings with various stairways leading onto roof terraces, where several people were working in unison and operating some sort of mechanism out of sight. Behind them was a much larger, longer building with a sloping roof, and through the windows she could see the glitter of several chandeliers, a voice shouting out instructions from within. The royal riding school? It was famous throughout Spain.

But there were other voices calling out, one she recognized much closer to hand. She turned right and stepped through another set of doors into the outer arc of the stadium itself. On either side, left and right, steps rose up in steady flights along the back wall, the timbers of the shallow roof which shaded the spectator stands looking like the gills of a mushroom from here. She went to climb the steps when she heard the voice again. It was Marina's.

She stepped forward instead and pushed up the latch of a vast wooden door in front of her; it led to a circular pathway that ran between the seating stands and the perimeter of the bullring. A wooden gate was closed and she opened it, her eyes up as she took in the sight of the dramatic colonnaded arches encircling the amphitheatre. She had never seen anything like it before. Of course, the generic image was familiar from old films, spaghetti westerns and Hemingway novels, but in the flesh . . . the sheer scale of it was impressive. She tried to imagine what it must have been like in days gone by, filled to capacity, the spectacle of colour, the pomp . . .

She realized she was walking on sand, some of it going between her toes in her open sandals. Painted wooden *barreras*, or wooden panels, dimpled and cracked from generations of fights, were set atop the stone wall which framed the ring, with four larger boards, *burladeros*, set out in intervals in front of them on the ground for the *toreros* to hide behind.

'Olé!' The excitable shout came from above her. She stopped walking and looked around and up. Marina. She was up there? Charlotte frowned. It had sounded like she was down . . .

Were the acoustics distorted by the shape of the—

'Charlotte!'

It was Nathan. He was standing up, his body tense and unnaturally still, like he'd been deep-frozen on the spot. He was with Marina and another man she didn't recognize. For a moment, the peace held as she looked up at them all and wondered what they were doing up there.

Then she heard the sound of chains, of mechanisms moving. She saw Nathan's head turn and something in his manner made her go cold. A door was being lifted up, like a guillotine being readied, and suddenly she realized what those men on the terraces outside had been doing, what they had been lifting: more doors. Creating a secure tunnel – to here.

'Shut the doors!' Nathan began yelling. 'Shut the doors!' He was waving his arms madly, trying to get someone's attention, but whose? No one could be seen from here behind the high walls; they had been designed to protect, to create a strong, safe seal.

The man sitting beside him was speaking rapidly into a radio, standing up too now and issuing urgent directives. 'Close the *toril*! Close the *toril*!' He listened to something that was said, his face slackening. He looked over to her. 'Run! Get behind the *burladero*!'

Charlotte stared at him. She knew what he was saying. She understood his command. She just couldn't seem to . . . move.

'Charlotte! Get behind the board!' Nathan hollered, his voice more like a bear's roar, as suddenly she heard a terrible sound – deep snorting, heavy shoulders barging against walls, the stamp of hooves. Getting closer, closer . . .

Here.

She felt all the breath leave her as the bull ran into the ring. It was a dappled grey, lighter in build than she might have expected and yet still so . . . huge. It barrelled through in an awkward up-down motion, not yet noticing her, pawing at the sand and snorting wildly. It was stressed and defensive.

She didn't move. Nor did anyone else. There was just a moment of utter stillness as the beast acclimatized to its surroundings, taking in the sudden space. And then her.

Her mouth dried up. There was nothing else now but her and it. She could see nothing, hear nothing. She wasn't aware of the screams from the stands, she didn't see the blur of motion as someone suddenly jumped down into the *callejón* pit, and up onto the defensive stone wall, vaulting the *barreras* and charging towards her. All she could hear was the sound of blood rushing in her head, all she could see was the animal beginning to run now, dipping its head, that vast bulk on stumpy legs, getting closer . . .

She felt hands slam into her, her feet leave the ground and suddenly she was in the air – for one, two, three seconds and then down again, landing heavily, rolling through the sand. She stopped face down, dizzy and disoriented. She looked up. The bull was still running. But not after her.

Nathan was heading towards the far side of the ring, leading it away from her, twisting back to see where the animal was, the sound of its snorts like a wind at his neck.

In sheer horror at the scene – he would be gored, trampled – she screamed for him, gathering herself up, her feet scrabbling to find purchase as she watched him run. He was agile, fit, staggering his direction like a switchblade.

He looked over at her. 'Get behind the board!' he shouted at her. 'The board!'

She heard him this time and she began to look. Where was the closest? But they were staggered in quarterly intervals and . . . this stadium, it had to be seventy metres wide. Nowhere was close.

She went to run but her ankle gave out from under her and she cried out. She must have hurt it in the fall.

'The board, Charlotte!' He had run out of stadium in the other direction and was running back towards her now. And that meant, so was the bull.

She began running as fast as she could, the limp bad, but adrenaline pushing her onwards. The *burladero* was maybe ten metres away, eight . . .

Underfoot, she could feel the vibrations of the animal as it got closer, the desperation in Nathan's eyes as he charged towards her . . .

Five, three . . .

He reached out, grabbing her arm and yanking her hard, pulling her with him behind the board just as the bull slid and slammed horns-first into it.

She screamed, trembling uncontrollably as Nathan pulled her into him, his back to the board and creating another layer of protection as the bull pawed and circled, snorting behind them out of sight.

'Fuck, Charlotte! Fuck!' he said angrily, the adrenaline still coursing, his breathing coming hard as he held her by the shoulders and looked her up and down, checking for injuries. She could see the panic in his eyes, the tension in his body as he checked and double-checked she was okay. 'Fuck—'

His gaze met hers, naked and true, and suddenly her world narrowed down to just the two of them behind that board – no bull, no baby, no wife, no reason why they couldn't be what everything was telling them they should be. He kissed her with all the urgency that had impelled him to cross a stadium to save her, to outrun a bull, his passion a need that she be okay, be here.

But they weren't alone and the sound of the bull running again made them pull apart again, jumpy. Nathan tightened his arms around her like a wall, holding her head to his chest as he looked around them, looking for help. 'It's okay, we're safe here,' he murmured. 'He can't get to us here.' But he was looking tense and every second seemed like a minute. What was taking so long? She was shaking still.

The rattle of chains made them both stiffen as they heard the door being winched back up, hooves at a canter. Voices.

'No, don't,' she gasped, as Nathan loosened his grip on her and leaned around the board to get a look.

She felt the tension leave his body as he caught sight of the action on the other side of the boards. He pulled back in, looking down at her. 'It's okay. The picadors are here. They're herding him out again. It's fine. It's safe now.'

She stared up at him, the episode already running in a loop through her mind – the silent image of him leading the bull away from her, the tone in his voice as he'd realized what was about to happen, the look in his eyes . . . In that moment, he'd dropped the story and it had all been there still. It didn't matter what he said or what she did, that he was married or she was about to be, they were connected by a thread of fire that hadn't been and couldn't be extinguished. She felt his hands press into her skin, his grip tighten as he stared down at her—

'Oh my God, Charlotte!' She heard the scratch in Marina's voice as she ran along the *callejón* pit, stepping up on the low stone wall and leaning over the wooden barriers. 'Are you okay?'

Nathan stepped back, away from her, the spell broken, his face impassive but his eyes burning with confusion.

'Yes, I'm fine. I . . .' She looked around in bewilderment. Everything had happened so fast.

'What were you doing down there?'

'I thought you were in here. Having a tour.'

Marina gave a surprised laugh. 'We already had the tour. They were just bringing in the novice bulls for the horsemen to train with.'

'. . . You're saying that was a baby?' she asked, beginning to feel foolish. Embarrassed.

'Four-year-old.'

'It was big enough from where I was standing,' she murmured, suppressing another shiver.

'You're still shaking,' Marina said. 'Are you sure you're okay?'

'Absolutely,' she lied, her eyes flickering to Nathan's and away again. 'Think I might have a sprained ankle though.'

'I'm sorry if I pushed you too hard,' he said, looking stiff, his reserve coming back down. 'I needed to get you out of its way. You weren't moving.'

'Thank God *you* were.' She frowned. 'I don't know why I couldn't move. Why couldn't I move?'

'It's a common stress response – flight, fight or freeze. You froze.' Their eyes locked once more but she could feel the distance between them widening again, normal service being resumed. He was married. She was about to be.

'Come, we should get some ice on your ankle,' Marina said, intruding. 'I fancy a coffee anyway.'

They moved to the cafe, Nathan looping her arm around his shoulder and helping her hop along. The manager – who she'd seen with the radio – ran to get ice and a compress, looking stressed. One of his VIPs quite literally having a run-in with a young bull was not what he'd needed.

'We didn't think you were coming back,' Marina said as they rearranged chairs around the table to make a leg rest for her.

Nathan looked down guiltily. Had he thought she'd taken him at his word on Saturday – fled from here, away from him?

'Mateo thought it was best if I was here for the reunion.'

'Yes, but Mayra thought you were due back yesterday,' Marina said.

'Well, I got a little held up. But the driver was taking me back from the airport and said you were here, so I thought I should rejoin you as soon as possible.'

Their coffees were set down and Marina gave the waiter a delighted smile, as though relieved that for once she wasn't the one serving it.

'. . . I assume your grandmother isn't here?' Charlotte asked her conversationally, seeing how Nathan stared into his coffee, lost in thought. Was he thinking about what had just happened between them – again? How it seemed unstoppable, no matter what he said?

'God, no.' Marina's expression changed. Charlotte looked back at her, hearing the note of concern in her voice. 'She is resting again. To be honest, she is not quite herself here.' She looked back at them both with a concerned expression. 'I'm worried this has taken more out of her than she will admit. Perhaps it was a mistake coming here. I shouldn't have pushed her—'

'Marina, you didn't push her – your grandmother came here because she wanted to see her brother again. She is a strong woman, here on her terms.'

'Mmm, maybe.' Marina gave a noncommittal shrug. 'She just seems so . . . quiet, here.'

'Has she left her room at all?'

'Once or twice. They take her out in the carts and she goes to the garden or the stables. Then she comes back and rests for the day. There are so many memories for her. Too many, I fear.'

'It's bound to be emotional for her,' Charlotte agreed, fiddling with the spoon on her saucer and glancing at Nathan again. Had he heard a word they'd said? He looked so . . . lost. 'And she's still said nothing to you?'

'Nothing.'

'Has there been any word yet when Mateo and his father are due to arrive?'

'Tomorrow now. Apparently there was a dip in one of his readings they weren't happy about and they decided to keep him in to run a few more tests.'

'Does your grandmother know he's coming tomorrow?'

Marina nodded. 'She has said barely a word today. I didn't want to leave her but she insisted. I think she wanted some time there alone before Carlos arrives.'

Charlotte frowned; they were still no closer to knowing the reason for their estrangement. 'Nathan?' Her soul stirred as his eyes met hers again. 'Have you found anything yet that could help?'

She watched him visibly pull himself back into the conversation. '. . . Perhaps.' He tapped his finger against the coffee cup as both women looked at him, gathering his thoughts. His focus. 'As you know, I've been principally looking into her husband – your grandfather, Marina. As a start point, I took a view that he may be the most likely antagonist for the breakdown in relationships between your grandmother and her family: his name, being foreign, immediately suggested he was one of the overseas volunteers in the International Brigades, which in turn meant he was Republican – and that would have been a big problem back then. So I dug around and, sure enough, found a Jack Charles Quincy, from Oregon. He was thirty-four when he joined the Abraham Lincoln battalion, one of twenty-eight hundred Americans volunteering to fight for the Spanish Republic. Thirty-four was pretty old for a brigader. Most of them were kids – seventeen, eighteen.

'Anyway, he was one of the first wave of overseas recruits, landing in Malaga in the autumn of 1936, and arriving soon after in Ronda. It looks like he was tasked with coordinating a local Republican militia run by a man called Santiago Esperanza who had been an active insurgent in the area.' He shot Marina a wary look. 'In particular, he was known for his antagonism towards the Mendoza estate.'

Marina frowned. 'You mean to say my grandfather fought alongside a man who had actively targeted my family?'

Nathan hesitated, then nodded. 'It's looking like that, yes.'

Charlotte frowned. 'So you think my grandmother left because she fell in love with a Republican?'

He gave an uncertain look. 'Certainly it's a possibility. It would have been a very volatile, if not outright dangerous thing to do. The political landscape back then was highly charged and inflammatory. The economy was dominated by agriculture, and the landowners – particularly those with estates the size of the Mendozas' – were autocratic and conservative with a small "c". They didn't take kindly to the Second Republic's radical reforms.'

'Sorry, but this isn't a period of history I'm familiar with,' Charlotte interrupted, hoping he might look at her again. 'What were their radical reforms?'

His eyes met hers, making her heart double-beat. 'Giving women the vote, protecting workers' rights, creation of trade unions . . .'

'. . . Right.'

He looked back at Marina again. 'The Mendozas were, predictably, staunchly Nationalist. Felipo Mendoza, your grandmother's father, had close links with the military. His eldest sons Valentino and Montez briefly fought under General Franco in Morocco. Franco was a personal friend of his.'

'That's a mighty ally to have.'

'Yes. But it still didn't save him,' Nathan shrugged apologetically.

'What do you mean?'

'Felipo, Valentino and Montez were murdered in the December of '36.'

'. . . Murdered – how?'

'A group of rebels broke into the compound one night and dragged them from their beds. They were bundled up here, to where a crowd was waiting and –' he nodded his head in the direction of the famous Puente Nuevo along the street – 'they were thrown to their deaths.'

Marina gasped, sitting back with horrified eyes. The monumental eighteenth-century bridge famously straddled a 120-metre-deep gorge that split the town into two encampments. '. . . Was my grandfather involved?'

Nathan hesitated, then nodded. 'I believe so, yes. It was widely understood to have been carried out by a group he was connected with, called Hijos de la Noche; they specialized in midnight raids.'

Charlotte looked down, stunned. If Marina's grandmother had fallen in love with the man who murdered her family, it was little wonder she had stayed away all these years. Her betrayal was unforgivable.

'And there was a crowd waiting? Like it was a spectator sport?' Marina repeated, aghast. 'I cannot believe my grandmother would have fallen in love with a man who tossed her father and brothers from that bridge! He was nothing more than an animal!'

'You need to understand that the relationship between your family and the workers had completely broken down. Tensions had been at breaking point for years beforehand and there had been a sharp increase in the number of altercations in the weeks before the outbreak of war. In the June, for instance, a report was made to the Civil Guard, alleging a man was shot in cold blood by Valentino and Montez Mendoza, but it was never followed up. Shortly after that, a grand fiesta at La Ventilla was disrupted by the slaying of a prize horse in the stables and then, a few weeks later, workers stormed the estate: they killed some of the bulls, plundered the kitchens, reclaimed some of the land. But it was a short-lived victory. Franco invaded the mainland around the same time, reaching Ronda by the end of the summer. When the Nationalists seized the area and the old paternalists' power was restored, retribution was theirs – and it was merciless.'

'Merciless, how?'

'This bullring?' He nodded his head in the direction from whence they'd come. 'If you looked closely – or had known to look – you would see the bullet marks still in the stone wall from where they had the Republican prisoners rounded up and shot.'

Marina's mouth opened. 'No . . .'

'They were herded in, in small groups, and . . . picked off, one by one. There was no escape. Over two hundred men and boys shot. They even invited other landowners and dignitaries along to join in as a way of showing thanks for their support of the rebel cause. Some of the prisoners were guilty simply of being a union member, or the brother of a union member. Or the uncle of a man who had stolen from the orchard because his family were starving . . .'

'"They"? You mean the Mendozas? My family did these things . . . ?' Marina looked aghast. Shaken.

'There were atrocities on both sides,' Nathan said quickly. 'No war is ever as bitter or bloody as a civil war and the Spanish war was no different.'

Charlotte didn't know what she could add. She had expected some uncomfortable secrets to be unearthed during this process; every family had them but particularly those that became dynasties – wealth and power were rarely accrued through wholly legitimate means. But this? It was a whole other level.

Marina looked at Nathan again, her features set in a grim expression. 'So what happened to my grandfather? After he killed my great-grandfather, I mean . . .'

'It looks like he got away from here and moved up to Madrid. From the records I've seen, Jack Quincy was killed in March '37 in Madrid. American, International Brigade ID, estimated to be mid-thirties. Everything suggests it was him.'

'What happened to him?' Marina asked.

'He was shot during a siege in a church.'

Marina nodded and fell quiet again. Every revelation was like a punch. To learn that so many of her family had been murdered, were murderers . . .

'So you think Jack and Marina eloped together,' Charlotte

said, seeing how his eyes flashed dangerously at her use of the 'e' word. 'They left Ronda and came to Madrid?'

'That's what I'm not sure about. I don't think *he* can have been the catalyst for her leaving – the dates don't fit. We know Quincy didn't arrive in Spain till autumn of '36 but your grandmother seems to have left the area just before that, in the summer. The last time she was seen publicly here was at the grand fiesta I mentioned. There's a notice in the local paper at that time speculating that she had gone missing, even rumours she had been kidnapped – this was big bandit country back then. But no ransom was ever demanded and the family made no public comment; war broke out literally a week later so it was forgotten, replaced by much bigger stories – the military campaign was waged in the countryside to begin with and the fascists were merciless: no prisoners of war were taken, there were no wounded. It was a purge. Every man was killed.' He looked at Marina again, trying to find a silver lining. 'I'm beginning to wonder if your grandmother left because she truly supported the Republican cause, rather than because she fell in love. If she did, then she almost certainly saved her own life by leaving when she did – the fate of Republican women was almost worse than for the men. Dying was often preferable.'

'How?' Marina asked, looking dumbfounded.

He looked down at the table before looking back again. 'Some were shot. Most were raped. Gang-raped to death. Their heads were shaved. Humiliated by being forced to drink castor oil and then marched around the villages as they lost control of their bowels.'

Marina slapped her hand over her mouth and closed her eyes, trying to push his words away. 'How do we not know about any of this?' she asked finally in a quiet voice.

Nathan shot her a sympathetic look. 'Because Franco won and ruled for another thirty years. And history is always written by the victors.' Charlotte looked up at his choice of words. 'The history he saw to it was written, was carefully edited and . . . sanitized to the fascists' benefit. The history you have been passed down is only one tiny perspective of how it really happened, written through a narrow, reductive lens. We know some of the truth but not all of it. The full story falls down into cracks we could never know to search. We never get to know everything about a story, even if we're there ourselves.'

Charlotte looked up at his words. He was staring at her, remembering too – she could see it in his eyes. That tutorial. Their first night . . .

She felt the current surge between them again. It was undeniable – and yet impossible too. She saw it all in his face: the longing. The conflict. The pain.

He was quiet for a moment before looking back at Marina. 'There's a lot that still doesn't make sense. Your grandmother doesn't appear to have met Jack in Ronda, yet Felipo Mendoza and his sons were murdered by him in December 1936, even though we know he had already left for Madrid by then – there was simply no way he could have still been in the area and not been caught in the reprisals in the bullring. *But*, for Quincy to come back here from Madrid at that time would have been incredibly risky. The capital was under siege by then and Franco's forces had surrounded the city, so crossing the Nationalist lines would have been very, very dangerous. He risked his own life to take theirs and that means it *has* to have been personal, it wasn't just war. Something else must have happened between them that we don't know about yet.'

Marina stared at him. 'I can't believe this is my grandmother we're talking about. That this was her life,' she said. 'How have you even been able to find out all this?'

'It's my job to know where to look, but I'm working from old military records, newspapers, civic photographs, church records, ledgers, files – but there's only so much that they will reveal. Like I said, the full truth falls down the cracks; there are some things only your grandmother will ever know and which only she can tell.' He looked at her closely. 'Do you feel you'd be able to bring it up with her, now that you have some background?'

'I don't know. She is always so adamant whenever I've tried.'

'But that was before you knew this. If she does feel guilty or ashamed of what her actions meant for her family – and we do know that her husband murdered them – then that may be why she doesn't feel she can explain them to you. But if you show her you already know, that perhaps you even understand . . .'

'Well, I guess I could always try,' Marina agreed, staring into her coffee sadly. 'After all, we can't help who we fall in love with, right?'

Chapter Twenty-One

Madrid, February 1937

Once, the kitchen had been a place from which to steal, small hands swiping strips of iberico ham as they coursed through in planned lightning raids. Once, the kitchen had been a place of refuge from their father when his temper saw him marching through the house, a stick in his hand, never thinking to check the staff areas for them. Once, the kitchen had been a place of comfort and homely aromas when their mother was at parties in the capital. But now, with the siege in full effect, it was the hub of war, the place where they made bombs.

Marina was boiling up the condensed milk, staring into the frothing whiteness as she stirred. Luciana stood beside her, measuring out the nails like she was sifting flour for a cake, crystals and rocks heaped in buckets beside her; the dynamite was kept in the pantry, away from the heat and any ignition sources. They made a good team: efficient, calm, dextrous, though they didn't talk much; there didn't seem to be much to say these days anyway, conversation had become transduced from a means of connecting with people to merely communicating ways to stay alive.

It was just the two of them now in the girls' bedroom. Marta's body had been found the day after she disappeared, a neat hole in her head that had gone in above one ear and come out below the opposite jaw. 'Sniper' was all Ivan had said, when he had come in with the news. He had seen a physical description that matched hers in the list that was published daily in the *Gaceta* newspaper, of the corpses collected off the streets. He and Paloma had followed it up, just to be certain, going to the Dirección General de Seguridad where photographs of the bodies were kept for relatives to check, hoping it was another twenty-one-year-old woman in a blue dress who had died of 'organic disintegration of the brain'. They had come back with no doubts – it was her.

That was when everything had changed, the gears shifting up. Paloma had joined the Batallón Femenino del 5th Regimiento de Milicias Populares, the band of women fighting on the front line. Something in her had changed with the death of her friend as she had realized propaganda and night-time excursions weren't enough any more; Modesto had been right – there was no time for ideological notions when bullets were being peppered from rooftops at women who had gone to buy tomatoes.

The government urged order and restraint but to Marina, it seemed they were more concerned with promoting their peaceable image to the international community than really eliminating the Nationalist rebellion. With the Assault Guard and Civil Guard defecting to the uprising and the loyalists that remained deployed to the front line, the citizens were sitting ducks: exposed, unprotected and vulnerable. The militias were stepping into the vacuum left by the disintegrating police forces but it was the *checas*, those political party and trade union squads set up to rout out the fascists in their midst, that had rapidly gained traction and power. Unchecked by any effective leadership or control from the Republican government, they were running wild and running the city.

Every day brought fresh arrests and executions of the pro-rebel supporters but far from feeling safer, Marina felt her inward terror grow – this was puppet justice, with just the mere suspicion of a right-leaning tendency being enough to condemn a man to death. Luciana had muttered one time, as they packed the bombs carefully as though they were stuffing chickens, that she had heard many of the denunciations simply sprang from sexual jealousy or attempts to evade debts. But in most other cases, it was enough simply to have owned a business or once opposed a strike, to have been a member of the clergy – or be their wife or daughter – or to have expressed support of the repression of the Asturian rising in 1934. If anyone was to discover then that she was a Mendoza of Ronda, a traitor by blood . . .

The threat of being exposed was ever present. Only last month, she had been shopping in the central market and as she left the meat stall, had bumped straight into two young sisters she immediately recognized from home. Their house had been on the same street as the Esperanzas', and they had played with Santi and his siblings. Marina had never been introduced to them formally but she knew exactly who they were, for she had seen them many times in church as her family passed by to their pews at the front. The sisters had always looked so neat and tidy in their Sunday-best outfits, with their combed hair and placid expressions, but they didn't fool her with their goody-two-shoes acts, for Santi would gleefully recount to her their swimming games down by the river, their hiding games in the gorge, their running games in the streets . . . Marina had hated them for it, getting to have the best of her best friend, the freedom to play with him while she was sequestered at La Ventilla with just a governess and her brothers. And she hated them still, for now Santi was dead and there was nothing left of him to be had at all.

As she had stood, toe-to-toe, with them in the street, there had been a moment of pure instinct in which they all recognized one another as Andalusian sisters, natives from the same homeland; she could see they recognized her but that they couldn't pinpoint where exactly. They half smiled, knowing they were kin but not yet realizing the bitter divide between them. Her hair, still roughly cut and short on the neck, was the most effective and immediate deterrent to revealing her identity and in the next instant, she had turned away, hoping the narrative attached to her 'look' would be enough to re-affirm their instinct that not only was she one of them, but that she had suffered for their shared principles. They would assume she had been captured. Tortured. Abused.

But she would take no chances – she no longer shopped at that market, nor did she frequent that district now for fear of seeing them again, for if they did subsequently place her, they would effectively be her executioners, of that she had no doubt. It meant she had to walk another two miles across the city to the next market, risking the snipers' bullets that had dispatched Marta so ruthlessly; it also meant she could no longer shop with her only remaining friend, for she could think of no viable explanation to give Luciana as to why the central market must now be avoided. She had escaped Ronda's borders but still, it seemed, she was tethered to her past.

Taking the milk off the heat, she walked into the pantry to get a stick of dynamite. As she came back out again, she heard the front door slam and she flinched, freezing on the spot.

'Relax, it's just Ivan,' Luciana murmured, without looking up. If she had noticed Marina's growing paranoia, she passed no comment on it. 'I heard his cough.'

A few moments later, Ivan walked into the kitchen. He let his bag slide off his shoulder onto the floor as he sank into the chair. His face was dusty, his eyes drooping at the corners wearily, one still puffy from a recent black eye that was taking longer than expected to heal. Marina had patched his shirt at the elbow two nights ago but already there was a fresh tear in it from another scuffle or interrogation and, like Santi's mother with his shirt, she knew there would be yet more repairs due before the week was out.

Ivan had been tasked with running a sub-section dedicated to rooting out snipers and saboteurs. He reported to Sindo, who in turn had been appointed deputy secretary of the Cine Europa *checa* in November, after the start of the siege. It was one of the most feared squads in the city and Sindo was second in the chain of command only to Miguel Modesto, who had finally cast off the pretence of official sanction for this far more powerful role.

'Are you thirsty?' Luciana asked him, setting down the bag of nails and retrieving a glass from the cupboard instead. It was cloudy with soap smears, the water supply increasingly erratic, interrupted by the fascist siege.

She poured a glass without waiting for his reply and handed it to him. 'Thanks,' he muttered, his eyes scanning over the worktop and seeing the boxes of bombs ready for the next mission. It would be the same again tomorrow.

'You look tired,' Luciana said, sitting down opposite him. 'Bad night?'

'No, it was good,' he shrugged. 'Seven dead and we got a cannon and a cache of guns off the bastards. They'd been holed up in the San Jerónimo Church on Moreto.'

'What kind of guns?'

'Mousquetons. Lighter than rifles but hell of a kick.' He patted his shoulder in warning.

Luciana nodded as though she was making a mental note,

just in case. Sometimes it struck Marina just how very far she was now from being the secretary she'd first met six months ago, swapping explosive words for packing nail bombs with dynamite. But then, weren't they all transformed by this war? Marina could hardly remember her old life at La Ventilla any more – the rolling green pastures and grazing animals, hand-made dresses and her mother's sweet perfume, her soft hands and slightly dulled eyes, those extravagant fiestas, almost too bright, too colourful even in memory for this bleached-out, dust-covered, shelled landscape.

'Mousquetons? They had been stolen from the barracks then?' Marina asked, sealing off the last bomb and putting it carefully in the box.

'That's my guess.'

'Did they give you anything useful? Besides the weapons?'

Ivan shook his head. 'There was no talking; they were determined to shoot their way out.'

Luciana gave a 'what can you do?' shrug. It wasn't an unusual situation: stories of torture were rife and no one on either side wanted to be a prisoner; it was better to be dead.

Marina leaned against the counter, brushing the powder off her hands and sniffing her fingertips – the smell always disturbed her sleep, as though war could permeate her dreams as well as her waking life. She sighed, feeling a wave of exhaustion break over her; her feet burned from standing on them so long, for she had finished a shift at the Palace hotel earlier. She and Luciana both worked there now: waitresses by day; *milicianas* by night.

Some sounds outside made her look up, alert again, and she automatically crossed the room, peering out carefully from behind the shutters. A black Rolls-Royce was parked on the street below, a pair of legs emerging from one side, Miguel

Modesto's impressive form already erect on the other. Notorious around the city, the car actually had a nickname – El Rayo, or Lightning – and was conspicuous for its presence at the highest profile 'trials'.

'It's the others,' she said, looking back to find Luciana already watching her.

The other woman simply nodded. 'I shall put the broth on.' She rose from the table again, her palms pushing down on the tabletop as though she needed help getting up. She looked older than her thirty-seven years.

Marina stood stiffly as she watched the men look around the empty street before entering the building, bracing for the sound of their footsteps on the stone floor, their keys in the door, the timbre of their low voices vibrating through the rooms before them. And then they were there, Sindo removing his hat and placing it on the hatstand with his usual precision, Modesto shrugging off his overcoat, his eyes falling immediately to her as they always did.

'Good evening, ladies.'

'Good evening,' Marina replied, forcing herself to walk across the room and take his coat from him – it was a courtesy, a sign of friendship, something which was ever more important these days as his power grew and her resistance showed no sign of waning. Several times he had made subtle approaches to her – offers for dinner, a new dress – but every time, she politely found an excuse, knowing all the while his patience was growing thinner and thinner, until one day, she would wake to find herself out of favour of one of the most powerful men in the city. And what would happen then?

'We were just hearing from Ivan about the day's successes,' she said, folding his coat and going to fetch him a *rebujito* without being asked.

'A modest gain. We had hoped they were storing a lot more guns in there. We have still lost thousands of weapons that should be ours, weapons that are killing our own.'

'The snipers though, they had been problematic, had they not?' she asked, handing him the drink and trying to find the positives.

He nodded, his stare weighty upon her. 'Their position had been favourable. The towers gave them a 360-degree view that was difficult to penetrate. Reclaiming the church brings back that corner of the district.'

'Well I'm glad.' She forced a smile, hoping he wouldn't misread it as something she didn't intend. 'It is an area of the city I like very much. It is good it belongs to us once again.'

'Then we should walk there some time. Perhaps when the flowers come into bud.'

Marina nodded, although she couldn't imagine anything flowering in the city ever again; corpses were more numerous than flowers these days, the fetid stench of death overpowering the delicate aroma of jasmine and oleander. 'I'd better help Luciana with dinner,' she said quickly, turning away and feeling how his eyes followed after her. She saw Ivan and Luciana watching him watching her too. Were they threatened by his interest in her, or was it her they were worried for?

'Miguel, come – the papers I mentioned are through here,' Sindo said, leading him out of the kitchen.

Wordlessly, Luciana pushed the bowl of onions her way; Marina began chopping, wishing Paloma was still here. There had been safety creeping about in her shadow, but now she was doing what she had been built for – fighting on the front line – and Marina was left blinking in the glare of a spotlight, hopelessly exposed.

Paloma had returned to the apartment only twice in the

three months since she'd left – the first in the dead of night, between operations, staying only for thirty-six hours and sleeping for thirty-two hours of that. The second time, she had returned injured, a flesh wound in her arm needing medical attention before an infection in it grew worse. Luciana had doused it with iodine and as Paloma endured the stinging agony, she tried to pass the time telling them about the regiment's exploits; they were working closely with a small unit called Hijos de la Noche who specialized in nocturnal exploits, sabotaging operations behind Nationalist lines, and led by an American captain, Jack Quincy, who had been attached to the unit from the International Brigade.

Each time, Marina had sat with her for as long as she could, revelling in the daring of their exploits and wishing she too could believe in something so passionately she was prepared to die for it. But sometimes she wondered if perhaps a part of her – the vital part – had already died, for it was becoming increasingly hard to feel; so much of her existence was concerned with surviving – and having to fight to survive – that ironically any joy in living seemed to have disappeared altogether. She couldn't remember when she had last laughed or smiled even, and hunger, tiredness and fear were her constant companions.

Had she made a terrible mistake coming here? Wasn't life continuing as it always had for her family? She didn't have to be living in this way. She could be safe. Protected. The Nationalists had control of Andalusia, the power balance remaining in the hands of her father and his friends; after a brief tussle with the reds, nothing had changed for them. Whilst the rest of the country struggled and fought, Left against Right, socialist against Nationalist, the battle was already won there, the status quo re-established. Santi's uprising had been quashed and he was dead.

Dead.

Santi was dead.

She blinked hard for a long moment, the knife slack in her hand as she steadied her breath. No matter how many months passed, no matter how many times she said the words, they never felt real – it was impossible he could be gone. And yet he was. It was the only thing that had changed: her father was still the landowner, the bulls still grazed the green grass and the workers were still hungry . . . She had left for nothing and he had died for nothing and that was the worst of it.

'Marina?' She looked up to find Luciana looking over at her. 'Are you okay?'

'Of course.'

'You are sure? You look pale.'

'I'm just so tired, that's all.'

'We will sleep when we are dead. Perhaps tomorrow,' Luciana said, tossing her a look. She had a dark sense of humour that unnerved Marina sometimes.

They continued chopping and slicing, the thin stock bubbling ferociously and spitting at their wrists as they threw in the vegetables.

'It is smelling good in here,' Ivan said, rubbing his hands together appreciatively as he walked back into the room.

'It won't be long now,' Luciana said. 'Another drink?'

'Why not? I believe I have earnt it,' he replied, holding out his glass and sinking back down at the table again.

'What were you doing through there?' Luciana asked over her shoulder as she poured the sherry.

'Looking through those old boxes in the study. There's been a high-profile arrest on the French border.'

'Oh. Anyone we would have heard of?'

'Heard of, no, but I thought it might be the previous owner

of this place. I thought I recognized her from the photograph on the arrest card. She's a beautiful woman even if she is a fascist.'

Marina fell very still as his words carried over to her. What?

'And is it her?' Luciana asked, scooping up a handful of chopped potato and dropping it in the pan.

'It looks that way. Sindo and Miguel are just going through the photographs now.'

'What photographs?' Marina asked, her voice sounding hollow. 'I thought Paloma said everything was burnt when you moved in?'

He shrugged. 'Not everything.'

'So who was the owner?' Luciana asked.

'Sofia Delgado – some socialite with links to Mola –'

Marina froze at the sound of her godmother's name, her past so close to her it was like breath on her neck.

'– The husband was a general in the army. Died several years back in Tangiers but he was top brass. Miguel thinks she could be valuable.'

'Valuable how?' Luciana frowned. 'Surely she doesn't know anything useful?'

'Probably not, but she could be a bargaining chip – her life for a cannon.' He gave a careless shrug. 'Something like that.'

Marina felt sick. She remembered her godmother's excited laugh as Marina had opened her present at Christmas, her pitiful tears when her husband's body had been brought back. She had been childless, kind, patient, a great storyteller . . .

The sound of more footsteps into the room prompted Marina to suddenly move again, to look busy and fuss with the meal preparations as Luciana poured them all fresh drinks. She sensed Modesto's presence rather than saw it.

'Dinner's nearly ready,' she said, forcing another smile as

she turned and went to move past him, reaching for a slotted spoon.

'Fascinating thing,' he said quietly, coming to stand by her and watching her with an intensity marked even by his standards.

'What is?'

'The likeness.' He pointed to a small photograph he placed on the counter. It was of a young girl, no more than thirteen. A confirmation photograph, the girl's hands were pressed together in prayer, a short veil settled like a cloud around her shoulders, long dark hair looped back in an intricate braid.

Marina could remember the exact moment the shutter had snapped – the photographer had said 'horse's bum' to get her to smile.

Her eyes drew level with his, the fear draining her of blood.

'I mean, clearly it's *not* you,' he said in a low, slow voice. 'That girl is fascist scum and this once beautiful apartment is now – for her – enemy territory. She wouldn't dare to remain here. She would know only too well what would happen to a girl like her if she was found: the utter desecration of innocence and piety that would await her, the many, *many* men who would mete out their revenge against her and the class she represents . . .' His eyes blazed, burning into her, his breath scorching her face. She didn't dare breathe back, she didn't blink, and it felt an age before he spoke again. She truly expected her heart just to stop beating, her knees to give way. 'But you agree, there's a likeness between you?'

He wanted an answer. She had to answer. Play this game. 'A little,' she whispered.

He looked from her back to the photograph, to her again. 'Yes. You're right. It is just a little. Around the eyes, I think. And maybe the mouth.' His gaze fell pointedly to her mouth as he slipped the photograph into his trouser pocket. 'But she is no match for you, of course. She is just a Nationalist whore, whereas you are a true beauty: classic, refined, timeless.'

She swallowed. '. . . Thank you,' she whispered.

His eyes roamed her face, mere inches from hers and she felt his hand creep over hers on the counter, his skin rough and calloused and hot. 'But let us talk of nicer things. The ugliness of the day is done and we both live to see another dawn. We are the lucky ones, are we not?' She nodded. 'Though this is a time of war, still there must be time for beauty, for love, don't you agree?'

'I do,' she whispered.

'So then, when *shall* we go for that walk we mentioned, Marina Marquez? I do not think we can wait for the flowers.'

Chapter Twenty-Two

'Oh, I'm sorry—' She stopped in the doorway, one leg lifted to keep the weight off her ankle as she caught sight of the figure perched at the end of her bed.

Señora Quincy turned her head fractionally. Her hands were folded in her lap as she stared out of the window. 'Oh, Charlotte, no. Forgive *me*,' she said, going to move. 'I should not be in here. I thought you were not coming back.'

'Please, stay sitting,' Charlotte demurred.

'I just wanted to see it again.'

'It used to be yours?'

The old lady nodded. 'And Arlo's was on the other side.' Where Nathan slept now.

'How did you manage to get up here?' Charlotte asked, hopping carefully into the room.

'Two of those men lifted me.' She tutted, displeased by the necessity of it. 'Still . . .' She raised her arms slightly to indicate the old-fashioned room. 'It was worth it.' She glanced across at Charlotte, seeing how her ankle was bandaged and held up. 'How did *you* get up here? You can hardly move.'

'Scooted up on my backside,' Charlotte grinned, hopping over to the small armchair opposite the end of the bed. 'Not very elegant. My mother would have died if she'd seen me.'

'Couldn't someone have helped you? Where are the others?'

'Marina's gone back to her room – she wanted to check on you obviously. And Nathan's still in town, working.'

The old lady rolled her eyes. 'Digging the dirt, is he?'

'Uncovering truths,' Charlotte said. 'He's not here to apportion blame but to unearth reasons that explain – even support – your actions.'

Señora Quincy stared out of the window again. 'Those who need to know, know,' she said quietly.

'He thinks you fell in love with the wrong man.'

'Oh, I did that all right,' the señora agreed, but she didn't add anything and she sat quietly instead for a long time, her awareness of her surroundings seeming to come and go.

Charlotte let her own gaze drift out of the window, over the gardens. The silence suited her too. She felt worn out and battered from the past few days: London, coming back here, facing off to a bull, that kiss, that kiss . . . what did it mean? There was unfinished business between them, Nathan's eyes had told her that much as they'd left him in town. But the facts were the facts, no matter how hard she wished them otherwise: he still had a wife and child. Surely that was their ending?

'It's funny, I can remember it all so clearly – that night I left,' the old lady said abruptly, cutting into her thoughts. 'I cut my hair at that basin through there, escaped through that window . . . It was all ahead of me. My life was beginning that night, I could feel it.' She looked up at the beamed ceiling, the shuttered window. 'He hasn't touched the room at all. It's just as it was when I lived here.' She patted the bedspread gently. 'I can even remember my mother making this.'

'Perhaps Carlos was hoping you would come back.'

'He knew that was never going to happen,' Señora Quincy

scoffed. 'He may not have been why I left, but he was the reason I never returned.'

Charlotte watched her closely, looking for clues, signals. 'So it *wasn't* to do with Jack, then?'

'Jack?' Señora Quincy looked at her sharply. It was another half-minute before she responded. '. . . No, not Jack.'

They fell quiet again. Charlotte didn't want to push. She sensed the old lady would reveal more through musings and recollections, than interrogations.

'Tell me, how did you find Ronda?' Señora Quincy asked. 'Did you like it?

'I didn't get to see much of it, sadly. The driver took me straight to the bullring from the airport and then, of course, I sprained this.' She kicked her leg forward. 'I couldn't really walk anywhere, but Marina and I did take a horse-drawn carriage tour. It's absolutely charming – all those white houses and tiny, tiny streets. I couldn't believe we could get through most of them. I fully expected the carriage to end up wedged between two walls!'

The old lady smiled. 'A great friend of mine lived in the *mercadillo*. I used to sneak down when I could as a girl. Those were the happy days.'

'Marina wants to go back in tomorrow; she's so keen to explore the town. I think she really wants to get to grips with her heritage.'

The old lady's smile faded. 'She will only be disappointed.'

Charlotte tipped her head to the side. 'Will she? From what I've observed so far, she's embracing this new life. You grew up in a different time, a time when the whole world was at war, and I don't doubt you had good reason for doing what you did. But Marina's a grown woman who can make her own choices. The world has moved on and the Mendozas are, after all, one of the most illustrious families in southern Spain.'

'Illustrious is not the word I would use for this family,' Señora Quincy said firmly.

Another silence.

'So you really don't see any sort of opportunity here for her? You don't think that the financial security that comes with being a Mendoza could give her a better life? A more comfortable one?'

'Of course you would say that. You are a – what is it again? A *wealth counsellor*. You are in the thrall of money, you worship riches and fame. It is your god.'

'Believe me, señora, it most certainly is not. I know very well that money can be something from which to escape, as much as it is to embrace. Yes, many of my clients actively chased what they now possess, wealth was their dream. But I'm not there to show them how to spend it. It's down to me to show them that they *won't* find fulfilment in those things. I want to help Marina, to make sure she doesn't get lost in the hype that is coming towards her – and it is coming. She can't unknow what she knows. She is a Mendoza by blood, a member of one of the most prominent families in the country. Her life has changed already but she cannot merely step from one world into the next, not without help.' Charlotte leaned forward slightly. 'Just the technicalities of being recognized as a legitimate heir mean she'll need to put a legal and financial team together. These are practicalities that can't be ignored. But where *I* can help her is with coping strategies for how to manage her personal relationships, her daily routine, now that she doesn't have to work – especially during this transition phase—'

'There will be no transition. We are not taking any money,

nor are we taking the Mendoza name. We are Quincys. The best thing I ever did for my family was to leave all this behind.'

'The best thing? Forgive me, señora, but I have seen first-hand the cracks in the walls, the broken-down washing machine . . . I have seen how your granddaughter works double shifts and two jobs to pay the bills each month. Can you really say that's better? Was it really worth it?'

'Yes.'

'Leaving your home? Your family?' she pushed.

'Yes.'

'So if you'd known then what you know now, you would still do it all again?'

She hesitated. '. . . I will not deny mine has been the harder path. It has been a burden on my own family, living with less.' Her gaze met Charlotte's. 'And many would say I am mad. You will. What did I give all this up for when the time I had with my husband was cruelly short? We had four days together and that was it. Four days in ninety-eight years . . .'

Her eyes swam with bitter tears and Charlotte felt her own heart stiffen at the sight of her still raw grief. 'But though they were only four, they were the days that defined my entire life. They were the days that explained my life: I was born to have his child, and I was spared to raise his child. There's never been anyone else for me.' When she looked back at Charlotte, her grey-green eyes were as clear as onyx. 'So when you ask me if I would do it again? Yes, in this life, and the next, and however many others might follow. I would always choose him.'

I would always choose him. What about when there wasn't a choice? Charlotte wondered. What about when he was married to someone else? A father?

One of the carers knocked on the door. 'Excuse me, señora, your granddaughter wishes you to rest now.'

Señora Quincy looked over at him and gave a nod. She did look weary. The medic wheeled a wheelchair into the room and carefully lifted her frail body off the bed. The old lady's eyes never left hers and Charlotte marvelled that though the flesh was weak, the spirit was still so strong.

'Please just consider this one thing, señora,' she said, as the carer turned to wheel her away. '*You've* got full disclosure on this situation. You know why you abandoned this life and chose another, harder path. Marina doesn't. She loves you but you also love her and maybe what was right for you all those years ago isn't right for her now. For your granddaughter's sake, at least tell her everything and allow her to decide for herself.'

There was no response.

'I will take Señora Quincy back to her room now,' the carer said, when his patient didn't reply. 'She must rest. Señor Mendoza is returning home tomorrow.'

Charlotte nodded. She already knew it was going to be a long day.

Marina was sitting in one of the red velvet carver chairs, nervously reading a magazine and looking like she was sitting in the dentist's waiting room when Charlotte hobbled into the room. She had managed to shower and change into a draped mocha silk dress, the elegant look rather undermined when one of the staff caught sight of her coming down the stairs on her bottom, leg outstretched.

Mayra appeared at the door. 'An aperitif, Señora Fairfax?'

She saw that Marina was drinking beer. 'Thank you. A negroni, please.' She needed something strong and swift. Nathan's continued absence was making her edgy. Where was he? They had to at least talk about what had happened between them at the bullring, didn't they? That kiss had been real, true.

There had been no lies between them then. Was he just going to avoid her? Stay out all night? Stay somewhere else instead? She felt desperate to just see him. Even just seeing him would suffice. But she knew in her heart it wouldn't stop there. Over and over she had replayed the look he had given her at Marina's words, *we don't get to choose who we fall in love with.*

Mayra nodded and left again.

'How are you feeling?' Marina asked, setting aside the magazine as Charlotte settled herself on the sofa; it was so low she wondered if she would ever be able to get up again.

'I had a quick nap. I don't know what it is about flying. I always need to sleep afterwards. How was your grandmother?'

'She had gone out for some air when I got in. She's resting now, though. She's going to skip dinner tonight.'

'Right,' Charlotte said, feeling a stab of guilt that she had pushed the old woman so hard.

She gazed around the room. It was all shadows and dark corners, mahogany timbers along the ceilings, console tables draped with heavily fringed damasks, the furniture hard and lean. It wasn't a room for slouching in; it demanded a straight back and shoes on, manners and a sharp wit – she had grown up in rooms such as this. On one wall, between the windows, flashed a set of matador's knives and above the fireplace was draped an opulent cape, silver and gold thread woven through carnation-pink silk.

'Incredible, isn't it?' Marina asked, looking around too. She was wearing tight black trousers, heeled ankle-boots and a strappy, shiny camisole with a trim of sequins along the top, kohl heavily inked around her eyes. She looked more like she was ready for a big night out than a quiet private dinner and Charlotte felt another stab of concern for how much she had coming her way in the future months. It wasn't just the right bank balance that would make her a Mendoza, it was the right manners too, knowing the right people, drinking the right wine, telling the right jokes. 'I can't believe this is . . . *me*,' she murmured, her eyes alighting on a portrait on the far wall. She frowned, getting up and walking over.

'What is it?' Charlotte asked, trying to twist in her seat.

'Is it just me or . . .' Marina lifted the painting off the wall – another no-no she didn't yet know about – and carried it over. '. . . Is she me?'

'Wow! She's the image of you. Or you are of her, rather.'

'Aren't I?' Marina said in amazement, her gaze travelling over the portrait. The woman was young, with a rope of thick dark hair twisted into an elegant looped braid, a hat angled on her head. She was sitting side-saddle and wearing a magnificent emerald velvet riding habit.

'She's so beautiful,' Charlotte said, admiring the artistry. This was no lucky likeness, the artist had been accomplished, masterful even.

Was that footsteps she could hear?

'Quick, put it back.'

'But who is she?' Marina asked, transfixed.

'My grandmother.'

The deep voice made them both jump, Marina almost dropping the painting on Charlotte's lap.

'Mateo,' Charlotte faltered, trying to recover herself, mortified to have been caught looming over a painting that should have been hanging in a museum, not being picked off the wall like a Beyoncé poster.

Seemingly from nowhere, Mayra appeared and discreetly took the painting from Marina's hands, returning it to its rightful position on the wall. Mateo walked into the room, looking imposing in a beige striped seersucker blazer and chinos. He was tanned, elegant, perfectly at home. Of course.

'Marina,' he said, holding out a hand and clasping the other around hers. 'My cousin.' He stared down at her, a benign smile on his face as he openly studied her, taking in the Mendoza features – heavy, planed bone structure, deep-set eyes. 'I must say, the likeness is striking. Did my aunt ever mention her mother to you?'

Marina shook her head, dumbstruck and forgetting for a moment to use her voice too. '. . . No.'

'No,' he nodded, the smile still in place. 'Well, she was a noted beauty. The most beautiful woman in Andalusia back then, they said.'

Marina looked like a rabbit in the headlights, her smile stuck on as Mateo overwhelmed her. As one of the wealthiest men in the country, his face was instantly recognizable but it was his smooth manners and utmost decorum that were the unexpected extra. Charlotte knew Marina would never have met someone of his calibre before and that to have been his waitress would have been somehow easier than sitting here as his new-found cousin.

'We weren't expecting you till the morning . . .' Charlotte said, rescuing her and wishing she could stand up.

Mayra returned with their drinks, including a martini for Mateo. They each took them and Mateo gestured for Marina to please sit too.

'. . . Is your father with you?' Charlotte asked.

'No, he is coming on with my wife in the morning. One more night's observation and paperwork.' He gave a light-hearted roll of his eyes as he crossed his legs, fussing slightly with the crease of his trousers. 'But I felt I ought to get here as soon as I could. I've been very aware that you've been gathered here for several days. I hope you won't think it remiss that we couldn't get here before now.'

'Not at all,' Marina said, perching at the front of her chair as if she was in a job interview. 'In fact, I think my grandmother has benefited from having a few days to recover first from the journey.'

'I'm glad to hear it. And she is quite well?'

'Very, thank you. She's resting in her room, getting ready I think for tomorrow.'

Mateo smiled. 'Is she nervous about the reunion?'

'I'm not sure. I think so, but then she's always been very self-possessed. It can be hard to tell.'

Mateo inhaled. 'I think my father is . . . relieved. I'd say that's the word. I think this is something he has wanted for a very long time.'

Charlotte saw how Marina's smile had become even more fixed and a small, awkward silence bloomed.

'I only wish we had known about each other sooner,' Mateo said, smoothly filling the void. 'We might have met under happier circumstances.'

'Yes,' Marina agreed meekly, looking intimidated.

Mateo looked around the room, as though noticing something wasn't quite right. 'Ah, but where is our professor?'

'Still working,' Charlotte said neutrally, even as her stomach clenched again at his prolonged absence.

'At this time of the evening?' Mateo frowned, checking his Patek Philippe watch.

She tried to look surprised too. It was growing late now, all the museums or institutions he would be visiting for work would be closed. He was deliberately avoiding her. Their kiss earlier had him running scared. Another mistake . . . In the heat of the moment it had been just that: heat. Hormones. Chemicals. Adrenaline was up. But in the growing coolness of these hours afterwards, the facts would be reasserting themselves to him with stark brutality: he had a family. It couldn't be changed.

'Well he took a few hours out this afternoon to join me on a tour of the bullring,' Marina explained. 'It was very kind of you to have arranged the private visit.'

'The least I could do,' Mateo said, spreading his hands wide in a generous gesture. 'We have, of course, very close links with them. I expect you saw the sculpture of the bull outside?'

Marina nodded.

'That was one of our bulls – Leviatan. Truly one of the most impressive beasts we ever bred: he weighed two tonnes and had shoulders wider than a car. He was the creature that inspired Ferruccio Lamborghini when he came to visit La Ventilla in the 1960s and decided to have an image of the bull as the marque for his cars.'

'Wow, I never knew that,' Charlotte smiled, seeing how Marina looked like she might burst with pride.

'That's very cool,' Marina grinned.

Mateo looked over at her. 'It *is* cool being a Mendoza,' he agreed, seeming pleased. He took a long sip of his drink. 'Well, it will be interesting to see what his research has uncovered. How *has* history remembered the Mendozas, I wonder?'

Charlotte and Marina glanced at each other, sensing he had no idea of the shadows behind the family's glittering name.

'Nathan told me once he sometimes feels like more of a detective than a historian,' Charlotte said lightly instead.

'That's a good analogy. Is there much of a difference, I wonder?'

Charlotte thought for a moment. 'I suppose the detective wants justice.'

'And the historian?'

'The truth.'

Mateo narrowed his eyes, regarding her interestedly. 'The truth, yes, there's no room for sentiment there. It's about the facts. The cold, hard facts.'

Mayra came in, announcing dinner was ready, and Marina gratefully finished her beer with one long gulp – prompting a look of bemusement from Mateo.

'By the way, Charlotte, I have something for you,' he said, shooting her a conspiring look. 'Come. It is out here.'

He put down his drink and walked out into the hall. Charlotte struggled to her feet and hobbled over, leaning against the doorway. There, a magnificent saddle gleamed astride the back of a chair. It was decorated with a Hermes-orange satin bow.

'To get you back in the saddle, so to speak,' Mateo said. 'You remember our first conversation?

'I do. And it's beautiful,' Charlotte gasped. 'But . . . *why*?'

'It's a wedding gift of course!'

What? She looked up at him, just as Marina joined her in the doorway.

'You're getting *married*?' Marina asked excitedly, placing a hand on her arm.

'In just a few days,' Mateo nodded.

'Charlotte, why didn't you say?'

But Charlotte couldn't reply, because the reason why was standing frozen on the spot at the other end of the hall, a jacket in one hand and eyes that told her he had heard every single word.

Dinner was brief. Mateo was a charming and self-assured host but even he was struggling to keep a conversation going single-handedly for more than three courses: Marina, overawed by the unexpected social situation, could only dumbly agree to anything he said, and Charlotte could scarcely hear a word that passed, her brain going into overdrive as she tried to think of ways to explain things to Nathan. But he wouldn't look at her; for the entire dinner he had kept his attention on either his plate or his host, smiling at Mateo's anecdotes and doing an all-round fantastic job of acting (as he had tried to in the jeep) as though she wasn't even there.

'Will you excuse me?' she said finally, as the dessert plates were being cleared and Mateo started making noises about finishing off the meal with some brandy. 'I think I need to get to bed. My foot is throbbing and I need to elevate it.' She didn't know how much longer she could sit there, pretending to be fine when she was anything but.

'Me too,' Marina said quickly. 'Not the foot. Just the bed bit.' She smiled nervously. 'Big day tomorrow.'

'Quite,' Mateo said, tipping his head in agreement and smiling broadly as she slipped from the room. 'You're sure we can't persuade you to stay for a nightcap, Charlotte?'

'I'm afraid not. It's Nurofen and an early night for me.'

'Well that is a shame. I had been hoping we might mix a little business with our pleasure and regroup on things before the big day.'

'First thing tomorrow?' she asked hopefully, standing up with a wobble.

Mateo saw how her leg was still held awkwardly off the floor and immediately, gallantly, relented. 'Of course.'

'Thank you for a lovely evening. Goodnight,' she said, her gaze coming to rest on Nathan, but he was busying himself with pouring the last of the red into his glass. He had drunk a lot over dinner, matching Mateo easily, who seemed to appreciate having an equally thirsty guest.

She began hobbling and hopping over the floor, aware she had an audience.

'My dear,' Mateo tutted to her back as she reached the door. 'How on earth are you going to walk down the aisle in three days' time like that?'

'Oh, it's . . .' She couldn't even finish the lie.

'More to the point, how on earth are you going to get up the stairs tonight?'

'I'm fine,' she said quickly. 'I have a system: bottom shuffling. *Not* elegant. *Very* effective.'

'Nonsense. You'll ruin that beautiful dress of yours. I'll ask for some of the carers to carry you.'

'Please don't. I hate a fuss,' she said quickly. 'And I'll be up in half the time it'd take them to get here anyway.'

'But . . .' Mateo looked floundered by her refusal. 'Nathan, talk some sense into her, please. Dior silk was not designed for sweeping floors.' He looked suddenly at his dining companion. 'Or of course, you could do the honours—'

'No, no,' Charlotte said firmly. 'He couldn't possibly—'

'Nonsense, he's twice your size. He'll barely know he's lifting you; isn't that so, professor? We can hardly leave a damsel in distress.'

There was an expectant pause.

'Yes. Quite,' Nathan muttered, setting down his napkin and scraping his chair back.

Mateo rose too. 'And then you can join me afterwards in the library for that drink.'

'Of course.'

The two men crossed the room and Charlotte began limping ahead as fast as she could, trying to get to the stairs first.

'I don't know. Modern women,' Mateo said, seeming amused as they reached her on the second step. 'They simply will not accept help.'

'Mmm.' Nathan stood before her, staring down with that inscrutable expression that was his speciality. Without another word, he scooped her up. She felt a blush of embarrassment and mortification as he began walking easily, carrying her as if she were a tray, his eyes dead ahead.

'As I said. Very good,' Mateo nodded, approvingly. 'The library's down here, professor. Second door on the right.'

'Really, I'm fine,' she murmured in a low voice as soon as Mateo turned away and began striding down the corridor. 'Please, you can put me down now. This isn't necessary. I'm quite capable—'

'Actually, I'm not sure you are capable,' he said tightly as he climbed the staircase without any apparent effort. 'You stood in front of a charging bull this afternoon, remember?'

Hearing the scorn, she looked up at him as he carried her, his head lifted, jaw thrust angrily. 'Nathan . . .' she faltered. 'I wanted to tell you.'

'Tell me what?' he asked stubbornly, pretending he didn't know what they were really talking about.

They were at the top of the stairs now but he made no attempt to put her down, striding down the corridor like she was a naughty child being sent to bed.

'. . . I wanted to tell you about Stephen.'

'You said he was no one.'

'I . . . panicked.'

He tossed her up slightly, readjusting his grip. 'If you're engaged, why aren't you wearing a ring?'

What? Oh. '. . . It's being engraved.'

He glanced down at her, gave a careless shrug. 'Well, it's

not my business anyway, I already told you that,' he said dismissively.

'That's right,' she said desperately. 'Because you're *already* married, something you conveniently left out of the conversation too! You can't put all of this on me.'

They were at her bedroom now, the door ajar, and he kicked it open so that it swung against the opposite wall. Without another word, he threw her onto the bed and stared down at her. 'Poor bugger. I wonder if he knows what he's let himself in for – marrying you in a few days when last week you were in bed with someone else.'

She gasped, furious at his double standards. 'You know it wasn't like that!'

'Actually, that's exactly what it was like,' he contradicted her.

'You're not . . .'

'What?' he prompted, throwing his arms out curiously.

'You're not just *someone*.'

He stared back at her, in the same room but further away from her than he'd ever been. 'No, that's right, I'm not. I'm the lucky bastard that got away.' He shook his head. 'You know, I pity him. I really do. You're so convincing, whichever part you're playing.'

'What do you mean by that?'

'Take a look at yourself, reinvented – working like you need to, helping people cope with being rich so that they don't make the mistakes you made. Making sure they don't end up as the party queen who goes off one weekend to a family friend's wedding and comes back as the fucking bride.'

She rose up onto her knees, trying to get to eye level with him, to get him to see . . . 'Nate, please—!'

'But you haven't changed at all, not inside; you're exactly

the same now as you were then – using people to make you feel better. I was your wild card – the poor boy who didn't give a damn about your rich friends and the right parties, and you liked that for a while. But I just couldn't quite cut it, could I? I couldn't save you *enough*. And so what's he now? Another safety net?' He held his hand up as she went to speak. 'No, don't even bother telling me. I'm not interested. Being with me, being with him, it makes no difference. You're still so beautiful Lotts, so broken, so fucking *tragic*, never quite getting over Daddy's death.'

'Don't you mention my father!' she cried, her hand automatically rising to strike him, but he caught it – this time – holding her tightly by the wrist.

'Still off-limits, is he?' he asked, seeing how the tears immediately budded in her eyes. 'You know, you can get married as many times as you like, but it doesn't matter how often you change your name, you'll still be his daughter.'

The truth of his cruel words hit like a whip, making her sting and flinch. 'I hate you,' she whispered, feeling the tears fall.

His eyes scoured her face, emotions he would never put voice to darkening his features and taking him far away from her. 'Good. That's for the best.' And he dropped her wrist and walked out of the room.

Chapter Twenty-Three

Guadalajara, outside Madrid, March 1937

It was a starless night, the moon a fragile silver curlicue in the unremitting black sky. She lay on her stomach, waiting as she'd been told, her eyes on the road as she recorded the number of vehicles coming up the pass. So far, she had counted nine armoured trucks, six panzers, and two armoured cars. And more were coming.

She shifted position, the cold ground chilling her through the thick blanket; it had been one of the coldest winters of the century and her arms ached from their splayed position as she looked through the binoculars. She watched the lights coming up the narrow road, saw the soldiers in their round helmets, heads dipped tiredly, rifles between their knees: all of them someone's son, someone's brother, someone's husband. A year ago it would have been her they were fighting for; now she was their quarry, hidden on a hillside under cover of darkness and counting them off as they headed straight into the ambush Miguel and the others had set for them, two miles from here.

It was the first mission on which she had been allowed to accompany them. Miguel, for all his cruelties in private, was surprisingly protective. He didn't want anything to happen to her – not by anyone else. She was *his* pet and he liked keeping her on a tight leash. But they needed more manpower; they had been badly hit by ferocious fighting in the Jarama valley, and even he couldn't reasonably argue against using her in the offensive – she was young and fit and strong. The fascists' hold was strengthening and they needed everyone they could get: man, woman or child.

Another convoy was coming, she could hear the rumble of the trucks before she saw them, and she dipped a little lower for good measure, wondering where the others were stationed. They were spread out all over this hillside, tired eyes watching from the darkness, plotting, waiting . . .

She knew Ivan was working up at the front with the American – a crack shot, he could keep his nerves cool and arm steady even when mortars were being shelled at him. Marina wasn't sure she would ever get used to the sounds of war, the sweet smell of cordite . . .

She had been told to watch out for the flare; that was the signal to abandon the raid and start running; above all to get back to camp with the machine gun strapped to her back. She wasn't sure which asset was more prized by them – her life or the gun. Weapons were in desperately short supply, making their sabotage unit ever more valuable to the Republican powers as they disrupted the fascists' infantry supplies and field operations.

Briefly it occurred to her she had become a bandit. They were notorious back home, the area such a stronghold that a hundred years earlier, the government had been impelled to create the Civil Guard just to deal with them. Arlo used to run around as a little boy, pretending to be one, until the day their father had roughly explained that they were exactly the people the bandits had wanted to rob and hurt; he hadn't slept for a week after that, waking in the night and crying, climbing into her bed.

Arlo. Her other half, her gentle-spirited twin. She closed her eyes, feeling the pain that always came whenever she thought of him. It was a physical ache, as though something had been bodily removed from her and left in its wake an endless hollow that couldn't be filled or replaced. Her mother had always said they were connected by an invisible thread and she could feel it now, a nerve ending, exposed and raw. 'You came into this world together,' she would say. 'And you must promise to stay in it together.'

Instead, they had been separated before they reached seventeen, already worlds apart. There had been no other way: he could not leave and she could not stay. His every decision was rooted in fear – of his father's anger, of his mother's disappointment – and one word of her plans would have sent him running to them, because losing her was his biggest fear of all. He would have betrayed her just to keep her safe and she couldn't allow that. She couldn't live that way any more.

But could she keep living like this? In the dark moments when Miguel took the pound of flesh that was the price for his protection, she made herself promises that she would see them again when the war was over. But it felt like an impossible dream. She was no longer the girl who had climbed out of that window. War had taken her innocence, her childhood, her hope—

A sound whistled past her, a bullet screaming into the nubby bark of a tree just ahead. She gasped and ducked, her hands instinctively covering her head as she heard another spinning at high velocity. Her cheek pressed into the dirt and she dared to look upwards: the sky was glowing red and the distant crack of gunfire, of shouts, splintered the still silence of the night.

She looked behind her but could see nothing. Not yet anyway. But those bullets had come from somewhere, someone was coming down and she couldn't afford to stay here. Abandoning the blanket and her coat, she quickly scrabbled to her knees and wrestled the machine gun onto her back using the makeshift harness she had made with some dead fascist soldiers' belts. It was heavier than she had expected and she struggled to stand; she was only supposed to have been safeguarding it here. Hers was the midway station – neither up nor down – and Quincy, the handsome American captain, had intended to bring it himself when he came back down. That was how he was: war hadn't diminished his manners; if anything, it seemed to magnify their importance for him, as if he believed that those alone were all that was left to distinguish them from the beasts. If he only knew what an animal he served beside, Miguel doling out a nightly torture to her under his very nose and against which he was supposedly fighting. But she could say nothing; to ask for his help would be to demand his suicide. She had chosen freedom but it had trapped her as surely as any cage.

As best she could, she began to run down the hillside, her feet slipping on the wet leaf mulch. She held her arms out, running from one tree to the next, partly to control her speed, but the legs of the tripod kept catching against the trees and alternately either wedged her in place or else sent her spinning. The mechanical *rat-a-tat-tat* of machine gun fire made her cry out in fear, unable to see where it was intended – her or someone else? Where was Miguel? Whatever else he was, he had kept his promise to her: he had kept her safe, kept her alive this long.

Her legs wheeled, her arms pumping, lungs burning, eyes tearing. She didn't know where she was, the road now out of sight and every tree looking like all the rest, but as the gradient steepened, the forest and needle-carpeted ground suddenly giving way to rock, she knew she was nearing the gorge. The cave was down there. Safety. Their agreed meeting point. She scrambled quickly around the boulders and granite outcrops that replaced the trees, grateful for the childhood that had given her a nimble agility, a childhood that could never have predicted she might one day be using those skills to run for her life with a machine gun strapped to her back.

Sure enough, the land dropped away suddenly – the undoing of those who didn't know to slow – and as she looked down she saw the oxbow bend of the river far below. The cave aligned with the three-quarter point along the top of the curve. She was nearly there.

Her nails broke as she dug her hands into the rock face, the so-called path used by the wild goats barely as wide as her foot. Facing in, she shuffled along, knowing that one strong gust of wind might be all it took to unbalance her with the alien weight behind. But within a few minutes, she could already see the tips of the olive branches ahead. Only the unnatural angle of them betrayed that they had been cut and wedged in around the boulder that doubled as a door. It was a much-used bolthole – barely evident from across the gorge, far less from the sky as the fascists flew over in Hitler's Luftwaffe planes.

Her hands felt the mouth of the cave, finding the blessed curve inwards that took her deeper into the earth and away from the danger of man – his bullets, his mortars, his knives. Panting, realizing she was weeping, she pushed against the branches, into them, feeling them scratch her face as she found just enough width to wedge herself in and fall to her knees, away from the drop.

Whimpers escaped her as she struggled with the harness; the ties had drawn tighter around her shoulders from where she had become tangled in the trees, the downward momentum drawing her onwards momentarily before being abruptly locked in place. Her fingers fumbled with the knots, still lazy with cold, and it was another few minutes before she freed herself and could let the gun fall. She cried out with relief, throwing her head back as she rolled her shoulders, easing out the cramps, before pulling the gun out of sight from the shelf and replacing the branches again. She squeezed sideways past the boulder into the black cavity, exhausted. It was damp, the air fetid, but she had done it. She was safe. She was—

Not alone.

A twig cracked underfoot and then she was thrown against the wall, a cold muzzle pressing against her head.

'State your name,' a male voice hissed, one hand grabbing her by the hair, holding her in place, the other reaching up and down her body, feeling for weapons. She did the same as she was pressed against the cave wall, reaching for something, anything – a stone as a missile, a stick as a knife . . .

'Marina. Marina Marquez,' she whispered, hating that she could hear her own fear. Taste it.

There was a palpable silence, and then she was spun around again. And suddenly nothing and everything made sense.

Chapter Twenty-Four

'Ah, Charlotte, you slept well, I trust?' Mateo asked as she appeared on the terrace and began hobbling over.

'Like the proverbial,' she smiled, even though the bags under her eyes clearly told another story. But if she looked bad, Nathan looked a lot worse. She could tell from a single glance that he was hungover: it was in the droop of his eyes, the stiff set of his shoulders. Not that she was surprised – she had been able to hear him and Mateo getting stuck in to the brandy, their voices drifting through the house in the early hours. It had been past two when he'd come up and she'd heard him go into the bathroom again at six so she knew he too had barely slept. At one point, she had heard the creak of the treads and seen his shadow stop by the bathroom door into her room. She had frozen, her eyes glued to the dim hovering shape, her heart beating like a jackhammer, all her anger beginning to ball in the pit of her stomach. If he so much as dared . . . She didn't want his damn apology, not after everything he'd said. But after a while – had he been listening for the sound of her breathing? Crying? – he had moved away, the soft click of his door closing telling her it was safe again.

She would have missed it had she been sleeping herself but she had forgotten to draw the curtains – hopping to the window had felt a hop too far last night – and she was stuck in that no-man's-land of physical exhaustion and mental mania. Her eyes ached, burning to sleep, as she stared at the wall instead, mind whirling as she listened to the sound of him in the next room but one. She had heard him on the phone to someone – *her?* – his voice low and even, and then, exercising – push-ups, sit-ups, pushing himself hard, driving on. She just lay in bed listening to it all, these unremarkable everyday sounds of the man who had once been her world, the man who in the space of single days had seduced and then abandoned her, who had rescued and then forsaken her. She had loved him once but now she hated him, and he wanted that? He welcomed it?

She sat down at the breakfast table with them both and poured herself a glass of juice, aware of Nathan's hooded gaze flickering on and off her – taking in her hobble, her dress, her pale face, her silent contempt . . .

The table was set out on the terrace below a rush-matted pergola, dappled light sprinkling through the slats onto the bowls of watermelon, peach, nectarines and plums. Jugs of freshly squeezed juices stood like rainbow chimes, grapefruits and oranges like bowling balls.

'It's good of you to join me early,' Mateo said brightly. 'I thought we should have a debrief before our guests come through.'

'You must be looking forward to meeting your aunt,' Charlotte said lightly.

'Let's say I'm certainly . . . interested.' He looked at Nathan. 'Now, we kept to our promise and didn't talk shop last night—'

'Your brandy was too good for that,' Nathan replied.

'Indeed. You must take a bottle when you leave. It's hard to come by.'

'Thank you.'

Charlotte watched the love-in with jaded eyes as she began cutting up a grapefruit half.

'But tell me now, where are we? What have you found?'

Nathan inhaled deeply, as though wondering where to start. 'Well, we think we know why your aunt left – she was a Republican sympathizer. And her husband was an American who came over at the start of the war to fight as part of the International Brigade.'

'. . . *Republicans?*' Mateo asked as though it was a dirty word.

'The political ideologies of the Left were pretty far-ranging – from socialism to full-blown anarchy; they could have been all-out communists or just forward-thinking liberals. But either way, that all came under the umbrella of Republicanism and that's the side they fought for.'

'Well, that would certainly account for things. Siding with the Left would have been a betrayal of all our family stood for – our principles. There would have been no way my grandfather could have condoned the match. He and all his sons fought valiantly for the Nationalists—'

'Wait – your father too?' Nathan frowned. 'You're sure?'

'Of course.'

'But I haven't found any reference to that. In the local records I've seen, your grandfather and uncles Valentino and Montez signed up to join the Cavalry Regiment on 27 September 1936 – but your father's name wasn't there.'

'No, he didn't join the fight till the beginning of '37. He was a lieutenant in the reconnaissance squadron of the National Infantry Division.'

Nathan looked at him intently. 'And why was that, do you know?'

Mateo shrugged. 'Age? My father was the youngest son; he would only have been sixteen when the war broke out.'

Nathan pulled a sceptical face. 'Many soldiers were that age though, or not much older.'

'Well, he was also fiercely pacifist. My father has always said there are causes worth dying for, but none worth killing for.'

'So then what changed?'

'He grew older? He grew up?' Mateo shrugged. 'Principles are well and good, in principle, but I suppose when men are dying around you . . .'

'Ah yes, that'll be it,' Nathan nodded. 'Your grandfather and uncles were killed in December 1936 – not fighting on the battlefield, but dragged from their beds and murdered. If your father signed up shortly after in '37, then that timing isn't a coincidence.'

'No, I don't suppose it would be,' Mateo agreed after a short pause, sitting back as Mayra came out with a steaming pot and poured him some coffee. 'So then my father joined the war to avenge his family, his sister ran away with the enemy and that's why they were estranged?' He seemed almost disappointed by the anti-climactic revelation. 'It makes sense. It just seems a shame they've drawn out the grudge for so long when the rest of the country has managed to move on.' He looked into the distance wistfully for a moment. 'Still, my father has reached out the olive branch and forgiven her. I only hope she will see the generosity of his act and behave likewise.'

Charlotte frowned as she ate her grapefruit, remembering something Señora Quincy had said to her in the bedroom yesterday.

'Charlotte? You seem unsure,' Mateo said, catching sight of her expression.

'Well, it's just that . . . your aunt said something yesterday that suggested it wasn't your father who was the one in a position to do the forgiving.'

Mateo's beneficent smile soured. 'And what did she say exactly?'

'That he may not have been why she left. But that he was the reason why she stayed away.'

There was a silence.

'Well I would take that to imply her continuing anger that her brother fought against her husband during the war,' Nathan said shortly.

'Quite,' Mateo agreed. 'Exactly.'

'But why be so angry at your father for that?' Charlotte said, keeping her gaze firmly on Mateo and away from Nathan. She didn't even want to look at him now. 'She had run away six months earlier, before he'd even signed up. Plus she had to have known that out of the two of them, she was the one doing the "betraying" – to her family, her heritage – not him.'

'Perhaps because she understood him to be a pacifist, learning that he was fighting at all was the betrayal,' Mateo suggested.

'Seems unlikely though, don't you think?' she asked. 'She's really going to hold on to that "moral disappointment" for eighty years?'

'Oh, I think people can hold on to their *moral disappointment* for a lot longer than you realize,' Nathan sneered, scorn dripping from his words as he savagely cut up a peach. He stopped suddenly. He looked at Mateo again. '. . . Wait – reconnaissance squadron, you said?'

'Hmm?' Mateo murmured, sipping his coffee.

Nathan sat back in his chair, concentrating hard, lost in thought.

'What is it?' Mateo asked him, setting down his cup.

Nathan was quiet for another moment, a deep frown creasing his brow. 'I'm pretty sure . . . in fact I'm almost certain that the attack in which your aunt's husband was killed was carried out by a recon squad.'

'How do you know?'

'There's a lot of paperwork on it on the Nationalist side. I've been looking up anything with Jack Quincy's name in it and it was clear from the report I saw that things had gone badly wrong. The unit was there only to assess potential screen barriers, guard cover and the area's security. The orders from the FSC commander were logged as purely a preliminary survey of the premises—'

'What's FSC?' Charlotte interrupted tersely.

'Forward Support Company,' Nathan muttered, as though that would mean anything to her. He looked at Mateo again. 'They knew the church was being used by a militia group they had been tracking – Hijos de la Noche – but the FOB wasn't in position to move. No one was supposed to die that night. It was information-gathering only.'

She didn't bother to ask what FOB stood for.

Mateo stared at him. 'So what happened?'

'One of the soldiers somehow got inside the church and killed the two men in there: Jack Quincy and another man, his accomplice – Santiago Esperanza.'

'Esperanza?' Charlotte murmured, forgetting her hostility for a moment. 'You've mentioned him before.'

'Yes, he's from around here. It was his father who was supposedly killed by Mateo's uncles and, in turn, he was reputed to have had a hand in their deaths. He had worked closely with Quincy almost from the beginning and we're pretty certain Quincy was involved in the midnight raid that saw them thrown from the bridge, so chances are Esperanza was in on it too.'

'And this soldier broke into the church and killed these two men?' Charlotte asked.

Nathan nodded. 'The army brass were not happy they had been killed – they'd wanted the men taken alive, believing they had valuable information about planned Republican attacks.'

There was a silence, everyone's minds whirring.

'. . . What was the soldier's explanation for disobeying his commander?' Mateo asked finally.

'That he had seen through one of the windows that they had taken a Nationalist woman hostage.'

Charlotte's eyes narrowed. '*Had* they?'

'Yes.'

'Was she killed too?'

'No, she was pulled out in a pretty poor state though. She was hysterical. Mad even, which wasn't particularly unusual given what she must have been made to endure. Sent to a psychiatric facility, the report said . . .'

Charlotte didn't reply. She remembered all too clearly his words at the bullring, and the fate of any captured woman, red or white. Death would indeed have been preferable.

'. . . But now I'm wondering if that was just a cover story,' Nathan murmured.

A low drone came into earshot and they all looked up into the faultless blue sky, a tiny speck in the distance growing ever larger, drawing ever closer.

Mateo looked back at him. Time was short now. 'What do you mean, professor?'

'I don't think the hostage was the reason he broke rank. Any soldier would have known that disobeying a direct order would risk his being shot for insubordination. But if revenge was what he had signed up for in the first place, if he had joined the recon squad with the sole aim of tracking and finding the men responsible for his family's deaths . . . ? For him, that was probably a price worth paying. What else did he have to lose? His parents were dead, his brothers were dead, his sister was missing, probably presumed dead. I think this was personal.'

There was a long silence, the two men holding each other's gaze, neither one wanting to say the words.

Finally, Mateo stirred. 'You're saying you believe that soldier was my *father*?'

Nathan nodded. 'I'm afraid I do.'

Charlotte stared into the distance, trying to run the images in a loop through her head – Carlos Mendoza, intent on revenge, had found his target, not knowing he was killing his own sister's husband. No wonder Marina had hated him; enough hatred to last a lifetime.

'Dear God,' Mateo murmured, sitting back in his chair and looking ashen, as the helicopter headed straight for the lush estate, an oasis in the arid sierra. 'What are we doing?'

He was carried off on a stretcher, a team of white-suited orderlies met by his domestic team and handing over notes, medical kits and bags.

Charlotte and Nathan stayed back, well clear of the down-draught and watching as Mateo ran in a half-crouch towards his father, his jacket splaying out in the wind. They saw him reach forward and clasp the old man's hand, leaning down to kiss his forehead as the medics carried him over the grass. Behind, Mateo's wife climbed down from the helicopter and hurried to catch up with them, trying with one hand to stop her long dark hair from flying everywhere.

The team hastened into the house – efficient, deft, silent, no commands needed, doors being held open automatically, everything prepared.

Gone again.

'Oh.' Charlotte sighed at the sheer speed of it, feeling somehow disappointed. All they had seen of him had been a shiny head and that thin, pale arm extending from the covers, holding Mateo's hand.

'Well, that's that then. The client's got what he needed,' Nathan said flatly, his words a gross understatement to the scale of the tragedy they had just unearthed. He turned and moved off. 'I can pack and get out of here.'

'Back to your family,' Charlotte called after him, a cutting edge in her voice, as he walked off without even glancing at her. She was perfectly aware of the scale of her betrayal, her personal shortcomings – perhaps everything he'd said last night had been true but where was his remorse? Why was he so determined to heap all the guilt onto her? She saw him falter, move as if to turn back and cut her down again, but instead – worse – he carried onwards, disappearing into the house too. Done.

She stared into the void he left behind. She wanted to scream at his back, claw at his skin. Make him react. Make him be sorry. But he wasn't. He'd done what he'd come to do and now he was leaving without a backward glance. He was packing right now. He'd be gone in the hour . . . It was done. Over. Finally, this was their ending.

Heart pounding, panic flooding her, she grabbed her phone and pressed redial, trying the number again. Forget the hotel room in Madrid, that kiss in the bullring, the way her skin prickled under his every gaze, the flip in her stomach every time he walked into the room . . . She wasn't Carlos Mendoza. She knew it was happiness that was the best revenge.

'Hi, you've come through to Stephen Rathbone. Leave a short message. I'll call you back.'

'Stephen, please . . .' she hesitated, not knowing what else to say. 'Please call me. We have to talk.' She sighed and hung up, sinking back into her chair in a defeated heap. Three days, twenty-four messages, no reply. Fish learnt faster than this.

'He's here.'

She was standing in Señora Quincy's room, watching as Marina brushed and styled her grandmother's hair. The omens didn't look good. She was wearing a funereal black linen dress, no jewellery today apart from a cameo brooch. It was a severe, unfriendly look. Hostile, even.

'How did he seem?' Señora Quincy asked, staring dead ahead as her granddaughter fussed over her.

'Weak. I could barely see him, to be honest. They carried him through on a stretcher.' She went and perched on the edge of the linen sofa, watching blankly. The bed had been made, the room so pristine it was almost as if everyone in it was hovering, not touching the surfaces.

'Awake?'

'Yes, seemed to be. I saw him grasp Mateo's hand.'

'That is awake enough then.'

Charlotte wondered what exactly the old woman planned on saying to her brother. What could she say to the man who had murdered her husband? What could he say to the sister whose husband had murdered their family? 'Do you know what you're going to do?'

'Of course.' But she offered no explanation. Instead she regarded Charlotte with her usual critical, clear-eyed gaze. '. . . You look pale.'

'Do I?' Charlotte's hand rose to her cheek.

'My granddaughter tells me you are getting married in a few days.'

Charlotte opened her mouth . . . but the lie stalled. What was the point? She was leaving now anyway. It was over – Carlos Mendoza had his sister back, Mateo had his answers, Marina's rights as an heir were automatically protected by law even if her grandmother rebutted them. There was no further reason for her to be here. 'Actually, no, I'm not.'

'But last night—' Marina protested, looking up.

'I know. It was called off at the weekend, that's why I was delayed coming back.' She bit her lip. 'I didn't feel like I could tell Mateo after he'd gone to the trouble of organizing the present.' She stared down at her hands. 'I won't accept it, of course.'

'What happened?' Marina beseeched her, looking concerned. 'Or shouldn't I ask? I shouldn't ask – it's personal.'

Charlotte gave a wan laugh. 'I think we're beyond that now, don't you?' She gave a sigh so weary, her shoulders rose two inches and dropped four. 'The truth is, I can't marry my fiancé – because I am still married to my first husband.'

'*First* husband?'

'A man not known for his organizational skills. Or any skills, in fact. He didn't "get round" to filing the decree absolute and now my fiancé thinks I did it deliberately.'

There was an astonished silence.

'But you're so young for—'

'A second marriage? I know. We got married at university.'

'That's still very young.'

'I thought it was the right thing to do at the time. I'd recently suffered a great loss and was struggling to cope, and marrying him seemed . . . well, I thought it was a way to be safe.'

'Safe from what?' Señora Quincy asked, watching her closely.

Charlotte was quiet for a moment. 'My past. My family. My destiny.' She stared at her hands, spying a tiny white crescent moon in the pinks of her fingernail, still able to hear her mother's words in the bathroom that night. She gave a sigh. 'My family is . . . prominent. Like yours, it's a name everyone knows and they all want a piece of you, the glamour by proxy.'

Marina gave a tiny gasp of understanding. 'So *that's* why you do this. You know what it's like,' she said quietly.

Charlotte nodded. 'People on the outside have no idea of what it's like to be born into a family with no purpose, no rules, no limits. No one ever said "no" to me, or even "later" – I could have whatever I wanted, whenever I wanted it. But the problem with that is when you can have everything, you value nothing. It was my problem – and it was my father's too.'

'It was him you lost,' Señora Quincy said, presenting it as a fact.

She nodded. 'He'd had a drug problem for a long time. My mother had finally had enough. She was leaving him . . . I found him.' She pressed her lips together firmly, taking another breath. 'And the papers loved it. As far as they were concerned, the story was heaven-sent – rich and sordid and wasted and debauched. They trailed us everywhere for months. Some of my friends who I thought were protecting me, I found out later were selling stories about me to the press. There was nobody I could trust.' She stared into the distance, remembering it again, the moment he'd batted away her games, seen through her act. 'Except one. He kept himself apart, he wasn't like the rest. He wasn't from my world and he didn't care about that stuff. He just seemed to like . . . me.' Her voice cracked on the last word.

'So what happened?' Marina asked, her jaw slack with concern.

She shrugged. 'I messed it up, I was papering over the cracks. I loved him but I hadn't come to terms with my father's death and the more I loved him, the more frightening it felt. Everyone thought I was with him for the sheer novelty, my mother, my friends, they all told me it was some sort of rebellion – me trying on a different life. And the more they said it, the more I began to believe they were right, that he was just another obsession and that in trying to escape being like my father, I had become more like him than ever.'

'And so you decided to marry the other guy? Go with convention.'

'It wasn't as conscious as that, but yes. We had both been invited to a mutual friend's family wedding in Edinburgh so we agreed to travel up together.' She shrugged. 'We weren't together at that point, but I drank too much, as I always used to back then, and he . . . he jokingly suggested we were bound to get married sooner or later and that we should just elope. Things were difficult for him with his parents too. It just seemed to solve so many problems at a stroke.' She shook her head. 'I really thought it was the best idea I'd ever heard in my life: it seemed so obvious, standing there in the registry office – if I could change my name, I could change my destiny.' She looked at Señora Quincy. 'You can understand that, can't you? You turned your back on your financial fortune, you changed your name, your politics. Your circumstances.'

The old woman nodded.

'And so you know that it makes no difference to who you are inside. That deep down we can't change our nature. The girl who left this house eighty years ago vowing never to return – she's still there, isn't she, though you've tried to hide her, deny her? Isn't that why you've come back?'

Señora Quincy was very still, before she nodded again. 'In spite of it all, he is my twin. We came into this world together.'

Marina looked between the two of them, seeing the affinity – the parallels – between them. 'So what happened to the ex? Boyfriend I mean, not husband.'

He's upstairs packing, she didn't say. 'He's moved on. He's living abroad and got a family of his own now.'

'Are you in touch?'

She swallowed. 'Not really.'

'. . . Probably for the best,' Marina said finally, looking for a positive outcome.

'Yeah.'

'It's such a shame though, about your wedding. Just when you'd got yourself sorted again. Why would your fiancé think you did it deliberately?'

'He's a very organized man. He thinks I must have known the divorce hadn't come through but that I just didn't want to marry him and this was my way out.'

'Pretty dramatic way out!' Marina scoffed.

'I know.' She saw that Señora Quincy was still watching her, as though assessing her, and she forced a smile. 'Anyway, that is quite enough about me and my disastrous life. We are here to get yours sorted out, at least. Are you ready to see your brother again, señora?'

The old lady nodded, taking a breath that swelled her up. As if on cue – had they been listening? – two orderlies came into the room and helped her into the wheelchair.

As she rose, a couple of objects fell from the folds of her dress.

'Oh, I'll get them,' Charlotte said, stepping forward to retrieve them. She held up a worn-smooth, pale stone. At a certain angle, it looked heart-shaped.

'Childhood relics,' the old lady said, taking it quickly, possessively.

'Is this a shark's tooth?' Charlotte asked with a surprised smile.

She nodded again, taking that too.

'Yours?' She watched as the señora anxiously smoothed her fingers over its glossy surface.

'It belonged to my best friend. It was the most precious thing he owned. I always promised I would bring it back to him.'

'Oh, he lives in Madrid now?' Marina asked.

'No. He's long dead.'

Charlotte and Marina shared confused looks.

'What about the stone?' Marina asked. 'Was that his too?'

'No. Arlo found it in the river in the gorge. It was in the pair of trousers I stole from him the night I left here.'

'And you kept it all this time?' Marina asked, smiling and placing a hand fondly on her shoulder. 'Abuela, you *do* love him.'

Señora Quincy turned her head away, as though trying to deny the words, but Marina met Charlotte's gaze and gave her a hopeful look.

'Charlotte would understand,' the old woman said quietly. 'We understand one another, you and I. We are cut from the same cloth. We have both come from money. We have both, in our different ways, run from it.' She looked straight at her then. 'And we have both loved men we have tried our best to hate. Isn't that right?'

Charlotte didn't reply. She didn't know how on earth the old woman knew but . . . She could see Marina's head turning left and right, trying to look at them both, to find a clue that could help her understand what was passing silently between them. But love stories like theirs were caught, not taught; they couldn't possibly be explained.

Chapter Twenty-Five

'Do you want us to wait outside?' Marina asked as they stopped outside the bedroom. They all stared at the closed door. On the other side of it was a dying man who had everything but peace. A rich man who had offered up his fortune for a final goodbye.

The moment was upon them. Destiny was here.

'No, come with me. I'm not ready yet. I need to be sure.' The old lady held her hand up; it was trembling, and Marina squeezed it.

'I'm here, Abuela. I won't leave you.'

The door was opened and the orderlies went to wheel her in. Charlotte stepped back, away. 'And you, Charlotte,' the señora added. 'I will value your support.'

They walked into the room. It was not large and it was surprisingly spare. Like their old childhood bedrooms, nothing was superfluous or fancy, just a vast, four-poster bed pushed against one wall and some handsome chests of drawers. A picture of the Madonna and Child was framed above the bed with just one glinting curved *estoque* sword hanging on a wall. On the surfaces were old pictures – a sepia-toned portrait of a family in formal Spanish dress, photographs of Mateo and his sister growing up, his many grandchildren. And one which was larger than the rest: a photograph of a young girl on horseback, sitting side-saddle on a magnificent black horse; she looked very like the young woman in the portrait in the drawing room. Almost the same but not quite, her cool, grey-green eyes looking detached from the camera's hungry gaze. She was already beautiful, already wilful, already strong . . .

Mateo was sitting in a chair beside his father's bed. He looked up as they entered and walked over to them. 'Aunt.' There was respect in his voice and Charlotte knew that what they had just learnt had changed everything. She was no Judas or Lazarus.

She squeezed his hand affectionately, looking for – and finding – the resemblance to his father. 'My nephew.'

At the first sound of her voice—

'Nene.' It came from the bed, beneath the blankets which, in spite of the heat, were heavy. He was rigged up to a heart monitor and blood pressure machine, a drip dangling beside him.

'Arlo.' She was wheeled beside him, the same pale arm Charlotte had seen earlier as he was carried off the helicopter, stretching out again now.

Marina and Charlotte hung back, giving them privacy as they took in the sight of each other for the first time in eighty-two years: their once-plump skin now crepey and loose, strong limbs thin and spotted, the sumptuous Mendoza manes now wispy and sparse. But the eyes – had they diminished? Charlotte couldn't see him from here but Señora Quincy still had the same, challenging stare apparent in her childhood picture.

'I thought you would be fat,' the señora said finally.

'I thought you would be ugly,' he replied.

Charlotte smiled to herself. Insults were the best start. It was manners that would be the concern.

'Still got your teeth?'

He laughed, the sound breathy and light. 'Barely got gums.'

The señora laughed too, her eyes raking over her big brother – older by six minutes. They were still clasping one another's hands.

Marina jogged Charlotte with her elbow, casting her an excited sideways glance.

'. . . Eighty-two years, Nene.'

'I know.' She closed her eyes and nodded. Silence filled the room. Sometimes words really couldn't say what needed to be said. Eyes did the talking. Hands.

As if remembering them, she turned slightly, beckoning. 'Come, Marina, meet your great-uncle. Arlo.'

Marina stepped forward, hesitantly offering a hand to one of the most powerful men in the country.

'Come here, child.'

She leant down as he kissed her on the forehead and clasped her face between cool hands, regarding her close-up. 'I can see him in you.'

'Who?' Marina asked.

'Your grandfather.'

'Me too. Every time,' the señora agreed, smiling warmly and reaching over for her own kiss on her granddaughter's cheek. 'And you too, Charlotte. Come here. Meet my brother.'

She limped forward, feeling intrusive in the family scene. She slipped her hand into the one he was holding out but he did not shake it, merely holding it with the other one too, like the pope to a child. 'A pleasure, sir.'

He was diminished, it was clear. His hands tremored slightly and there was a gentle droop to the left side of his face. He was almost completely bald, with even his snow-white eyebrows meagre, a wan yellowish tint to his complexion.

But his eyes were the same as his sister's: bright and direct and challenging, and from them she could superimpose who he had once been over the frail body in the bed here now.

'Charlotte works with the bank. She has been advising us, trying to make me want to be rich again,' the señora said wryly, meeting Charlotte's eyes with amusement. 'But she has also been helping Marina adjust to the idea of having Mendoza blood – and for that I am grateful. Perhaps there will be *some* advantages.'

Charlotte smiled and hobbled back. The old man looked weaker than she had been led to believe by Mateo's reports. This reunion surely couldn't be a long one.

Carlos looked back at his twin again. 'You made it almost impossible, Nene. I had all but given up. I thought you must be dead. I *never* would have thought to look for that name.'

'I know . . .'

Charlotte cocked an eyebrow.

'But still you found me,' the señora shrugged, almost carelessly, as though it had been a game of hide and seek. She tipped her head to the side. 'How *did* you do it?'

'Sheer luck. Or perhaps serendipity?' His voice was raspy and weak. 'We were in Bilbao, for a gala at the Guggenheim. A tyre on the car burst.'

'Ah,' she nodded, seeing immediately.

'We called out a mechanic and I saw the name on his van: S. Quincy. I had never considered it and yet – how could I ever forget it?'

She stared straight at him, both of them remembering something shared, a common memory. 'No.'

'After that, it was easy. The lawyers had it done in a day.'

'And now here we are,' she said, patting his hand affectionately again.

Charlotte watched on, their half conversation weaving in and out of public comprehension. Was it a twin thing? She could feel the past pulsing in the room with them. It clung to every word, look.

There was a sound of footsteps, bounding up the stairs as though at two at a time, striding down the hall.

'I . . . Oh.'

She turned. Nathan was standing in the doorway, his fist held up ready to knock. He looked into the room with dawning realization. 'My apologies . . . Sorry. I came to say goodbye.'

'As have we all,' Señora Quincy smiled.

'I'm leaving now. I'm sorry, I didn't realize you were—'

Charlotte felt her heart race as she watched him, the embarrassment evident on his face. It made him look young, boyish, innocent. The earnest academic she had first met. Forever the odd one out with his hand-knit jumpers, regional accent, true heart.

'Please come in,' Señora Quincy said. 'Before you leave, you should at least meet the man who has been behind your hard work.'

Nathan set down his bag by the door and walked in. He had changed into jeans and a t-shirt, already off-duty; in his head, she knew, he had already left. Charlotte watched his every footstep, feeling her heart might leap out of her chest. These were their dying moments. Their final few minutes. She knew when he left here, she would never see him again.

'A pleasure, sir,' he said, gently shaking Carlos Mendoza's hand.

'The professor has been researching us, Arlo,' her voice almost teasing, as though she was reverting to the girl she had once been, the naughty little sister. 'Digging into our pasts.'

'Then I pity you,' Carlos replied. 'That must have made for difficult reading.'

'In places, yes,' Nathan replied with characteristic directness.

'... Try living it,' the old man replied, a half-smile on his lips.

Nathan shook his head. 'I can't. It's impossible to imagine. War makes ordinary lives extraordinary in a way that's impossible to understand during times of peace. But in some ways, you're almost lucky. You have lived harder, lived bigger lives as a consequence.'

'I like that. I have lived hard,' Carlos said, looking at the young academic intently. 'I would agree with it. Perhaps they should put it on my tombstone.'

'I hope not for a long while yet.' Nathan smiled and held out his hand to shake it again. 'It's a pleasure to have been able to meet you in person, señor.' He looked at his twin. 'Señora, I hope we part as friends? I wish you well.'

'Goodbye, professor, you have made this last week very ... interesting.'

Nathan turned away, stopping in front of Marina and Charlotte too. 'Marina, the best of luck. I think you're in for a hell of a ride.'

'I think you're right,' she grinned. 'Let's have that drink sometime.'

'Yes.' He nodded, his eyes sliding slowly to Charlotte. 'Charlotte.'

'Nathan.'

They stared at one another, both stripped of platitudes as they wordlessly uttered their final goodbye before an audience. But what more was there to say between them anyway? Over the course of their relationship they had run the gamut and said it all: I love you; I hate you. What else was left?

'I will walk you out,' Mateo said politely.

Nathan held her gaze for another moment more, then turned and left. Charlotte felt the air leave the room with him but somehow she continued to stand, she continued to breathe. After a moment, she realized the señora was watching her and a tiny beat of understanding flickered between them. 'I'll give you some privacy,' she smiled.

'Nene, would you leave us now too?' the Señora said to her granddaughter. 'There are some things I wish to say to Arlo alone.'

'Of course, Abuela,' Marina nodded. 'Can I get you anything?'

'Just ask the orderlies to come in and help me up onto the bed. I want to be closer to my brother.'

'Sure.'

'You are the sweetest girl,' Señora Quincy smiled, reaching up to kiss her on the cheek, before she and Charlotte left the room.

'Help my grandmother onto the bed, please,' Marina said as they passed the two men waiting patiently outside.

Together, they headed downstairs – Charlotte shuffling on her bottom – automatically heading for the cool terrace. After the intensity of that cloistered room, they both needed some fresh air.

'Well, I think that went better than expected,' Marina murmured.

But her voice sounded far away. Charlotte could see the dust plumes billowing up from the distant estate road and knew the red jeep was heading for the airport, taking him far away from here. '. . . Yes. Very positive.'

'He's not at all what I expected. I was thinking he would be . . . grand.'

Charlotte glanced at her. 'That's one of the assumptions

people make with great wealth. You'll have to start getting used to people foisting expectations on you too.'

Marina's face fell. 'I suppose so. It's hard to imagine.'

Mayra came out with a tray of drinks. 'Iced coffee?'

'Thank you,' Charlotte murmured, taking hers, grateful not to have even had to make a choice.

They sipped in silence for a few minutes. 'What do you think they're talking about?'

'Who knows? I don't think they'll be short of conversation. Eighty-two years is a long time to have to catch up on.'

'It was sweet he called her Nene. She always called me that growing up. I didn't know it was her nickname too.'

'I've never heard it before. What does it mean?'

'It's more a term of affection. Darling. Baby.'

'Ah.' Charlotte stared ahead, watching as one of the groundsmen worked in the flowerbed around the jacaranda tree. He was digging slowly, making shallow cuts into the hard earth.

She gave a small gasp of recognition, remembering something suddenly. 'Oh . . . That must be what the initials were.'

'What initials?'

'In that tree over there, someone's carved some initials into the bark: NM and SE. I couldn't work out who NM was. But it must be her – Nene Mendoza.'

'Oh. I guess so.' Marina looked over at the tree curiously. 'What about SE?'

'I don't kn—' Charlotte shrugged. But as she did so, a name floated to her as though brought on the breeze. '. . . Santiago Esperanza.'

Marina looked sharply at her. 'The man who—?'

Had murdered her family? Had died beside her grandfather? Had been killed by her great-uncle? Nathan's words reverberated in Charlotte's head: *This was personal.*

'It can't be,' Marina said dismissively. 'Why would his initials be beside my grandmother's? He was one of the workers. They can't have been friends.'

'No,' Charlotte murmured, even as her brain asked, couldn't they? The señora had mentioned her best friend lived in the *mercadillo* – but that was the peasant district of the town. And the . . . the shark's tooth she had been holding. A childhood relic, she had called it. Her best friend's. *It was the most precious thing he owned.* Was that what she had retrieved from the tree, the first day here? Wasn't it extraordinary she should have even remembered it after so many years? Charlotte could still see how she had pressed it to her lips and kissed it as she was driven back to the house again. It meant a lot to her. *I promised to bring it back to him.*

Charlotte shifted uneasily in her chair. Something was nagging at her.

'Charlotte?'

'Mmm?'

Marina was looking thoughtful. '. . . Do you think it was strange that she said "this last week"—?'

'Huh?' On the table Charlotte's phone rang.

'As opposed to "this past week"?'

'Hang on—' She answered it.

'Charlotte, it's me.'

'Nathan?' Her heart broke into a gallop. 'Where are you?' She closed her eyes, willing him to say he was sorry, for all of it, that he loved her and only her, that he was coming back. In the background she could hear the sound of the car engine, the radio playing quietly. But which way was he going – to or from her?

'Something's been bothering me since the talk with Mateo earlier. It's made me wonder something.'

Despair washed over her. '. . . Wonder what?'

'The woman that was taken hostage in the church, the night Quincy was killed.'

She closed her eyes. '. . . What about her?'

'What if it was Marina?'

They flew open again. '*What?*' She frowned, lost. '. . . What on earth would make you think that?'

'Because I think she was in the church that night, not because she'd been taken hostage – but because she was getting married.'

Charlotte froze. 'You're saying Carlos killed his sister's husband at their *wedding*?'

'Yes. Except I don't think it was Quincy she was marrying. He was marrying her.'

She wasn't marrying him but he was marrying her? She squinted her eyes shut again, tired of his theories, tired of trying to keep up. 'You're not making sense.' Why couldn't he let this go now? They'd done their jobs. It was over, all of it.

'From the very start, I've been working on one basic assumption – that Jack Quincy was Marina's husband. But I overlooked one critical detail: before he signed up to serve, Jack Quincy was a Baptist minister. Quincy wasn't the man she married. He was the one *marrying* them.'

Them? Charlotte shifted uneasily, she could feel something gathering . . . 'Who . . . ?' But even as she asked the question, the name came to her.

'Santi Esperanza was the other man killed alongside Quincy that night. Just like he was there with Quincy the night the Mendoza men were murdered. He blamed the Mendozas for his father's murder. He was implicated in the slaughter of Marina Mendoza's treasured horse the night of the fiesta at La Ventilla – just over a week before she disappeared.'

We have both loved men we have tried to hate.

'But his name. She took Quincy's name.'

'Yes. To protect her child. If Carlos had found out she was having Esperanza's child, do you think he would have allowed that? He'd killed the father, do you think he would allow the son to live too—?'

Charlotte gasped as she remembered the señora's words in her bedroom: *He may not have been why I left but he was the reason I never returned.*

'. . . After everything that had passed between their families, at the *very* least he would have put the child up for adoption. But Franco's government legalized changing the names of Republican orphans and children of prisoners; if Marina Mendoza was in a psychiatric hospital when she gave birth and he was adopted, she never would have found him again. Now I've just double-checked the paperwork – the hospital she was sent to was bombed and burnt down in '38, the year after she was admitted; many of the inpatients were killed, but others fled and disappeared. If she was one of them, by taking Quincy's name and not Esperanza's, she protected her child *and* found a way to ensure her brother could never find her.'

Charlotte felt herself go cold. Carlos had said it himself, right there in that room. *I never would have thought to look for that name.*

She stared over at Marina, words running through her head. Omens. Clues. *Both loved men we have tried to hate . . . This last week . . . Bringing it back to him . . . He's long dead . . . We came into this world together.*

She stiffened suddenly. They came into this world together and, it was implied—

'Oh my God!' The phone dropped from her hand as she

began to run, limping badly but the adrenaline lifting her as it had in the bullring.

'Charlotte, wait! What is it?' Marina cried, panic suffusing her voice as she raced after her.

She limped up the stairs, not caring about the searing pain that shot through her with every step. 'No! No-no-no!' she cried, seeing the two orderlies sitting outside the room, leaning against the wall and scrolling on their phones. They had been sent out too? They looked up in alarm at the sound and sight of her.

'What's wrong?' they asked as she tore past, throwing open the door so that it banged hard against the wall.

She felt the breath knocked out of her as she took in the sight on the bed. Marina was only a moment behind her and she screamed, her legs giving out as saw the growing red stain, the two pale frail bodies lying beside one another. Two letters in separate handwriting were propped on the side table, an all but empty bottle of pills tipped on the floor and a vivid red cut on each one's wrists; the stained shark's tooth was on the blanket, and their hands tightly clasped as the blood pooled between them.

They had come into this world together. And now they had left it together.

One blood.

Guadalajara, March 1937

She stared at him, the black eyes that were seared onto her soul – awake or dreaming, ever-present – burning back at her. 'You're alive,' she whispered, her hand reaching out to touch his skin, to check he was real.

His flinch told her he was, the warrior more threatened by the tear than the spear. 'I couldn't die yet. Not until I found you again.'

The words rocked her, turning her heart upside down, the world. '. . . You've been looking for me?'

'Almost since you left.' His voice was thick, the initial shock marbling now with shame. 'I tried not to. I tried to let you go. I told myself it was better you were gone. That it was safer that way.' His eyes raked over her, taking in the short haircut, and she saw the emotion spring to his face as he realized—

'No,' she said quickly, seeing the horror form like a cloudburst. 'I did it. When I escaped. I was trying to disguise myself.'

He studied her face, looking for the kind lie, and when seeing none, turned away, his back expanding and contracting in broad, relieved breaths as his fist pulled into a punch before he splayed his palm flat against the wall of the cave again.

'Santi, I'm okay. Really.' She placed her hand on his shoulder, feeling the muscles and scars beneath her palm. What horrors had he lived through? What atrocities had he seen?

'What I did . . .' he said quietly, his head bowed.

'Don't. You don't have to say it.'

He turned his head fractionally, still not facing her. 'No, I must. I have to . . . I was angry. I *needed* to avenge my father and yet . . . I couldn't do what I needed because of you. I hated that I couldn't hate you too. And when I saw you at the church, saw how sorry you were, it only made it harder. I thought that if I pushed you away and made you hate me, then I would be free to do what I had to do.'

She dropped her head, realizing then that her father was

dead. Her hand, still on his back, felt the rapid thud of his heartbeat echoing through his bones, the ropes of old scars still visible to the touch. '. . . I understand.'

Slowly he turned. 'But can you forgive?'

'I'm not sure. I tried to hate you too. I tried to be glad when I thought you were dead. They told me they rounded you all up in the bullring.'

Pain crossed him like a shadow. 'Quincy and I had already left. He had been ordered up to Madrid and agreed to take me with him so I could find you . . .' He took a breath. 'I really thought I could do it – live with you hating me – but that last time I saw you, in the field . . .' He met her gaze then looked away again. 'You'd never looked so beautiful. The image of you haunted me . . .'

She stared up at him. 'And you me,' she said simply. 'I hated that I loved you.'

Shock made him startle. '. . . You loved me?'

'And still do. You were the only one who ever let me be me. There was never going to be anyone but you,' she whispered, seeing how her words made him tremble, her touch made him shiver. She stepped closer, her finger tenderly tracing the sweep of his cheek, before she reached up on tiptoe and pressed her lips to his – gently, lest he might break.

When she pulled away, his eyes were shining. 'I'll never leave you again, Nene,' he said, his voice hoarse. 'I'll protect you now. We'll always be together, I promise.'

'We always were,' she smiled, feeling his arm hook around her waist and pull her closer to him, their bodies pressed together, exhausted and thin, bloodied and desperate. He kissed her again, more urgently now, his hands gripping her to him and she felt her body respond, softening, yielding . . .

The punch, when it came, sent them both flying. Marina found herself on the ground, Santi spun into the wall, dazed. She looked up and cried out in fright to see Modesto bearing down upon them both, his bloodied fist unnoticed as his chest heaved with terrifying anger.

'Miguel,' she beseeched, holding her hands up placatingly. 'Please—'

'You little whore,' he snarled, his words a hiss as he spat at her, kicking out with a booted foot. 'I should have known.'

'No!' Santi cried, launching himself at him, throwing a punch that connected with Miguel's jaw, but made little impact – there was at least five inches and twenty kilograms' difference between them.

'Stop!' Marina shouted as they wrestled, fists flying, missing, connecting, a melee of limbs sending them both careering into the wall and off again.

She scrambled away from them desperately as they brawled, tears streaming down her face in horror as Miguel landed one, two blows, sending Santi sprawling to the floor. He was bleeding from the nose, one brow cut, but he got up again, his black eyes blazing as they always did. Often down, never out.

'Please! Miguel, stop! You'll kill him!'

'That's the idea,' Miguel snarled, raising his hands up in a fist, ready to go again.

Santi rushed in at him again – fearless, furious – this time getting one up on the bigger man by kicking his feet out from under him and sending him flat on his back, winding him momentarily. He kicked out, catching him in the ribs, the head, but Miguel – a seasoned thug – caught his leg and flipped him up like a twig.

Both men lay dazed for a moment and Marina scrambled

to her feet, looking around for something, anything, with which to fight. She saw the pistol which Santi had tossed away in alarm when he had realized it was her, half buried in the dust. She ran towards it but Miguel caught her foot, as if realizing her intent, sending her sprawling again.

'Get back here, you fascist bitch,' he said, closing his fist around her ankle just as her fingers made contact with the cold steel. With hands shaking violently, she grabbed it, pointing it straight at him as he flipped her over onto her back.

He froze momentarily as he looked down the barrel of the frantically shaking gun, a cold smile gradually spreading across his lips. 'You wouldn't dare. You don't have it in you, Marina Mendoza. You can't even kill the enemy.'

'You *are* the enemy!' she screamed – and pulled the trigger.

The sound of the gunshot ricocheted around the cave, deafening, amplified. She dropped the gun like it was hot, staring down at her captor with horror and relief.

'Nene!' Santi cried, running over to her and enfolding her in his arms. 'Don't look, don't look,' he said as she began trembling violently. She had killed a man.

The sound of voices, of footsteps, made them both turn, as Sindo and Quincy burst into the cave, pistols pulled, faces set for battle.

'What the hell . . . ?' Quincy cried, seeing the two of them standing there, Miguel's slumped corpse on the ground, blood soaking into the earth, the metallic smell of it already filling the confined space.

Marina felt her terror heighten. This was it, they'd both be shot now, killed for treachery when they'd only just found each other again. 'He was . . . he was . . .' she stammered, but she was too shocked to form the words.

Slowly, the two men dropped their guns, Sindo replacing his in his belt.

'We know what he was,' he said quietly, his eyes meeting hers in perfect understanding. 'Come. We need to get rid of the body.'

Chapter Twenty-Six

Madrid, October 2018

'It's a triumph, Marina,' Charlotte smiled.

They stood together, looking back at the party. Guests were mingling, talking and laughing as they moved around the exhibition, admiring the photographs, poems and artworks and reading the brief histories that had been compiled for each one. Marina and Mateo had worked tirelessly together trying to find the best material to sum up the project's theme – Love and War – and it had been a particular coup getting the rival Reina Sofia museum to lend Picasso's masterpiece *Guernica* as the centrepiece; Katerina had pulled in more than a few favours to make it happen and she had been key in helping draw the whole show together, not least in enabling the party to be held here, at the museum. Such was the power of the Mendoza name.

'I can hardly believe it is happening,' Marina said, watching as the catering staff attended to the guests as per her instructions. This was her fledgling company's first big event, and with such a high-profile guest list, she needed it to go off without a hitch; between setting up the company and compiling the memorial exhibition, she had been working fifteen-hour days for the past few months and Charlotte knew that was, in part, a way to fill the void left by her grandmother's death.

'Well, you've worked so hard for this. You deserve the success. Enjoy it. Let your team take it from here now.'

'You're right, it's –' She bit her lip anxiously. 'It's just hard to step back, that's all. I'm so used to doing everything myself, I'm not good at delegating.'

'It'll come. You're doing brilliantly,' Charlotte said reassuringly. 'You're learning to be the boss. A Mendoza.'

Marina turned in to face her, dropping her voice. 'Talking of that, I thought you'd want to know – we had the coroner's report back.'

'Oh?'

'Stage-four breast cancer.'

'Oh.' Charlotte's mouth parted in surprise. 'And she never said?'

'Not a word. Her carers never knew either. She refused all medication.'

'. . . She didn't want to worry you?'

'Probably.'

'Well . . .' Charlotte said after a pause. 'I suppose there's some comfort to take in that. If she didn't have long either . . . at least they were together at the end.'

Marina nodded, looking pensive. 'I've been thinking about this a lot actually, and I think . . . I think she knew that was what she would do, as soon as she heard he was dying too.'

'Do you think that's why he was trying to find her?' Charlotte frowned. 'Could it have been some sort of pact?'

'I think it was more of a promise, if anything. Before you came into the room that day, I asked her why she was going through with this. He'd caused her such pain and it was clear she was tormented by the prospect of seeing him again.'

Marina took a breath, emotion taking grip of her once again as she remembered the events of that fateful day. 'But just before you came in, she told me that as a little girl, her mother had made her swear to always protect him, that he wasn't as strong as she was.' She bit her lip. 'I think she felt there was comfort in going together, that he wouldn't be alone. No matter what had happened between them and how bad things got, they looked out for each other at the end. They kept the promise.'

'Oh, Marina,' Charlotte said, placing a hand on her arm, her voice thickening with emotion.

Marina looked at her with teary eyes, the pain still fresh. 'I know Nathan did a great job but I'm still not sure we got to the bottom of what really happened between them.'

Charlotte managed not to react at the sudden mention of his name. 'Well, to be honest, I don't think anyone ever could – they may not have even known the full truths themselves. So much of life is influenced and dictated by chance details that get lost in the retelling.'

'Hey.' Lucy Santos came over, her eyes bright. 'So I think they're ready for the speeches. How are you feeling?'

Marina and Charlotte both recovered themselves with quick smiles, Marina dabbing at her eyes quickly and pulling a nervous face. 'Terrified.' The two women had become fast friends when Charlotte had introduced them, sensing that they shared more than just fat bank accounts: both had been pulled into this new world by means outside their control and they had bonded immediately over the etiquette perils and paparazzi pitfalls, trying to navigate it together; Lucy was even helping Marina find a new apartment.

'You'll be brilliant,' Lucy said confidently. 'Is Mateo going first?'

'Yes. Oh God, they're all going to be staring at me.' Marina went to bite her nails but Lucy pushed her hand down again.

'Of course they are. Everyone wants to see the long-lost Mendoza heir,' she shrugged. 'But remember why you're doing this: for your grandmother, you're honouring her life and the sacrifices she made. You've got this.'

'You're right,' Marina nodded as Lucy winked at her.

'Ladies and gentlemen—' The voice made them turn, the rushing babble of conversation diminishing to a trickle. 'I give you this evening's co-host, Mateo Mendoza.'

Everyone clapped politely as Mateo took to the podium, looking utterly at ease. Charlotte surveyed the room again, aware of a vague sense of being watched. But then she knew a fair few of the guests gathered here tonight, many of them were clients.

'Standing here before you tonight is, it is no exaggeration to say, one of the great honours of my life,' Mateo began. 'As you will all be aware, it was a difficult summer for our family, losing my father, and we feel the loss greatly. He was an exceptional man who lived an extraordinary life. The Mendoza name casts a long shadow but I think, in many ways, he often felt like he was the one standing in the shade. Despite the public perception of him as a business *titan* or *mogul* – descriptions he abhorred – he was in private a very humble and modest man. Family was everything to him and my sisters and I grew up knowing we were deeply loved.'

He inhaled, looking slowly around the room. 'But if we suffered a great loss this year, we have also made gains, and discovering my father had a twin sister, Marina, was a shock that has since become a joy. Lucky is a word that is used a lot in connection with our name but my father came of age in a time of war when the certainties of life shifted on an hourly basis and there wasn't much luck to be had by anyone. And although ours was certainly not the only family to be ruptured during those dark days of the late thirties, having had these past few months to ruminate on the discoveries made this summer, I do believe that losing Marina was the great tragedy of his life. They were apart for eighty-two years out of ninety-eight. Those are very sad odds for two people who came into the world together; things should have been different for them and in another time, I think they would have been.'

He looked out at the gathered guests, speaking easily, without notes.

'But I take comfort in an interesting conversation I had this summer, one which has stuck with me, to do with the course of life and how it unfolds. I was drinking brandy – rather too much brandy – in my library one evening with a history professor –'

Charlotte stiffened at the reference to Nathan again. It had been difficult enough flying back into Madrid, just knowing he was here.

'– and he said that through his work, he had come to see that life is not linear, but rather weaves and meanders in loops that sometimes touch to make a complete circle, connecting us back to a seminal point in our past. Many times it doesn't, of course, snaking away again in different directions, a series of near-misses, if you like. But he said, occasionally, if we are lucky, the points can touch again and we get to close off a circle. And I believe that is what my father managed to do this summer. It was his last act of will, bringing his twin back into his life and coming full circle . . .'

Charlotte stepped back like she'd been pushed, knowing she hadn't been so lucky. It had been a near miss for her, Nathan back in her life, in her bed, just fleetingly before he meandered away again, back to his family, his work, his life here . . .

'Are you okay?' Marina whispered, seeing how she pulled at the neck of her dress.

'Yes, I . . .' She felt eyes upon her. She felt hot. She cleared her throat. 'I'm just going to freshen up. I'll be right back.'

'Okay, but be back for my speech,' Marina said anxiously.

'I will, I promise.'

She moved as discreetly as she could through the crowd, hurrying away from the congregated mass and down the marble corridors, following the signs for the Ladies. She needed to splash some water on her face and just take a moment. It was the surprise of hearing his name again, that was all. She should have known he would be mentioned tonight. After all, it was his work that had given the family answers and resolution.

Her shoes tapped rhythmically as she hurried past the priceless masterpieces, not seeing them. She turned the corner and rushed down the next hall, knowing her way around here so well; she and Mouse had been brought here so many times as children to see the various paintings the family had sold to 'return them to the public gaze' but which she had later come to realize was a cover for settling her father's numerous drug-related debts. She didn't need to turn her head to know that the copy of *La Joconde* was just down here on the left or that—

Suddenly she remembered again. With everything that had happened, she had completely forgotten, but she walked over now and stopped in front of the little Chardin, still sitting unobtrusively and discreetly amidst the splashier works. She stared at it in silence. It had been the painting he had most admired in her parents' home, the only one that had seemingly touched him. She had barely ever noticed it, screaming past as a child on rollerskates with Mouse, blind to it as a sullen teen. But he had seen the world through a different gaze to her and he'd been drawn to how it showed 'beauty in the small things'. She had sent it to him as a last-ditch attempt to reach out to him after she'd destroyed everything between them, after he had transferred to Oxford, ignored every message she left, returned every letter she wrote . . . and now it was here too, as tossed away as all her apologies. She realized she had forgotten to chase Katerina on it, both of them overtaken with other events.

'It's on loan.'

The voice made her jump and she whirled round. Nathan was standing a few feet away, watching her. Time stopped. What was he doing here? Or should she have been so surprised? Mateo must have invited him, or Marina?

Her body loosened treacherously just at the sight of him. It was a moment before she could speak. '. . . Because you didn't want it.'

'Yes.'

The flat rejection stung her – he was always so direct – and she turned away. No matter what physical effect he had on her, she wasn't going to stand here and let him give her an emotional drubbing all over again.

'. . . It was too painful having it hanging on the wall,' he said to her back. 'Every time I looked at it I was reminded of you – and I just wanted to move on and forget you.'

She almost gave a laugh. Was that supposed to make her feel better? She turned back to face him. 'Right,' she said sarcastically. 'Thanks for clearing that up.'

She wanted to leave but her feet didn't move and they stood staring at each other, like flies caught in a web, helplessly awaiting their fates.

His gaze fell to her hand. 'No ring.'

She stirred, immediately on the defensive. Was he really going to bring all that up again? '. . . No.'

'Being engraved?'

Was that supposed to be a joke? '. . . No.'

His eyes locked with hers, probing for answers without asking questions, but she remained silent. It was none of his business that Jules had signed the papers and Stephen had returned her call. It wasn't his concern that she had chosen this single status. He may not be free but she was, and she would find her path, no matter what he or her mother or anyone else said to the contrary.

She shifted weight. 'I didn't know you were going to be here.'

'Or else you wouldn't have come?'

'Probably not, no.' He wasn't the only one who could be blunt. 'Why are you here?'

'I helped Marina find some of the archive footage,' he shrugged. 'We've met for drinks a couple of times now.'

'That's nice.' Another tinge of sarcasm coloured the words.

'She said the wedding was cancelled – that Jules pulled off another of his cock-ups.'

She turned away angrily. 'Oh, you really can't help yourself, can you?' she chided. 'You just have to gloat.' She tipped her head to the side, turned the tables onto him. 'And how about you? Cheated on your wife lately?'

'I don't have a wife,' he replied calmly.

'. . . Fine, girlfriend. Fiancée. Whatever the hell she is.'

'Ex-girlfriend. Currently staying at mine with her baby boy while she tries to get an apartment sorted. Her boyfriend's left her.'

Charlotte stared at him, stunned, his words and their ramifications rebounding around her head. '. . . So then . . . why did you say—'

'Actually I didn't. You assumed. And it seemed better that way. I thought it would keep you away. I didn't want to be back here again.'

She frowned. 'Back where?'

He shrugged. 'Loving you.' The simplicity of the words stilled her as they stared at one another. She saw the vulnerability come into his eyes, the sangfroid dropping away. He glanced back down at her again. 'Look Lotts, it's true that for a long time, I wanted to hate you and hurt you; I didn't think I could ever forgive you for what you'd done. You didn't just break my heart, you tore it up.' His month set into a grim line. 'But when I got the call about the case . . . I had to see you again. I needed to prove to myself that I could walk away, show that it was finally over for me.' He gave a dry smile and shook his head lightly. 'Bad move. Really fucking bad move.' He shrugged his eyebrows. 'So when I saw that name come up on your phone . . . it was like it was happening all over again. I couldn't believe I'd actually put myself through it.' He looked straight at her, the hurt shining like a lamp in his eyes. 'I wanted you to know what it felt like to be betrayed like that too.'

'Nathan . . .' she faltered. How many times had she hurt him?

'But I'm tired of pretending I don't love you or that I don't miss you. I lost you once, only to find you and then immediately think I'd lost you again.' His voice broke and he glanced at his feet, her earnest academic again, unsure and hesitant. 'The short story is, I can't keep doing this. I need to know once and for all – do you want to be with me or not?'

'Yes.'

There was no hesitation, no ambiguity in her voice and he gave a surprised smile. 'You can take a moment to think about it, you know. I'm not holding a gun.'

'I've had five years to think about it.' She sank onto one hip and tipped her head to the side, letting her hair slide a little over one eye. '. . . And, frankly, it's getting a little boring.'

He arched an eyebrow, hearing that old provocative tone in her voice, the past reaching into the present with fresh green shoots. 'I'm *boring* you?'

She gave her most bored shrug.

He strode over and scooped her up in one fluid movement, making her shriek with delight. 'Well then I guess we'll have to see what we can do about that.'

'Where are you taking me?' she smiled, clasping her arms tightly around his neck as he began marching down the corridor with her.

'Somewhere you've never been before.'

'Fiji?' she quipped, her eyes teasing. 'The pope's private apartments? The men's loos?'

He looked down at her with glimmering eyes that sent her world spinning off its axis. 'Let's start with my apartment,' he grinned. 'And take the rest from there.'

Epilogue

Madrid, 12 March 1937

They were using rams now, the ancient iron bolt groaning in its casing as the doors bowed and heaved. The two men looked at each other. There wasn't much time. A few more runs and the soldiers would break through. And what would they see?

His own gun by a pillar, too far to reach. The bodies on the floor – the American stretched out and staring unseeingly at the vaulted ceiling where angels were dancing above his head. A woman. *Marina.* His breath tore at the sight of her. She was here. She was alive. It was still too much to comprehend.

She was beginning to come round, her hand beginning to close up protectively, soft groans coming from her splayed form. He could see the cut on her scalp where the door had hit her, dark almost-black blood matting her short hair. But it was a graze, possible concussion. If they could get her out of here, she would be fine. He had to get her out of here.

He looked back at Santi. 'Give yourself up,' he implored him. 'I will speak to them. We can come to some arrangement. They want information from you – tell them what you know.'

Santi shook his head, the gun trembling in his hand. 'I can't.'

'Yes, you have to. It is the only way. She needs you to survive. You're her husband now.'

'And if I do survive – what does that mean for her? She's a red, like me. You know what they would do to her. We both do.'

A white-hot spear of fury trammelled through him at the thought. 'No! I would tell them.'

'You are a lieutenant,' Santi said scornfully. 'Who will listen to you? You think they'll believe she is your sister?'

'I will make them!'

'How? How can you explain that she is *your* sister when she is here with *me*? That she is my wife?'

He had no reply. There was no way to explain it. She was as guilty as Santi and they would treat her as such, his friends, his brothers in arms.

There was another ram, the doors bowing again, wood beginning to splinter and creak. He could hear their shouts, the bloodlust high. Many times he had been on the other side of that door with them.

Santi stepped forward and held out his gun, his eyes blazing. 'Do it.'

'What?' He stared at it in horror. 'No!'

'Yes, it is the only way.' Santi walked up to him and thrust the gun into his hand, forcing his fingers to close around it, pointing it back out towards him. He took three paces back and jabbed his chest, above the heart. 'Right there.'

'Santi, no!' He stared down at the gun in his hand, which was shaking violently now, just as it had the first time he had ever held one, Vale coaxing him, urging him to take the shot.

Santi stared at him with calm, cold eyes. 'You came here to kill me, Arlo. Kill me.'

'But that was before I knew—'

'It is *because* you know that you must do it. For her sake. You know what they'll do.'

The doors were rammed again and, this time, it was as though the whole church shook, the doors splitting and tearing, the men roaring like warriors. One more and they'd be through.

'She'll never forgive me,' he protested.

'If you love her, you'll do it anyway.'

On the ground, Marina was stirring, trying to lift her head. He already knew what would happen if she had a choice, which side she would choose and what that would mean for her . . .

He raised his arm, staring down the length of his arm at his old friend. Santi gave a tiny nod as their eyes met. 'Thank you.'

Arlo nodded back. And fired.

Acknowledgements

It's true what they say – it takes a village. It may be my name on the cover but there's a behemoth of a team behind me providing guidance and support all the way – be it editorial, grammatical, logistical or moral – so thank you to all the gang at Pan Mac Towers; to my super agent and RNA Agent of the Year no less, Amanda Preston; and to my beloved family, including the gingery, whiskered, four-legged members on whose daily walks the creative magic usually strikes.